About the A

From as far back as she can rer... dreamed of being a writer. She penned the first chapter of a romance novel just out of high school, but it took much study, many (varied) jobs, one ultra-understanding husband, and three gorgeous children before she finally sat down to turn that dream into a reality. Michelle lives in Australia, and when she isn't busy plotting, she loves to read, ride horses, travel, and practice yoga. Visit Michelle: michelleconder.com

Chantelle Shaw enjoyed a happy childhood making up stories in her head. Always an avid reader, Chantelle discovered Mills & Boon as a teenager and during the times when her children refused to sleep, she would pace the floor with a baby in one hand and a book in the other! Twenty years later she decided to write one of her own. Writing takes up most of Chantelle's spare time, but she also enjoys gardening and walking. She doesn't find domestic chores so pleasurable!

Mills & Boon novels were the first 'grown up' books **Julia James** read as a teenager, and she's been reading them ever since. She adores the Mediterranean and the English countryside in all its seasons, and is fascinated by all things historical, from castles to cottages. In between writing she enjoys walking, gardening, needlework, baking 'extremely gooey chocolate cakes', and trying to stay fit! Julia lives in England with her family.

The Crown

Duty to the Crown

MICHELLE CONDER

CHANTELLE SHAW

JULIA JAMES

MILLS & BOON

First Published in Great Britain 2023
by Mills & Boon, an imprint of HarperCollins*Publishers* Ltd,
1 London Bridge Street, London, SE1 9GF

www.harpercollins.co.uk

HarperCollins*Publishers*
Macken House, 39/40 Mayor Street Upper,
Dublin 1, D01 C9W8, Ireland

ISBN: 978-0-263-31893-7

DUTY AT
WHAT COST?

MICHELLE CONDER

To Paul, with love.

CHAPTER ONE

AVA GLANCED OUT of the car window at the sparkling summer sunshine bouncing off the exquisite French countryside and wished herself a thousand miles away. Maybe a million. That would land her on another planet where no one knew her name. Where no one knew the man her father had expected her to marry was about to marry another woman, and felt sorry for her in the process.

'It's time you stopped messing around in Paris, my girl, and came home to Anders.'

That particularly supportive comment had come only this morning, making her blood boil. His condescending words filled her head, drowning out the singer on the car radio who was warbling about wanting to go home. Home was the last place Ava wanted to go.

Not that her father's anger was entirely unexpected. Of course he was disappointed that the man she had been pledged to marry since she was a child had fallen in love with someone else. The way he'd spoken to her—*'A woman your age doesn't have time to waste!'*—as if turning thirty in a year meant that she was over the hill—made it seem as if it was her fault.

But Ava *wanted* to fall in love! She *wanted* to get married! She just hadn't wanted to marry Gilles—a childhood friend who was more like a brother to her than her own— and he hadn't wanted to marry her. The problem was they had played along with their fathers' archaic pledge for a little too long, sometimes using each other for a fill-in date when the need arose.

Oh, how her father would love to hear *that*… Somehow, after her mother's death fifteen years ago, her relationship with him had disintegrated to the point where they barely spoke, let alone saw each other. Of course if she had been born a boy things would have been different.

Very different.

She would have had different choices. She would have been Crown Prince, for one—and, while she had no wish at all to rule their small European nation, she would at least have had her father's respect. His affection. Something.

Ava gripped the steering wheel of her hatchback more tightly as she turned onto the narrow country lane that ran alongside Château Verne, Gilles's fifteenth-century estate.

For eight years she had lived a happy, relatively low-key existence in Paris; finishing university and building her business, stepping in at royal functions when her brother Frédéric had been absent. Now that Gilles, Marquis de Bassonne, was set to marry a friend of hers, she had a bad feeling that was all about to change.

Ava crinkled her nose at her uncharacteristically gloomy mood. Gilles and Anne had fallen in love at first sight two months ago and were happier than she'd ever seen either one of them before. They completed each other in a way that would inspire songwriters and she wasn't jealous.

Not at all.

Her life was rolling along just fine. Her art gallery, Gallery Nouveau, had just been reviewed in a prestigious art magazine and she was busier than ever. It was true that her love-life was a little on the nonexistent side, but her break-up three years ago with Colyn—the man she had believed she would eventually marry—had left her emotionally drained and a little wary.

At nearly twenty years her senior he had seemed to her to be the epitome of bourgeois intellectualism: a man who didn't care about her heritage and loved her for herself. It had taken a couple of years to figure out that his subtle criticisms of her status and his desire to *'teach'* her all that he knew made him as egotistical and controlling as her father.

And she really wished he hadn't popped into her mind, because now she felt truly terrible.

The only other times she'd felt this miserable had been during gorgeous evenings wandering by herself along the Seine, when she was unable to avoid watching couples so helplessly in love with each other they couldn't walk two paces without stopping to steal another kiss.

She had never felt that. Not once.

She frowned, wondering if she ever would.

After Colyn she had been determined only to date nice men with solid family values. Men who were in touch with their feelings. But they hadn't inspired much more than friendship in her. Thankfully her business kept her too busy to dwell on what she lacked, and if she was getting older...

Pah!

Stamping on even more mood-altering thoughts, she adjusted the volume dial on the radio and wasn't at all prepared when she put her foot on the brake to slow down for a bend in the road and nothing happened. Imagining that she had put her foot on the accelerator instead, she'd moved to correct the oversight when the car hit a patch of gravel and started to slide.

Panicking, she yanked on the steering wheel to keep the car straight, but the car had gathered momentum and in the blink of an eye it fishtailed and rammed into some sort of small tree.

Groaning, Ava clasped her head where it had bounced off the steering wheel.

For a moment she just sat there. Then she realised the

engine was roaring, took her foot from the accelerator and switched the car off. Her ears rang loudly in the sudden silence and then she caught the sound of one of her tyres spinning in midair. Glancing out through the windscreen, she realised her car was wedged on top of a clump of rocks and heather plants in full bloom.

Talk about a lapse in concentration!

She blew out a breath and gingerly moved her limbs one at a time. Thankfully the car had been going too slowly for her to have been seriously hurt. A good thing—except she could picture her father shaking his head at her. He was always telling her to use a driver on official engagements, but of course she didn't listen. Arguing with him had become something of a blood sport. A blood sport he was so much better at than her. It was one of the main reasons she'd snuck off to study Fine Arts at the Sorbonne. If she had stayed in Anders it would have been impossible to keep the promise she had made to her dying mother to try and get along with her father.

His earlier edict replayed again in her head. She couldn't return to Anders. What would she do there? Sit around and play parlour games all day while she waited for him to line up another convenient husband? The thought made her shiver.

Determined to stop thinking about her father, Ava carefully opened the car door and stepped out into the long grass. The spiky heels of her ankle boots immediately sank into the soft earth.

Great. As a gallery owner it was imperative that she always look impeccable and there was no way she could afford to ruin her prized Prada boots. Since she'd decided a long time ago not to take any of her father's money she didn't have any spare cash lying around to replace them. Another decision that had displeased him.

She stood precariously on the balls of her feet and leaned in to retrieve her handbag. Her phone had fallen out and when she picked it up she saw the screen was smashed. Unable to remember Gilles's mobile number, she tossed it back in the car in frustration. She could always call emergency services, but then her little accident would be all over the news in a heartbeat—and the thought of any more attention this week for 'the poor jilted Princess' made her teeth gnash together. Which didn't help her sore head.

No. She'd simply have to walk.

But standing on the grassy verge with her hands on her hips, she realised just how far it was to the main gates. Her beloved boots would be destroyed. Not to mention how hot and sweaty she would be by the time she got there. This was not the graceful and dignified entrance she had planned to make. And if one of those media vans she had seen loitering a few miles back saw her...

Wondering just what to do next, she had a sudden brainwave. A sudden and slightly crazy brainwave. Fortuitously—if she could describe running her little car into a ditch in such terms—she'd crashed right near a section of the outer wall that she had played on with her brother Frédéric and her cousin Baden and Gilles during family visits to the château in her childhood. Scaling the wall as revolutionary spies had been their secret game, and they'd even scraped out footholds to aid their escape from imaginary enemies.

Ava felt a grin creep across her face for the first time that day. She had to concede it was a tad desperate, but with Gilles's wedding only hours away that was exactly what she was. And, anyway, she had always loved to climb as a kid; surely it would be even easier as an adult?

'There's a woman stuck on the south wall, boss. What do you want us to do with her?'

Wolfe pulled up in the middle of an arched hallway in Château Verne and pressed his phone a little tighter to his ear. '*On* the wall?'

'The very top,' repeated Eric, one of the more junior members of Wolfe's security team.

Wolfe tensed. Perfect. Most likely another interfering journalist, trying to get the scoop on his friend's extravagant wedding to the daughter of a controversial American politician. They hadn't let up all day, circling the château like starving buzzards. But none had been brazen enough to go over the wall yet. Of course he'd been prepared for the possibility—the reason they now had this little intruder in hand.

'Name?'

'Says she's Ava de Veers, Princess of Anders.'

A princess climbing over a forty-foot brick wall? Wolfe didn't think so. 'ID?'

'No ID in her handbag. Says she had a car accident and it must have fallen out.'

Clever.

'Camera?'

'Check.'

Wolfe considered his options. Even from inside the thick walls of the château he could hear the irritating whine of distant media choppers as they hovered just outside the established no-fly zone. With the wedding still three hours away he'd better extend the security perimeters before there were any more breaches.

'Want me to take her back to base, boss?'

'No.' Wolfe shot his hand through his hair. He'd rather turf her back over the wall than give her even more access to the property by taking her to the outer cottage his men were temporarily using. And he would—after he had established her identity and satisfied himself that she wasn't a real threat. 'Leave her where she's perched.' He was about to ring off when he had another thought. 'And, Eric, keep your gun on her until I get there.' That would teach her for entering a private function without an invitation.

'Ah...you mean keep her *on* the wall?'

When Eric hesitated Wolfe knew right then that the woman was attractive.

'Yes, that's exactly what I mean.' For all he knew she could be a political nutcase instead of an overzealous journo. 'And don't engage in any conversation with her until I get there.'

Wolfe trusted his men implicitly, but the last thing he needed was some smoking Mata Hari doing a number on their head.

'Yes, sir.'

Wolfe pocketed his phone. This would mean he wouldn't be able to start the pre-wedding game of polo Gilles had organised. Annoying, but it couldn't be helped. He'd offered to run security for Gilles's wedding because it was what he did, and the job always came first.

Once outside, Wolfe found Gilles and his merry band already waiting for him at the stables, the horses groomed and saddled and raring to go. Wolfe ran his gaze over the roguish white Arabian that Gilles had promised him. He'd missed his daily gym workout this morning and had been looking forward to putting the stallion through his paces.

Hell, he still could. Taking the reins from the handler, he swung easily onto the giant of a horse. The stallion shifted restlessly beneath his weight and Wolfe automatically reached forward to pat his neck, breathing in the strong scent of horse and leather. 'What's his name?'

'Achilles.'

His mouth quirked and Gilles shrugged. 'Apollo was taken and he's a bloody contrary animal. You should enjoy each other.'

Wolfe laughed at his aristocratic friend. Years ago they had forged an unbreakable bond when they had trained together for selection on an elite military task force. They'd been there for each other during the tough times and celebrated during the good. Inevitably Gilles had started sprouting reams of poetry and Greek myths to stay awake when they'd spent long hours waiting for something to happen. By contrast Wolfe, a rugged Australian country boy, had used a more simple method. Sheer grit and stubborn determination. A trait that had served him well when he had swapped special ops for software development and created what was currently the most sophisticated computer spyware on the planet.

Wolfe Inc had been forged around that venture, and when his younger brother had joined him they'd expanded into every aspect of the security business. But where his brother thrived on the corporate life Wolfe preferred the freedom of being able to mix things up a little. He even kept his hand in on some of the more hairy covert ops some governments called consultants in to take care of. He had to get his adrenaline high from something other than his beloved Honda CBR.

'Always the dreamer, *Monsieur le Marquis*,' he drawled.

'Just a man who knows how to have balance in his life, Ice,' Gilles countered good-naturedly, calling Wolfe by his old military nickname. He swung onto the back of a regal-looking bay. 'You should try it some time, my friend.'

'I've got plenty of balance in my life,' Wolfe grunted, thinking about the Viennese blonde he'd been glad to see the back of a month ago. 'No need to worry your pretty head on that score.'

Achilles snorted and tossed his nose in challenge as Wolfe took up the reins.

'I won't be joining you just yet. I need to check on an issue that's come up.' He kept his tone deliberately bland so as not to alarm his friend, who should be concentrating on why he was signing his life away to a woman in matrimony rather than why a woman was currently sitting on one of his outer walls. 'Achilles and I will join you in a few.'

The horse pulled against the bit and Wolfe smiled. There was nothing quite like using all his skills to master a difficult animal, and he wondered if Gilles would consider selling him. He already liked the unmanageable beast.

* * *

Okay, so maybe it wasn't that much easier to scale a high brick wall as an adult, Ava conceded. In fact it had been downright scary and had shown her how unfit she was. Her arm muscles were aching in protest. It hadn't helped when she'd discovered the ancient chestnut tree she had been relying on to help her down the other side had been removed, and then two trained security guards wielding machine guns had happened upon her.

She hadn't considered that Gilles would have hired extra security for the wedding, but in hindsight she should have done. Naturally the men hadn't believed her about the car accident, and now all she needed was for one of those media helicopters she could hear to zero in on her and her joyous day would just about be complete.

It was all Gilles's fault, she grouched to herself, eyeing the uneven terrain at her feet where the magnificent tree had once stood. And surely they'd raised the height of the wall since the last time she'd climbed it as a tearaway twelve-year-old.

Shifting uncomfortably, she eyed the two killers camouflaged in street clothes below, glad she was conversant in English. She knew no self-respecting Frenchman would ever be seen mixing flannel with corduroy. 'If you would just check a couple of hundred metres up the road you'll find my car and realise that I am telling you the truth,' she repeated, struggling to hold back the temper her father had often complained was as easy to strike up as a match. Which actually wasn't true. It took special powers to induce her to lose the plot.

'Sorry, ma'am. Boss's orders.' That from the one who looked slightly more sympathetic than the other—although that was like saying snow was colder than ice.

'Fine. But I have a headache and I'd like to get down.'

'Sorry, ma'am—'

'Boss's orders,' Ava finished asininely, wondering what

the two men would do if she decided to jump. Not an entirely practical option since she would likely break her ankle.

It had clearly been an oversight on their part as children only to whittle footholds on *one* side of the wall. A mistake no self-respecting spy in their right mind would have made!

Ava briefly closed her eyes and gently tested the injury on her forehead. It felt so large she was sure the House of Fabergé would weep to get their hands on it.

A wave of irritation threatened to topple her off the wall and impale her on one of those raised guns, and as much as she told herself it was irrational to be irritated with these men, since this whole situation was her own fault, she couldn't dispel her growing agitation. In truth, she felt like a fool sitting atop Gilles's wall like a silly bird.

'And where is this boss of yours?' she queried, injecting her voice with a calm she was far from feeling.

'Coming soon, ma'am.'

So was Christmas. In four months' time.

A low rumble of thunder brought Ava's head around as she tried to locate the sound. Her view was hampered by soaring parkland trees and wild shrubbery, and the only thing visible in the distance were the rounded red brick towers of the château and a picture-perfect blue sky beyond.

Then a flash of white amongst the trees caught her attention, and she couldn't look away as a purebred stallion galloped into view. Ava's eyes drank in the beautiful creature—and then she felt slightly dizzy as her eyes took in its handsome rider.

Windswept sandy hair was brushed back from a proud face with a strong nose and square jaw, wide shoulders and a lean torso rippled beneath a fitted black polo shirt, and long, muscular legs were outlined to perfection in white jodhpurs and knee-high black riding boots.

She sensed he was absolutely furious, even though he hadn't moved a well-honed muscle. His narrowed eyes were boring into hers with the intense focus of a natural hunter. Even when the horse stamped impatiently beneath him, its nostrils flaring and its tail flicking with irritation, the man remained preternaturally still.

Ava's heart pounded and she found her fingers gripping the stone wall for support. Heat was turning her limbs soft. Of course it was the sun making her hot, not the ruthless-looking warrior staring at her with an arrogance that bordered on insolence.

'Are you the reason I'm still on this wall?' The confrontational words were out of her mouth before she'd known they were in her head and she could have kicked herself. She had meant to be pleasant, to make sure this ordeal was over as quickly as possible. She knew instantly from the firm jut of his jaw that she had well and truly put paid to that.

Wolfe didn't move a muscle as his eyes swept over the fey gypsy on the wall. He'd been wrong. She wasn't attractive. She was *astonishingly* attractive, and his soldier's eyes noted everything. High cheekbones, honey-gold skin, eyes as dark as night and thick sable hair pulled into a ponytail, wisps from which floated around a lush, sulky mouth that looked as if it was waiting to be kissed.

By him.

Impatiently discarding the unexpected thought, he let his eyes drift lower over a white cotton shirt the gentle breeze was using to outline her rounded breasts, and fitted jeans that hugged long slender legs. And bare, stocking-clad feet!

Achilles swatted the air with his tail, as if he too was disturbed by the vision, and then Wolfe registered her haughty, royally pissed-off question and recovered himself. She was an intruder, and she was ruining a rousing game of polo, and if she was upset she could stand in line.

'No.' He shot her a cursory look. '*You* are the reason you're still on that wall.'

Ignoring her hissed exhalation he swung out of the saddle and approached his men. He could feel her eyes following him and wondered at their exact colour, immediately irritated at the irrelevant thought.

He waited for Eric to fill him in on how they had come across her, and then indicated for him to pass over the leather handbag he held in his hand.

'Is the gun absolutely necessary?'

Her slightly bored question floated down from the wall.

'Only if I have to shoot you with it.' He didn't bother looking at her when he spoke. 'And keep your hands where I can see them.'

'I'm not a criminal!'

He ignored her little outburst and inspected her handbag. 'Find anything interesting in here?'

'No, boss. Usual women things. Lipstick, tissues, hair clips. No ID, as I said.'

He heard her exasperated sigh. 'I already told your watchdogs I had a car accident and my purse must have fallen out of my bag.'

'Convenient.'

'For whom? You?'

Wolfe gave her a stare he knew from experience made grown men think twice. 'You have an awfully smart mouth for someone in your predicament.' And he wished she would close it. The husky quality of her lightly accented voice was having an adverse effect on his body.

'I am Princess Ava de Veers of Anders and I demand you let me down from here immediately.'

Wolfe ran his eyes over her again, just for the sheer pleasure of it and because he knew it would put her on the back foot. 'What are you doing on a wall, Princess? Learning to fly?'

'I am a guest at this wedding and you are likely to lose

your job if you insist on leaving me up here. I'm probably sunburned by now.'

'By this watered-down version of the sun?' And on that golden skin? 'Unlikely. And honoured guests usually approach by the main gates. What outlet do you work for?'

Her brow crinkled. 'I don't—'

'Newspaper? Magazine? TV station? Nice camera, by the way. Mind if I take a look?'

'Yes, I do.'

He dumped her handbag on the grass and started checking through her photos.

'I said *yes*, I do mind.'

'Whether I look or not isn't contingent on whether you mind.'

'Why bother asking, then?'

He nearly smiled at the exasperation in her voice. 'Manners.'

She made a cute noise that said he wouldn't know what manners were if they conked him on the head.

Frowning at the photos on her camera, he glanced up at her. 'Nice celebrity shots on here. I repeat—what rag do you work for?'

She rolled her eyes. 'I am not a member of the paparazzi, if that's what you're suggesting.'

'No?'

'No. I own an art gallery. Those were taken at a recent opening night. Not that it is any of your business.'

Wolfe rubbed his jaw and pretended to consider that. 'Really? Given your current predicament, I'd say it's very much my business.'

She looked as if she was holding on to her temper by a thread. 'I do understand how this looks. And I even appreciate how efficient your men were at spotting me—'

'I'm so happy to hear that.'

'But—' she carried on as if he hadn't interrupted '—I am

who I say I am. My car is a couple of hundred metres that way, and your men would already know this if they had bothered to go and find it instead of holding their weapons on me as if I was a terrorist.'

Wolfe handed the camera to Eric. 'Oh, I'm sorry.' He didn't bother to hide the contempt he felt for her type. Haughty princesses—real or imagined—who thought their needs took preference over everybody else's. 'Did I forget to tell you? My men take orders from *me*, not you.'

Her pout turned even sexier. 'Convenient.'

He wasn't in the frame of mind to appreciate her wisecrack and nearly reconsidered his need to verify her identity before tossing her back over the wall.

'Eric. Dane. Take the Jeep and find her car. If it exists.'

She sniffed at his instructions and shifted her bottom on the wall. She must be completely uncomfortable by now. Serve her right.

'I told you to keep your hands where I could see them.'

She rolled her eyes. 'Do you think it might be at all possible that I could wait on the ground for your men to return? I promise not to overpower you while they are gone.'

The air seemed to buzz with the antagonistic heat she imbued him with, and her accent lent her sardonic words a sexy edge. She was a wicked combination of beauty and spirit, and not even the way she spoke down to him was enough to keep his libido at bay. A truly annoying realisation.

'I think I can handle you.'

Her eyes dropped to his mouth and Wolfe felt a kick of lust all the way to his toes. He waited, breathless, for the heat in his groin to dissipate, but if anything it got worse. Then her eyes blazed into his and the chemistry he'd been trying to ignore sparked like a live wire between them.

The way her eyes widened he thought perhaps she had read his thoughts, but that was impossible. Fourteen years in the business and Wolfe knew how to hide what he was feeling—hell, he'd learned how to do that by the time he could walk.

Perhaps she'd just felt the same burn he had. And had liked it just as little, if her wary gaze was anything to go by. Which gave him a moment's pause. If she was a journalist—or, worse, some sort of political stalker—she'd have already used that connection to manipulate him, not shy away from it as if she'd just been singed.

His eyes took in wrists that looked impossibly slender within the cuffs of her masculine-style shirt, then moved down along fine-boned hands and nails buffed to perfection. She didn't do hard labour. That much was obvious.

He knew instinctively she was who she said she was. It was in her regal bearing, the swanlike arch of her neck, in her sense of entitlement and the way she looked at him as if he was staff. His mother had often looked at his father like that and Wolfe had always felt sorry for the poor bastard.

She shifted again, her eyes on the ground. 'Do you have any suggestions on how I might get down from here?' And with a degree of dignity, her tone seemed to imply.

'Perhaps you'd like me to unfold my trusty ladder from my back pocket?' Wolfe mocked. 'Oh, dear. Left it at home.' He opened his hands, palms facing upwards. 'Guess you'll just have to jump into my arms, Princess. What a treat.'

His horse snickered and her eyes used the excuse to glance at the stallion before returning to his. 'Channelling your inner Zorro?' she asked sweetly.

His lips twitched. 'Only because I left my Batman tool belt at home.'

'With Robin?'

Despite his less than stellar mood he chuckled. 'Cute. Toss down the boots first.' The last thing he wanted was to be stabbed by one of those dangerous-looking heels, and by the gleam in her eyes that was exactly what she was considering.

'I have a better idea. Why don't I just go back down the way I came up?'

'No.'

Her lips tightened. 'It makes perfect sense. I can—'

'Try it and I *will* shoot you.'

'You don't have a gun.'

'I have a gun.'

She paused, her stillness telling him she was weighing up whether he was telling the truth or not. Her eyes slid down his torso and over his legs and he felt a rush of unexpected excitement, as if she'd actually touched him.

'You are being overly obnoxious about this,' she fumed.

'Not yet, I'm not.' Wolfe barely managed to suppress his rising aggravation at this physical response to a woman he already didn't like. 'But I'm getting close.'

'If you drop me I'll sue you.'

'If you don't hurry up and get down from that wall I'll sue *you*.'

Her dark brows arched imperiously. 'For what?'

'Trying my patience. Now, pass down the boots. Nice and easy,' he warned softly.

With an audible sigh she dropped her boots one after the other into his outstretched hands. The kid leather was warm from her touch.

'Now you.' His voice had grown rough—a clear indication that some part of him was looking forward to holding her in his arms. And what was wrong with that? He might not be interested in starting up another affair straight after his last one had ended so tastelessly, but he *was* male and this woman *was* beautiful.

'I'd rather wait for a ladder.'

So would he.

'Then you'd better settle in. I run security, not rescue.'

Again she glanced dubiously at the ground. 'It didn't seem

like such a big drop when I was younger. And what happened to the chestnut tree that used to grow here?'

'Now you're mistaking me for a gardener, Princess. What next?'

Her eyes narrowed. 'Certainly not for a nice man. Rest assured of that. And my correct title is Your Royal Highness.'

He knew the correct title. He might not be royal himself, but he'd met enough in his lifetime to know how to address one. 'Thanks for the tip. But I don't have all day. So let's go.' Time to stop thinking about the tempting swell of her breasts and her hot mouth.

'*You* don't have all day? Thanks to you, I'm impossibly late now,' she complained.

He beckoned her with his fingers. 'My heart bleeds.'

'You're really very rude.'

'Want me to leave you up there?' he prompted, fresh out of patience.

'Excuse me for being a little uneasy.'

Wolfe sighed and held his hands up again. 'I've never dropped a princess before.'

'You've probably never had the opportunity before now.'

He shook his head. 'You sure do know how to make yourself vulnerable, Princess.'

She muttered something in French, making him want to smile. She was all fire and...*attitude*!

Balancing on her hands, she carefully swung her leg over the wall, so that she was perched on it like a little chipmunk, her fingers turning white as she gripped the edge. Still she hesitated, lifting first one thigh and then the other to make sure the fabric of her jeans didn't catch.

'Want me to count to three?' he drawled.

She threw him a dark look, her eyes fixed firmly on his, and then they snapped closed and she launched herself off the wall.

Wolfe felt her svelte torso slide through his hands as he

caught her, his arms winding around her before she hit the ground. Her rib cage heaved as she dragged in an unsteady breath, the movement flattening her soft breasts against his hard chest.

Her arms clung tight around his neck, holding his face against the warm pulse at the base of her neck. His senses instantly filled with her heat and sweet perfume. He usually found perfume cloying. Hers wasn't, and was probably the reason he held her longer than he needed to. Held her moulded against him as if he'd been doing it his whole life. Held her long enough to wonder how it would feel to fit himself deep inside her.

Tight. Hot. Wet.

Wolfe's head reared back as his senses took over and he found himself staring into exquisite, wide-spaced navy blue eyes that made him feel as if he'd been hit by a land-to-air missile.

'You can put me down now,' she said a little breathlessly.

He could slide his hands down to her butt and wrap her legs around his waist, as well.

As if he'd spoken out loud the air between them thickened, and he felt every hot inch of her go impossibly still against him.

Almost embarrassed by a stupefyingly strong urge to crush her mouth beneath his, which had held him spellbound for—God—he hoped only seconds, he none-too-gently set her on her feet and stepped back from her.

It was only then that he noticed the slight swelling above her right temple.

'You should get that looked at,' he instructed roughly.

Her eyes licked over his face before meeting his, her breathing as uneven as his heart rate. 'I'm fine.'

'Put your shoes on. It's time to go.' He busied himself with collecting Achilles while his mind came back on line. By rights he should search her, to make sure she was clean, but, *hell*, he wasn't touching her again. Bad enough he'd have to put her on the back of the horse since Eric and Dane had yet to return.

He frowned, wondering what was taking them so long.

'I'd rather walk.' Her eyes flitted from the stamping stallion and back to him.

Realising he was functioning below par, and that had he been on a real military expedition he might well be dead now, Wolfe re-engaged his instincts and gave her a hard stare. 'You can try my patience, Princess, but I wouldn't recommend it.'

She blinked, as if she hadn't expected his curt tone. 'Unlike your men, I don't take orders from you.'

Wolfe widened his stance in a purely dominant move he knew she hadn't missed. 'We have yet to establish your real identity, so you either get on that horse or I'll use one of these reins to bind your hands and drag you behind.'

'I'd like to see you try,' she invited him coolly.

He couldn't believe this posh piece of work was calling his bluff. 'Would you, now?'

She balled her hands on her hips and drew his sight to her slender curves. Not a clever move in his currently cantankerous state of combined anger and arousal. Of course he wouldn't drag her, but he'd subdue her and throw her over his saddle.

He saw the moment she realised his threat wasn't entirely idle.

'Only men with very small appendages play the tough guy.'

'And only women who are incredibly stupid challenge a man they've never met to prove his masculinity. Fortunately for you, I don't feel the least threatened to prove myself by shrewish females.'

'What can I say?' She cocked her hip towards him insolently. 'You bring out the best in me.'

Wolfe breathed deep at her intentionally provocative manner. 'I'm sure that's very far from your best, Princess,' he drawled.

Her brows slowly rose and Wolfe realised he'd inadvertently revealed how attractive he found her. No doubt it was something she was used to and, like all women in his experience, would take absolute advantage of it given half the chance.

Something he didn't plan to do.

Aggravated by his one-track mind, he was about to end her rebellious stance by physically dumping her onto the horse when his phone rang.

'We found the car, boss. She's legit. Her purse must have been thrown from her bag because it was lodged under the front seat.'

Wolfe grunted a reply and told his men to meet him at the cottage.

He looked up in time to catch her superior expression and knew that she'd overheard his conversation. 'Seems you are who you say you are. Next time use the gate.' He brought Achilles alongside her and grabbed the stirrup. 'Give me your leg.'

'You're not even going to apologise?'

Her tone spoke of generations of superiority that made any apology Wolfe might have given die on his lips.

'Your leg?' he repeated, his eyes cool and guarded against the fire pouring out of hers.

Moving forward, she tossed her ponytail over her shoulder, caught her heel on a rock and pitched straight into his arms.

Already highly sensitised to her touch, and not sure if the move had been deliberate, to throw him off balance, Wolfe immediately set her away from him. 'And don't try using that sexy little body to garner any favours, Princess.'

'Trust me when I say that touching you is the last thing I would want to do.'

She presented him with her stiff back, gathered the reins

up in one hand and stamped her foot into his hand. Wolfe didn't know whether to be amused by her or angered, and perhaps if he hadn't been about to head off after Gilles's wedding to oversee an important software installation he might have hung around to test her lofty challenge. But he was, and he wasn't stupid enough to get involved with another highly strung female.

'Shift back,' he grated. No way was she riding in front, where she would be cradled between his hard thighs.

'You know, all that masculine muttering is entirely uncalled for. You are unquestionably the most irritating individual I have ever had the misfortune to come across.'

Wolfe was just about to tell her the feeling was entirely mutual when she twisted the reins out of his slack hold and dug her heels into Achilles's side. The horse responded like the thoroughbred it was and sprang into an instant gallop.

Wolfe couldn't believe it!

Not only had the little spitfire turned him on just by breathing, she had completely got the better of him. Neither of which had happened to him in… It had *never* happened before!

'Dammit!'

Cursing under his breath, Wolfe whistled sharply. If Gilles had trained his animals correctly the horse should come to a complete stop.

CHAPTER TWO

ONE MINUTE AVA was flying across the uneven ground with breathless speed and the next she wasn't moving at all. The horse did little more than twitch its majestic tail as she tried to urge him forward. By the time she worked out what had happened the overbearing *inbecile* was almost upon her.

'Come on, horse. Do *not* listen to him. He is nobody.'

'You look like butter wouldn't melt in your mouth, but you're a bossy little thing aren't you, Princess?'

'You are so arrogant.'

He settled his hands on his hips. 'That's rich, coming from you.'

'I am not arrogant,' she said in a voice that would have made her father proud. 'I am confident. There is a difference.'

He had the gall to laugh. 'And the difference would fit inside a flea's arse.'

Ava used her sweetest voice to call him a foul name in French, knowing he probably wouldn't understand her.

He shook his head and tsked. 'Temper, temper.' His gaze lifted to her hair. 'If I didn't know better I'd say there was a red streak running through that glossy mane of yours.'

A chauvinist. How original. 'I suppose you think I should be flattered you didn't say blond?'

'No, I would never confuse you with a blonde,' he said with mock seriousness. 'I like blondes.'

'Then I *do* consider myself flattered!'

She thought about flicking the reins to try and ride off again, but he read her mind and his jaw clenched. 'I don't make the same mistakes twice. Shift back.'

Ava noticed how big the hand was that gripped the reins and instantly recalled how they had felt on her body as he'd caught her. Once again her pelvis clenched, sending delicious ripples of sensation through her whole body. Surprised, and a little breathless, she berated herself for the physical reaction. He was Neanderthal man two million-odd years later, his blood supply no doubt taken up by all the muscles in his body instead of his head, where he needed it most.

He moved a small handgun out from under the back of his shirt and tucked it inside his boot, and she felt another traitorous thrill shoot straight to her core. Peevishly she hoped the gun went off and shot him in the foot.

'I'm sure many women get turned on by your barbaric tactics, but I can assure you I am not one of them.'

'Good to know.' He stroked the horse's neck in long, smooth sweeps. 'Since I'm not trying to turn you on.'

His eyes glittered up at her and made her heart pump just that little bit faster. Lord, she hoped he didn't know she was lying, because she *shouldn't* find this uncultured beast of a man so attractive.

Grabbing the pommel, he fitted his foot into the stirrup. 'Now, you can ride up in front between my legs if you want to, Princess. Who knows? It might be fun.'

Ava quickly scooted back and ground her teeth together when he gave a low, sexy laugh. His voice was rich and totally indolent, as if he was always thinking of ways to pleasure a woman.

He swung easily onto the great horse, his large frame filling the saddle. The horse shifted as it readjusted to take their weight. 'You might want to hang on.' He shot over his shoulder, drawing up the reins.

'I am.'

He glanced to where her hands gripped the saddle blanket before raising his eyes back to hers. Ava drew in a sharp breath at the impact.

'I meant to me.'

Ava had no intention of holding on to him. 'Dream on.'

He gave a half smile, as if he might do exactly that, clenched his powerful thighs, and the horse sprang forwards as if it had nothing more than a child on its back.

Instinctively Ava clutched at his shirt and found herself plastered up against the back of him. He was hard! And hot! Unable to help herself, she widened her fingers over his abdominal muscles as if she needed to do so to prevent herself from falling off. Colyn had always bemoaned the fact that she wasn't tactile enough for him, but right now she could barely resist the urge to explore this stranger's muscular physique. She thought she heard him blow out a hard breath and, slightly embarrassed at her temerity, quickly moved her fingers to his narrow hips. The roll of muscle there told her that he worked out. A lot.

Fortunately it took no time for the spirited stallion to make it to the main buildings. Unfortunately it was still long enough for the friction from the saddle and his body to make the space between her legs feel soft and moist.

Mon Dieu.

Yes, it had been a long time since she had been intimate with a man, but this one was *so* not her type...

Focusing on her surroundings, instead of the man she could feel with every cell of her body, she realised they weren't at the stables but at one of the side entrances to the main building.

About to ask what they were doing there, she stopped when he twisted around in the saddle, grabbed her under her arm and effortlessly lifted her off the horse. Ava felt the slide of his thigh all the way down her body and closed her eyes briefly to block out the rush of heat coursing through her. When her feet finally touched the ground she locked her knees to take her weight and had to force herself to push away from his heat.

'Any time you want to learn how to fly again, Princess, you just call me, okay?'

Ava curled her lip, but before she could come up with a pithy retort he had dug his heels into the stallion and was gone.

Thank God. It would take two top-of-the-line masseurs to work the tension out of her back after that!

'Ma'am? Are you lost?'

A footman materialised at her side, and it was only then that Ava registered that her 'captor' had set her down in a private part of the castle, far from the prying eyes of arriving guests. It was probably more because he was used to using the servants' entrance than out of any actual consideration for her, but even as she had the ungrateful thought she had a feeling she was wrong.

Wolfe stood on the lime-green lawn at the side of the white marquee set up as a servers' area under the shade of a weeping willow. He wasn't on duty, but his eyes scanned the throng of wedding guests holding sparkling glasses of wine and champagne and recapping the beautiful service they had just witnessed.

The men mostly wore classic morning suits, as he did, and the women were tastefully attired in afternoon dresses and sunhats. Later, at the evening reception, they would all change into their ballroom best.

It was only when his eyes finally found the Princess, in a small cluster of women waiting to talk to the bride, that he realised he'd been searching for her.

He cursed under his breath. His reaction to her was annoyingly primal. And annoyingly still present. The problem, he decided as he studied her, was that she had an element of the conquest about her. All that snooty standoffishness combined with her natural beauty was like a summons to any man who had red blood pumping through his veins. But while he enjoyed a challenge—possibly more than most men—some inner sense of self-preservation warned him to keep his distance.

He had very firm rules when it came to women and he never deviated from them. Keep it short, keep it sweet and, most importantly, keep it simple. This posh princess had *complicated* written all over her pretty face.

He'd seen enough relationships fall apart to last him a lifetime, and while logically he knew not all couples ended up on the scrap heap he wasn't prepared to take the chance. It was probably the only risk he wasn't willing to take, because when it all went pear-shaped the fall-out was usually devastating.

'I know that face. You're brooding about something.'

Wolfe glanced at Gilles, who had ambled up with two glasses of champagne in his hands. Wolfe took one and smiled. 'Just enjoying the frivolities.'

Gilles gave him a droll look. Previously they had both bemoaned any wedding they'd been forced to attend. 'I thought you were bringing someone with you today?'

Wolfe took a sip and tried not to wince as the warming liquid pooled in his mouth. 'Not while I'm working.'

Gilles lowered his own glass, amusement dancing in his eyes. 'She dumped you?'

Wolfe recalled the look on Astrid's angry face when he'd told her he wouldn't be seeing her again. 'Yep.'

'In…' Gilles glanced at his watch '…how many hours?'

Wolfe chuckled. He'd enjoyed Astrid's company for five busy nights while he was working in Vienna a month ago, and she had enjoyed his. When he'd tried to say goodbye she'd kicked up a stink. Accused him of using her. Wolfe's anger had surfaced then. He knew he had a name for being a heartless womaniser but he was simply honest. He didn't see the point in beating around the bush and pretending to feel things he didn't. And nor did he sleep with as many women as his reputation would suggest. He wouldn't have any time left over for work if he did.

'What can I say? She was one of the smart ones.'

Wolfe waited for his friend to start up another good-natured lecture about settling down. Anne, it seemed, had reformed the once bad-boy Marquis to the point where Wolfe now almost preferred her company to his.

'Well, that works out well for me.'

'It does?'

Gilles chuckled. 'Don't look so relieved. I wasn't about to try and reform the unreformable.'

'Thank God.'

'But I do need a favour.'

Favours Wolfe could do.

'Sure.'

'There's a girl I need you to keep your eye on tonight at the reception.'

Wolfe didn't exactly look at the sky, but he came close. 'Friend of Anne's, by chance?'

'Yes, actually. But, no, I'm not trying to set you up, you suspicious clod. She's the woman my father wanted me to marry.'

Gilles's words sparked a distant memory of a late-night chat from years back that Wolfe had completely forgotten about. He took another pull of his drink and wished it was beer in an icy bottle instead of champagne in a tepid glass. 'I'm listening.'

'Years ago my father and hers came to the decision that we would forge a strong union if we married when we came of age.'

'I think you "came of age" about ten years ago, my friend, and isn't that a little last century?'

Gilles's mouth twisted into an ironic smile. 'You've met

my father. Hers is worse. Anyway, the media have done a good job beating some life into the old story this past week, playing up the whole jilted fiancée thing, and Anne said it's been a bit rough on her.'

Wolfe knew what it felt like to be talked about behind his back. Even if the people in the small town he'd grown up in had been doing so out of sympathy rather than slander. At least for him and his brother, at any rate. 'What's wrong with her?' he asked suspiciously.

Gilles scoffed. 'Nothing. But I don't want you to sleep with her. Actually, I'd be downright angry if you did. She's gorgeous, and way too good for you. I just want you to keep an eye on her. Make sure she's having a good time.'

'Who is she?' he asked, premonition snaking down his spine.

'See the woman talking to Anne now?'

Wolfe didn't have to look to know it was the Princess from the wall and he nearly groaned. Anyone but her. But at least now it made sense why she had been so familiar with the estate. They were family friends.

Wolfe turned his back on the woman he was intent on avoiding for the rest of his life. 'I'm sure she can take care of herself.'

Gilles gave him a quizzical look and Wolfe cursed his curt tone. He had nothing against the Princess, really. Except for the fact that she'd occupied his mind all afternoon and made him want to push her sweet skirt up around her waist and take her up against the nearest hundred-year-old oak. He definitely didn't want to find out that Gilles had once been with her. Had they been lovers? The thought left a sour taste in his mouth.

'I'm sure she will, too, but as she's attending the wedding alone I thought you could keep your eye on her for me. You know—ask her to dance, make sure she has a drink.'

Today he'd been mistaken for a rescue service, a gardener

and now… 'You've got waiters for that, and I'm not a damned babysitter.'

Gilles's eyebrows shot up, but before he could say anything his new wife stepped around Wolfe and curled her arm through Gilles's. 'Babysitting who?'

Her green eyes met Wolfe's speculatively and Wolfe saw Gilles's eyes fall guiltily on someone behind him.

'I hope you do not mean me, Gilles?' Ava's tone was as lyrical and as superior as Wolfe remembered it.

Gilles stepped forward and kissed both her cheeks. 'Ava, you look as beautiful as ever.'

'I can see that you *do* mean me,' she berated lightly. 'And I can assure you I do not need babysitting.'

Her eyes briefly cut to Wolfe's with such aloof disdain it made him want to smile. He remembered her hands splayed over the ridges of his abdominal muscles as she'd clung to him on the horse. She might not like him very much, but he knew dislike wasn't the *only* emotion she felt.

'Of course you don't, *ma petite*.' Gilles humoured her. 'Now, let me introduce you to Wolfe, a good friend of mine.'

Unable to prevent himself from ruffling her regal feathers, Wolfe tilted his head. 'We've met. How's the head?' His eyes drifted to the wide-brimmed hat, tilted to one side to conceal the bruise on her forehead. The pale pink exactly matched a flirty two-piece suit that followed the line of her curves all the way to her perfectly shaped calves and slender ankles.

Exceptional legs, he thought, his gaze trekking slowly back up to her face.

She arched a brow that told him she hadn't taken kindly to his once-over, or to the implied intimacy in his tone.

'You know each other?' Gilles regarded Ava in surprise. 'No.'

'Oh?' Gilles cut his curious gaze back to Wolfe.

'Shall I tell him, or do you want to?' Wolfe drawled.

After briefly glaring all sorts of retribution his way, she

turned a serene smile on Gilles and Anne. 'It was nothing. I had a small problem with my car and your friend *kindly* provided me with a lift to the château.'

'A small problem with your car?' Gilles frowned.

Wolfe held her gaze as he felt the others turn to him and told himself to leave well enough alone. Ruffling her glorious feathers was not on his agenda, even if his body was demanding that he forge a new one—preferably starting with her naked on top of a set of silk sheets. 'What Her Highness means is that she had a car accident, climbed your outer wall and got captured by my men—'

'And stole your horse because you were being incredibly rude!' she provided, cutting Gilles's blustering in half.

Wolfe shifted his weight and stuck one hand into his pocket. 'And here I was thinking you stole him because you wanted to go for a ride.' He rubbed his hand across his abdomen, unable to stop himself from teasing her a little.

'I did think about it,' she murmured huskily, the quick dart of her pink tongue caressing her lower lip and sending a bolt of lust straight to his groin. 'But since he wasn't up to my usual standard I thought why bother?'

Wolfe laughed at her bald-faced put-down. Gilles was fortunately too worried about her accident to pick up on the subtext, but Anne's interested glances told him that she wasn't quite as obtuse.

'You weren't hurt?' Anne queried, concern lacing her words.

'A bump on the head,' Ava dismissed casually. 'Really, the whole thing was *incredibly* insignificant.'

Wolfe's lips quirked. 'You know, I wouldn't have described it that way myself.'

'No?' Ava held his gaze. 'Maybe you need to get out more.'

'Maybe I do,' he agreed, noting the line of pink that highlighted her lovely cheekbones. Maybe he needed to get out with *her*. No. He'd already decided not to go there. But, damn, he was enjoying sparring with her.

'But what were you doing on the wall?' Gilles interrupted with a frown.

'Well, trying to get down, obviously,' Ava returned pithily. 'Which would have been a lot easier if you hadn't removed that lovely old chestnut tree.'

Gilles gave a typically Gallic shrug. 'I had no choice. It was a security risk.'

Wolfe laughed right up until the moment she shared a warm smile with Gilles. Again he wondered at their history. Had she been in love with his friend? Was she still? Was that why Gilles had asked him to watch out for her? Was it possible she would cause trouble if he didn't? Questions, questions, questions. And there was really only one he wanted answered.

How responsive would she be in his bed?

His name suited him, Ava mused absently, nursing a flute of champagne as she willed the evening reception to finish.

Predatory.

Intense.

Arrogant.

And utterly transfixing when he turned those molten toffee-coloured eyes on her. Not to mention aloof and emotionally unavailable if the evening gossip was to be believed.

'They call him Ice, and apparently he has a heart as hard to find as a pink diamond,' one woman had said, giggling as she'd gazed longingly across the room at him.

Ava had rolled her eyes. She knew many women saw an unattainable man—especially a wealthy alpha male like Wolfe—as a personal challenge to go forth and rehabilitate, but she wasn't one of them. She was only interested in a man who was caring and considerate and who respected a woman as more than just a trophy to be admired and trotted out when it suited him. A gentle, sophisticated man, who was looking for love and companionship more than short affairs with a variety of women.

That thought reminded her of the luncheon she'd had with Anne last month. 'Hot' and 'divine' were words that had been bandied around when she'd talked about a friend of Gilles's called Wolfe. As had 'confirmed bachelor'. Ava remembered zoning out at that point, telling her friend she wasn't at all interested in commitment-phobes like her ex. Which put Gilles's 'hot' friend with the beautiful eyes and corrugated abdominal muscles firmly off her Christmas list.

Even if he *did* looked incredible in a custom-made tuxedo.

Oh, stop, she scolded herself. Lots of men looked incredible in tuxedos; they were the equivalent of a corset for women.

Of course lots of men hadn't made her burn just by looking at her, or made her want to touch them all over, but that was just bad luck. Or maybe it was more to do with how uncomfortable she felt tonight. Maybe she was just looking for a distraction from all the polite smiles and curious stares from many of the other guests.

Those who were friends knew that she'd never seriously been involved with Gilles, but they were intent on having a good time and she felt curiously lonely in the large crowd.

Her mind was intent on remembering the way Wolfe had held her in his arms that morning, with such breathless ease she hadn't been able to stop herself from imagining what it would be like to kiss him. Embarrassingly, she had even held herself perfectly still as if in anticipation of that kiss!

Pah!

She was just feeling a little strained after having to put on a brave face all day. And, okay, she was also a little intrigued by Wolfe. It had been a long time since a man had caught her attention. A long time since she had wondered about his kiss. A long time since she had felt the warmth of a man's loving embrace. Not that Wolfe's would be loving—but it would be warm…

Ava pulled a wry face at herself. Before today she wouldn't have said she had missed a man's embrace at all. But right now, watching this one they called Ice nonchalantly circle the room but not quite participate in the frivolities made her ache for it.

And don't try using that sexy little body to garner any favours, Princess.

Ava's lips tightened.

Arrogant.

Rude.

Unsophisticated.

Uncultured.

So why had she surreptitiously touched his body at the first opportunity?

Ava shivered and raised her champagne glass to her lips. Empty. *Drat.*

The doctor Wolfe had sent to see her—an unexpectedly nice gesture she still had to thank him for—had told her it would be best if she didn't drink tonight. Her position as 'jilted fiancée' in a room full of her peers told her it would be best if she did.

Taking another glass of Gilles's best from a passing waiter, she took a fortifying sip. It didn't surprise her that Wolfe had a reputation with women. A man who could lift a fully grown woman off a horse and lower her slowly to the ground with one hand held a certain *earthy* appeal.

For *some*, she reminded herself firmly. Not for her.

'My dance, I believe?'

For a minute Ava imagined the deep voice behind her was Wolfe, but it lacked a certain velvety-rough tenor and hadn't sent any delicious tingles down her spine so she knew it wasn't. Turning, she smiled at a nice English Lord who had been hounding her all night.

She didn't feel like dancing with him, but nor did she feel like triggering more gossip by refusing every man who approached her. Smiling with a polite reserve she hoped he read as, *Lovely, but be assured I'm not interested in furthering our acquaintance*, she stepped into his arms. Which was when she caught sight of Wolfe, watching her yet again from across the room. Her eyes immediately ran over the woman at his side, who looked young, happy and relaxed. By contrast Ava felt old, surly and uptight. Which was partly Wolfe's fault, she thought churlishly, because she couldn't seem to stop thinking about him.

And the fact that he had a beautiful woman at his side while he held his eyes on her only confirmed that the talk about him playing the field was true. Unless he had been watching her all night because of Gilles's silly request that he 'babysit' her. For some reason the latter thought aggravated Ava more than the former.

Five minutes later, feeling as graceful as a goose under Wolfe's constant regard, she sent her dance partner to fetch her a glass of water so she could find out. She didn't need an audience when she told Wolfe that his attention was not only supremely annoying but totally unnecessary.

Orientating herself in the vast room, she located him lazily propping up a wall in a dimly lit section of the ballroom, feeling ridiculously elated when she found the bubbly blonde was no longer running her fingernails up and down his powerful forearm.

He didn't say anything when she stopped in front of him, just looked down at her through a screen of thick dark lashes that made his mood impossible to gauge. Not that it mattered. She was here about *her* feelings, not his.

'You are eyeing me off because Gilles asked you, too, no?' She knew she'd mixed up her words—her English was always clumsy when she was agitated.

'I think the term you're looking for is *watching over you*.'

Amusement laced his tone and her spine stiffened in annoyance.

'I don't need watching.'

'I thought all women liked to be watched. Isn't that why you wrap yourselves up in those slinky dresses?' His drink swayed as he made an up-and-down motion with his hand.

Ava glanced down at her strapless jade-green gown, which was fitted to the waist and then fell to the floor in silky waves. 'My dress is elegant, not *slinky*.'

'Why don't we agree on elegantly slinky, for argument's sake?'

He was smooth, this handsome Australian, very smooth. 'I do not need babysitting,' Ava said, reminding herself that she had not approached him to flirt with him.

'I never said you did. In fact I told Gilles you could take care of yourself.'

'Presumably because I made off with your horse?'

'You didn't make off with my horse.' The pitch of his voice dropped subtly. 'But you did play a pretty dangerous game on him.'

Ava's heart kicked up a notch at his silky taunt. 'I'm quite sure I don't know what you mean.'

Wolfe smiled. 'I'm quite sure you do.'

He took a lazy sip of his beer and her eyes were drawn to the strong column of his throat when he swallowed. She looked up to find that his eyes had closed to half-mast as she watched him and her breasts grew heavy.

Determined to ignore the sensation, she continued. 'So, if you are not doing Gilles's bidding, why do you watch me?'

'Why do you think?'

His eyes toured over her body and she had a pretty good indication of why. Something hot and quivery vibrated up and down her spine. The memory of the feel of his hands on her torso returned. They were so large they had almost swallowed her whole.

Perturbed by the physical response he so effortlessly created in her, Ava shook her head. Compared to her he appeared so cool and relaxed, and yet she was sure if she touched him he'd feel as tightly coiled as a spring.

'I think you are a man who gets what he wants a little too often, Ice!' she challenged, deciding that he was messing with her head. The way he looked at her. The way his eyes lingered on her mouth. She knew he felt the chemistry between them and she wondered why she wanted to push him to show her. Even more she wondered what it would take to make this self-contained man lose control.

'Is that so?'

'Yes.' Ava tried to match his careless tone even though her heart was thumping inside her chest. 'The word in the powder room is that you steal hearts wherever you go.'

'Have you been talking about me, Princess?'

Ava felt her temper spike at his evasiveness. 'That's not an answer.'

His eyebrow rose at her sharp tone. 'You didn't ask a question.'

Wanting to stamp her foot in frustration, she decided the smart thing to do was to bid him goodnight. She'd already decided to ignore the way he made her feel, and yet here she was almost begging him to make her change her mind.

Dragging her eyes from his sensual half smile, she took a step back and curled a stray wisp of hair behind her ear. 'Fine. If you'll—'

His hand shot out and snagged her upper arm. His hold was gentle, yet uncompromising, and she couldn't prevent a gasp of surprise at the unexpectedness of it. 'Don't play games with me, Rapunzel. I guarantee you'll lose.'

Ava barely contained her temper. If anyone was playing games here it was him, not her. And if a small voice in her head was asking her if trying to get the better of him on the lawn earlier had not been a game—well, she didn't much care right now.

'You have that wrong.' She lifted her chin. 'I am not the

one playing games here.' Because deep down she knew it would be beyond stupid to invite this man into her life in any capacity.

He stared at her, finally letting the sensual heat she had felt in him all night shine through in his eyes. She couldn't look away, like a deer caught in headlights as he inexorably drew closer—only realising it was she who had swayed towards him when a glass of mineral water was thrust in front of her face.

'There you are,' Lord Parker puffed, pushing his chest out in Wolfe's direction.

Half expecting Wolfe to challenge him, Ava was absurdly disappointed when all he did was slide a thumb across the rampaging pulse-point in her wrist before releasing her. As if as an afterthought he bent towards her, his mouth close to her ear, his intoxicating scent making her breathless.

'Careful what you wish for, Princess. You just might get it.' He straightened and inclined his head in her direction. 'If you'll excuse me?' He mimicked the cool words she'd been about to serve him moments earlier before striding across the marble floor and into another room.

Ava let out a long pent-up breath. She should be glad he was gone. He was arrogant, obnoxious, and too cool for school—and yet he made her burn hotter than any man ever had before. It was a powerful aphrodisiac. All-consuming and tempting. And despite the fact that he had just warned her off some obtuse part of her still wanted to know what it would feel like to have those capable hands on her heated skin—her *naked*, heated skin.

'Ladies and gentlemen...'

The MC interrupted Ava's conflicting thoughts.

'The bride is about to throw her bouquet before the couple departs for the evening.'

A triumphant squeal rent the air as the bouquet was caught by one of Anne's American friends, followed by a stream of synchronised clapping as the bride and groom made their way upstairs. They would be spending the night at the château before leaving for their honeymoon after luncheon the following day.

Ava joined in the well-wishing but her chest felt tight. Anne and Gilles were so happy. So in love. An old fear that she would never get to experience that depth of emotion with someone special cut across the happiness she felt for them both.

Realising she must be more out of balance than she'd first thought, she decided to call it a night. Glancing around the room, she noted that Wolfe was nowhere to be seen and felt another stab of irritation at herself. She was torn between wanting him to want her and wanting him not to. It was as if she was somehow in thrall to him. As if her brain no longer functioned, or it functioned but was stuck in one groove, like the needle on an old-fashioned record player. The word *sex* was going round and round in her head like an endlessly exciting mantra.

Ava stared at her water glass and wondered if someone had drugged it. The last thing she wanted was sex with a man completely unsuitable for her hopes and dreams. Wasn't it?

Annoyed, she pivoted on her heel—and gasped when she nearly ran smack into the man who had occupied her mind pretty much the entire day and night.

'You're leaving before our dance,' he murmured silkily.

The balls of her feet hurt and she didn't want to dance. 'I did not think you played games.' She could barely hear her own voice above the sound of her thundering heartbeat. Had he been toying with her to heighten her awareness of him? If so, it had worked. She had never been more aware of a man in her life.

She saw his nostrils flare at her confrontational tone and something primal unfurled low in her pelvis, because she knew that he *did* play games. And even though it went against all her principles part of her wanted to play—with him—tonight.

'Maybe I want to feel you in my arms one more time.'

Heat rushed through her body as his husky words burned her up inside. *How did any woman stop herself from drowning under such blazingly sexual intensity?*

'Do you?'

As if sensing her near capitulation, he gave her a lupine smile. 'Yes.' He set her drink aside and swept her into his arms.

Ava's stomach flipped. She'd like to think that she'd *let* him walk her backwards onto the dance floor—although that would imply she still had some influence over her actions and she wasn't sure that she did.

'What about what *I* want?' The question was meant to establish some sense of control on her part, but she suspected that he knew what he did to her and had seen right through it.

He brought the hand holding hers towards her face and rotated it so that his knuckles gently drifted across her cheekbone. 'This *is* what you want, Princess.'

A cascade of sensations made her shiver and she told herself to tread carefully. Told herself that there was only one kind of man who parried around a woman all night and then approached her at the end. The kind her mother would have told her to steer well clear of. What it said about her wanting him regardless she didn't want to think about.

He was so sure. So confident. She should shoot him down in flames. Using his own pistol to do it.

Instead she braced herself against his magnetic sensuality and told herself she would walk away at the end of the song.

'One dance.'

CHAPTER THREE

DANCE? WOLFE DIDN'T want to dance with her. He wanted to possess her. And for a self-confessed non-game-player he had played a game of parry and retreat with her to rival all others.

Not intentionally.

His *intention* had been to avoid her. But once she'd entered the ballroom in a green dress that flowed around her body like a caressing hand he'd been lost.

Well, maybe not lost. More like mesmerised. And it had annoyed the hell out of him that he'd noticed that every other male in the room felt the same way. The married ones couldn't do anything about it, but the single ones had been lining up as if she was a participant in some secret speed-dating service.

He, on the other hand, had spent most of the night fighting the urge to muscle his way through the throng of wedding guests and throw her over his shoulder like the barbarian she had accused him of being. Hell, his body had been so attuned to hers he'd practically known every time she'd blinked.

Chemistry. He'd never experienced it quite so strongly. But he knew the quickest way to appease it would be to have her. So far he'd steadfastly stuck to his plan not to go near her but, hell, why not? He was only responding to her like any other healthy male who had held a beautiful woman in his arms and wanted her. Nothing complicated about that.

In fact it was so simple he didn't know why he was dwelling on it so much.

He would have had more to dwell on if he *hadn't* wanted her. And as for that instant tilting of the world he'd felt earlier when he'd caught her…well, it was only lust. Raw, pagan, blow-your-head-open lust. Perfectly rational. Perfectly normal.

Wolfe looked down into her face. Her cheeks were pink and her lips were softly parted as she breathed shallowly. His gaze drifted lower, to the firm thrust of her breasts, her aroused nipples, and then back up. Her gaze was slumberous but slightly guarded, as if she too were a little taken aback by the strength of this thing between them.

Without making a conscious decision to do so, he spread his hand possessively over her hip, pressing her closer. He knew the minute she felt his hardness because she made one of those softly feminine sounds that had his body jerking in response.

It made him want to spear his hand in her upswept hair and drag her mouth to his, but at the last minute the sounds of the party still in progress penetrated his desire-drugged mind. Instead he cupped her chin in his palm and brought her eyes to his. 'I want you, Ava. I want to kiss you until you can't see straight and make love to you until you can't move. I've thought of nothing else all day.'

A shiver raced through her and Wolfe felt as if he was poised on the blade of a knife as he waited for her response.

'I…' She blew out a breath. Swallowed heavily. 'Okay.'

Exalted, and no longer questioning his need for her, Wolfe grabbed her hand and fought to keep his steps measured as he led her off the dance floor.

She'd been allocated a room in the east wing of the château and he didn't pause for breath until, on the second-floor landing, he felt a soft tug on his hand.

Turning, he watched her run her hands down the sides of her dress, the nervous gesture only serving to mould it closer. 'Wolfe.' She cleared her throat. 'I'm not sure this is such a good idea.'

Wolfe wasn't sure about anything except that the sound of his name in her husky, accented voice twisted his insides into a mess. A very hot mess. 'Not sure what is such a good idea? This?'

He backed her against the stone wall and raised his hands to frame her face. Then he used every ounce of skill he possessed and leant down to claim her mouth with his.

Immediately his senses became overloaded with the rich, intoxicating taste of her. He'd known it would be like this. Overpowering. Overwhelming. Her ruby lips were so much fuller and sweeter than he had imagined, and when she parted them and pressed closer the instinct to ravage her consumed him.

His fingers dug into her scalp to hold her steady as he deepened the kiss, his tongue sweeping into her mouth to explore every corner.

'Wolfe, please…'

Her soft whimper of need inflamed him to the point of madness. He couldn't get enough of her. His hands shaped her slender curves, desperate to delve under the dress, and he was keenly satisfied when she ardently returned his hunger. Her uncertainty of moments ago was flung into the flames of a desire so bright it burned him alive.

She was sensational, and he ground himself against her in ardent anticipation. He couldn't remember ever feeling this frenzy of need before, and it was just dumb luck that a door banged somewhere along the corridor and brought him back to his senses.

Fighting for control, he grabbed her hand again and didn't stop until they were both breathless and inside her bedroom, the door firmly closed behind.

He hit the light switch and stared at her.

She stood in the centre of the historically preserved room like a pagan offering, her lips already moist and swollen from his kisses. She sucked in a deep breath and he thought he saw a shadow of vulnerability chase itself across her face.

It gave him a moment's pause.

He had avoided thinking about a woman in any serious capacity his whole life, after having to clean up the damage his mother had caused by her actions. But this wasn't serious. Making love—having sex, he amended—with Ava de Veers was not a threat to his wellbeing in any way, shape or form.

It was about pleasure. Mutual, unadulterated pleasure.

'I like the light on,' he rasped.

She moistened her lips. 'I don't…mind.'

Satisfied that he knew exactly what he was doing, Wolfe shoved away from the door and paced towards her. He stopped a breath from touching her and gazed into her wide-spaced smoky eyes, searching out any further signs of apprehension, promising himself he would stop if she showed even a hint of uncertainty. Fortunately he didn't have to test that theory, because her gaze could have melted iron when it met his.

His iron will.

Shaking off the insidious devil of doubt that told him once was never going to be enough with this woman, he curled one hand around the nape of her neck and pulled her up onto her toes. She steadied herself by placing her hands on his shoulders. The air between them turned to syrup as she tilted her head back into his hand, presenting him with the elegant arch of her neck.

Wolfe felt his lip curl upward as he thought of the recent vampire craze in the cinemas. Suddenly he understood the draw. Lust pounded through his blood and he brought his other hand up to trace the tender skin she had exposed to his hungry gaze. She opened her eyes, stared into his, and then did something he hadn't expected—she took charge and pressed her lips to his.

He let her sip and nibble at his mouth for maybe ten seconds before that primal feeling she dredged up in him took over. Then his hands and lips firmed and he forced her mouth wide, demanding that she cede everything to him.

And she did. Without hesitation. Her slender arms snaking behind his neck, her body arching into his.

Wolfe told himself to ease off before he scared both of them, but her mouth angled more comfortably under his and he didn't know how it was possible but she took the kiss deeper. Wrapped her sweet tongue around his and made his head spin.

Without really being aware of his surroundings he wrenched his jacket off and pushed her fumbling fingers aside to tear at the buttons on his shirt. Shucking out of it, he welcomed the bite of cooler air on his overheated flesh and the layer of sensation it added.

He released the dark mane of her hair from its tight coil and felt his heart wrench as it cascaded past her delicate shoulders.

Ignoring the swirling emotions ebbing and flowing through his mind, he cupped her breasts and moulded them in his hands. Soft and round, the nipples already poking through the silky fabric of her dress like tiny diamonds. He kneaded and shaped her, his eyes on her face as he roughly dragged his thumbs across both her nipples at once.

'Oh, Wolfe. *Mon Dieu.*'

Her husky groan urged him to draw the hidden side-zipper of her dress down until her pale, perfect breasts stood proud and taut in front of him.

'Ava, you're—' He swore as words failed him and bent to draw a dusky pink nipple into his starving mouth. The taste of her made him throb, and when she clutched his head to hold him closer he gave up any pretense of finesse, scooping her into his arms and yanking off the ugly floral bedspread before depositing her on crisp white sheets.

She leant up on her elbows and watched him through heavy-lidded eyes as he dragged the silky gown from her long legs and tossed it aside.

Wolfe took her in as he stripped off his remaining clothing: her wavy hair a dark ripple down her back, her sweet breasts rising and falling in time with her heavy breaths, her narrow waist, and the sheer purple panties that revealed more than they hid.

Her woman's scent rose up to tease him and he climbed onto the bed and came over her, his hands braced on either side of her face. 'Now, my lovely, I have you right where I want you.'

Her hands came up between them, curling into his chest hair. Her smile was full of womanly provocation. Her actions thankfully belying her earlier hesitation. 'You like to think you're in control, but I am stronger than I look.' She scratched her nails lightly against his skin like a cat.

She shuddered beautifully beneath him and turned her head to capture his mouth with hers. He groaned, sank into the kiss, let himself become absorbed by it. His free hand smoothed down over her torso, learning her wherever he went.

Her own hands were busy, stroking up over the muscles of his arms. When she pushed playfully against his shoulders he didn't budge. 'It feels like you're made of steel. You're completely immovable.'

'Where do you want me to go?' he growled with husky promise. 'Up?' He kissed his way along her neck and bit down gently on her earlobe. 'Or down?' His tongue laved her collarbone and dipped lower, circling ever closer to the centre of her breast.

Her eyes glazed over with desire.

'Ava?'

'Quoi?' She arched off the bed, her breasts begging for his mouth.

'Which way?'

She gave a low moan as he continued to tease her, and when she wrapped one leg around his lean hip he guessed her intention and let her flip him onto his back. She pushed up until she straddled his waist. 'Now who's got whom exactly where they want them?' she said, a look of triumph lighting up her face.

Wolfe grinned and repositioned her until her hot centre cradled his erection. 'That would be me.'

'Ohhh.' Ava spread her palms wide over his chest. 'I know you think—'

Wolfe leant up and suckled one of her peaked nipples into his mouth, cutting off whatever she was about to say. Her wet heat was shredding his control and the time for banter was well past. 'I think you're sensational.' He switched to her other breast and realised that he meant it.

Usually a woman was content to let him lead all the play in bed, but this was much more fun. And the taste of her cherry-red nipples blew his mind.

While she was distracted by his mouth he smoothed his hand down her belly and cupped her where she was open and already wet for him, her filmy panties no barrier to his questing fingers. Her eyes flew open as he found her and pushed a finger inside her slick centre. She cried out his name and balanced over him as she rocked against his hand.

Wolfe's erection jerked painfully but he forced himself to wait, enjoying having her at his mercy. Enjoying the astonished look of pleasure that came over her when he lightly circled her clitoris. And especially enjoying the way she flung her head back in ecstasy and screamed his name as she came for him.

He rode out her orgasm with her until her head flopped

forward, her long hair falling around his face like a silky veil. Needing to be inside her with an urgency that was shocking, Wolfe flipped her onto her back, chuckling softly when she just lay there in silent supplication.

'At least I know how to get your absolute cooperation now.'

Ava pushed her hair back from her face and stretched sinuously. 'What did you just do to me?'

'I made you come.' He rolled on the condom he'd pulled from his wallet and nudged her thighs wider, entering her on one slow, luxurious thrust. 'And now I'm going to do it all over again.'

It took every ounce of control he possessed to keep his movements even and gentle until her body had grown accustomed to his size, but when he felt her completely relax and take all of him fully he couldn't hold back, driving them both to the edge of reason a number of times, until with a sob she gripped his hips and forced him over the edge into a space that was so white-hot he felt as if their bodies would be fused for eternity.

His last coherent thought was, what did he do after an experience like that?

With sexual release came clarity, and Ava could barely believe what had just happened. Had she *really* just had sex with a man she'd met merely hours ago? A friend of Gilles's, no less?

Yes, she had. The evidence was still there in the tiny aftershocks of pleasure rippling through her core, not to mention the harsh breaths of the man lying beside her who looked as if he was choosing his best exit line.

She made a small sound in the back of her throat. 'I told myself I wasn't going to give in to this.'

Her voice had him rolling towards her and the bed dipped under his powerful frame. Ava's skin burned where his eyes raked over her, and as casually as she could she pulled the top sheet up to cover her nudity.

'Why did you?' His voice was gravelly. Sexy.

Was that a serious question? She'd done it because at the time she'd felt she didn't have a choice. As soon as he'd taken her into his arms she hadn't been able to help herself.

'Curiosity,' she said, the word sounding much better to her ears than, *I couldn't help myself.*

'That sounds a bit calculated.' His eyes narrowed as if he was assessing her. Judging her.

'Hardly.' Did he think she had set out to sleep with him?

Embarrassed by the thought, Ava wondered what happened now. Did they engage in polite conversation? Did he get up and leave? Well, he had to, because this was her room, but...

Unsure of herself, and hating the way that made her feel—as if she was standing in front of her father about to be told off for not living up to his expectations—she decided that she had no choice but to fall back on her usual tricks of feigned indifference or taking charge. Since indifference seemed too far out of her reach right now, she chose the latter.

'Please do not feel like you have to stay around because of me. You must be tired, and I'm not the sensitive type.'

Wolfe propped his hand on his elbow, a lazy smile curling his lips. 'This is your idea of pillow-talk?'

No. It was her idea of self-defence. She feigned a yawn. 'Or if you're not tired, I am.'

His golden-brown eyes grew flinty. 'Are you asking me to leave or telling me?'

'Isn't that what you were just thinking you should do?'

His eyes flickered from hers for the briefest of seconds, but it was enough for her to know she had been right in her assumption.

'Actually, I was thinking of inviting you out to dinner.'

His comment took her by surprise, and she was sure he was making it up. She swallowed heavily and pushed aside the tiny kernel of pleasure his words had imbued her with. 'I'd love to, but you're about five hours too late.'

He shook his head in amusement. 'Are you always this prickly after a bout of hot sex?'

Ava swallowed. She didn't know. She'd never had sex like that before. The whole thing both alarmed her and set her body on fire in equal measure. What had happened to her promise only to go out with men who wanted the same thing she did? Love. A family.

Hating the feeling of uncertainty that had her in its tight grip, and hoping she appeared as casual as Wolfe, she let her eyes drift over his stubbled jaw and broad shoulders. When she noticed a small patch of puckered skin right beneath his collarbone she frowned.

'That was a bullet from a semi-automatic.'

Ava's startled gaze met his. Was he serious?

He'd said it as if he was ordering a sandwich from a deli.

'Ouch!' Keeping her voice light to match his as she noticed another scar lower down, she said, 'And this?'

He wrapped a lock of her hair around his finger and started to play with it. 'Shrapnel.'

She pointed to another small mark on his arm. 'Spurned lover?' she queried flippantly, understanding on some level that these wounds weren't badges of honour for him, but represented the deep pain and suffering brought by the uglier side of the life he had once led.

'Accurate sniper.'

He brushed the ends of her hair across her upper chest, where the sheet stopped. Ava felt goose bumps shimmer across her skin and hoped he didn't notice.

'I take it you're not very good at your job?' she teased.

His eyes glittered with amusement. 'That's one way of looking at it.' He let go of her hair and replaced it with his fingers, his movements causing the fabric to drag across her sensitised breasts.

Anticipation made her body throb and, powerless to stop herself, she let her eyes drift lower, taking in the thin trail of hair that bisected his ripped abdomen and moving towards the magnificent erection rising straight out from his body—which was when she saw a jagged white scar that ran along his outer hip towards his thigh.

Her attention torn between the two, she was only vaguely aware of him chuckling. 'You sure you want to know about that one?'

'The scar?'

'That, too,' he teased.

She shook her head. 'What happened?'

'An unfortunate rendezvous with a piece of barbed wire, thanks to one ferociously competitive younger brother. Not very glamorous.'

'Glamorous!' Her brows drew together. 'None of them are *glamorous*!'

'You'd be surprised how many women find them a turn-on.'

She shuddered. 'I don't.'

'No?' He touched her face almost reverently, gently stroking around the bump on her head that—thankfully—pain-killers had taken care of.

Ava smiled and again surprised herself by touching her lips to his. Something flickered in his darkened eyes as she pulled back. It was some unnamed emotion, and the air between them seemed to pulse. She saw the instant Wolfe rejected whatever it was he was feeling and then, in a move that startled with its swiftness, she found herself flat on her back, with him once again braced over the top of her. He captured her hands in one of his and raised them above her head, the completely carnal smile on his lips making her heartbeat quicken.

'Wolfe, we probably shouldn't do this again,' Ava breathed, wishing there was a little more conviction behind her words.

Wolfe lowered his mouth to hers and nudged her thighs further apart with his knees, grabbed his last condom and slipped inside her wet, welcoming heat. 'We probably shouldn't have done it in the first place,' he said on a long groan.

CHAPTER FOUR

WOLFE SCOWLED AS he marched across the circular driveway of the château towards the outer cottage, the quartz driveway crunching loudly beneath his boots in the morning air. It was still early, the sky etched in palest blue with a ribbon of orange rimming the horizon.

Why the hell had he invited her to dinner? And would she take it to mean tonight?

He wasn't even meant to be in town tonight. He had a huge meeting first thing tomorrow morning in Hamburg. He didn't have time to wine and dine a woman. So he'd tell her. Apologise. Explain that he'd forgotten about the business meeting.

He winced inwardly. She'd no doubt think it was an excuse…but what else could he do?

An image of waking up beside her caused him to clench his jaw. After years of practice his body had clicked on just before dawn, and he'd come instantly awake to find a warm, sexy woman curled into his side, with her head cushioned on his numb shoulder and her hand curled over his heart, the soft skin of her upper back silky smooth beneath his rough hands.

No.

There was no way he could have dinner with her—tonight or any other night. The sex had been great—more than great—but he rarely visited Paris, and even if he did he'd have very little time to see her again. And the last thing he needed was another ear-bashing from a woman who wanted more than he could give.

Would Ava be like that? Start accusing him of using her even though they'd both agreed on short-term? He didn't know. And then he almost missed a step as he realised that he and Ava hadn't agreed on anything last night. They'd been too busy ripping each other's clothes off.

Wolfe grinned. Blew out a short breath. Last night had been something else. *She* had been something else. Hot beneath all that regal perfection. He knew if Gilles found out he'd slept with her he'd hop into him, but... His smile turned to a frown. Had Gilles ever held her so intimately? Come to think of it, had *he* ever held a woman so intimately after sex? Didn't he sleep on his stomach as a general rule?

No.

Entering into an affair with his friend's ex-fiancée wasn't going to work for either of them. Better to nip it in the bud now. Tell her it had been wonderful—more wonderful than he'd had in... What did that matter? It had been great. She had been great. But they were adults whose lives were vastly different.

Hell.

He stopped with his hand on the cottage doorknob.

He *had* to take her out to dinner. He might not have been one hundred percent truthful when he'd told her he had been thinking about asking her last night, but he wasn't a complete bastard. The least he could do after the night they'd shared was take her out for a meal.

So, okay, they'd go out. He'd choose a nice little out-of-the-way restaurant, make her feel special, take her home, maybe finish the night off with more sex—not that *that* was a deal-breaker—then he'd leave and his world would be right again.

Nice and simple. Job done.

He turned the knob and greeted his men as he entered the

cottage, not at all sure whether he should be bothered by the unusual level of excitement he felt at the thought of seeing her again.

Ava woke alone and realised immediately from the heat in the room that it was late. Then memory kicked in, facilitated by the lingering scent of Wolfe on the other pillow and the fact that she was naked.

She didn't know what had possessed her to sleep with him last night, but she knew she had definitely not been thinking with her head screwed on straight. No way would she have done all those things if it had been. No way would she have given herself so completely to a man she hardly knew if… A wicked thrill raced through her as images of Wolfe's magnificent body filtered through her mind and she frowned. She wasn't into cavemen, no matter how charismatic, and she had never been one to drool over a gorgeous face and body.

Before, a little voice chirped annoyingly.

Ever, Ava countered decisively.

She pushed her hair back from her face and smoothed out some of the knots caused by Wolfe's warm fingers. Her core pulsed with remembered pleasure and she groaned at her body's willingness to relive every erotic moment. Yes, there was definitely something to be said about all the dips and bulges of warm, sold muscle, and the man certainly knew his way around the female body. But so he should. According to Anne, he had enough experience for ten men. And she didn't have time in her life for someone like that. She was over shallow hook-ups where the male wanted sex and the female wanted a relationship.

Last night had been… Last night had been sensational, yes. But it was an aberration. One of those things out of the box that you couldn't quite explain but you knew you probably shouldn't have done. Too much champagne, too much anxiety about being at the wedding, too much overpowering testosterone in the form of one blond, godlike male.

Jumping out of bed to distract herself, Ava winced as long-unused muscles registered all that godlike male possession. He was just so big. So strong. When he'd manacled her hands and held her prisoner... Ava shivered and rejected her body's instant softening. But he'd just played with her and then he'd left. His actions spoke more loudly than his words ever could.

That old insecurity she'd thought long gone raised its knobbly head like a sleepy dragon and yawned. But she wouldn't go there. She'd dealt with that childish feeling when she'd moved to Paris, and it was no longer relevant to who she was now.

Maybe this whole business—her father's phone call combined with her emotional response to the wedding—had affected her more than she'd allowed herself to consider, made her act out of character.

Another one of Anne's comments snuck into her consciousness. 'Women drop like lemmings around him,' she'd said at lunch. 'But he lives a fast-paced life. According to Gilles, the man is never in the same city for longer than a few days at a time. It's like he's combing the globe for some holy grail.'

More like variety in his bed, Ava thought with a burst of asperity. And good luck to him. She hoped he enjoyed himself.

He did invite you to dinner, that devil's voice reminded her.

Yes, out of some sort of guilt, she told herself. He'd sensed her uneasiness after the sex and had made the invitation on the spur of the moment. It had been a nice gesture but his voice had lacked conviction. And his actions this morning only backed that up.

No.

She wouldn't be having dinner with Wolfe. He didn't really want to take her out and it would only be prolonging the inevitable. Also, she could think of nothing worse than forcing someone to do something they didn't want to do. That was her father's *modus operandi*, not hers.

Okay.

Shower. Get dressed. Hire a car. Drive back to Paris. She had a meeting with a new artist she was sure was going to be a pain in the backside but who had the potential of van Gogh and she couldn't be late.

She didn't have time to dwell on a man who had taken as much pleasure as she had without any promises for the future.

When the right one came along she would know it, and until then—well, she was nearly thirty. She didn't have time to waste time on casual encounters with ripped Australian security experts. And if fate was kinder than it had been yesterday she wouldn't run into him this morning and would be spared the whole awkward morning-after thing.

Feeling more like her normal self after a shower, she smiled as she crossed the marble foyer and propped her small suitcase beside the front door. Bending down, she'd retrieved the thank-you note she'd written to Anne and Gilles, which she planned to leave with Gilles's butler, when she heard a dark voice behind her.

'Leaving so soon?'

Ava wheeled around, her hair flying over her shoulders in a slow arc. Wolfe stood in the arched doorway, ruggedly handsome in worn boots, black low-riding denims and a basic white T-shirt that drew her eye to every solid inch of him.

Placing her hand against her chest, Ava tried to smile into his hard face. 'You scared me.'

He crossed his arms over his chest. 'Obviously.'

'I…ah…' God, she sounded like a silly debutante! And why did he look so angry all of a sudden? It wasn't as if she had been the one to walk out on *him* before the birds had started chirping. 'I have a busy day lined up.'

* * *

Wolfe could tell instantly that Ava had put last night behind her. It was in the regal tilt of her head, the squared shoulders and the way her gaze didn't quite meet his. Not to mention the small, reserved smile she bestowed on him, as if all that had passed between them last night had been polite conversation instead of intimate body fluids. It was the same smile he'd seen her give plenty of other men the night before, and to say he felt infuriated by it would be a grand understatement.

He recalled the way she'd told him he could leave her room after sex. At the time he'd thought she had been politely trying to *give* him an out, but what if she'd been trying to *get* him out instead?

'On a Sunday?'

Her chin came up, most likely because of his sceptical tone. 'Yes.'

'And what about dinner?' he asked casually.

It appeared she had a guilty conscience, because her gaze cut to the left before returning to his. 'Tonight?'

Damn.

Wolfe read her meaning in that single word and knew she had no intention of having dinner with him, that night or any other. He didn't like it. 'Yeah. You, me, a bottle of red. Or do you prefer champagne?'

'Actually, I have a meeting with someone this afternoon, so I won't be able to make tonight.'

Someone she was sleeping with, perhaps?

Wolfe raked her slender figure in a floaty summer dress and lightweight sandals and tried to rein in his uncharacteristically possessive response as his mind immediately stripped her naked.

On some level he knew he was behaving completely irrationally. Really, he should be rejoicing that she didn't want to complicate things between them by prolonging the inevitable, because—well…he knew his interest in her would wane at some point.

'And it's probably better this way, don't you think?' she said a little too quickly.

'Better what way?' He refolded his arms and rocked back on his heels. No way would he make this easy for her.

Her gaze snapped irritably to his and then cast over him, lighting little bushfires in its wake. 'Better if we forget dinner. Forget last night.'

'Forget last night?' Wolfe wasn't sure if this had ever happened to him before. A woman waking up after a night of phenomenal sex who not only didn't want to have dinner with him but looked as if she never wanted to see him again either.

'Oh, come on, Wolfe.' Her slender hands fitted around her hips just as his had done last night. 'I'm sure this isn't a novel concept for you. In fact it's probably a relief.'

His eyes rose to hers as he forced himself to focus. A relief? Yes, it *should* have felt like a damned relief. The fact that it felt more like an insult only increased his aggravation.

'You think I pick women up and sleep with them every time I go out?'

'I don't know.'

And she didn't care, if he read her tone correctly.

'But why are we arguing? Did you want more from last night than just sex?'

He stiffened, suddenly uncomfortable as she turned the tables on him. Saying no just felt wrong, but… 'No.'

She nodded quickly, as if she'd expected his answer. Wanted it, in fact. Did *she* do this all the time? Pick up men for a night of no-strings sex? The idea made his stomach knot.

'Great, so we're on the same page. Last night was lovely. I had a good time. Hopefully you did, too.'

She shrugged almost apologetically and he had an unpleasant moment of wondering if this was how women felt when he walked away from them. But then with all the previous women in his life he'd established the parameters from the start. Perhaps he was just reacting badly because this time he hadn't done that.

'What more is there to say?'

Ava's challenging question brought his mind back to her.

'Clearly nothing,' Wolfe ground out. 'You seem to have it all worked out.'

She mashed her lips together, as if confused by his tone, and Wolfe warned himself to stop being stupid. This was the perfect scenario, wasn't it?

The sound of footsteps coming down the grand staircase drew his eye, and then he heard Ava swear in French.

'Gilles is coming. I don't want… Can we just pretend this never happened?' She tinkled a laugh. 'Yes, the wedding was gor— Oh, Gilles. *Bonjour*. Where's Anne?'

Wolfe thought about telling her never to try her hand at acting. She looked as innocent as someone trying to make off with the family jewels.

He narrowed his eyes as Gilles put his hands on her waist and gave her a kiss on each cheek, disturbed by the unexpected urge to pull him off her.

'As quaint as Anne finds the ancient staff bell in our room, it didn't work this morning—so I've been sent in search of coffee.'

'What a fantastic idea.' Ava nodded enthusiastically. 'I think I might join you.'

'You want one, Wolfe?' Gilles rubbed his eyes, as if he hadn't had much sleep.

Wolfe knew how he felt.

'No. I've had enough coffee to last me a lifetime.' Ava's pout firmed, and Gilles threw him a quizzical look.

Deciding it was past time he left, he shoved his hand into his pocket for his keys and felt the phone he'd put there to give to Ava.

'This is for you.' He held out a silver smartphone. 'I took

the liberty of placing your SIM card into a spare after my men found yours broken in your car.'

'Oh.' She looked confused by the gesture. 'You didn't have to do that.'

He knew he didn't. He'd wanted to.

He turned it on and passed it to her, before informing Gilles of his plans to hit the road earlier than he'd intended.

While Gilles tried to convince him to reconsider, Ava's phone beeped a string of incoming messages. They both turned to see her frowning at it.

Wolfe immediately felt his guard go up. 'What's wrong?'

'My father has left ten messages. Excuse me while I retrieve them.'

She dialled a number and pressed the phone to her ear at the same time as Gilles's butler hurried into the foyer.

Momentarily distracted when he handed Gilles a piece of paper, Wolfe returned his gaze to Ava in time to see the colour leach out of her face.

She turned almost blindly to Gilles, her breathing erratic. 'Frédéric has been involved in an accident. Gilles…' Her voice trailed off when Gilles looked at her, and if possible she lost even more colour. *'Quoi?'*

Wolfe didn't think she'd realised that she had reached out and was gripping his forearm in a talonlike hold.

Gilles shook his head as if in a daze.

Hell.

'I need to speak with my father. Find out what hospital he is in.' Ava's shaky hands fumbled with the phone, and it would have dropped if Wolfe hadn't swiftly bent to catch it.

'Ava, he's not in hospital.'

'Ne sois pas absurde, Gilles. The accident sounds serious.' She shook her head, unable to say more.

Wolfe cursed under his breath.

'Ava—'

'No.' She held up her hand and cut him off, backing away

from both of them, so disorientated she would have bumped into the wall if Wolfe hadn't reached out and grabbed her by the elbows.

'Breathe, Ava,' he instructed levelly. 'In. Out. That's it.'

Her gaze cleared a little and her body went rigid as she pushed his hand away. 'I'm fine.'

Wolfe's mouth tightened. 'Give me the phone,' he ordered. 'I'll call your father.'

She swallowed heavily, her navy eyes bruised. He would have wrapped his arms around her then, pulled her in close, but she was so rigid she might as well have been wearing armour. He'd thought he'd sensed fragility in her—the same as he'd sensed last night—but if he had it was long gone.

Ignoring the voice in his head that told him he should butt out of her affairs and mind his own business, he scrolled through her phone. When he couldn't find an entry under 'Dad' or 'Father' he glanced at her. 'What's his name?'

'It's listed under "The Tyrant".'

Her chin came up, as if defying him to make a comment; the action told him that the moniker hadn't been given in jest. But was her father really a tyrant? Or was she just another spoilt little girl who threw tantrums when things didn't go her way? And why did he even care?

Dumping a lid on the list of questions forming in his mind, he quickly dialled the number and introduced himself when the King answered on the first ring. 'Your Majesty, this is James Wolfe, head of Wolfe Inc. I have your daughter here. Yes, Gilles is with her. Ava?'

She took the phone with a shaky hand. 'Sir—'

Her voice trembled and despite trying to keep himself detached the sound of it cut Wolfe to the quick.

'Of course. *Oui.* I can get a flight. Yes. Okay.' She rang off and frowned at the phone as if she didn't know what it was doing there.

'Ava?'

She glanced at Gilles as if she didn't know what he was doing there either.

Shock. She was going into shock. Wolfe recognised the signs.

'I have to…' She gave a tiny shake of her head, collected herself. 'I… Frédéric has died. He… I have to organise a flight home.'

Gilles barely blinked, but Wolfe could see his friend's utter devastation below the façade of calm. 'Wolfe, can we borrow your plane?'

'Of course. But there's no we, Gilles. I'll take her.'

'Frédéric was a good friend. I'll—'

'You should be with Anne—'

'I can organise myself,' Ava cut in.

Wolfe's hands clenched into fists when Gilles put his arm around her shoulders. 'Don't be silly, Ava. You can't be alone at a time like this.'

'Shouldn't your priority be to your new wife and your house guests?' Wolfe hated himself for reminding Gilles so flatly. Hated himself for the stab of jealousy over a woman he'd never planned to see again.

'Would you two stop?' Ava demanded. 'I am more than capable of—'

'Getting on my plane and letting me escort you home,' Wolfe commanded.

She scowled up at him. 'I don't want to put you out.'

Wolfe didn't know if she was being stoic or just obstinate, but he knew he wasn't letting Gilles take her to Anders. 'Too late,' he growled.

When the butler approached Gilles again Wolfe stepped closer to Ava, invading her personal space. 'Is that your only suitcase?'

She stepped back. 'I told you before. I don't get off on barbaric men.'

Her view of him grated but he pushed his feelings aside. 'Do you really have time to argue?'

'No.' His words seemed to trigger something inside her and her eyes grew distant. She paced. Looked at Gilles and then turned back to him. 'Fine. You may take me.'

Wolfe mentally shook his head, almost awed at the way she'd managed to turn her acceptance into an order.

Ava was functioning on autopilot and barely registered Wolfe buckling her seat belt while the plane taxied down the runway. Somehow he had got her to Lille and on board a plane without her conscious awareness of it.

Her brother was dead.

The news was shocking. Indescribable.

A helicopter accident. Ava couldn't think about it, her mind incoherent with grief. Her brother was the rock of the family. The future heir. He was five years younger than her and, while they had struggled to be close after her mother died, she had always looked out for him. Anticipated that he would always be there. He couldn't be gone. He was only twenty-four.

She shivered and felt a soft blanket settle over her shoulders. She clutched it.

Wolfe placed a glass of water on the table in front of her. 'Do you need anything else?'

She shook her head. 'I'm fine.'

'So you keep saying.'

But he didn't push it, and Ava was grateful. She watched him return to his seat. When he'd come across her in the foyer her heart had turned giddy at the sight of him. It had taken a lot of effort to remind herself that there was no point in seeing him again and even less in sleeping with him! His increasing anger at her response had thrown her a little but then he'd confirmed that, no, he didn't want more than sex from her, and she'd known she had made the right decision.

After they arrived in Anders she would likely never see him again, and that fact made her feel instantly bereft.

Her mind linked the feeling with a time when she was fourteen and her father had continued with a state trip even though she'd been hospitalised with chicken pox. He'd monitored her condition from afar, as usual, but coming so soon after her mother's death his behaviour had done little to alleviate her loneliness and her sense of powerlessness at being alone.

That same sense of helplessness and loneliness engulfed her now, and she pushed it back. Her father would expect her to demonstrate more fortitude than that.

More childhood memories tumbled into her mind, like dice on a two-up table. Memories of Frédéric as a boy. Of her mother.

Rather than becoming *more* available after her mother's death from cervical cancer, Ava's father had withdrawn and focused on his work, seeming not to know how to connect with her. He had been fine with Frédéric. Ava had grown more and more resentful of the disparity in the way in which he treated his children, and more and more determined to show him that his views of women were archaic and demeaning.

But nothing she did ever seemed to be good enough for him. Perhaps if she'd been more like her mother, had been able to put his needs first, they might have seen eye to eye. But Ava couldn't. She had witnessed her mother's sadness whenever her father chose duty over family, and it had made her want something entirely different for herself.

Now, with Frédéric gone—a thought that just wouldn't stick in her head—she was next in line to the throne. She could only imagine how her father must be cringing over that, and she felt slightly nauseous at the prospect of having to step into the role.

Wolfe's voice telling her to refasten her seat belt cut across her tumultuous thoughts, and she glanced outside her window and saw the Anders mountain range as they came in to land.

Imposing a rigid shut-down on her fears about being home, she blanked her mind and switched to cool indifference. From the plane doorway she could see her father's royal guard standing alongside a line of official black cars, and she nearly turned and asked Wolfe to restart the engine and fly her some place else. Really, she felt about as strong as a daisy in a hailstorm—and she hadn't even seen her father yet.

Sensing Wolfe directly behind her, Ava had a debilitating urge to turn and rush into his arms, have him tell her that everything would be all right. But that was weak, and Wolfe was the wrong man to lean on in this situation. She wasn't special to him, and he wasn't the type to sit back and go unnoticed. He was used to taking charge, and there was no way she was going to let him sideline her in front of her father. She had been handling things on her own for a long time now, and she could handle this, as well.

Images of last night, of falling asleep in his arms after their wonderful lovemaking, filtered through her mind and made her pause. Then the empty space he'd left in the bed that morning intruded and stiffened her resolve. It would be a mistake to think she could rely on James Wolfe even for a short time.

'Thank you for the use of your plane but I can take it from here.'

'I told you I would take you home and I will.'

His hot toffee eyes glittered down at her dangerously, and his controlled voice told her he was as determined to have his way as she was.

'I am home.'

'Ava—'

'Wolfe. I'm fine. Really.'

'You don't look fine. You look like you're about to break apart.'

Did she? She'd have to work on that between here and the palace. Practising now, she squared her shoulders and stared him down. 'I'm not. I thought I told you already. I am not the sensitive type.'

Wolfe arrogantly slashed his hand in the air to cut her off in a move that was reminiscent of something her father would do. 'It's not open for discussion.'

That was *exactly* what her father would say, and *exactly* the reason she couldn't have Wolfe with her. That and the sudden sense that if she let him Wolfe would hurt her as Colyn never had.

'No. It isn't,' she agreed tightly, hardening herself against the sheer force of his will, the sheer force of her desire for him, which appeared to be even worse now that she had experienced what passion really was.

For a moment neither one of them moved, facing off against each other like two adversaries in a gunfight.

Wolfe's mouth tightened as he made to turn away from her. Then his fist clenched and his eyes, when he brought them back to hers, were seething with frustration. 'You are without a doubt the most infuriatingly stubborn female I have ever met.'

His voice, for all its aggression, was as soft as silk and sent a flash of fire beneath the surface of her skin.

He was without a doubt the most beautiful, the most powerfully dangerous male she had ever met, and she was afraid she would dream about him for ever.

CHAPTER FIVE

'DID MATTHIEU SAY what my father wanted to see me about, Lucy?'

'No, ma'am.' Lucy, her new lady's maid, returned from the wardrobe with two jackets for her to choose from.

Ava shook her head and immediately felt terrible as Lucy's face fell. Two weeks home and she still wasn't used to being waited on hand and foot again. She felt sorry for the young girl whose services she'd barely used.

She glanced at her reflection and smoothed her messy ponytail. She hadn't done her hair properly in days, but her father had requested her presence and she would not let him see her as anything less than perfect.

'You don't like my choices, ma'am?'

'I love your choices.' She gave Lucy what she hoped was an appreciative smile. 'But it's hot. In fact, why don't you take the afternoon off? Go and see your boyfriend.'

The girl bobbed her head deferentially and Ava sighed heavily and headed out.

She hated being home.

Hated the cold stone walls of the palace that felt more like a prison. She had barely seen her father since she'd returned, which wasn't necessarily a bad thing—except she had barely seen anyone other than staff, and it had given her far too much time to dwell on her grief.

Glimpsing bright summer sunshine through the long row of Gothic windows as she moved from one hallway to the next made Ava feel bleak. It just felt wrong. The sky should be grey, not blue.

Her brother was dead. The royal duties she had always shied away from were upon her, and there was no escape.

As her father had said, the people needed hope in these black times and she was it. They looked upon *her* to lift them out of the bleak mood caused by the loss of her brother—and, more than that, Ava now knew that her father was ill. One day, sooner than she had expected, she would be Queen—and the thought was completely overwhelming.

What did she know about running a country? Having all those people depend on her? It was criminal how little she knew, and even though that was mainly due to her father's chauvinistic views that women were trophies, not leaders, it gave her no pleasure that he now had to rely on her to preserve Anders' future as an economically viable entity.

And what of her gallery? It was closed for the whole of August, but she had dithered about what to do with it. Although of course she knew in her heart that she would most likely have to close it. It was devastating to think that the life she had built for herself could be so easily dissolved. As if nothing she had done in Paris mattered.

Steadying her breath, she hid her pangs of dismay and a gnawing sense of foreboding behind a smile as she stepped inside her father's plush outer office and greeted his personal assistant.

'He's waiting, Your Royal Highness.'

'Thank you, Matthieu.'

She tried to relax her face as Matthieu opened an inner door and Ava saw her father, as always, behind his enormous rosewood desk. He looked pale and more drawn than usual, and Ava tried to keep her immediate concern from showing in her voice. 'You wished to see me?'

'Yes, Ava. Take a seat.'

'You're starting to worry me, sir,' she said, sitting in one of the leather-bound chairs opposite, wondering why he had greeted her in English. 'Have you received bad news from your physician?'

'No.' Her father's response was clipped. 'I've received disturbing news from the security expert who brought you home from France.'

Wolfe?

Ava's heart leapt behind her rib cage as an image of him that seemed all too close to the surface of her mind clouded her vision. For two weeks he had filled her thoughts right before sleep took her, and he was the first thing she thought of when she woke up. Even on the morning of Frédéric's funeral, when she had felt at her lowest.

Ava sighed. She really needed to stop thinking about those hours they'd spent in bed together. Her dreams of him left her feeling weak and needy, and the man probably couldn't even remember her name, let alone conjure up her image in his head.

Unlike her good self, who could not only conjure up his image oh, so easily, but his scent as well—woodsy and masculine. It was so vivid that he might as well have been in the room with her right now.

'What does Wolfe have to do with anything?'

She had tried to keep the query light, but a sudden fear that her father knew that she had slept with him came at her from left field. Surely Wolfe hadn't told anyone? The tabloids? Could her father's health withstand a salacious story about her at this time?

'I have to do with a lot of things, Your Royal Highness.'

The deep, familiar drawl from the man filling her head space had her twisting around in her seat to where he stood across the room, his body half turned away, as if he'd been doing nothing more than studying the scenery outside the high arched windows.

'But in this case it's about your safety.'

Her eyes drank in his beautifully cut black trousers and white dress shirt that pulled tight across his wide shoulders. He'd had a haircut, the shorter style drawing even more attention to the roguish quality of his perfect bone structure.

Those remembered toffee eyes were fixed on her face, touching her mouth ever so briefly, and Ava felt singed all the way through.

'What about my safety?' She hated that she sounded as breathless as she felt.

'Monsieur Wolfe has some news concerning your car crash at Gilles's château.'

She heard the underlying censure in her father's tone and guessed that he was angry she hadn't told him about the accident herself, but she had no time to ponder that as Wolfe prowled towards her, his loose-limbed gait impossibly graceful for a man his size.

He effortlessly dominated the large room and as he drew closer she realised that her heart was racing. He, of course, could have been a mummy for all the emotion he displayed.

Using years of practice to keep her expression from revealing any of her inner turmoil at having this man—her one-night lover—in the same room as her father, Ava forced herself to maintain eye contact with him. 'Such as?'

'Yesterday I spoke to the mechanic who repaired your car,' he informed her, a touch of fierceness lining his words.

'Why would you do that?'

'A hunch.'

'A hunch?'

'Yes. One that paid off. You didn't crash because of a loss of concentration. You crashed because a vial of potassium permanganate mixed with glycerine had been dropped into your brake master cylinder.'

Ava's brow furrowed. 'Is there a layperson's version of that?'

'Your brakes were tampered with.'

Did he mean deliberately? 'Maybe they were worn.'

'Yes. With a special chemical compound that, when it got hot enough, rendered your brakes useless.'

Ava struggled to digest what he was saying. 'You think my car was deliberately sabotaged?' The very idea was ludicrous. It was true that Anders had once experienced conflict with the neighbouring country of Triole, but that had died down years ago. Her brother had even been set to marry the young Princess of Triole when she came of age.

'Not only that,' her father interjected. 'We now know that Frédéric's helicopter crash was not an accident either.'

'What?' Ava's startled gaze flew to her father. 'I… How is that possible?'

Wolfe's voice was hard when he answered. 'A section of the rotor was altered in such a way that the pilot had no chance of detecting it.'

'You're suggesting Freddie was *murdered*?'

'Not suggesting. Stating. And whoever did it went after you, too.'

Ava reflexively pressed her hand into her stomach. This was too much to take in. 'But that is absurd. Who would do such a thing?'

'Enemies. Freaks. Stalkers. Shall I go on?' His tone was deadly serious.

'Monsieur Wolfe has kindly agreed to investigate that side of things.'

'Wolfe.'

He'd corrected her father. Something no man ever did. Half expecting him to put Wolfe in his place, she was surprised when her father nodded.

Men!

'Really? You volunteered?' Ava didn't bother hiding her incredulity. 'Why would you do that?'

'Ava!' Her father's reprimand at her outspokenness was loud and clear in the still room. 'Wolfe hasn't volunteered. I have hired him.'

Of course. She thought asininely. *Why would a man who keeps his affairs short and shallow volunteer to help out a woman he is clearly finished with?*

It galled her to recall just how many times she had checked her mobile phone for a missed message from him over the past weeks. She could have called him, she supposed, but pride had stopped her from even considering it. Calling him would only prove that she hadn't been able to move on from their night together while he had.

'Why would you do that, sir?' Ava turned her back on Wolfe to try to block out the overwhelming physical attraction she still felt for him. 'Why not use the local police?'

'It's a question of trust, Your Highness,' Wolfe answered.

His frigid formality made her feel despondent, and that in turn made her feel annoyed. 'We don't trust our own police force now? We're a peaceful nation, *Monsieur* Wolfe,' she said, stamping her own formality on the situation. 'No political uprisings anywhere.'

'True. But in this situation you don't know who is intending to hurt you. I won't.'

His tone was bold and confident and she wished she shared his assurance. After the way she had dreamt about him for two weeks she wasn't so sure. Although she did believe he wouldn't hurt her in the way he was referring to.

His thick lashes acted like a shield against his thoughts and Ava couldn't wait for the meeting to end. 'I'm not sure I believe this.' She appealed to her father. 'It could just be coincidence.'

'Chemical compounds kind of mitigate that possibility, Your Highness.' Again Wolfe answered for her father.

'I trust Wolfe's judgement on this, Ava.'

Over her own? What a surprise.

'Fine.' She waved her hand dismissively. 'Is that all, sir?' She needed to get out. Back to the sanctuary of her suite. Wolfe's steely indifference was like a red rag to her overly sensitised senses.

On the one hand she was glad he was treating her like a stranger, but it made her feel inadequate when all *she* could do was remember the feel of his body when it had been joined to hers, his hands on her skin, his mouth... Oh, his mouth!

And Frédéric had been *killed*. Someone might be trying to kill her as well...

'No, that is not all.' Her father brought her attention back to him. 'Wolfe has also been hired as your personal bodyguard for the duration of the investigation.'

The breath stalled in her lungs and the room spun. 'I don't think I heard you correctly, sir.'

Neither did Wolfe.

Her *personal* bodyguard?

He glanced at Ava's shocked expression and hoped his own didn't mirror it. The King had requested that he organise personal security for her, not that he be responsible for her himself. He didn't have time for that kind of grunt work on top of his corporate responsibilities. And guarding a woman who already occupied too much of his head space was not something he'd let any of his staff do.

'I know you don't like security being assigned to you Ava,' the King said. 'But things have changed. You are now the Crown Princess and you need to be protected at all times. This situation highlights how important that is.'

'Yes, but we have our own security detail.'

Her father sighed, as if he was settling in for a familiar battle. 'I believe hiring an outsider is the best course of ac-

tion until this situation is resolved. Wolfe comes highly rec-
ommended and is a personal friend of Gilles.'

'I disagree.'

Determination vibrated through her voice and got Wolfe's
back up.

The skin on the back of his neck prickled and he resisted
the urge to rub it; he was a master at not giving in to those
physical signs that demonstrated when a man was under extreme stress. He had tried to convince himself that his sleepless nights with Ava on his mind were just because he had a
niggle about her accident. He'd assumed that once that niggle had been investigated and the King was apprised of the
danger surrounding his daughter he'd be able to re-establish
his normal routine.

The driving need that had hit him in the gut as soon as Ava
had stepped into the room made a mockery of that. It wasn't
ruminations over her accident that had kept him awake—and
hard—for the past two weeks. It was her.

Absently Wolfe wondered if she had relived their night
together as much as he had, and whether she'd be interested
in taking up where they had left off.

What?

He silently mocked his wishful thinking. By the look of
her she'd prefer to run him through with one of those swords
lining the King's private study.

Maybe he just needed to get laid.

And, no, not with her. If he took her on as a client—

'Wolfe is clearly too busy, sir. But I'm sure there's another
person out there just as capable.'

She was right about him being too busy, Wolfe thought,
but there really was no one else he would trust with her life.

Feeling that he no longer had a choice, he gave the King
a curt nod of acceptance.

'No!'

The King cut an irritated look at his daughter. 'Ava, this

is not open for discussion. My word is law, and it's time you realised that you have a responsibility, a *duty*, to your country. You *will* do it.'

Did that mean she didn't want to? Wolfe wouldn't have been surprised. He understood the fickle nature of women better than most.

She stood beside the window with her arms crossed and the afternoon sun turning her hair a deep glossy brown. Wolfe could feel her frustration, her fury, in every tautly held muscle of her slender body.

His own body flushed with heat as he took her in, and he couldn't help resenting the effect she had on him. He didn't want to be this caught up by the sight of a woman. *Ever.*

'I'll need absolute control,' he said, overlaying unwanted thoughts with the professionalism he prided himself on. 'Access to everything.' Wolfe addressed his words to the King. 'Every nook and cranny and secret entrance and exit to the castle. Ava's diary. Her itinerary. I'll employ my own chef to do her meals, and I want the final word on everything she does and every person she sees.'

'You're asking a lot.'

Wolfe knew what the King was saying. *This is my daughter and you'd better not stuff up.* 'Yes, I am.'

'Perhaps Monsieur Wolfe would like my firstborn, as well?' Ava said, injecting her voice with bored insolence, tapping her foot agitatedly on the marble floor.

The King nodded his agreement before addressing his mutinous daughter. 'I have organised a ball in your brother's honour this coming weekend and you will need security for that.'

'It's too soon,' Ava whispered softly.

Her arms enfolded her waist in a protective gesture her father didn't seem to notice, but it tugged at some unwanted place inside Wolfe's chest.

'It's not too soon. And the ball is not only to honour your brother's life—it is to find you a husband.'

A *husband*?

Wolfe's eyes locked on Ava's face, which had suddenly turned ashen. His own gut felt as if it was twisted up with his intestines, and a flash of adrenaline rushed through his system as if he'd just been physically assaulted.

'I can find my own husband, sir.'

'Not now that you're Crown Princess, you can't,' the King rasped. 'The stakes have been raised, Ava, and you've had more than enough time to find a suitable partner and Anders badly needs a celebration *and* an heir.'

The tension in the room as Ava stared at her father could have cracked the Arctic shelf. Wolfe thought of the island paradise he had planned to visit next week, after his round of meetings. The warm sparkling blue waters of the North Atlantic. A new set of sun loungers that edged one end of his lap pool.

'Do I even need to be in attendance, sir?' Ava stared down her nose at her father with bored enquiry. 'I'd hate to mess around with your plans.'

The King's eyes hardened. 'Don't be smart, Ava. You have a duty to do. You know that.'

'And is it *my* fault that I am entirely underprepared to carry out that duty?' she retorted.

Her words were underscored by a subtle vulnerability that called to every one of Wolfe's protective instincts and threatened his determination to remain detached from everything at all times. It was an aspect of his nature that had never been challenged before—regardless of what he had seen and experienced. It was the reason he had acquired his nickname.

Instead of following that troublesome thought down what could only be a dead-end street set with an ambush, he focused on what he could see and hear. The facts.

'You chose to run around Paris for eight years.' The King's face had the motley hue of a man on the edge.

'Because I didn't have any choices *here*,' Ava returned icily.

'I won't argue with you, Ava. You need a husband. Someone who understands the business and can support you when you need it.'

Wolfe noticed the King's hand shook slightly as he picked up his water glass. 'Wolfe, if you would accompany my daughter back to her quarters? I'm sure you'll want to get started on the best way to carry out your duties as soon as possible.'

Wolfe wasn't sure about anything right now except two things. His need for this woman was stronger than it had ever been, and taking on the role of her personal bodyguard was absolute insanity.

Ava rounded on him as soon as he'd followed her into her private sitting room. *'"I'll need absolute control. Access to everything."'* She mimicked his voice, her tone scathing. 'Are you kidding me?'

Wolfe couldn't stop himself from running his eyes over her slender curves as she stopped in the middle of the room, her body vibrating with tension.

Had she lost weight?

He studied her face. Her cheeks were flushed, her mouth was tight and she had dark smudges under her eyes that told him she had been sleeping as poorly as he had. All the same, she looked magnificent, and he wanted to take her in his arms and kiss her so soundly it was all he could do to remain where he stood. 'It's for your own good.'

'According to some so is whale oil, but you won't find me firing a harpoon any time soon.'

Wolfe sighed, realising this meeting was going to be even more difficult than he had anticipated. 'Ava, this doesn't have to be awkward.'

She paced away from him and then turned back sharply.

'Don't mistake my fury for awkwardness, Wolfe. I can't believe you've agreed to take this job.' She paused and locked her eyes on his. 'You know, if you wanted to see me again you could have just picked up the phone.' Her navy eyes glittered challengingly.

'My taking this job has nothing to do with whether I want to see you again. And I believe it was you who cancelled dinner,' he reminded her stiffly.

She gave a dismissive shrug. 'I didn't see the point in going out with you when it was a spur-of-the-moment request made out of guilt.'

Wolfe contemplated her answer. Was that why she'd cancelled? 'It wasn't guilt.'

She arched a brow. 'No? So why run off so early? I don't even think the birds were up when you left.'

Wolfe's mouth tightened at the insouciant boredom he heard in her voice. It was the same tone she'd used with her father before. 'I left because I had to provide last-minute details to two of my men before they left on another job.' And he'd wanted to surprise her by replacing her damaged phone with one of his.

Her eyes flicked to his briefly, as if she hadn't considered that. But why would she? In hindsight, it had probably looked bad to her, waking up alone after the passionate night they had spent together. Which, he acknowledged to himself now, was another reason he'd left. He'd woken up with such a strong sense of wellbeing his instinct had been to pull back. It was so ingrained in him he hadn't even thought to question it at the time. Hadn't *wanted* to question it. Now, looking at it from her point of view, her reactions that morning made more sense.

'I'm sorry if I hurt you,' he murmured sincerely.

Ava's chin came up and her eyes shot sparks at him. 'Hurt me? You didn't *hurt* me, Wolfe.'

Wolfe's mouth tightened at her vehemence.

'Quite the contrary. In fact you did me a favour, because I didn't have time to have dinner with you and...' She shrugged again. 'It's too late now anyway.'

Was it?

Yes, of course it was.

'You're right.' For one thing he was now her bodyguard and she was his client, and for another he wanted her just a little too much for comfort. 'That ship has definitely sailed.' Wolfe paced the length of an antique rug, agitated by the situation he had inadvertently created for himself. 'And your father wants you to marry!' Which would effectively remove her from his orbit altogether.

'Something you'll never do!' The heated statement was almost a question.

'Something I'll never do,' he agreed. He'd spent his adult life avoiding that particular institution, and he'd never felt any need to reconsider his views.

Ava nodded sharply, as if somehow his response had been predictable, and Wolfe ground his teeth together. This situation—his total physical awareness of this woman, his total *agitation* at this woman—was going to make his job almost impossible. Never before had he felt as if he was at the mercy of his emotions as he did with Ava, and he hated the feeling that he was not as in control as he would like to think he was. So much for his old nickname. Thank God his army mates couldn't see him now!

Ava started pacing in front of the high bevelled windows again, as if she had too much energy that was searching for an outlet. Her fitted trousers pulled tight across the rounded curves of her backside.

'You do realise if my father knew of our history together there is no way he would let you guard me?'

Wolfe brought his attention back to her face. 'So will you tell him or will I?' he asked silkily, irritated with himself and

with her hot-headed stubbornness. She threw him a look and
he swiped a hand through his hair. 'Will you just sit down?'

'Another order? Let me just set you straight on something,
Monsieur Wolfe.' She set her hands on her sexy hips. 'If you
think I am going to do everything you tell me to do you have
another thing coming.'

Her accent had thickened with her agitation and it drove
his mind right back to the bedroom.

Wolfe released a slow breath. 'Believe it or not, I'm trying to help you.'

'Oh, that's right—my own personal protector.'

He crossed his arms and waited for her to run her anger
out, determined not to get into any more arguments with her.

Seeming to sense his newfound resolve, she prodded at it
like a child poking its fingers inside a lion's enclosure. 'So,
do I get to order you around, as well?'

'I work for your father.'

Her gorgeous mouth thinned. 'Two peas in a pod. How
cosy.'

'All that energy you're burning up is just going to tire you
out unnecessarily,' he offered amiably.

'You should be glad I'm using it up on pacing,' she snapped.

Wolfe's body caught fire at her words. *Down, boy.* She
didn't mean *that* was an alternative. It would probably never
be an alternative again after today. No, it definitely *couldn't*
be.

He watched her ponytail trail over the soft skin of her neck
before he sat on the edge of the low, plump sofa that was surprisingly modern in a room that dated back centuries. 'Take
your time. I have all night.'

She crossed her arms over her chest, pushing her breasts
up so they swelled just above the opening of her shirt. 'Well,
I don't. So I'd like you to leave.'

'I need to ask you a few questions first.'

'You're really pushing your luck.'

'Maybe we should clear the air about that night at Gilles's wedding.'

'Us having sex, you mean?'

Her cool indifference again made him wonder just how many other men she had spent the night with, and the fact that he was at all interested only added another layer of heat to his spiralling annoyance. Was she just like his mother, willing to slake her lust whenever the urge arose and with any man handy? The thought made him sick.

'Yes.'

Her eyebrows rose at his churlish tone and she leant back against the windowsill. 'What's to clear up? Have you forgotten how it's done?'

'Ava—'

'Oh, don't worry, Wolfe. I'm not about to strip off my clothes and ask for a repeat. Unless that's what *you* want? Is that why you took the job?' Her voice dropped, lowering to a sultry purr. 'Are you going to order me to take my clothes off, Monsieur Wolfe?'

'I don't sleep with my clients,' he informed her sternly, ignoring the lie his body's response begged him to make of that statement.

She raised a mocking brow. 'My father will be chuffed to hear that. He's not into men, as far as I know. Although every family has their secrets.'

Her unexpected humour broke the rising tension between them and Wolfe laughed. 'Tell me, Princess, what is it about me being your bodyguard that you hate the most if it isn't our history?'

She threw him a droll look. 'Do you have a spare year?'

Wolfe took a deep breath and offered up an olive branch. 'Why don't we start over?'

'Pretend we've never met?' she asked, somewhat dubiously.

'If that works for you.'

She shrugged. 'As long as you don't order me around I can do that.'

Could she? He wasn't sure he could. 'Good. Take a seat.' He spoke briskly, indicating the sofa opposite him. 'I need to ask you some things to help my investigation.'

When she didn't move Wolfe frowned. Was their cease-fire over so soon?

'Ava?'

'You can call me ma'am. And I believe you just issued another order?'

Yes, perhaps he had.

'So did you,' he ground out.

'You didn't say I couldn't order *you* around.'

'Av— Dammit, you need to cooperate or I can't do my job.' His mind conjured up the last time he'd teased her by telling her that he knew how to make her cooperate and he swallowed. Hard.

'So quit.'

'No.'

'Why not?'

'I've given my word to your father and there's no one else I'd trust with your safety.'

'What do you care about my safety? We're strangers.'

Wolfe sucked in a silent breath. Seriously, the woman would try the patience of a saint. Reminding himself to keep control, he settled back more comfortably on the sofa. The cat sleeping in the corner rose and stretched, sniffed him and then crawled onto his lap.

'Hey, mate.' He stroked it absently. 'You look like you've seen better days.'

'He belonged to my mother.' Her mouth turned down slightly at the corners, indicating that she was still affected by the loss. In some way he envied the fact that she cared.

The cat nudged his hand. 'I take back what I said,' he told the cat. 'You're in top condition for a man your age.'

He looked up to find Ava watching him. When their gazes collided she flushed, and he wondered what she had been thinking.

'I think I hate you.'

Well, that was definitive, and unfortunately the feeling wasn't mutual. 'I'm not your enemy, Ava,' he said softly.

The words *but someone is* lay unspoken between them.

Her shoulders slumped as if she had the weight of the world bearing down on her. 'Can't my father answer your questions?'

'That depends on whether he knows anything about your love-life. From what I saw of the interaction between you two before I would have said you're not that close.'

Her eyes narrowed suspiciously. 'Why do you want to know about my love-life?'

'Everyone in your sphere will be investigated.'

'Even you?'

'I have an alibi for the night Frédéric was killed.'

'Really?' She finally sat down and crossed her legs. Slowly. 'What is it?'

Wolfe regarded her wryly. 'And I don't have any motive for wanting to kill you.'

Yet.

She smiled, clearly sensing his frustration. 'Am I getting to you?'

'You don't want to get to me, Princess.'

'No, I want you to quit.'

'Get over it.'

Suddenly her gaze turned serious. 'Are you planning to investigate my artists?'

'Of course.'

'Be nice. Some of them are sensitive.'

'Unlike you?' It was both a statement and a question.

'Unlike me.'

He didn't believe her. Just the fact that she cared about her artists told him more than anything else. And then there was the look of concern that had briefly crossed her face when she'd first walked into the King's office. She had a heart. She just guarded it well. He could relate to that. He'd put his in a box years ago, and that was exactly where he intended it to stay. It was a timely reminder to keep his head on straight around this woman. She got to him as no one else ever had, and that made her dangerous and him volatile.

'Who was your last lover?'

She threw him a look.

'Before that,' Wolfe said gruffly.

Her eyes widened. 'You want a list?'

No, he did *not* want a damned list. 'Yes.'

She looked as if she was about to tell him to take a hike. 'A lovely American took my virginity when I was eighteen because he thought it would be fun to bed a European princess. Then I met a novelist who wanted to write the great Parisian novel. We were quite serious—unbeknown to my father—but three years ago I realised that we weren't after the same thing and we broke up.'

Wolfe could tell that both men had hurt her and he wanted to run them through with a blunt instrument.

'Did you love him?' The question was irrelevant and he hoped she wouldn't pick up on that.

'How is that relevant?'

Damn. 'If you're going to question me at every turn this won't work.'

'I already know it won't.'

'Ava…'

She huffed out a breath. 'I thought I did at the time. Now… I'm not so sure.'

He wanted to ask what had happened since to make her question that but he wasn't sure he really wanted to know. 'And since then?'

The look she gave him made his stomach knot.

'Apart from the Anders football team…' She recrossed those long legs in the other direction and stared straight at him. 'You're the lucky last, Monsieur Wolfe.'

Wolfe sucked in a litre of air at her admission, ignoring her snipe about the football team. How had he so completely misread her? But he'd known, hadn't he? He'd needed to believe she was as sophisticated and jaded in the art of seduction as he was. It had made it easier to let her go after the night they'd spent together. Made it easier to believe that what was between them was nothing more than mutual biological gratification. Not that it had worked exactly…

He stood up and startled the cat, who promptly jumped down and crossed to Ava. She reached down, her movements as graceful as the animal she scooped into her arms to cuddle.

'I'll need to see your itinerary for the next few days,' he said gruffly.

She didn't look up. 'I'll have Lucy forward it to you tomorrow morning.'

Wolfe moved to the picture window and stared out at the acres of grass that ringed the palace to the sprawling mountains beyond. Incredibly, he was thinking how happy he was that she'd never slept with Gilles.

Hell.

If he was going to protect her he had to stay on task. He had to stop thinking of her as a person. As a desirable woman. And he especially had to stop thinking of her marrying some stupid fool her father was planning to choose for her.

CHAPTER SIX

AVA WASN'T SURE how she was supposed to find a husband when she compared every man she came across to Wolfe. Not that she had taken her father's oppressive statement seriously. She had no intention of letting herself be bullied into a convenient marriage just to suit his wishes. Not on something this important.

Fortunately she was getting a reprieve from having to pretend to go along with it in the arms of her debonair cousin Baden.

'Quite the *soirée* your papa has put on for you, cuz.'

'Yes,' Ava agreed flatly, glancing around the gilt-edged ballroom filled to the gills with beautifully attired guests. Alcohol consumption had lifted the mood considerably since the beginning of the night, and even though she hated being here she had to admire her father's opportunistic streak.

He was a man who didn't stop until he got what he wanted. And he wanted her married, it seemed. In a hurry. Of course the supreme and lately suppressed romantic in her knew that there was every possibility she would meet someone tonight and fall in love at first sight. After all it had happened to Anne and Gilles. But... Her eyes drifted to Wolfe, standing nonchalantly towards the back of the room.

There was her problem, right there.

He was supposed to look like one of the guests. Undercover. What he looked like was a man who could kill with his bare hands and not put a crease in his bespoke tuxedo. But perhaps that was only because she knew it was true. Perhaps to the other women watching him so closely he just looked like a sexy, rakish male who was good in bed. Something else she knew to be true…

As if sensing her appraisal, he meshed his eyes with hers. Ava felt the impact of his stare from across the room. She couldn't fathom the effect he still had on her. It was instantaneous and totally consuming. She sensed that he felt it, too, but he had much more control over it than she did. Or the attraction just wasn't as strong for him as it was for her. Given that he was only here because her father was paying him, she put more weight on the latter.

And at night dreamt of shedding him of the former…

'Who is he?'

'Who?' Ava gripped Baden's hand and swung him so that Baden had his back to Wolfe.

'The cowboy leaning against the wall who hasn't taken his eyes off you all night.'

Ava glanced over Baden's shoulder as if she was searching for whoever he was talking about. 'I don't see anyone special, but then Father has every single man on the planet in attendance tonight. How are you enjoying the evening?'

Baden scoffed. 'It's a little soon after Freddie's death, but… You're trying to change the subject, dear cousin. There's a story here you don't want me to know about. Come on.' He tickled her ribs as he'd used to do when they were children. 'Tell Cousin Baden.'

'*Arrête*, Baden. This is hardly the place.' Ava hadn't meant to snap, but Baden wasn't the most socially savvy individual at the best of times. 'You're letting that wild imagination of yours run away with you again.'

'I don't like him.'

'I don't either,' she grumbled, knowing that it wasn't dislike she felt for James Wolfe, but something else entirely.

If only he wasn't so arrogant. So self-assured. So lethally male. Ava sighed. Who was she trying to kid? She loved those aspects of Wolfe's nature. Colyn had never been so overcome with passion that he had dragged her from a dance floor and kissed her senseless the way Wolfe had.

'You slept with him, didn't you?' Baden mused. 'I can see it in your eyes.'

Pressing her fingers to her forehead, Ava wondered if it was possible for a headache to materialise out of thin air. 'Please, Baden...' There was no way she was going to confirm anything to her blabber-mouth cousin. 'Keep your voice down.'

'You don't want your papa to find out?'

'He's...' Ava struggled to come up with some plausible reason as to why Baden might see Wolfe around the palace over the next little while without informing him as to why he was really here. 'He's trying out for a staffing position, I believe.'

'You slept with the hired help. You naughty girl.' Baden laughed. 'Not that I can't see the attraction. All that hard muscle!'

Ava cringed as she realised that Wolfe had moved to within hearing distance. 'Would you *please* keep your voice down?' she pleaded.

'What position is he going for?'

'I don't know and I don't care. Ask Father.' Ava knew that he wouldn't, because he had never had an easy relationship with her father.

Baden sipped his wine. 'How is the old tyrant bearing up?'

Relieved to be talking about anything other than Wolfe, Ava latched on to the change in topic. 'You never know with

Father. But honestly I think he's in denial. Hence the party tonight.' She swept the lavish ballroom with a rueful glance.

'And you? How do you feel about being Anders' first Queen?'

Baden knew her life at the palace had never been easy. It had always been something that had bonded them together since he had lost his own father, her father's twin brother, when he was five. Then his mother had deserted him, taking his baby sister with her, and he hadn't seen either of them since.

'Oh, I'm definitely in denial.' She gave a dismissive shrug, not wanting to dwell on the future when she still had no answers about how to handle it. 'Can you excuse me? I need the powder room. Why don't you ask the lovely Countess over there to dance?'

Baden followed her gaze and raised an eyebrow. 'Because she's ugly.'

'Baden!' Ava rebuked him again. 'That's a terrible thing to say.'

'If you don't like the truth, don't get in the way of it.'

Ava gave him a look that told him exactly what she thought of his tasteless comment, and then kept her gaze down as she wound her way purposefully through the throng of guests. She didn't have a specific destination in mind but somewhere quiet and—

'I told you not to go outside.'

The sound of Wolfe's deep voice directly behind her shimmered down her spine.

Ava looked up and realised she had been so preoccupied with Baden's horrible comment that she had walked outside the glass doors leading to her mother's rose garden. A golden moon hung like an enormous balloon on the horizon, and fairy lights twinkled strategically from various trees and bushes, giving the summer evening an ambient glow.

'I needed some air.'

'Is it any wonder?'

She stopped walking and looked back at him. 'What does that mean?'

'It means I'm surprised you're still standing after all the dancing you've done. Husband-hunting looks like difficult work.'

Ava glared at him. Really, she wasn't in the mood for the uncivilised version of Wolfe tonight. 'Why are you even here still?' she asked, her English skewed by her testiness. 'I thought you were the best, but so far you haven't come up with anything, and it has been a week already.'

A long week, in which she had once again locked herself in her room in a petulant sulk. Partly she still wasn't ready to embrace the duties her father wanted her to take on, and partly she had been hoping that Wolfe would get so bored he would quit.

'Unfortunately the invitation I put out over the internet for the bastards responsible to come forward hasn't seemed to work. Maybe I'm losing my touch.'

'Maybe you never had it.' As soon as the words were out she regretted her provocative tone because his golden eyes sparkled with amusement. 'Now, that's just plain nasty, Princess. Fortunately my ego is strong enough to withstand that kind of a slur.'

She snorted. 'Your ego is like a cockroach. It could withstand a nuclear holocaust.'

Completely unprepared for Wolfe to throw his head back and laugh, Ava struggled to prevent a smile from forming on her lips. 'Stop that.' She absolutely loved his deep chuckle. 'People are looking.'

Not waiting for him to follow her instructions, she continued down the stone steps past small clusters of guests enjoying the fragrant garden.

'So, any contenders you need me to vet for you?'

Wolfe's lazy drawl sounded too close, and Ava stopped and swung around to face him.

It took a minute for her to ascertain his meaning and when she did she gasped. '*You're* vetting my future husband?'

'It's part of the package.'

Ava bit back the first retort that came to mind, knowing it wouldn't lead anywhere good. 'Well, it's a useless part,' she informed him shortly. 'Just because my father says something should happen it doesn't mean that it will.'

'You're against marriage?' His brow rose in surprise.

'No, I'm against marriage without love.'

'Ah, a romantic. I somehow didn't take you for that.'

'You don't know me very well, that's why,' she said stiffly.

The look he gave her told her that he knew part of her very well, and was remembering it just as vividly as she was.

Ava felt a blush creep up her neck and quickly added, 'And you don't have to be romantic to want to fall in love.'

'No, just deluded.'

The wealth of emotion behind his brief response made her hesitate. Everyone had a story that coloured their actions and decisions, and she had a sudden urge to know what his was. 'Is it that you're afraid of intimacy, or that you like variety too much to settle down?'

'Since I'm not afraid of anything, and I move around continuously, I think it's safe to go with the latter.'

Ava studied his brooding expression and knew he was afraid of one thing at least—revealing anything personal about himself.

'Choosing that kind of lifestyle would indicate that you're running away from something.' She watched his response to her comment and just saw bland enquiry. Then another idea popped into her head. 'Or is it more that you're searching for something to add meaning to your life?'

The slight narrowing of his eyes was the only sign that she might have punctured his cool reserve in some form.

'Why complicate things unnecessarily, Princess? It's always better to lead with the head, not the heart.'

His use of the word *Princess* in his sardonic drawl told her it would be pointless to push him. He was a man who did what he wanted regardless of anyone else. 'You should take coffee with my father,' she said with measured indifference. 'You'd get on well.'

His piercing gaze scanned her face and she knew he'd picked up on the bitterness that was never far from the surface at the mention of her father.

'What's up between you and your old man?'

About to tell him that she didn't answer personal questions either, Ava found herself responding anyway. 'The truth is we've never seen eye to eye. He is a man who is very set in his ways. Very practical and logical. I was never his idea of the perfect daughter.'

'Why not?'

She could see his curiosity was well stirred and paused. She never talked about her relationship with her father—or lack thereof. Ever. But some small part of her wanted Wolfe to understand her. She'd seen the look on his face when she'd revealed how few lovers she'd had in her twenty-nine years— as if he'd expected there to have been a cast of thousands— and she hated that she cared what he thought of her. But it was senseless to deny that she didn't—at least to herself.

'I was too much of a tomboy growing up. Too impetuous. I liked bareback horse-riding and climbing trees and he wanted me to dress in pretty clothes and speak only when spoken to. I did like the pretty clothes, but...' Her voice trailed off.

Wolfe gave her a small smile. 'The speaking when spoken to...?'

She returned his smile, but it felt hollow. The pain of the past still had too tight a grip for her to find any lightness in those memories. 'Not so much. When my mother died he got worse. My brother was sent to a military academy to start his leadership training and I was home-schooled because my job was to look pretty, not to go out and work. Nothing I ever did was good enough in his eyes. Do you know he's never once visited my gallery in Paris—?' She cut herself off with a self-conscious laugh when she realised just how much she had revealed to him. Why not blurt out that she was afraid she'd never find love either, and tell him *all* her deepest fears?

'Does that make you feel like you're still a disappointment to him now?'

Ava felt her stomach churn. 'No. I don't need his praise. I'm not a child.' She cleared the strident note out of her voice. 'But I resent that he wants everything his way.' She bent and sniffed at one of her mother's prized flowers, the scent faint now in the late evening. 'Why do you think he wants me to marry?'

'To make sure the monarchy is secure.'

'To make sure there is someone beside me who can do the job, you mean.'

'You think he doesn't believe you're capable?' Wolfe's brows rose in surprise.

'I'm a woman. That speaks for itself as far as my father is concerned.'

Wolfe seemed to consider this and Ava moved farther along the path, wishing she'd never let this conversation progress as far as it had.

'Do you?'

His question stopped her and she glanced back at him. 'Do I what?'

'Think you're capable?'

'Yes,' she said, internally cringing at the defensiveness in her tone. She had a Fine Arts degree and a Master's in Business and while she might not know everything involved in running a country, she... 'I run a successful gallery.' Which surely counted for something.

'A small business,' he dismissed, shoving his hands in his pockets and strolling closer. 'It hardly translates, wouldn't you say?'

A wave of heat coursed through Ava at the slight. She might struggle to feel worthy in her personal relationships, but hadn't she always backed herself professionally. 'No, I would not say that.' She didn't even try to keep the indignation out of her voice. 'Do you know how hard I had to work to prove myself in Paris? To make my *"small"* business successful?' She straightened her spine. 'How difficult it was to get anyone to take me seriously? To get artists to trust me to work for them when everyone just expected me to be a vacuous party girl?'

She was breathing so hard when she'd finished she nearly missed Wolfe's soft grin.

'Oh, you are *horrible*!' she spluttered. 'You were playing devil's advocate with me!'

'You have a fire in your belly I guess you would never show your father.'

It pained her to acknowledge he was right. She had built a wall up where her father was concerned and she used it to keep him out. To show him that she didn't need him. More than that, she was afraid he would shoot her down in flames if she tried and failed in replacing Frédéric.

She was a grown woman who had never got over wanting her father's approval. She'd moved to Paris so she could avoid facing that.

Feeling dismayed by her unexpected realisations she shook her head. 'He doesn't respect me.' And, boy, did that hurt.

'So make him.'

Ava's startled gaze connected with Wolfe's.

'And if you stop pretending you're not sensitive about things when you are, that might help.'

She felt her mouth fall open at his gentle ribbing and quickly snapped it closed. She wanted to argue that she'd mastered that unwelcome aspect of her nature years ago, but just looking at Wolfe made her awash with a certain type of sensitivity she couldn't deny.

She turned away, only to have him grasp her shoulders and turn her back before she'd taken a single step. He reached out and secured her chin lightly between his fingers, his eyes glittering down at her in the glow of the mood lighting. 'Maybe you need to think of your duty as being to your people now, Ava, not your father.'

Her breath caught. He hadn't called her Ava since that morning at Gilles's. Trying to hold on to her equilibrium, and reminding herself that there was nothing intimate behind his unexpected tenderness, she gave a rueful quirk of her lips. 'I never looked at it like that.'

'Because you're focusing on the past. That's gone. It's only the future that counts.' His tone was firm, the words delivered with such a resounding sense of resolution she knew he had said them before.

'You're right.' She let the silence build between them as her head spun with ideas. His words *'make him'* settled inside her. Perhaps if she stopped reverting to the recalcitrant teenager she had once been that would be a start. 'I cannot keep fighting my father. It is not only futile, but he's sick. And I do have obligations now that require my full attention.' She released a noisy breath and smiled wearily. 'Do you think perhaps I have felt sorry for myself for long enough?'

Wolfe's head came up, surprise lighting his gaze, as if he hadn't expected her to admit to such a flaw. Then he laughed. 'You're one out of the box, Princess.'

She smiled back at him, warmed by the admiration in his voice. Warmed by the fact that he somehow made her feel valued.

She was instantly transported to the single night they had

shared together. As much as the passion between them had shocked her, it had also thrilled her. She wondered— *No, Ava.* Not only was Wolfe not interested in fostering a long-term relationship with a woman, he had said himself that their *'ship'* had *'definitely sailed'*.

CHAPTER SEVEN

'WE ARE NOT stopping, Ava, and that's that.'

Ava knew her father's face had taken on the stony hue that had used to scare her as a child, but she steadfastly kept smiling at the sea of people waving flags along the tree-lined boulevard as the royal coach trotted slowly down the centre of Anders.

Every year citizens and tourists came out in droves to celebrate Anders Independence Day, with a plethora of sumptuously themed floats and gaily designed costumes. This year there was a more sombre mood to the proceedings, with many of the floats carrying her brother's picture. It made Ava want to reach out to her people to make up for Frédéric's loss. After her conversation with Wolfe three nights ago she knew that she could either let her insecurities control her or...try.

So she had.

And it felt like a blessed release finally to make some of the hard decisions she hadn't realised she'd been actively resisting. One had been to inform her artists that she would be helping them find new representation when her gallery closed down the following month, and the other had been to start sitting in on business meetings with her father's advisors. The workload was intense, and there were aspects of ruling her country that made her head spin, but she felt as if she was making inroads. Slowly.

Slow inroads into everything except her relationship with her father. Just this morning he had been lecturing her about making a decision on the five 'expressions of interest,' as he referred to the marriage proposals he had already received on her behalf, without even considering her view. As far as he was concerned she should bow down to her destiny, and he saw nothing wrong with the fact that one of those proposals had arrived from a man she hadn't even met!

But Ava wasn't ready to compromise on that point. And with Wolfe sitting opposite her, sublime in a designer suit, his gaze scanning back and forth over the joyous crowd, she didn't even want to think about it.

Instead she marshalled her determination to make her father respect her and kept a calm smile on her face as she addressed him. 'I need to walk some of the way.'

Her father nodded benevolently to his people. 'I won't repeat myself, Ava.'

'I know it's not the way we've traditionally done the avenue ride,' she said. 'But if I am going to rule Anders it's important to me that our people don't see me as a distant figure. Especially since I have lived in Paris for so long.'

Her father glanced at Wolfe. 'Tell her it's too dangerous.'

'The King has a point,' Wolfe conceded. 'It is never a good idea to make last-minute changes to your itinerary.'

Ava felt her stomach plunge as he sided with her father, instantly recognising the emotion that gripped her as a feeling of betrayal. After the gala ball she felt as if they had formed a friendship of sorts. She had enjoyed his company as he had escorted her to and from meetings, had enjoyed him sitting in with her to ensure her safety, and been surprised and thankful when on a couple of occasions he'd offered some keen business insights that had been beyond her understanding at the time.

Most of all, though, she loved how when everyone else had left for the day he brought her a cup of her favourite tea without her having to ask. Nobody, she had realised that first time, ever did anything for her without her having to ask first.

She looked across at him, willing him to understand. 'But it *can* be done.'

Her father's face tightened. 'Why are you always so determined to defy me?'

'This is not about defiance, sir,' Ava insisted, holding back her tendency to disconnect from her father in order to keep her goal in sight. 'If you can give me one good reason why I shouldn't walk amongst our people then I'll listen.'

'It's a break in tradition.'

'Why can't I start a new one?'

'A safety risk, then.'

Of course Ava knew he was right, but she also recognised that fear was debilitating. 'Is it important to rule safely, Father?' she asked softly. 'Or with integrity?'

Her father turned from the window and stared at her, his expression pained. 'You always were a smart child, Ava, but you're still not leaving this carriage. Wolfe—' he spoke while still smiling and waving '—stop her before she does something stupid.'

Ava hated the fact that yet another man held something so important to her in his power. She lifted her chin, wondering how she would react when Wolfe sounded the death knell to her idea. It was important to her on so many levels...

Fortunately her determination wasn't to be tested on this as Wolfe, his expression stern, broke her steady gaze to address her father. 'My job is to keep her safe, Your Majesty, not to stop her.'

'Thank you.'

Wolfe turned from the narrow window that had once formed part of a parapet when he heard Ava step into the small room he was using as an office. He'd thought she would want to make an early night of it, worn out after walking for miles that day and thrilling her people with handshakes and good wishes. On the contrary, she looked fresh and still buzzed, dressed in some sort of yoga outfit that left little to his hyperactive imagination.

He knew why she was thanking him, but she'd put him in an impossible position with her earnest request and he was still fuming about it. 'It was a foolish thing to do.'

'Maybe.' She threw him a brief smile. 'But I needed to do it and you understood that.'

'I understood you had a crazy idea and it came off okay this time. Next time it might not.'

'Life's a risk, no?' She cocked her head. 'I would have thought your job was full of them.'

'Calculated risks are different from spontaneous reactions.'

'It wasn't a spontaneous reaction,' she said indignantly. 'I'd thought about it all morning.'

'Next time you might want to share that,' he said dryly.

'Okay.' She shrugged. 'I take your point, but it doesn't stop me from being happy that I did it.'

Wolfe grunted in response and made the mistake of moving to stand behind his desk. He'd had to train himself to ignore her delicious scent all week, but this close, in the confines of this suddenly overheated room, it was nearly impossible to do.

When she didn't make a move to leave he glanced at her. 'Was there something else?'

'Yes. Do you have any news on who might have killed my brother?'

'No.' He had some leads to go on but he had no intention of telling her that. Keeping a client apprised of his intel was not the way he operated.

'Okay, then.'

Her slender fingers trailed over the top of his desk, but just when he thought she was going to give him a break and leave she swung back towards him.

'I'm going for a walk outside. Just in case you need to know.'

Of course he needed to know.

'If you go I'll have to go with you.'

Her eyes met his. 'Okay.'

Her voice had a husky quality, and all he wanted to do was haul her across his desk and push that stretchy top up her chest. 'I suggest you get a jacket. It's cold outside.'

'I don't know where you get your weather information from,' Ava said ten minutes later, her sneaker-shod feet crunching the gravel footpath underfoot. 'It's not cold at all.'

She shrugged out of her lightweight jacket and draped it loosely over her shoulders. 'I love these cloudless summer nights in Anders. The cicadas singing and the mountains in the background. When I was small I used to lie on the grass with my mother and count the stars. It's not possible to do that in Paris.'

'No stars?'

'It's not the stars; it's the grass. If you so much as look the wrong way at the lush lawns in a Parisian park a *gendarme* will come over and slap you with a misdemeanour charge.' She wagged her finger playfully. 'One can look but never touch.'

Wolfe knew exactly how that felt.

'Even princesses?'

She threw him an impish grin. 'Afraid so. The only people who get special treatment in Paris are the Parisians.'

Wolfe laughed, finding himself relaxing under the vast velvet sky, intrigued as Ava relived her time in Paris and made comparisons between France and Anders. He'd found himself making similar comparisons between Australia and Anders during the week. It was most likely because it had been years since he'd spent so long in one place, but as much as he would have said he was a beach lover he found the small mountainous nation of Anders surprisingly serene and peaceful.

'How do you feel about being back?' he asked.

Ava stopped walking and turned to face the mountains, their high peaks barely discernible in the night sky. 'Two weeks ago I would have said I hated it, but now...now it's growing on me again.'

She hesitated, and he could see her wrestling with herself about whether to continue. Surprisingly he wanted her to. He liked listening to her talk.

'Because?'

'Because I've missed the fresh scent of pine in the air and the tranquillity of being surrounded by every shade of green. It feels like home, and being here has made me realise that I miss that more than I allowed myself to think about.' Her hand trailed a clump of lavender and she raised her fingers to her nose and inhaled the sweet scent. 'The only fly in the ointment is my father,' she continued, almost to herself. 'He's so determined that he's always right it becomes exhausting trying to deal with him at times. What about you?' she asked lightly.

'No. I find him easy to get along with,' Wolfe deadpanned.

She stopped in the middle of the path and arched her brow. 'You know what I mean.'

He did. He just had no intention of talking about his parents.

Stepping off the path onto the well-tended lawn, he walked a short distance and laid his palms against the trunk of an ancient pine tree. He wasn't sure if she would follow, but then he heard her soft tread on the pine needles and felt glad that she had. 'They say if you hold your hands against the trunk like this you can feel its secrets.'

'Really?'

She spread her fingers wide against the trunk beside his and stirred up all sorts of unwelcome responses inside his body.

'What do you feel?'

Wolfe paused, quite sure she didn't want to hear what he was really feeling. 'Bark.'

She laughed and shook her head. 'And for a minute there I thought you were going to go all deep and meaningful on me.'

'Mmm, not me.' Wolfe caught her lingering gaze and moved back to the worn path.

'You grew up on a farm, didn't you?'

'Yep.' He hoped his short answer gave away just how little he wanted to talk about his past.

'What was it like?'

No such luck...

'Dusty.'

'Pah!'

He glanced at her and couldn't help chuckling at her disgusted expression.

'Do you know you close up like a crab whenever I ask you anything personal?'

'Clam.'

'That's what I said.' She studied him as if she was trying to work him out. 'Why do you make it so hard to know you?'

Wondering what to say to that thorny question, Wolfe was relieved when his cell phone vibrated in his pocket. He pulled it out and saw that it was his brother. 'Excuse me, but I have to take this.' He pressed the answer button. 'Ad-man, what's up?'

His brother hesitated on the other end of the line. 'Oh, sorry, bro. Have I caught you in the middle of a run?'

It took Wolfe a second to understand his brother's comment, and then he became conscious that his breathing was tense and uneven. *Great.* 'Just work. Don't tell me you're still in the office, too?'

'With you living it large in a European castle, guarding a beautiful maiden, where else would I be?'

Wolfe told his brother he'd trade places with him in the blink of an eye but even as he said it he knew he was lying. Quickly changing the subject, he tormented his brother a little more and then ran through a few work-related issues before ringing off.

'Well, that was convenient.'

Wolfe lifted his gaze to the woman who was slowly driving him mad and realised that other than his brother she was the only person who had ever teased him about his behaviour.

Feeling overly hot, even though the air temperature had dropped a couple of degrees, he focused on the small cluster of flowers she held in her hands, not unlike a bride waiting to walk down the aisle. Shaking off that disconcerting image, he made his voice curt when he spoke. 'We should head back inside.'

'Okay.' She sniffed the small posy and fell into step beside him. 'Was that your brother?'

He thought about changing the subject, but knew if he did her interest would only grow, not wane. 'Yes.'

'You sound close to him.'

'I am.'

'So, no sibling rivalry?'

He shook his head. 'We're less than two years apart so we did everything together.'

'Does he travel around like you?'

'No. He's based in New York.'

'Does he have a wife? Kids?'

Wolf stopped so abruptly she'd taken two more steps before she noticed.

'This is starting to feel like an inquisition.'

She shrugged one slender shoulder. 'I'm just trying to know you a little better.'

'By asking questions about my brother?'

'You won't answer questions about anything else.'

That was because he had never seen the point in talking about himself. And, if he was completely honest, because he was starting to like her in a way that transcended the physical and that scared him. It was dangerous to bond with a client. It caused sloppy work and unrealistic attachments to develop.

'Look, don't worry about it.' She gave him a half smile that seemed paper-thin. 'When you're like this…' She gave another one of those Gallic shrugs that drove him bonkers. 'I forget you work for my father.'

If she had tried to wheedle information from him, or tried to make him feel guilty, he would have held his line. Faced with the stoic indifference he now knew she used to mask her true feelings, he caved. Or perhaps it was just that she looked so beautiful in the light of the crescent moon.

'What do you want to know?' he asked, not a little gruffly.

'What do you want to tell me?'

Wolfe blew out a breath. It was so typical of her to make him work for something he didn't even want.

'My father died ten years ago.'

Ava stopped and looked at him. 'I'm sorry. Were you close?'

Had they been close? Probably not, if he had to think about his answer. 'At times.'

'And your mother?'

Wolfe turned to continue walking. 'I don't know where she lives. She left when I was younger.'

'Oh. That must have been hard.'

'It is what it is.'

He felt her glance and knew she was seeing more than he wanted her to. 'Is she the reason you avoid long-term relationships?'

There was a lengthy silence in which he realised even the cicadas had stopped singing. As if they too were waiting with bated breath for his answer. Wolfe made a sound in his throat at the uncharacteristically fanciful thought and nearly missed her next word.

'Love?'

He did not want to talk about this with her. It was time

to end the conversation. 'Love is the most unstable emotion I've ever come across,' he said fiercely. 'My mother didn't just leave once. She left over and over. And every time she returned she told us how much she loved us. It was the only time she ever said it.'

As soon as the bleak words were out he regretted them. The look of pity on Ava's face only made the feeling ten times worse.

'Where did she go?'

Wolfe thrust his hand through his hair and promised himself next time he'd stick to monosyllabic answers or none at all, as he usually did. 'We never knew. Sometimes she would meet a man in town and take off, other times she just went on a "holiday".'

'But that's awful. What did your father say? Was he even there?'

'He was there,' Wolfe said grimly. *Usually out on his tractor, ignoring reality.* 'But he didn't say anything. When she came back, sometimes months later, we all just pretended she'd never left.'

'That hurts the most, no?' Her delicate brows drew together in consternation. 'I used to hate it when my father would go off on extended business trips, or lock himself away in meetings and then totally ignore how it made us feel.'

'I wasn't hurt by her actions,' Wolfe denied. 'But Adam was. Whenever she'd go he used to run away and try and find her.' He hated remembering those hours of searching for his brother, worried about whether he'd find him alive or dead in the hot, arid bushland that surrounded their farm.

'But not you?'

Wolfe realised with a start that she had somehow sucked him back into the past against his better judgment, and he felt excessively relieved to find they had arrived back at the palace. 'No. Not me. I was older. I understood.'

She looked up at him with such a penetrating gaze he felt every one of his muscles grow taut.

'Understood what, Wolfe?' Her gaze bored into his. 'That you were a child who couldn't rely on his mother's love?'

CHAPTER EIGHT

AVA VACILLATED BETWEEN the two evening gowns laid out on her hotel bed. She could smell the fragrant Parisian air through her open window, and outside she knew the night sky was streaked with pink and orange, the Seine sparkling under the glow of the street lamps that had just gone on.

She tapped her foot in time with her favourite jazz album, blaring from the hotel's sound system, trying to feel okay about her coming dinner with Prince Lorenzo of Triole and not to torture herself about where Wolfe had got to last night.

For a whole week he'd barely uttered a word to her—ever since he'd opened up about his childhood and she'd made that rash statement about his mother. The words had been out of her mouth before she'd thought it through, but she had felt so outraged on his behalf. And clearly he'd felt outraged by what *she'd* said, because he had stopped sitting beside her in meetings and had even stopped making her evening cup of tea. It was a silly, inconsequential thing to care about, but it had come to mean a lot to her. His support had come to mean a lot. Somewhere along the way she had forgotten that she was just his client. Forgotten that, although they had been lovers, they had nothing else between them.

The devil on her shoulder told her he'd been out with a woman. That he was a man with a large sexual appetite he had not slaked for weeks. Her hands knotted into fists and she forced herself not to think about the heaviness in her heart. Forced herself to concentrate on the *crucial* task of choosing a gown for the evening. She smiled wryly at Lucy, who clutched the ornate mahogany bedpost with a dreamy expression on her face.

Ever since Ava had submitted to the changes in her life and accepted Lucy's help their relationship had blossomed into the beginnings of a genuine friendship.

'Which do you think, Lucy?'

'Depends on the look you're going for. The silver is stylish and understated, while the red is very "look at me". Very racy.'

Which would Wolfe prefer? The thought winged into Ava's mind before she could stop it. The silver. He'd want her to blend into the background.

'The red,' she said decisively, angry with herself for wanting to dress to please Wolfe. And *racy* might help pick up her mood. Ava rolled her shoulders to ease the tension her warm bath had failed to alleviate.

'Great choice.' Lucy beamed. 'Prince Lorenzo will find you irresistible!'

The sound of the music being clicked off made Lucy's last words ring loudly in the sudden silence. Lucy gasped, her hand pressed against her chest. 'Monsieur Wolfe!'

'Leave us, Lucy,' Wolfe commanded icily.

Lucy hesitated, her eyes darting to Ava's.

Ava handed Lucy the red gown. 'If you could have this pressed and return it when it's done, Lucy, that would be lovely.'

She could tell instantly that Wolfe was in a dangerous mood; the expression on his face was as black as his clothing.

After waiting for Lucy to close the sitting room door, she turned to face him. 'I didn't hear you knock.'

'That's because I didn't.'

Their eyes connected and Ava couldn't have looked away

to save her life. Then he prowled to the other side of the room and slammed her window closed before turning to face her. 'Big night tonight?' His eyes fell on the silver dress draped over her bed.

'A state dinner is always important.' Her heart thumped in her chest and she moved to sit on the stool facing the dressing table, started unwinding her hair from the topknot she'd put it in while she bathed. If nothing else it gave her hands something to do. Although she knew he was angry, she had no idea why. 'Did you want something?'

Now, *there* was a loaded question. But it wasn't one Wolfe was in a state of mind to answer. Not with her wearing that flimsy midnight-blue kimono that perfectly matched her eyes and most likely nothing underneath.

He was in a foul mood and he knew why. He was frustrated with the lack of progress he'd made on her case—and frustrated with himself. He'd lost focus somewhere in the middle of last week and stopped thinking of her as a job. Somewhere along the way he'd started to admire her work ethic, her commitment to master a duty she'd never thought would be hers…and then he'd gone and exacerbated the situation by spilling his guts to her.

'Understood what, Wolfe? That you were a child who couldn't rely on his mother's love?'

Wolfe silently cursed as her nosy question replayed once again inside his head. That's what you got for opening up to a woman. Psychobabble and a week-long headache.

He'd made a mistake—too many where she was concerned—but as long as he made the other night his last he could live with it.

Now all he had to do was to reinstate the cool professionalism he was renowned for and get back on task.

In some ways he had hoped taking last night off would help with that. He'd met a mate in Rome at a nightclub he'd hated before he'd even made it past the officious bouncer. When he'd hit the dance floor with a super-sexy Italian girl his head had started aching from the loud music and his body had all but yawned with boredom. Boredom? At breasts bursting out of a short dress that would send any normal man into a frenzy of desire? Ridiculous. Or so Tom had informed him.

'Wolfe?'

His name falling from Ava's delectable lips was like a husky invitation to his senses. In his mind's eye he imagined her rising gracefully from the cushioned stool on which she sat. Saw her loosen the sash on her robe, knew that it would fall halfway open, catch on the crest of her nipples and hold, revealing the temptation of her flat belly and the brunette curls he longed to bury his face in. She would hold his gaze, tilt her cute nose and saunter towards him. Then she'd arch her imperious brow, wrap her arms around his neck and pull his mouth to hers.

Of course she didn't do any such thing.

Instead she picked up her hairbrush and ran it through her hair in long, languid strokes. Wolfe glanced sideways and saw the discarded jodhpurs and billowy white shirt she had worn riding earlier that day with suitor number two hundred and one, and all he wanted to do was ride *her*. Hard.

For nearly three weeks he'd held it together. Held his desire for her at bay. Held his self-control in check. Why was it pulling at him now? Making him sweat?

But he knew, didn't he?

Lorenzo, the urbane Prince of Triole, wanted her—and her father had decided he was the one. He'd asked Wolfe to do a special security check on him to clear the way. Tonight Lorenzo would no doubt try to stake his claim on her. Knowing how much she sought her father's approval, how much she wanted to do the right thing by her country, he was very much afraid she'd go along with it. Not that he should care. It wasn't as if he had made a claim on her himself.

'Wolfe?' Her voice had risen with concern at his delayed response to her question. 'Do you have news about who caused Frédéric's accident?'

'No.' Wolfe grated harshly, holding up the crumpled piece of paper he'd printed out five minutes ago. 'I'm here about this.'

She glanced at the document before cutting her eyes back to him. 'Am I supposed to know what *"this"* is?'

'Your itinerary.'

'Oh, that.' She turned back to the mirror dismissively. 'You told me to tell you in advance when I planned to make changes to it.'

'I remember telling you it was dangerous to change it.'

Her nonchalant shrug ratcheted up his tension levels. 'It's going to be a lovely day tomorrow and—'

'You've been to Paris before,' he interrupted impatiently. 'Hell, you lived here for eight years. Why do you need to go on some convoluted walking tour?'

'I have not been here for nearly a month. I want to see the city again.'

Wolfe bit back a string of curses at her determined expression. 'Look out of the window.' He gestured to the one behind him without really seeing anything. 'To the right the Eiffel Tower, to the left Notre Dame.'

'Actually, that's Hôtel de Ville to the left. You cannot see Notre Dame from that window.' She regarded him steadily. 'Have you ever actually walked around Paris before, Wolfe?'

'Sure. I've strolled from the airport to the car and from the car to whatever building I needed to enter.'

'Well, that at least explains why you don't understand my need to reconnect with the city,' she said. 'I might not be back here for some time and I want to wander up through Montmartre to Sacré Coeur, have lunch, and check out the new installation in my gallery before it is disassembled.'

'You agreed to let *me* decide when you could visit your gallery.'

'I've changed my mind.'

'You're angry because I'm calling the shots.'

'That has nothing to do with it. Did you have fun last night?'

The unexpected question threw him, and he watched through narrowed eyes as she rose and slowly approached the bed, gripping the bedpost in a provocative pose he wasn't even sure she was aware of.

'I can fit in Sacré Coeur, but you're not walking around Montmarte and your gallery is off-limits until I say so.'

He had leaked a fake itinerary to a couple of key suspects and the one she had devised for herself came too perilously close to it for comfort. Letting her have her way would put her in danger, and he couldn't live with himself if something happened to her. If she should—

'Look at you,' she said testily, her knuckles white where she gripped the bedpost. 'You are frustrated and angry with me and yet you won't show it. So controlled. So cool under pressure. Maybe the rumours are true and you *are* made out of ice.'

She turned, flicking her hair back over one shoulder in a quintessentially feminine gesture that dared a man to follow through with his baser instincts. Wolfe was not in the mood to let such a direct challenge go uncontested.

Within seconds he was on her, the flat of his hand slamming loudly against the wardrobe door as she was about to open it. 'You think I'm made out of ice, Princess? How quickly you forget.'

She spun around, her eyes wide, her breaths punching the air. Was that fear or anticipation he read in her dilated pupils?

He looked at her. At the silvery striations in her dark eyes and the tiny row of freckles that lined one side of her upper lip. Unable to help himself, he slid a hand into her hair and tilted her face up to his. Their eyes clashed in a battle of wills. He told himself to back off, settle down, but his gaze dropped to her soft mouth and he couldn't think of anything else but kissing her. Taking her.

Her nostrils flared as if sensing his need, and instead of crushing her lips beneath his he lightly brushed against them.

Once.

Twice.

She moaned and tried to draw his tongue into her mouth, but he'd thought about kissing her like this for weeks and now he didn't want to be rushed. He slipped his other arm around her waist and drew her against him, all the while teasing her lips with his. She twisted in his hold, her mouth moving beneath his as if she was as desperate for the contact as he was. As if she'd thought about this as often as he had. His hands swept over her back, cupping her firm butt and bringing her in closer against his pulsing hardness.

Her own hands were just as busy, roaming his chest, curving around his shoulders, burning him wherever she touched.

The sensation of her velvet tongue flicking against his threatened to drive him to his knees, and he pressed her against the wardrobe and wedged his leg between her thighs to keep them both upright. Her head thudded lightly against the wardrobe door and he cupped the nape of her neck and urged her mouth to open wider. She was like molten silk in his arms, sliding against him, urging him on with her husky whimpers for more.

Wolfe had felt his control slipping the moment he walked into the room. Now he had none. Even the thin barrier of their clothes was too much between them, and his hands stroked over her, shifting the slippery fabric aside as he sought the sweet perfection of her breasts.

For God only knew how long he was lost. A slave to sensation. A slave to her soft scent and even softer body. A slave to her heat, to the tug of her feminine fingers in his hair. If there was some reason he shouldn't be doing this he couldn't think of it.

Behind him he heard the snick of the latch as the door was quietly opened.

Thrusting Ava behind him he spun, his gun drawn, but even as he did so he knew he was at least two seconds too late.

The maid gasped softly and nearly fainted, but other than the sound of his own ragged breathing you could have heard a feather float to the floor.

So much for not making any more mistakes, Ice.

Hell.

If he needed a clearer example of just how poorly he was doing at the job of protecting her he didn't want to know what it was.

Wolfe stood motionless at the back of yet another extravagant ballroom and knew that despite donning yet another squillion-dollar tux he was doing nothing to blend into the glitterati of Paris. He was too angry with himself to care.

He should never have kissed her.

Now it was not only uncomfortable to watch her in the arms of another man, it was downright impossible. How his father had taken his mother back time after time Wolfe didn't know. He only knew he couldn't do it. If Ava chose someone else—Lorenzo—then she could have him.

Hell.

Of *course* she was going to choose someone else. That was the whole point of these elaborate tea parties and gala events. She was husband hunting and he thanked God he wasn't on her list.

Didn't he?

Of course he did. Even posing that question was a sign that he needed to step back. A very long way back.

And he would. In fact he already had. In—he checked his watch—fifteen minutes everything would have changed for the better. He blew out a long breath and dragged in some perspective with his next inhalation.

He knew how it felt to feel that someone you loved didn't love you, and… Oh, hell. He couldn't keep thinking like this. It felt as if his precious rules were in tatters, and he'd already thought and spoken more about his past in the last week than he had in twenty years. Next he'd be imagining that lust was love, and then where would he be? Hung out to dry like his old man, that was where. Talk about perspective.

It was a cliché that the client often fell for the bodyguard. It was just a hot mess if the opposite occurred, and he *fixed* hot messes—he didn't create them.

Telling himself she was just like any another woman wasn't working either. He wanted *her*. Not just any woman. *Her*.

When he had taken this gig his arrogant fat head had led him to believe he could control himself around her. *Yeah, right*. He'd proved in her hotel room two hours ago that he showed about as much control around her as a shark in a blood bath.

As a special ops soldier he had been trained to dig deep when every bone, muscle and tendon in his body was screaming for rest. He was trained to hold his line under extreme forms of torture no man should ever have to face. Apparently they hadn't thought to train him to resist desire of this magnitude. Of course in reality he *could* resist her—there was simply some part of him that didn't want to. And that was the part that scared him the most.

Ten minutes.

He shifted his weight to the balls of his feet and searched the baroque-style ballroom for her. She wasn't hard to find in that showstopper of swirling scarlet that hugged every inch of her lush curves—those it managed to contain anyway. If she'd wanted to make a statement of availability she'd succeeded. And Lorenzo was in the market and had the correct weight to buy.

But not Wolfe. His life was mapped out just as surely as hers. Work, women and play—in that order. It was a great life. A life any man with his head screwed on right would envy. A life he had never questioned before and, dammit, still didn't. That soft, sexy sound she made every time he slipped his tongue into her mouth was nothing he wouldn't forget with time.

Raucous laughter from somewhere behind him brought him out of his daze. Where the hell was she? The ever-moving crowd kept blocking his view, but even so his sixth sense told him she wasn't there.

An icy chill slid down his spine.

Glancing to the left, he caught the eye of one of his team acting as a waiter. Jonesy subtly signalled towards the patio doors leading to the gardens. His mouth tightened. He'd told her not to leave the room. No doubt the perfect Prince of Triole had taken her outside, and that wasn't going to happen on *his* watch.

Furious with himself for yet another lapse in concentration, Wolfe wove a determined line through the throng of guests until he was outside. Giving his eyes a moment to adjust to the dim light, he strained his hearing for the sound of her voice. Then he saw the flash of her strapless gown through the trees and the matching red stripe down the side of the Prince's trousers. His and hers. Perfection in the making, he thought acidly.

Lorenzo had caught her hands in his, the expression on his face one of earnest concentration. Was he about to propose? Wolfe didn't wait to find out.

'Nice night for a stroll, *ma'am*.'

Ava stiffened at the sound of Wolfe's voice behind her and tugged her hands out of Lorenzo's. She knew Wolfe was reprimanding her for going against his orders, but she didn't care. Since he'd walked out of her hotel room she'd been more determined than ever to find Lorenzo attractive. She didn't want Wolfe to be the only man who could make her melt with mindless passion, because she knew he was determined to stay unattached for ever and she needed the opposite. She *wanted* the opposite! And wanting something more with him was just asking for heartache. Especially when the look on his face as he'd stormed out of her hotel room had left her in no doubt as to how appalled he was by the attraction that still simmered between them.

He moved now, blocking her way, his legs set wide apart, his hands clasped behind his back. He was so intensely male he took her breath away and, try as she had all night, she couldn't forget the way it felt to be pressed up against all that hard muscle.

Previously she would have said she wasn't a woman who could get turned on by a powerful man. But of course previously she hadn't met Wolfe. Hadn't felt this explosion of chemistry that made her tingle and burn. Hadn't felt such a strong need to be with someone not just sexually but…always.

She let out a silent, shaky breath she hoped he wouldn't notice and stared him down.

'Prince Lorenzo and I would like some privacy, Wolfe.'

'I need to talk to you.'

Ava shook her head. Talking was a bad idea. Forgetting about what had happened in her hotel room was what was required. 'Not now.'

Wolfe cut his eyes to Lorenzo and she knew he was on the verge of ordering him to leave. Only Wolfe would consider doing that with a man who was second in line to the throne.

'Wolfe, please.' She hated the way she sounded as if she was begging but she was. She couldn't do this any more. First thing tomorrow morning she was going to contact her father and tell him to organise another bodyguard. Wolfe could still head up the case if he liked, but she knew there was absolutely no way she could feel anything more than friendship for any man she met while Wolfe was by her side. Even when he wasn't with her she thought of him, ached for him. She was starting to fear that no one would measure up to him. *Ever.*

His jaw clenched, as it always did when he was annoyed with her, and if possible his expression grew even more remote.

God, he was impossible! That kiss back in her hotel room... Her lips parted...

Don't think about it, she ordered herself.

Not easy when he blocked her path, giving her no choice but to either wait for him to step aside or turn around with her tail tucked between her legs and retreat back inside as he wanted her to do.

Ava knew which option she *wasn't* going to take.

Stepping closer to him was a mistake, though, as her senses became immediately overloaded with the faint trace of musk and man—a combination that instantly flooded her body with heat and need.

She shivered and Lorenzo placed his hand on her shoulder. Straight away her undisciplined mind compared its size and texture to Wolfe's. It felt cool, where Wolfe's always felt so warm it bordered on hot, and it didn't make her want to wind herself around him until she didn't know where she ended and he began.

'Are you cold, *piccolina*?'

For a minute Ava thought Wolfe might do Lorenzo damage, and she quickly smiled her reassurance at Lorenzo before throwing Wolfe a baleful stare. 'We can talk later. Right now I need you to move out of my way.'

In more ways than one, her mind quipped unhelpfully.

Ava waited, remembering the time he had threatened to toss her onto his horse. Back then she hadn't believed he'd really do it. Now she knew better. Wolfe always got the job done, no matter what.

He glanced at his watch and then stepped aside, but it didn't feel as if she had won a major victory.

In a fit of frustration she tightened her hold on Lorenzo's arm in an attempt to disconnect her senses from Wolfe.

Oh, who was she kidding? She'd done it to send a message to Wolfe that his rejection of her hadn't affected her in the slightest. That she didn't *need* him. But silently she accepted that if Lucy hadn't interrupted them they'd have made love again. And she couldn't dislodge the sensation that it just felt so right to be in Wolfe's arms.

'Ava?'

'I'm sorry, Lorenzo. I was…you were telling me about how we could integrate the telecommunications networks between Anders and Triole?'

Ava let him fill her head with possibilities and murmured appropriately, but her heart wasn't in it and, feeling Wolfe's steely silence behind her, she experienced an overwhelming need to escape both men and take stock. And she would have done exactly that if Wolfe hadn't cleared his throat and stepped forwards again.

'Ma'am.' His voice was dark and official. 'We need to have that talk now.'

Ava glanced from Wolfe to the burly man in an expensive suit and with a grim expression standing beside him. Did he have news about her situation?

Excusing herself from Lorenzo, Ava waited for Wolfe to speak.

'Ma'am, this is Dan Rogers. He's a security specialist who has worked for me for a number of years. He'll be taking over your security detail from now on.'

It took a minute for Wolfe's words to sink in, and when they did Ava's stomach bottomed out. 'You're quitting?' She couldn't believe it. He'd told her he would *never* quit, and she realised with a start that she'd come to rely on that.

'Not quitting. I'm rearranging the team to better utilise our skill-set.'

Ava heard what he said but she didn't believe it. This wasn't about skill-sets. This was about that kiss in her hotel room.

With her thoughts and feelings swirling around inside her like leaves in a whirly wind, she said the first thing that came to mind. 'My father won't like it.'

Wolfe's jaw clenched and released. 'I'll deal with your father.'

Before she could think of anything else except the sick feeling growing in the pit of her stomach he turned to the other man.

'Take care of her. Once she's secure for the night call me and I'll come and give you a complete brief.'

The man nodded.

Wolfe nodded and then turned his eyes briefly to hers. 'Goodbye…ma'am.'

Ava closed her eyes and leant her head back against the butter-soft leather seats inside her limousine. She was alone in the car, having forbidden her new bodyguard from riding with her. He hadn't liked it, but she'd given him the super-special superior look that had never worked on Wolfe and he'd acquiesced.

Now she felt horribly alone and hankered for something familiar. Something to anchor her in a world that kept moving and changing at a pace she was struggling to keep up with. She'd had so many decisions to make lately she was completely exhausted. No wonder she felt so out of sorts. Life-changes usually happened one at a time and with some sense of order. Didn't they? At least that had been her experience to date. But these past few weeks nothing had been as it should. Least of all her.

In a split-second decision she knew Wolfe would call a

'spontaneous reaction' Ava instructed the driver to take her to her gallery, and immediately felt better.

The restless energy flowing through her was somewhat appeased at the thought of seeing Monique's new works. They'd been installed two weeks ago, and viewing them on her smartphone wasn't the same as standing back and inspecting them in person.

She smiled as her change in plans was relayed to the other two cars. No doubt Wolfe would have a kitten…but he had chosen to abandon his post and there was nothing he could do about it. She imagined the conversation they might have if he were here. Was it wrong to enjoy their mental tussles with each other so much?

When the car stopped Ava didn't wait for her chauffeur to open her door but did it herself, breathing in the sweet damp air of Place des Vosges.

Her new bodyguard stopped beside her. 'Ma'am, I'd like you to wait a few minutes before heading inside.'

Ava considered that briefly and then realised why. 'Is Wolfe on his way?'

'Yes, ma'am.'

Ava cursed. 'I thought you were in charge now?'

'I am. However—'

'Never mind. And, no, I won't wait for your boss to join us.'

Pivoting on her heel, she set off across the square to the row of shops she knew like the back of her hand. Her footsteps echoed in the quiet night that was only broken by the low hum of fast-moving cars on the main road and the squeak and clunk of a garbage truck as it rattled along the cobbled streets.

Dan reached the solid metal door to her building before her and held his hand out for the key. 'I'll do that, ma'am.'

A car door slammed somewhere close behind her but she ignored it.

'I can do it.' It might be the last time she ever did, and she wanted to take in every moment.

'Ava!'

Wolfe's hard, angry voice made her fingers fumble the key, and that made her mad. He wasn't going to ruin this for her by muscling his way in. She wouldn't let him.

Of course her stupid key chose that moment to become stuck and, frustrated, she twisted it in the opposite direction. Wolfe's harsh, 'Get back!' confused her, and then a strong arm wrapped around her middle and yanked her sideways seconds before a deafening bang exploded in her ear.

CHAPTER NINE

SHE SCREAMED AND then lost her breath as she felt as if a giant boulder had fallen on top of her.

'Secure…the…area.'

Wolfe's deep voice, laden with pain, instructed the men running towards them. Ava coughed as she tried to breathe the filthy air around them, but her lungs were constricted. Feeling winded, she tried to twist onto her back and realised that it was Wolfe who was smothering her with his body.

When he shifted she dragged in a bucketload of acrid-smelling air. 'What…?'

'Ava. Don't move.' Deft hands ran over her body with mechanical efficiency, and when he was satisfied she wasn't seriously injured he hovered over her, his movements somehow lacking their usual fluid grace.

Hearing a ringing sound in her ears, she peered around to see that the front of her building was completely blown apart. The fire door she had installed as a precaution lay crumpled as if a giant fist had tried to punch holes in it.

Bewildered by the chaos and devastation around her, and only peripherally aware that Wolfe's men surrounded them, Ava glanced at Wolfe. '*Mon Dieu*, you are hurt.'

Ignoring the pain in her hands and hip where she had hit the pavement, she reached out to the jagged tear down the sleeve of his jacket. The white shirt beneath was already turning crimson under the glow of the street lamp that remained intact like a silent sentinel above them.

'Get her…into the car,' Wolfe rasped, shrugging out of his torn jacket.

'No.' Ava tried to reach for him, her only thought to help him, but he slashed his hand in the air.

'Now.'

His voice brooked no argument and before she could do anything his men had gripped her arms and steered her back towards the limousine. She could hear Wolfe ruthlessly issuing orders and the distant wail of a police siren. Concerned voices filtered through the dust and smoke and then faded away as Wolfe's men held back any curious onlookers drawn by the explosion.

Within minutes of the police arriving Wolfe was beside her in the car, wearing a black leather jacket; nothing about his appearance suggested that he'd just thrown himself on top of her as a bomb had blasted glass, bricks and plaster all over him.

He seemed calm and eerily controlled.

By contrast Ava couldn't stop trembling. She was to blame for what had happened. Wolfe had told her not to change her itinerary and she hadn't listened. She had wanted—what? The comfort of the familiar? To get back at Wolfe for leaving her? To make him come after her?

She let out a shaky breath. Right now all she knew was that she had put those assigned to take care of her in danger and she felt awful.

On top of all that the threat to her life was obviously real! Somehow she had held on to the notion that Wolfe was wrong. But it wasn't he who had been wrong, it was her.

'I'm sorry,' she whispered helplessly. 'I feel terrible.'

'It's not your fault.' His voice was clipped, withdrawn. It made her feel worse because she could tell he was blaming himself.

Tears welled behind her eyes but she told herself not to get emotional. That now was not the time. But emotion was stronger than logic even on a good day. 'That is nonsense. I should have—'

'No! *I* should have.' His eyes met hers and he stopped. 'Where are you hurt?'

'I'm okay.'

'Ava.' The way he said her name was a warning that he was going to go completely macho if she didn't cooperate, but all she could think about was how much she loved the way it sounded on his lips.

'My wrist.' And her hip. And she could really use a glass of water.

As if she'd spoken out loud he retrieved a bottle from the mini-bar and untwisted the top.

'Merci.'

After she'd finished he took the bottle. 'Give me a look at your hands.'

Shaking, Ava held them out and he gently felt along her wristbones. She winced as he pressed on her tender palm, but he continued his inspection undeterred.

'I don't think bones are broken, but your palms are badly scraped.'

'They'll heal,' she dismissed, catching his brooding frown.

'Thankfully.'

His phone rang before she could ask what would happen next and he released her hand to answer it.

She closed her eyes as the night-dark city whisked by. Wolfe didn't try to touch her or talk to her again but she wanted him to. She felt chilled, as if she'd never be warm again. And for once she didn't argue when he took complete control of the situation. Right now it was easier to sit back and let him do what he did best.

She stole a glance at his austere profile. His jaw was packed with tension, his expression tough. He would do anything to keep her safe because he *had* to, and all she wanted was for him to do it because he *wanted* to.

With a start she realised just how much she trusted him to take care of her. How much she trusted him to have her best interests at heart.

'Please don't be angry at Dan,' she said, suddenly realising that she might have put the other man's job at risk. 'He tried to stop me.'

'I'm not angry at Dan,' he said flatly.

No. He was angry with her. With himself, perhaps.

'You won't fire him?'

'Your concern for his future is a little misplaced. Your behaviour tonight could have got him killed. It could have got you— Hell! What were you thinking?'

Although his words were angry his tone sounded more... devastated. And that sent her own sense of guilt higher.

'I wanted...something familiar. Closure.'

'Closure?'

'I felt restless after you left and I knew I wouldn't sleep. It seemed like a good idea.'

He shook his head. 'I should have told Dan to physically waylay you.'

'Why didn't you?'

His gaze was intense when it connected with hers. 'I didn't want him touching you.'

Ava swallowed at the raw admission.

'Just another mistake on my part.' He blew out a breath and turned away from her, his hands knotted into fists on his thighs.

'Do you think any of Monique's paintings survived?'

He looked at her as if she'd grown another head, but then his expression softened. 'Unlikely. Your fire door sent most of the explosion inward instead of outward. It tells me that whoever set it was more rank amateur than stalwart professional.'

'Do you have any idea who it might be?'

'If I did I'd have my hands around their throat right now.'

'Me, too.'

He shook his head at her, a reluctant smile forming on his lips. 'You are one tough lady, Princess.'

Ava's nose crinkled. She wasn't great at accepting praise even when she felt like she deserved it, but she couldn't deny the warm glow Wolfe's words lit up inside her.

When the car stopped it was a good excuse to refocus her thoughts. Glancing outside, she could see they were on some form of airstrip, but it was too dark to make out exactly where they were. The only source of light was coming from the open rectangular door of Wolfe's private plane.

Wolfe waited for his men to flank the car before opening the door. He glanced around, his eyes scanning the darkness. He was so fierce. So sure. He braced himself against the car as he leant down and beckoned to her. 'This way.'

Careful of her injured palms, Ava scooted across the soft leather, still warm from his body. The softly falling rain chilled her bare shoulders and arms as she stepped out of the car.

Immediately Wolfe moved into her space and lifted her into his arms.

'I can walk.'

'My way is quicker.'

His tone told her he was readying himself for an argument, but frankly Ava didn't have the energy and wasn't sure of how capable she was of making it up the steps under her own steam anyway.

She sighed and rested her head against his chest, her eyelids too heavy to stay propped open. No doubt he was taking her back to Anders, but she'd much prefer a tropical island far away from the outside world if she was given the choice.

Once on his plane she kept her eyes closed, and only opened them when she felt Wolfe gently lower her onto a soft mattress.

The doctor Wolfe had sent to her at Gilles's was waiting and Ava struggled to a sitting position, with the reams of fabric from her torn and dirty gown twisting around her legs.

He followed Wolfe's instructions and checked her wristbones before efficiently sticking a number of plasters over her scraped palms. 'These will feel stiff and sore for a couple of days, due to the bruising beneath the scratches, but they should heal fine.'

'Check her left hip. It's bothering her.'

Her eyes flew to his. How did he know it hurt? 'It's fine.'

'Check it.'

Ava only flinched once during his gentle ministrations, grateful when he deemed it only a light bruise.

'What about you?' She glanced at Wolfe but he was busy checking an incoming message on his phone.

'I'm fine. Thanks, Jock. Tell Stevens to get us airborne as quickly as possible.'

It was only after he said it that Ava became conscious of the whine of the aircraft. Seconds later they were racing towards the sky.

Her eyes traced the smudges of dust covering Wolfe's sandy-blond hair and moved down over his snowy-white shirt beneath the leather jacket.

'You're shivering. Here.' Wolfe pulled a brand-new white shirt out of a small closet, his movements as clipped as his tone. 'I don't have anything for you to wear and both your clothes and your lady's maid are back at the hotel. Can you get changed yourself?'

'Into a shirt?'

'It's all I have here.'

Ava stared at it, the events of the night crashing in around her. Tears pricked behind her eyes and she bit her bottom lip. Hard. She felt scarily vulnerable and needy. The feeling brought both Frédéric's and her mother's death into sharp focus inside her mind.

'Come here,' he said gently.

Wolfe gripped her shoulders, but Ava was afraid if she gave in to the comfort he was offering she would break down completely and never let him go. She shook her head. 'I need to use the bathroom. I'm filthy.'

He looked as if he wanted to argue but then released her. 'Bathroom's through there.'

As the enormity of what had happened hit her full-on Ava had to concentrate to make her legs carry her the short distance across the plane.

Once inside the pristine bathroom, she used the amenities and eyed the shower stall despondently. It would take too long to shower with her hands bandaged, but she would love to just wash the night away if she could.

Don't think about it, she ordered herself. *Then maybe it will all go away.*

She felt like crying.

Reaching around to the side of her gown, she let out an impatient growl as her clumsy fingers fought to drag the zipper down. Then she heard the unmistakable sound of fabric tearing and a sob rose in her throat. The once beautiful gown sagged and fell to the floor and it took all her effort to remain standing. Crying over a dress when someone was trying to kill her…when someone had killed her brother… Pathetic.

Telling herself to get a grip, she kicked off her heels and stuffed her arms into Wolfe's shirt. She knew immediately by the linen smell that he'd never worn it, and that made her want to cry even more.

Dashing at her useless tears to hold them back, she nearly screamed aloud when she couldn't even do the simple task of sliding buttons into buttonholes. Her fingers were hampered by the thick bandages and the length of the shirtsleeves that dangled past her wrists and refused to stay pushed up her arms.

'Oh, damn, damn, *damn.*'

'Ava? Are you okay in there?'

Ava stopped cursing and stilled. '*Oui*. Fine.'

The door opened regardless and Wolfe stood framed in the doorway, with his hands on his hips. He'd changed into a clean shirt that hung out over soft denim jeans. *Magnificent* didn't even begin to describe him.

Wolfe felt as if someone had just tried to squeeze every drop of blood out of his heart as he took in the sight of her standing in the middle of the bathroom, pale and regal, clutching the sides of his shirt together, her torn gown like a puddle of blood circling her bare legs and feet. Tear-marks tracked down her dirty face and her lower lip was trembling as she tried to hold herself together.

He'd never met another woman like her. One who faced life's challenges with grit and determination. One who wasn't afraid to face the truth about herself and, when she set her mind to something, just gathered her courage, rolled up her sleeves and got on with it.

Something tugged in the region of his heart. She was beautiful and strong and...*special*. The word anchored inside his mind and wouldn't budge. It didn't help that she looked as sexy as hell in his shirt.

'I can't do up these damned buttons,' she complained, her voice rough as she worked to hold back tears, her brow furrowed.

'Oh, baby...' Wolfe didn't have a lot of experience dealing with female tears but he acted purely on instinct as he stepped into the room and closed his arms around her. Something satisfying was released inside him when she buried her head against his chest and sniffed. It felt as if she belonged there, but he immediately dismissed the rogue thought. That kind of thinking was totally against his rules.

Her arms slid around his back and he ignored the bolt of discomfort that shot up his spine as she inadvertently touched muscles that had been crushed when part of the wall of her gallery building had landed on top of him.

'Do you know why I chose Paris?'

Her soft voice was muffled against his shirt front and she reminded him of the bunch of newborn kittens he and his brother had once found abandoned in one of the back sheds on their farm. He and Adam had secretly fed them until they had grown too big to be contained. His father had wanted to drown the lot of them, but both of them had begged him to reconsider. Then they had made signs and taken the kittens to the local mall, and stayed all day until the last one had been given away.

The stupid memory made him feel suddenly vulnerable, and he cleared his throat and smoothed his hand up and down Ava's back to distract himself. 'No. Why?'

'It's my mother's city. She grew up here. After she died my life became like something out of a Dickens novel. My father didn't know how to deal with a teenage daughter so he didn't. Since Frédéric had been sent to military school, I...I...'

'You had no one.'

'No.'

A raw sob ripped from her throat and, remembering her stoic reaction to the news of Frédéric's death, Wolfe guessed that she had probably never let herself grieve the loss. The futile destruction of her gallery would be just one more injury for her to try to cope with.

The need to comfort her overrode any sense of self-preservation he had left. Gathering her close, he cradled the back of her head and soaked up her tears, absorbing as much of her pain as he could. When the storm had passed she shifted even closer and every muscle in his body tensed in response.

'You must think I'm a weak foo— Oh, my God. Why did you not tell me I looked like this?'

Wolfe glanced over his shoulder and saw her horrified

reflection in the small bathroom mirror. He eased her away from him and pushed her mass of hair back from her face. 'Really? I thought you were just going for the Panda of the Year award.'

'Yes. With dreadlocks,' she scoffed, dashing at the dusty tear-smudges on her cheeks with the back of one hand. The other was holding her shirt blessedly closed.

'Here, let me.' Still taking most of her weight, and trying not to think about how good she felt leaning into him, Wolfe reached around her and wet a facecloth with warm water. He tilted her chin up and gently wiped as much of the grit and smudges from her face as he could. His muscles knotted as he thought of how close she had come to dying, but he forced himself to relax. Right now her needs took precedence over his rage.

She must have sensed the change in him because she gave him a half-hearted smile and started fumbling with the tiny buttons on his shirt.

Damn, he was going to have to do that for her, as well.

Gently knocking her hands aside, he reached for the top button of the shirt. 'Let me do that. It will be quicker.'

Her beautiful red-rimmed eyes met his and sweat broke out on his forehead. He needed to think of something else.

First, remove the dust cover, then release the tension on the recoil spring.

Okay, he started disassembling an AK47 in his head. That was definitely something else.

His fingers felt feeble as he forced the buttons into their holes and he paused when he accidentally brushed the sweet-smelling skin between her breasts.

Slide the hammer back.

What the hell were these buttons made of anyway? Plasticine?

Gas tube off—

No, idiot. Adjust the front sight post first.

Oh, what the hell.

There was no way cold hard metal could compete with the memory of the weight of those round breasts in the palm of his hands and he gave up, giving his mind permission to conjure up the bumpy texture of her nipples when they were aroused into tight peaks, their colour, their flavour...

Finally reaching the last button, and completely disgusted with himself, Wolfe was glad he didn't have that useless AK47 handy or he might shoot himself with it. He'd been as good as useless to her tonight anyway.

With professional detachment he ignored the question in his head about whether she was wearing panties and lifted her into his arms, hoping to God she couldn't feel his thundering heartbeat. He strode into the plane's bedroom and placed her quickly on the turned-back bed.

About to tell her he'd leave her to rest, he realised she hadn't moved, but sat huddled right where he'd put her.

'Ava...' He said her name on an exhalation. She looked so washed-out and unhappy he couldn't stop himself from placing his knee on the bed beside her and rubbing his hands over her shoulders. 'Baby, lie down.'

She shook her head and her lower lip wobbled again.

'Come on, Princess. Time for sleep.'

He eased her down on the pillows and smoothed her hair back from her face, determined to let that be the end of it.

'Wolfe?' Her voice, barely a whisper, was laced with fatigue and shock. 'Could you stay with me? I mean...just for a minute.'

Could he stay with her? Sure. *Should* he stay with her? No.

Wolfe closed his eyes and held himself still. It would be a monumental mistake to say yes. He wanted to stay. All too much. Which was why he shouldn't.

'Okay.' His hand slipped to the side of her face, caressing the cool skin of her cheek, her jaw. Before he had time to think about it he eased in beside her and leaned his back against the headboard. Without a word he gathered her close and felt her whole body sigh as she arranged her limbs to slot perfectly against his own—as if he'd been made specifically for this purpose. Specifically for her.

A sensation of warmth spread inside his chest and a lump formed in his throat. Without being truly conscious of it he stroked her back. 'Sleep, Princess. I'll be here.'

Had he really just promised that?

After promising himself he'd keep as much physical distance from her as possible?

Well, yes, but there was time to re-implement that plan once he had her on his island. His house wasn't huge, but it was big enough to get lost in, and once he had her safe he'd be able to lock himself away and get to work.

So, yes, he would stay for now, give her the comfort she had sought and failed to receive as a lonely teenager, and then he'd get up. Pore over the intel his team would have sent him about the bomb. He had a suspicion he knew who was behind the attack on her life, given the people he had deliberately leaked Ava's bogus itinerary to, and it was time to find out if his instincts were correct.

Releasing a slow breath, he willed his pain-racked body to fake relaxation. Earlier, when he had spotted Ava in front of her building it had been like running over moon grass instead of smooth pavement trying to reach her. His instincts had been screaming that he should have sent somebody over to check the gallery earlier that night. He hadn't—another slip-up—and he'd nearly lost her. Hell, a newly minted grunt could do a better job of protecting her than he had.

She made a light snuffling sound in her sleep and he realised he'd been stroking her hair. He untangled his fingers and pulled his hand back, wincing when a strand caught in one of his chipped fingernails.

Seriously, it was time to stop mooning over those blue,

blue eyes and the honeyed taste of her mouth and remember she wasn't a goddamned date.

He cursed low under his breath as he realised he'd given himself this same pep talk once before. Then it had been as effective as trying to milk a cow while wearing gardening gloves. Something else he and his brother had tried once. And what was with all these childhood memories streaming into his consciousness as silent and insidious as floodwater?

His gaze slid to Ava's face. A soft wave of her hair had fallen across her cheek and he gently moved it back. The lump in his throat returned with interest.

Dammit, he had to pull back. If he didn't do white picket fences he certainly didn't do bluestone rock with a moat and a drawbridge! But there was nothing he could do to stem the flood of feeling her near-death had opened up in him. He'd do anything to protect her. He knew it. And it was only sensible that he hated that feeling.

About to move off the bed, he felt her arm stretch and settle across his waist. Helpless to do anything else, Wolfe watched her sleep.

CHAPTER TEN

AVA HADN'T HAD any time to feel embarrassed over her crying stint. Once they'd landed Wolfe had hustled her from the plane and led her to a waiting Jeep. She knew instantly that they weren't in Anders, where she had assumed he had been taking her. It was the humid night heat and the smell of eucalyptus in the air.

'Where are we?'

Wolfe stopped beside the black Jeep. 'An island.'

Ava gave a short laugh. 'You're kidding?'

'No. Why?'

She shook her head, wondering if she was still dreaming. 'No reason.' She knew she must have been dreaming that Wolfe had sat with her during the whole flight and stroked her hair. Ava hesitated before preceding him into the car. 'Which island?'

'Cape Paraiso. It's a small private island off the west coast of Africa.'

She studied the carved planes of his profile in the starry sky, noting the sense of ownership in his voice. 'Yours?'

'It was on sale. Get in.'

Ava already knew that Wolfe hadn't grown up wealthy, which meant he was a self-made man, and she couldn't help but like how unassuming he was about his success.

She stifled a yawn as the car zoomed along a rough track.

She gingerly held on to the door to stop herself from sliding against Wolfe's solid frame, but he didn't even notice as he scrolled through some sort of document on his phone.

'Do you have any ideas as to who is responsible yet?'

He glanced at her briefly, his expression guarded. 'I'm working around the clock on it.'

Ava let him read. The wind was up and it rustled through towering hardwood trees. The glint of the moon shone silvery streaks on the inky ocean. She could just make out a solid stone house that looked to be set into the side of a cliff, and as they drove closer she saw that it was finished with a tiled roof and acres of glass.

When the car had pulled into a short circular driveway Wolfe jumped stiffly from the Jeep. Her eyes followed him as he walked around the front of the car. If she wasn't mistaken he was very much a man in pain. She remembered the blood on his torn jacket before he'd changed out of it and reluctantly acknowledged that she had become so absorbed in the horror of what had happened she hadn't thought about his injuries at all.

Wolfe hovered by her side.

'I'm okay. I can walk.'

After a brief pause he nodded. 'Follow me.'

The tiles were cool and slightly gritty with sand beneath her bare feet, but Ava had only a moment to admire the massive front door before she was inside a foyer-cum-living area that could comfortably house his plane and the Jeep and still have room to spare for an ocean liner.

'Wow!'

'You like it?'

Ava glanced at him. 'It's enormous.'

'The size is deceptive. This is the largest area because of the aspect. Are you hungry?'

Her hand went to her belly and she shook her head. 'I couldn't eat anything.'

He nodded. 'I'll take you to your room.'

She followed him along the narrow hallway.

'This corridor leads to the bedroom. The other one leads into the kitchen, gym and pool area. The house is all on one level so I doubt you'll get lost.'

He led her down a long hallway that had various other hallways leading off it and she wondered absently if they shared the same idea of size. 'Is it just us?'

He stopped outside a closed door and threw it open. 'Yes. The island is completely private. The couple who caretake for me live on a larger island about an hour away. Wait here.'

He stepped into the room, flicked on the light and checked the double glass doors leading to an outdoor area. When his gaze returned to her she became intensely aware that she was standing in the middle of a bedroom wearing nothing more than one of his shirts and a teensy pair of knickers. Every cell in her body seemed to vibrate on high alert and she wondered if he was at all affected by her. On some level she knew he had to be, but he was so good at controlling himself. It made her want to rip her shirt open and push all that stony self-control to the limit.

'I don't have any women's clothing and I can't send out for any. That shirt should do you tonight. In the morning I'll lend you some T-shirts and shorts of mine.'

'Merci.'

'I'd also prefer you didn't go outside. The whole house is alarmed and I don't want you tripping it.'

Without waiting for her acquiescence he strode to the door. 'You should have everything you need in the *en suite* bathroom, but I will be next door if you should need anything else.'

Like him?

The impulsive thought jumped into her mind and she smiled brightly. 'I'm sure I'll be fine.'

Or at least she wouldn't tell him if she wasn't.

Wolfe nodded. 'Goodnight then.'

Feeling wired after her rest on the plane, Ava turned her interested gaze to the room. It was large and airy and continued the strong Spanish feel of the other rooms, with terracotta floors inlaid with handcrafted mosaics, brightly coloured rugs and light timber furniture.

She'd dearly love to take a shower, but that seemed impossible with her bandaged hands. Nor could she go outside. Glancing around the stylishly furnished room she found nothing to distract herself, not even a TV.

With nothing to do she freshened up in the bathroom as best she could with her cumbersome bandages and lay down on the comfortable bed, willing herself to sleep again. Her mother had always said she could do anything if she put her mind to it, but it seemed that sleep on command wasn't one of those achievements.

Thinking of her mother made her feel sad again. Sad and alone. She had been the only person who understood her need to shine in her own right. Her need to stand on her own two feet.

Wolfe understands you.

The sneaky little thought crept sideways into her brain and transported her back to the bed on his plane. Rolling sideways, she shifted restlessly and felt bereft in the empty bed. Snuggling into his big body had been... It had been... Ava felt her pelvis clench in response. Yes, it had been heavenly. He was so warm. So solid. And this bed in comparison was cold. Empty. Exactly how she felt right now.

What would he do if she went to him...naked? Would it matter that he would never love her the way she desperately wanted to be loved?

Irritated with herself, she rolled onto her back and stared at the dark ceiling. Why, oh, why couldn't she get that man out of her head?

And why couldn't Lorenzo affect her half as much? Marrying him would solve every one of her problems. He was the spare to the heir in his own country, so he understood the pressures she would face as Queen. And he was kind. Considerate. The perfect gentleman.

But she didn't love him and he didn't love her. Although it was possible that love would grow; it often did in arranged marriages.

And it often didn't either.

'Oh, shut up!' Ava told the insistent voice in her head.

She would have to sleep with him. Take him into her body. And that just felt…

Wrong.

'Yes, yes. I get it.'

And talking to an empty room wasn't going to change anything. Feeling horribly alone, and miserably vulnerable after the night's events, Ava felt a desperate urge to leave a message for her father. To reconnect with him in some small way. Something her mother would no doubt be immensely happy with.

About to reach for her phone, she realised she had no idea where it was. She knew she'd had it in the limousine on the way to her gallery because she'd ignored an incoming message. Or had that been during the dinner earlier? She couldn't remember, but no doubt if she had left it in either place one of Wolfe's efficient men would have picked it up for her.

If they had where would they have left it? The living room? The kitchen? No way would they come to her room and disturb her.

Mulling over her options, Ava decided to take a look; she knew she wouldn't sleep anyway, and maybe she would fix herself a glass of warm milk in the process.

Feeling marginally better now that she was taking action, she stepped out of her room, feeling a bit like a thief as her bare feet padded silently on the tiled floor.

Hoping she was headed in the right direction, she stopped

when she noticed a triangle of light spilling into the hallway ahead of her.

Wolfe obviously wasn't in bed yet. Or maybe it was the driver of the Jeep. Maybe he could help her.

Cautiously moving forward, she felt a sense of trepidation tightening her throat as every horror movie she had ever seen vied for supremacy in her head. She leaned around the open doorway and her hand flew to her mouth to stifle her shocked gasp.

Wolfe was standing in a small utility room, naked to the waist, his back covered in a crisscross pattern of fresh welts and bruises. A large medical kit stood open on the marble benchtop, bandages, scissors and blood-covered swabs strewn around it. A white gauze bandage he had clearly applied himself ran the length of his left triceps.

As if in a daze she connected her eyes with his in the wide mirror. 'Oh, my God. That looks terrible.'

When it had felt as if a wall had fallen on her it *had*, she realised, but Wolfe had taken the brunt of the impact. Broken pieces of brick, wood and plaster had turned his bronzed flesh into a checkerboard of pain. The shock of the night returned full force and, feeling sick to her stomach, Ava moved into the room.

Wolfe spun around, presenting her for the first time in weeks with the sight of his magnificent hair-roughened chest.

Ava barely noticed.

Her eyes slid past his impressive pectoral muscles to where his bruised back could be seen as clear as day under the fluorescent light.

'It looks worse than it is.'

Her eyes met his. 'I very much doubt that.' Her hand covered her mouth again. 'Wolfe, I am *so* sorry.'

Swearing softly under his breath, he reached for the shirt he'd dropped onto the floor.

'I told you it wasn't your fault.' The words were more like

a grunt, but he didn't move to cover himself with the T-shirt as she stepped into his personal space.

'Much.' She gave him a stilted smile. 'What is this cream for?' She picked up the opened jar on the vanity behind him and smelt it.

'It's arnica. It's a natural remedy that takes a lot of the pain out of bruises.'

'So you *do* feel pain?' She tried to make light of it to curb how truly awful she felt about his injuries.

'Not if I can help it,' he said flatly.

She cocked her eyebrow at him and noticed him stiffen when she dabbed her finger into the jar. 'Turn around,' she instructed on impulse.

He shook his head, swallowed heavily. 'I can take care of myself.'

Ava understood his need for self-sufficiency. On a much smaller scale she too had decided it was safer to rely only on herself, but for some reason she wanted Wolfe to know that she was there for him just as much as he had been there for her.

Finding it hard to maintain eye contact with him as he towered over her, Ava nevertheless held her ground. 'Everyone needs someone, Wolfe.'

'I don't.' His words sounded gritty. Empty.

'Yes, you do. You're just too afraid to admit it.' Ava twirled her finger. 'Now, turn around. Please,' she added when it looked as if he wouldn't comply.

He shook his head in mock resignation. 'Anyone ever tell you you're a bossy little thing?'

'Hmm, there was a man once who might have uttered something similar.'

'What happened to him?'

'I threw him in my dungeon.'

'Then I better not cross you,' he said gravely.

'A smart man.' She laughed. 'Who knew?'

He scowled at her but there was a twinkling of humour in his toffee eyes. Her breath caught as she took in his male beauty, but then he turned and she could barely stop herself from wincing when she saw his back again. 'Tell me if I hurt you.'

'You won't.'

Their eyes met briefly in the mirror and she knew he was right. If anyone was going to get hurt here it would be her.

Ignoring the maudlin thought, she concentrated on being gentle as she touched him.

She felt him tense up at her first touch. His hands braced against the vanity unit, but other than that he didn't move as she worked the cool cream into his discoloured skin. 'Weren't you wearing one of those special vests?' she asked to distract herself while she worked.

'Kevlar is better against bullets than bombs. Although it hurts like a son of a bitch to get shot.'

And she knew he knew what *that* felt like.

He was so strong, this warrior of a man who had shielded her so well all she'd ended up with was a bruised hip and sore hands.

Fortunately her plasters didn't hinder her fingers from spreading cream onto him, and by the time she'd worked her way down to the base of his spine she felt his muscles start to relax.

And then other sensations started to creep into her consciousness. Sensations like the fact that his warm, toned flesh was beneath her fingertips. Like his size. The fact that she was standing so closely behind him she would only have to move a centimetre to be plastered against all that heat.

Just like that lust unfurled like a flower low in her pelvis and turned her insides to liquid. She glanced at his face in the mirror and found his eyes were shut tight, his knuckles as white as the basin he gripped. It was as if he was holding on to his control by a thread. As if her touching him was affecting him the same way it was affecting her.

Without allowing herself any time to think about it, she leant forward and placed her lips along the indent of his spine, feeling rather than hearing his sharp inhalation. He smelt of soap and the cream now absorbed into his skin. And all man. Ava breathed deep, careful not to press against his bruises but unable to stop kissing him on every undamaged section of his back.

He was tall, so much taller than her, and she had to stretch to reach the base of his neck. As soon as her lips found their mark a deep sound rumbled through his body and he spun towards her, his hands gripping her waist to hold her back.

A tap dripped in the quiet room but neither of them paid it any attention.

Ava knew her eyes showed how aroused she was but she didn't try to hide it from him. She knew he would never want a future with her, but at this point she didn't care.

Last week she had pledged that she would dedicate her life to her country. But that seemed irrelevant tonight. Tonight they had both nearly lost their lives. Tonight she just wanted to be a normal woman with a man who made her feel so much.

'What are you doing, Ava?'

His deep growl sent a frisson of awareness straight to her core.

She spread her hands wide over his magnificent chest. 'What does it look like?'

'It looks like trouble.'

She smiled. 'I want to make love with you, Wolfe.'

His nostrils flared and his fingers bit into her waist. Like a sinuous cat Ava arched towards him, powered by the knowledge that he seemed to be as aroused as she already was.

When he continued to stare at her, unmoving, she wondered if perhaps she'd misjudged him. Misjudged the depth of the chemistry between them. Misjudged his infinite self-control. The old feeling of not being good enough swamped her, but just as she might have withdrawn he hauled her up onto her toes and claimed her mouth with his.

Ava sighed blissfully against his lips. Her body knew his, trusted his. When he groaned and slanted his mouth to widen hers she didn't even think of holding back. She had wanted him to touch her—had wanted to touch him—for weeks, and it felt as if her whole body just melted into his like a boneless mass.

Possibly she was just being driven by the need to be physically close to someone right now. The ghosts of those she had loved and lost lay heavy in her heart after her horrifying ordeal. But she didn't care. She had never wanted a man the way she wanted James Wolfe.

'I want you, Ava.' His voice was as rough as a cat's tongue against her ear. 'God knows I've tried to resist you. Tried and failed. If you don't stop me now I won't be able to.'

Ava gazed into eyes as black as the night sky outside. He was giving her a message, she knew it. He wasn't the one for her no matter how good it felt to be with him.

Maybe it would have been smarter to heed that warning. Maybe it would have been smarter to push him away. But her body refused to cooperate. Something inside her sensed that he needed her equally as much as she needed him, and that feeling was stronger than any maybe.

'I don't want you to stop.'

CHAPTER ELEVEN

IT WAS AS if those passion-drugged words had unleashed a beast inside him. Wolfe forgot all about the gut-wrenching pain in his back and instead could only feel the gut-wrenching ache in his body. For her. Only for her.

Before, when she'd looked at him so guilelessly and told him that everyone needed someone, he had vehemently denied that he did. But right now his body made a mockery of those words. Her concern over his injuries had completely undone him. No woman had ever treated him so tenderly before and it was appalling how badly he wanted to soak that up.

As if in a dream state Wolfe smoothed his hands down over her thighs, encouraging them up around his hips. 'Put your legs around my waist.' His voice was so rough it was barely recognisable as he hoisted her higher.

'I hate it when you get macho,' she teased, locking her ankles together and squeezing his hips.

Wolfe's eyelids grew heavy as he felt her heat against his abdomen. Her breathlessness inflamed him even further. 'You want me to put mine around yours?'

Her husky laugh turned into a low, keening cry as he adjusted her so that she rocked against his erection exactly where he knew she needed it the most. A deep sense of satisfaction hit him hard at the thought that he could please this spirited woman so easily.

He kissed her all the way back to his room, only breaking contact to switch on the side lamp and lie her back on his bed.

This was what he wanted—what he had dreamt of since Gilles's wedding. Ava, hot for him. Spread out on his bed, aroused and waiting for him to take her. To possess her.

The warning in his head that he wanted her just a little too much was driven out by the sheer, unequivocal desire to take and brand her as his own.

Forgetting all about technique and—heaven help him— finesse, he pulled the front her shirt open, uncaring as some of the buttons tore free.

Her breath caught, pushing her breasts higher. Her nipples were already standing up and begging for his mouth. 'I need a shower.'

'No.' He shook his head slowly, his eyes drinking in her naked perfection. 'You need me.'

And he needed her. So badly it was a physical pain. He needed to be inside her and he gave up trying to work out why.

When she was naked, spread out before him like this, it would take a whole army to pull him off her, and he had the insane urge to beat his chest and chain her to the bed so that she could never leave.

More than a little disturbed by that gut-wrenching notion, Wolfe shoved it aside along with his jeans. Nothing, not even the whispered warnings of self-preservation in his head, was going to stop him from taking her now. He climbed over the top of her, his mouth nipping her skin wherever it landed.

Her hands stroked up his arms, trying to pull him down over her, but he resisted. He had no intention of rushing this. Instead he straddled her hips, imprisoning her legs with his and brought his hands up to cup and pleasure her breasts.

She tried to arch into his caress, but she was effectively trapped and he smiled. 'I know you hate this type of macho stuff.' He lightly brushed over her nipples as if by accident, enjoying that little catch in her breath. 'So feel free to tell me to stop at any time.'

Her eyes flew open. 'I should…I should…'

She stopped breathing again as he circled ever closer to her rigid peaks. She squirmed, making his erection throb, but he deliberately held off giving her what she wanted—what he wanted—building the anticipation between them, making them both burn.

Her hands stroked down over his chest towards his throbbing erection, a look of power and delight tilting her smile.

'Uh-uh.' He secured both her wandering hands in one of his above her head and dropped a kiss on her open mouth, lingering long enough to tease her with his tongue.

'You said "I",' he reminded her.

'I will never speak to you again if you don't put yourself inside me right now,' she vowed.

'What about this?' he asked, watching her face as he rolled a nipple between his thumb and forefinger.

She sighed in rapture, her body tightening as if she was a weapon he was fine-tuning.

He let go of her wrists and brought both his hands into play to pleasure her gorgeous breasts. The sight of her like that was highly erotic. He let his eyes roam over her flushed face and chest, enjoying her pleasure as he slowly increased the pressure to a torturous level.

'Oh, that. Oh, yes. Don't stop. Wolfe!'

Her arms fluttered and moved down, her hands sculpting his chest and abdomen until finally one was cupping him while the other palmed his aroused length. The bandages on her palms were cool where her fingers were hot. He bit back a pleasurable oath, his eyes closing as he continued to tug on her sweet nipples and absorbed her sensual touch at the same time.

'Wait,' he advised softly. 'Ava, baby, if you keep doing that I'm going to lose control.'

He shifted out of her hold, smiling as the sound of protest she made in the back of her throat turned to relief when he took the tip of her breast into his mouth.

She writhed beneath him and he released her imprisoned legs to stroke his hand between her thighs. She was hot and wet, so close to her climax he could feel the tiny tremors of her release beneath his fingers.

'Not yet, baby. I want to be inside you when you come.'

'I can't help it,' she moaned. 'You've pushed me too far.'

'Not yet, I haven't.' He urged her legs wider and positioned himself at the apex of her body. 'But I intend to.'

On a single powerful thrust he surged deep, pausing just long enough to let her expand around him before moving again. She whimpered desperately and dragged his face down to hers.

A primal sense of satisfaction rushed through him as he established a steady rhythm, rolling his hips against hers and causing a string of sensual spasms throughout her body that sucked him in even deeper.

Driving into her, Wolfe didn't stop until he felt her go still, poised on the edge of her release. He held her there as long as he could, but she moved against him, sobbing as her climax consumed her, her inner contractions forcing his own body to speed towards a release that burned hotter than the West Australian sun.

Wolfe woke and knew instantly that he'd overslept—something he hadn't done since before his army days. And in his arms was a woman who twisted his insides into knots Houdini would struggle to break out of. He thought about his inflexible rules: short, sweet and simple. Only one of them had been upheld last night, and it wasn't short or simple.

He lifted a strand of her hair and closed his eyes as he breathed in the soft floral fragrance, ignoring the screaming pain in his back from muscles still stiff from lack of use.

He'd ignored them the night before, too, when they'd been screaming from overuse. He'd lost track of the amount of times they'd made love, each time eclipsing the last in a way he would have said was impossible. And it wasn't just the sex he'd wanted, he realised uneasily. He liked her. He liked spending time with her. Watching her. Listening to her. Being challenged by her. Somehow, in a short space of time, she had come to mean more to him than any other woman ever had. More than he wanted her to. More than he was willing to think about.

She gave a small moan and snuggled deeper into his shoulder. Irresistible.

'What time is it?'

He glanced down and smiled as her eyes remained scrunched closed. 'I take it you're not a morning person?'

She rolled onto her back and shifted her head onto the pillow. 'Not really. You?'

'Always.' He propped up on his side. 'In fact I'm never up late, even after spending most of the night awake. I think you're making me soft.'

She glanced briefly down his body. 'I hope not.'

Wolfe gave a chuckle. 'Witch,' he said against her mouth, and her lips opened under his in a way that made him think about taking her again.

Remember the rules, a timely voice reminded him forcefully.

Yeah, the rules. The ones he was breaking faster than a politician broke election promises.

He jumped out of bed and reached for the jeans he'd discarded on the floor the night before. 'How about you take a minute to wake up while I fix something to eat?'

'Oh, Wolfe, your back looks terrible.'

He glanced over his shoulder. 'It'll heal.' He yanked a T-shirt over his head and his belly clenched as he saw Ava staring in that region. 'How are your hands?'

'*Quoi?*'

He couldn't prevent a crooked smile from curling one side of his mouth when she looked at him with dazed eyes. 'Your hands? How are they?'

She made a great show of looking at them, but he suspected she was trying to hide her blush from him. She never blushed, as far as he knew, and the sight was pleasing on a purely male level.

'Sore.'

'I'll take a look at them after breakfast,' he promised, grasping her wrists lightly and dropping a kiss against each bandage before he thought better of it.

Ava paused in the doorway of the kitchen and watched Wolfe flip something in the frying pan. His lithe, narrow-hipped frame drew her eye like a flame drew a moth.

He turned as if sensing her and gave her a lazy grin. 'The clothes fit, then?'

Ava glanced down at the oversized T-shirt and board shorts she'd had to roll twice at the waist to keep them up. 'I think that might be a grave exaggeration, but they're not falling off.'

His gaze lingered on her legs. 'Eggs, bacon.' He cleared his throat. 'Tomatoes in two minutes. It's not *nouvelle cuisine.*'

'I don't need anything fancy,' she assured him.

He gave her such an open, clear-eyed smile before turning back to the stove that Ava felt something inside her shift and fall into place. Shell-shocked, she couldn't move.

She loved him.

She had been trying to ignore the feelings burbling away inside her for so long but…*mon Dieu*, she had loved him from that first night. Had she? A lump rose in her throat as she recalled how gentle he had been with her mother's cat. At the time she'd told him that she hated him but she hadn't. Not even then.

'You okay?'

Ava glanced up from the terracotta tiles to find Wolfe holding a spatula and wearing a frown. 'Fine.'

'Well, that's a surefire answer saying that you're not.'

'No. I am.' She strolled into the room as if she hadn't just made a discovery that would irrevocably change her for ever. She couldn't tell him. Not only were her emotions too new, she didn't know how to tell him. And she was pretty sure he wasn't feeling the same thing she was, so she smiled instead. 'Really. I was just thinking of last night.'

'Good to know I make you scowl.'

'The other part.'

'Come here.' He pulled her in close. Kissed her mouth.

His warmth made her heart swell but she didn't let herself think it was more than it was. 'The eggs are burning,' she said faintly, wanting space.

His gaze was piercing, as if he was trying to read her, and she painted on another smile. 'I'll get the orange juice.'

'I've made fresh coffee, as well.'

Coffee. Yes. That would help her jumbled thoughts.

She opened the fridge. Funny, but when she had imagined realising she was in love with someone it hadn't been anything like this. She'd imagined she might be at a restaurant, or in bed, somewhere cosy, wrapped up in her lover's embrace. One of them would say it and then the other...they'd smile, share the moment...

'It's right there.'

Ava started as Wolfe reached around her and pulled a carton from the door, his other hand resting on the small of her back.

'Are you sure you're okay?'

'Positive.' Positive she might never be okay again. That was what she was positive about. Because Wolfe wouldn't want her love. He wasn't a man who wanted any woman's love. In fact if she told him how she felt it would probably send him running in the other direction.

* * *

Ava pulled her foot up onto a wooden chair and hooked her arm around her knee, nursing what remained of her coffee in both hands. They'd decided to eat their food outside by the infinity pool, but although the view was magnificent she had barely paid it any attention.

'So, tell me why you joined the army,' she asked, intrigued by some of the stories he'd told her about the time he'd spent with Gilles when they were younger.

Wolfe set down his fork and pushed his empty plate away, reaching for his own coffee. He took his time stretching out his long legs, his jeans riding so low she could just see the ridge of that fascinating muscle that wrapped around his hip-bones where his T-shirt didn't quite cover him.

'Couldn't think of anything else to do with my time.'

'Really?' She dragged her eyes back to his face as if she hadn't just been ogling him. She didn't believe a man with his keen intelligence would make such a decision so casually. If she had to guess she'd say it had something to do with his need to protect everyone around him. Like his brother. His father. 'That was it?'

His eyes narrowed, as if he could discern her thoughts. 'Don't make me out to be some sort of hero, Ava, because I'm not.'

Even without the cool words she could see the sudden tension in him and wondered if it was because this was the first personal question she had asked him since that night he had talked about his family.

Trying not to let his response completely ruin the mood between them, Ava cast her eyes over the golden cliff-faces and tiered flowerbeds that tripped down towards a horseshoe-shaped blue lagoon. 'Wow, this view is really something. Is the whole island this beautiful?'

'The other side gets the wind straight off the Atlantic, so it's a bit scrubbier, but basically yes.'

'Do you come here often?'

'Not as often as I'd like.'

Ava sighed. 'It's so relaxing here. It's as if the real world is another planet. If I had my way I'd stay for ever.'

The scrape of wood against terracotta brought her eyes back to him.

'It's deceptively dangerous. That cove down there is relatively sheltered, but the island can get twenty-five-foot waves at times, and then the beaches are littered with seaweed.'

His tone was much darker than it needed to be and Ava suspected he was talking about more than just the island. She suspected it was a warning for her not to fall for him, but if it was it was not only too late but completely unnecessary. What did he think she was going to do? Stalk him?

'And speaking of for ever…we didn't use protection last night.'

Ah, so *that* was what had triggered his tension. Ava felt her stomach bottom out. She hadn't even thought of it. She'd been so absorbed by her feelings for him, by her anxiety about what to do…

'I can see you're shocked.' He gathered up their plates, the harsh sound of cutlery sliding against porcelain jarring her. 'If you're pregnant it will change things.'

She *was* shocked—but more because the prospect didn't make her nearly as unhappy as he thought. In fact it made her feel elated to think of herself carrying his child. Something she definitely wasn't prepared to admit when his face had taken on all the levity of a thundercloud.

'What do you mean?' And still her silly, hopeful heart beat just a little faster as she waited for him to declare his love for her. Ask her to marry him.

'You'll have to cancel any plans you have to marry the Prince of Triole, for one thing.'

Quoi?

Ava stared at him. He thought she was going to marry Lorenzo? And he'd still slept with her! Controlling her temper by a thread, Ava arched her brow. 'No?'

One of the knives on the plate he was holding clattered onto the tiles but neither one of them broke eye contact to locate it. 'No. You'll be marrying me.'

'You?' She hadn't expected him to say that and it threw her off balance. 'I already told you I wouldn't marry without love.'

He paused, his brows pulled together. 'Not even for a child?'

Dull colour flooded her cheeks and a breeze rustled the nearby shrubs. Trap a man who so clearly wanted his freedom? 'I'd rather be a single parent.'

He glared at her. 'Since I don't hold the same view you'd better hope you're not pregnant. Because if you are you *will* marry me, Ava.'

'You'd better hope you're not pregnant. Because if you are you will *marry me.'*

Wolfe leaned his elbows on his desk and cupped his face in his hands. What an idiot.

Before, when she'd been sitting on his deck, he'd been looking at her and thinking how lovely she was. How much he enjoyed having her in his home. In his life. Then she'd mentioned for ever and he'd broken out in a cold sweat. It was as if she'd read his mind.

Panicked, he realised that in making breakfast and playing house with her he was not only still breaking all his rules with her but grinding them into the dust for good measure. This must have been how his father had felt about his mother. How else to explain why he'd taken her back over and over? Wolfe had vowed never to let a woman mean so much to him that she weakened him in the same way. But that had nothing to do with Ava, did it?

Hell, he'd acted like an ass and he owed her an apology.

A big apology.

After checking once more for updates on the bomb blast that had ripped her gallery in half, he scoured the house and found her walking on the beach.

She was a vision of loveliness, with his large blue T-shirt swamping her lanky frame and her mane of dark hair rippling down her back. Watching her, Wolfe felt a now familiar tug in his chest and knew he was in trouble. Deep trouble.

Not that it would do him any good to think that way. She'd made it pretty clear before that she saw him as nothing more than a temporary entity in her life.

'I'd rather be a single parent.'

Just the thought of her vehemence made him see red. Made his anger— He stopped. Blinked. What the hell was wrong with him? Had a brick from her building landed on his head last night and messed with his brain? Surely nothing else could explain his seesawing emotions.

Ava's soft laugh reached him from across the sand and forced his attention back to the present moment.

She turned slightly to twist her hair out of her face and Wolfe forgot all about his apology when he saw that she was on her phone.

When had she got that? And, more importantly, hadn't he told her not to use it while she was here?

Totally off balance, he let his frustration and volatile emotions morph into savage anger. 'Dammit, are you stupid? You don't make calls on a mobile phone.'

Ava spun round at the sound of Wolfe's harsh voice and nearly dropped her phone in the water. She could still hear Baden's voice but could no longer make out the words, her attention totally focused on the furious expression on Wolfe's face. Her breath caught and she felt as if she was thirteen years old and being confronted by her disapproving father.

'I have to go.' She disconnected the phone just as Wolfe reached her.

'What do you think you're doing?' he said, breathing fire and brimstone at her.

'Ice-skating?'

'Dammit, Ava. I told you not to make mobile phone calls from the island.'

She frowned, pretty sure that he hadn't. 'No, you didn't.'

'Yes. I. Did.'

'No. You. Did. Not. But anyway I didn't make a call. I received one.' She'd found her phone on Wolfe's chest of drawers after breakfast and checking her messages had helped take her mind off just how futile her feelings for him were.

'Answering it works the same way,' he said through gritted teeth. 'It gives away our location to anyone with the equipment to utilise it.'

'You use yours,' she felt stung into retorting.

'Mine's encrypted.'

Ava shoved her hands on her hips. 'Well, nobody told me that.'

Wolfe shook his head and ground his jaw as if she were a complete imbecile. 'I *knew* this wouldn't work.'

'I have no idea what you're referring to, but I've had enough of your overbearing attitude for one day,' she fumed. 'And, so you don't have to worry, it was just Baden checking up on me after the bomb. I hope that is not against your rules?'

She stalked off in the direction of the house. This was exactly like her father, judging her and finding her lacking. It hurt. Despite everything she had promised herself she had given Wolfe the power to hurt her. She had no one else to blame but herself.

As she passed the pool she glanced down at the phone in her hand and in a fit of pique her father would say was incredibly impulsive tossed it into the water.

'Dammit, that was a fool thing to do.'

She spun around, not realising that Wolfe had followed so

closely behind her. 'Like climbing that dumb wall at Gilles's. I wish I'd never done that either. Maybe then we would never have met.'

'We would have met.'

Caught off guard by his brooding tone, she felt all her anger leave her body and for a minute stood in front of him feeling strangely lost.

She needed a cup of tea. Yes, that would help her regroup. She glanced once more at the rippling pool as she stalked off. It *had* been stupid to toss her phone in it, particularly since she still had messages to check.

'What are you doing now?'

Ava opened a cupboard near the kitchen sink in search of mugs. 'Making tea. Do you want some?'

'No. The cups are above your head.'

'Do you have lemon verbena, by any chance?'

Wolfe expelled a long breath and some of the tension seemed to leach out of him. 'I have no idea.' He strode to a cupboard and started rifling through containers. 'No. Will peppermint do?'

'Yes.' Their eyes connected. Held. 'Thank you.'

Wolfe watched her pour boiling water into a mug and berated himself for letting his frustration at the situation cloud his objectivity. No wonder he hadn't located her brother's killer yet.

And she'd been right before. He *hadn't* told her not to use her phone. He'd *meant* to. But that wasn't the same thing. And mistakes like that got people killed.

Could get her killed.

Now he'd have to change their location. Find another safe place. Because he wouldn't risk her life, no matter how small the chance that the killer had the skills to track her to the island. He didn't know who he was dealing with and it was time to act as if he had some sort of a clue as to how to do his job.

He blew out a breath.

He needed to apologise to her. Again.

Without giving himself time to decide if it was a bad idea, he wrapped his arms around her from behind.

She stiffened but he didn't let go.

'I'm sorry for yelling at you. I behaved like a jackass.'

'Yes, you did.' She sniffed. 'Why?'

Now, there was the million-dollar question. 'I was jealous.'

Her eyebrows shot up. 'Of Baden?'

'I thought you were talking to Lorenzo.'

Her eyes softened and Wolfe felt more vulnerable than he ever had, even as a kid walking up to the front door of his house after school and wondering if his mother would be home.

Her throat worked and he was sure she was about to say something soft and mushy. He wanted to hear it so badly he ducked his head and kissed her breathless. He wasn't sure if she had been about to tell him that she loved him but he couldn't have coped if she had.

Because it wouldn't be real. They had grown closer through forced proximity and sex, but that wasn't love. And he couldn't bear to hear her say it when she didn't mean it.

A memory of his mother tucking him into bed and kissing his forehead when he was about five punched him in the head. Her warmth…her soft touch…

He felt a yearning open up inside him and doused it by slipping his hands beneath Ava's baggy T-shirt and appeasing a much more basic need. He stroked her breasts until she arched into him.

This.

This was something he knew he could trust in.

He lifted her onto the bench and yanked the shorts down her long legs, shifting her forward so that his erection was cradled in the notch between her thighs.

'That feels so good,' she groaned, wrapping her arms around his neck.

Wolfe kissed her like a starving man and carried her back to his bedroom.

'After the bomb?'

'Mmm?' Ava felt Wolfe shift to his side and let her body collapse against him.

'Ava, baby, wake up. I need to ask you something.'

'Mmm? Do I have to?'

'Yes, come on, baby. Back to the land of the living.' She sighed, enjoying the way his hand stroked her hair from her face.

'Okay, I'm back, General. What it is you want to know?'

'You said before that Baden was checking on you after the bomb?'

Ava frowned. The urgency in his voice was more than clear. 'Yes.'

'Did you tell him about it?'

'No.'

'You're sure? Now, think, baby. I need you to be certain.'

'I'm not a child, Wolfe.'

'Don't go getting surly on me again.'

She arched a brow. 'Me? Get surly?'

'Okay, okay.' He cupped her face in his hands. 'This is important. I need you to be one hundred percent certain.'

'Why would I tell Baden when he already knew about it?'

Wolfe closed his eyes briefly, as if he was in pain. Which he might be considering his bruises and their recent lovemaking. 'He shouldn't know.'

Ava pushed his hands aside, the nape of her neck tingling. 'I don't see how he couldn't. It must be all over the media, and my father would have told him.'

Before she'd even finished speaking Wolfe was off the

bed, shucking into his boxers and jeans. 'Dammit, where's my phone?'

'I saw it in the kitchen. Wolfe…?'

'Stay here.'

Ava stared after his departing figure and only paused to sweep up the T-shirt he hadn't bothered to put on before racing after him.

He was on the phone but speaking too quietly for her to take in more than, "Yeah…" and, "Get back to me."

'Want to tell me what's going on?'

Wolfe had his soldier's face on when he turned to her. 'You might want to sit down.'

Ava did, but only because his intensity was starting to make her legs feel rubbery. 'You think it's Baden.'

Wolfe pulled a chair in front of hers and sat down, his hands gentle as he held hers. 'I know you don't want to believe this, but your father just confirmed that Baden hadn't been told about the explosion.'

'But it must be all over the internet by now at the very least.'

He shook his head. 'No. I had it suppressed. As far as anyone knows a car ran into the front of your gallery.'

Ava stared at Wolfe's hands, absently noting how beautiful they were. Then her eyes rose to his. 'Baden would never have hurt Frédéric.'

Wolfe sighed. 'I'm sorry, Ava. I know you won't want to hear this but my team have been closing in on him for a few days now. He's mentally unstable. Did you know that?'

Mentally unstable? Ava shook her head.

'He's been diagnosed with schizophrenia. And his psychological transcripts reveal that he blames your father for the death of his.'

Stunned by what he was telling her, Ava shook her head. 'No. His father died in a boating accident.'

'Your father was driving it.'

'I know, but... You think Baden believes *he* should be the heir to the throne in Anders?'

'That's what it looks like.'

'But why do something now? Why not get rid of me and Frédéric years ago?'

'He might not have considered it. He might be off his meds. Or perhaps your father's illness has made him panic.'

Ava refused to countenance Wolfe's ideas.

'How could he expect to get away with such a thing?'

'That's the part only he knows.'

His expression grew remote and she felt him mentally withdraw from her when he stood up.

'All you need to know is that it's over. You can go home.'

CHAPTER TWELVE

'IT'S OVER. *You can go home.*'

Ava shivered. She knew Wolfe meant more than the threat to her life was over, and it made the four-hour flight to Anders interminable. She spent the whole time thinking about every way imaginable to tell him that she loved him and didn't want him to leave, but came up empty.

She'd nearly blurted it out in his kitchen, when he'd told her he was jealous, but he'd tensed up like a lone lion with a pack of hungry hyenas approaching and distracted her. She suspected that move had been because he had guessed what she'd been about to say and didn't want to hear it. And why would he? It wasn't as if she would be giving him some prized gift he'd waited his whole life to receive.

And on top of that her period had arrived midflight. She didn't know how she felt about that, having thought all afternoon about what it would be like to carry Wolfe's baby. But she knew she hadn't been relieved to find his bathroom well stocked with female hygiene products. Though that had been a timely reminder that he was a man who enjoyed women. And plenty of them. And knowing why, knowing that his mother had left him over and over and no doubt given him a healthy dose of abandonment issues in the process, didn't make the reality of his choices any easier to bear.

Still feeling torn about what to do when the plane finally

landed, she moved to the open doorway and paused. A fierce wind whipped her hair around her head. She saw her father and, surprisingly, Lorenzo waiting beside one of the palace cars, and she wished she was wearing more than one of Wolfe's shirts tied in a knot at the waist and a pair of his jeans rolled at both ends.

She felt Wolfe come up behind her and turned, expecting that he would accompany her down onto the tarmac. As soon as she saw the remote expression on his face she knew instantly that he wasn't going to. And, unlike the last time he had flown her home, she would have welcomed his support now.

'You're not coming,' she said unnecessarily, straightening her spine as if his actions meant nothing to her.

Wolfe hesitated and then shook his head. 'No. I have another job to go to.'

Oh. She hadn't thought of that. 'Where is it?'

'That's confidential.'

And dangerous. He didn't have to add that.

Ava gripped the inside of the open doorway, remembering all those scars on his body.

'I won't be back.'

She nodded slowly, feeling as if her stomach was about to upend its entire contents all over his shiny shoes. He looked at her warily, as if he was expecting her to kick up a fuss and stamp her feet—beg him to stay, perhaps. And she wanted to. She wanted to do all those things. But she wouldn't.

For one thing her father was waiting with what looked like the entire police force in attendance, and for another…Wolfe was too closed. Too distant.

Saying *I love you* seemed like too big a leap to make in the face of his implacable regard, and it wasn't as if it would change the outcome in any way. He was leaving. He couldn't make that any plainer.

'I can see that.'

His eyes snapped to hers, as if he was surprised by her lack of argument. 'I can't give you what you want, Ava. I'm sorry.'

He was sorry?

Ava shook her head at his pitiful comment. No way was she accepting that cop-out. 'How do you know? You haven't even asked what I want.' She knew there was an edge of frustration in her voice but she couldn't contain it. 'The truth is, Wolfe, you don't want to give me what I want because you have trained yourself not to need anyone. To be like that island you own. But you're not, and if you're honest with yourself you'll realise that your mother's actions hurt you just as much as they did your brother. Maybe more.'

She glanced up quickly, wondering if her words had affected him at all. If he got just how ruthlessly he'd disconnected himself emotionally.

'I'm fine as I am.'

That would be a no, then…

Ava sighed. He really was like an immovable rock, and she realised there was nothing left to say. The fact was Wolfe didn't love her and, as she had so often had to do lately, she had to face the reality of her situation.

Closing her eyes briefly against the quivering sensation in her bottom lip, she straightened her spine, marshalling her indifference to protect herself as she had so often done in the past. But it wasn't easy. Wolfe had crashed through her protective walls with the force of a military tank and all she wanted was for him to take her in his arms and tell her he loved her.

'Okay, then.' She turned to go, her feet leaden.

She hadn't made it two steps when he grabbed hold of her arm and stopped her. Ava felt her heart soar and searched his face for some sign that he was about to—

'You'll let me know if there's a child, won't you?' His voice was gravelly, strained.

Right then her hopes and dreams were well and truly shattered. She knew he would have 'done the right thing' if she *had* been pregnant, and it was with some irony that she realised that while she had fought marrying someone else for convenience she had never considered that the opposite could happen. That someone would have to marry *her* for convenience.

'There won't be,' she replied woodenly.

He frowned and dropped her arm. 'You can't know that for sure.'

'Yes, I can,' she said wearily. 'I got my period on the plane. Nice stash of female hygiene products, by the way.'

'My staff stock my plane, not me.'

Okay, that was something…sort of.

When he didn't immediately walk away she glanced up again and found his expression fierce.

'Ava, I still want you.'

She stared back at him while those words sank in and then she just felt angry. 'I don't know what you want me to say to that, Wolfe.' Because apart from begging him to stay what could she say? That he should do what she wanted him to do? Be what she wanted him to be? Wasn't that what she had railed against her father for her whole life? 'It doesn't mean anything. It's only lust and lust fades over time. Isn't that what you believe?'

'Yes.'

God, she hoped he was right. Because she felt as if her heart was being cleaved in half with a toothpick.

'Ava?' Her father materialised at her side. 'Is there a problem?'

'No.' Swallowing hard, she braced herself to look at Wolfe one more time, her eyes tracking over his features like a laser beam, trying to trace every fine detail of his handsome face. 'Goodbye, Monsieur Wolfe. I hope you find what it is you are searching for.'

Turning away before he saw how painful it was for her

to walk away from him, Ava let her father escort her from the plane, resolved to face whatever the future had in store for her with the same dignity and grace her mother would have shown.

CHAPTER THIRTEEN

WOLFE HAULED HIMSELF out of the sparkling blue sea and flopped onto the hot sand. The sun beat down on his head with relentless precision and a hermit crab scurried towards the ocean in search of safety.

The only sounds he could hear were the languid ebb and flow of the incoming tide and the intermittent squawk of overhead birds as they dived for fresh fish.

By rights he should have felt happy and relaxed, but he didn't. He hadn't felt that way for three days. Not since flying out of Anders and ordering his pilot to return to Cape Paraiso instead of flying him to the round of meetings he'd had to put off to guard Ava.

Ava.

When he'd left her back in Anders he had somehow convinced himself that he would be fine. That he would get over her. Right now he felt very far from fine. And his sense of loss when she'd told him she had got her monthly period on the plane made a mockery of his assertion that he would get over her.

'I hope you find what it is you're searching for,' she had said at the end.

The trouble was he hadn't been searching for anything. She'd been right in her first assumption that night at the gala ball. He was running. Filling up his life with work and activities so he would never have to face how empty his existence really was. So he'd never have to think about what he really wanted.

But that was unavoidable now, it seemed, because he couldn't think about anything else. He couldn't think about anything other than Ava.

He shook water from his hair and let his hands dangle over his knees.

The fact was he missed her.

She was everywhere on the island. In his kitchen in the morning when he made coffee, on his deck when he stood beside the pool and searched for the silver phone he'd removed a week ago, in his bed at night when he rolled over and found it empty, on the beach... He wasn't sure how she had infiltrated every part of his mind so profoundly in such a short space of time but there was no doubting that she had.

And if he kept up obsessing about her like this the next thing he'd think was that he was in love with her.

Hell.

He *was* in love with her.

Why keep denying it? He'd known it for a long time—he'd just refused to face it. Fear had kept him immobile. Fear of needing her more than she needed him. Fear of ending up a lonely shell of a man like his father. Fear of facing the fact that, yes, he *had* been just as devastated as his brother every time his mother had done her disappearing act.

'Understood what, Wolfe? That you were a child who couldn't rely on his mother's love?'

Oh, hell.

His heart had known the truth. His heart had kept pushing him towards her. His heart had wanted to protect her and care for her. His heart had insisted that he trash his dodgy rules every time he'd looked at her. It was his head that had come late to the party.

But was it too late?

Wolfe stared blankly out to sea. The way he saw it he had two options. He could take the risk, tell her how he felt and hope she didn't have guards cart him away, or he could keep his pride intact, travelling the world by himself until he slowly did become that empty shell of a man he had spent his life trying not to be.

He ran his hand through his hair. Hell, that wasn't even a real choice.

'I think we should make the announcement about your engagement to Lorenzo at the same time.'

Ava paused in the middle of scanning the acceptance speech she would read after her father announced his impending abdication and stared at him. 'I disagree.'

'It makes sense to combine the two. It's more efficient.'

Ava's lips pinched together. 'That may be so, but I need to do this my way.'

Her father made a grievous noise that sounded suspiciously like a snort of disgust, but he didn't push it, fussing instead with his military uniform before heading off to the state room where invited guests and the media waited for their arrival.

After double-checking her own outfit—a royal sash pinned diagonally to a satin gown—Ava followed him.

In the past few days they had grown closer than they'd ever been, drawn together by the devastating impact of Baden's actions and a mutual commitment to ensure that he received the best psychiatric care possible. Her father had shown great fortitude in the face of his nephew's betrayal, and Ava wished that she could grant her father this last request of her. But how could she?

Not only did it go against all of her hopes and dreams for herself, but her heart was so heavy she couldn't imagine she'd ever be happy again.

Wasn't it only fair that she worked to get over Wolfe before making the ultimate commitment to another man? Even if that man knew she didn't love him?

But, really, she asked herself, did it matter? Her father's illness had worsened with the stress of everything that had happened, and he was being forced to abdicate. Anders needed an heir... She sighed and came to a stop behind her father's straight figure as he waited for the state room door to be opened. Her pining for unrequited love seemed trivial by comparison.

And Lorenzo was a wonderful man. He would make any woman an excellent husband, and maybe if she committed herself to him the pain of losing Wolfe would start to fade.

'Okay.' She stayed her father with her hand on his arm just before he entered the room. 'Announce it.'

Her father frowned and swiped at the beads of sweat on his brow. Then he nodded. 'You've made me very proud.'

Ava gave a small smile. She hoped her mother had heard that.

Thirty minutes later the large room was buzzing with energy after her father officially announced that Ava would be taking over as Queen in exactly a month's time. Ava's own speech, pledging to uphold and expand on her father's absolute dedication to their country, had been a resounding success. The funny thing was she hadn't once felt nervous or overwhelmed. Either she was more ready to take on this job than she had thought, or all of her nerves had been cauterised when she had walked away from Wolfe.

'And on top of that—' The King waited for the crowd to subside into silence. 'On top of that it is with great pleasure that I also announce—'

'Before you do, Your Majesty, I need a word with your daughter.'

Ava glanced up and gasped as Wolfe strode into the room, the outer door swinging closed behind him. Every head swivelled towards his voice and two of her father's personal guards rushed him—only to fall back when they recognised who he was.

Ava's traitorous heart recognised who he was as well, and started beating heavily in her chest. Her eyes ate him up exactly like that first morning when she had met him as she sat on top of that wall at Château Verne. Only this time he wasn't on a white horse and he wasn't wearing jodhpurs. Instead he stood before her in a business suit and tie that did little to civilise the lethal glint in his golden-brown eyes.

Her father scowled at the interruption and Lorenzo shifted nervously at her other side.

'This had better be good, Wolfe,' her father said.

'It is.' Wolfe's eyes never left hers. 'Ava?'

Ava's heart did a mini-somersault at his commanding tone; shock and surprise that he was standing directly in front of her was making her feel light-headed.

'Surely whatever you have to say to my daughter can wait until after these proceedings are over?' her father said impatiently.

'Not if you're about to announce what I think you are,' Wolfe returned emphatically.

His expression was perfectly urbane but it reminded Ava of the time he had threatened to drag her behind his horse weeks ago. She knew it would be pointless to argue with him in this mood—at least in public. 'It's okay, Father. I'll speak with Monsieur Wolfe in private.'

Lorenzo half rose out of his seat, as if he might object, but one look from Wolfe had him reluctantly subsiding.

'Just tell me this.' Wolfe rounded on her as soon as the footman had closed the door to the small salon she had chosen further down the hall. 'Are you marrying Lorenzo because you love him or because your father wants you to?'

Ava frowned at him. 'Since I know your earlier experiences have given you a very skewed view of how women can be, I'm going to let that slide. But you need to know that question is incredibly insulting to me.'

Wolfe surprised her by shaking his head and laughing. 'Princess, you do have a special way of bringing me back down to size. But the fact that you didn't answer with an emphatic *I love him* gives me hope.'

'Hope about what?'

'Hope that there's still a chance I can convince you to fall in love with me.'

Ava stared at him blankly and then blinked as his words stopped spinning inside her head. 'Why would you want me to do that? You don't even believe in love,' she challenged softly.

A rueful smile formed on his lips. 'I didn't until I met you.'

'You're not making any sense.' Ava didn't dare let her mind head down the track it had veered on to in case the excited beating of her heart was wrong. 'What does that mean?'

It took him three long strides to reach her, and when he did he gripped her fingers in his, his eyes searching hers. 'It means you have opened my eyes to everything that has been missing in my life and why. It means I've been a fool to even think that I could let you walk out of my life.'

He stopped and she watched his throat work as he swallowed, a fleeting moment of nervousness crossing his face.

'It means that I love you, Ava. More than I ever thought possible.'

Ava's mind felt as if it was churning through butter as he said words she'd stopped letting herself imagine would ever fall from his lips. 'Are you serious?'

'About loving you?'

She nodded, lost for words.

Wolfe's lips twisted into a wry smile. 'Absolutely. But I don't blame you for doubting me. I fought my feelings for you the whole way—imagining that they would weaken me, imagining that you would be as flighty and as unpredictable as my mother.'

'I'm not like her, Wolfe,' Ava assured him vehemently. 'I would never abandon my husband. *My child.*'

'I know you wouldn't, baby. You need to know that when I was younger—about twelve or thirteen—and out looking for my brother for the hundredth time, I made a promise to myself that I would never let myself fall in love. That I would never make myself that vulnerable. And until that bright blue-sky morning at Gilles's wedding I've never had cause to reconsider that promise.' He paused, drew her hands up to his lips. 'Then I saw you and...you simply stole the breath from my lungs.'

'You left before I woke up that first morning,' she reminded him.

'That would be one of those foolish moments I was referring to,' he said a little sheepishly. 'And I'm sorry I hurt you. Truthfully, the way you made me feel scared me senseless. Just looking at you makes me burn up with need. When I woke with your head on my shoulder...I admit it—I panicked.'

Ava gave him a lopsided smile. 'I did think it was nice when you fixed my phone.'

'And that was when the trouble really started. After you got the news about your brother you became so withdrawn and I didn't know how to reach you. I tried to tell myself that I didn't want to, but I couldn't stay away from you, Ava. I thought about you constantly.'

'Why didn't you call?' she demanded fiercely.

'Because I didn't *want* to think about you constantly.' He groaned. 'I was still fighting the inevitable at that time...but that's done. Gone.'

'And you don't like talking about the past.'

He loosened his grip on her hands and hauled her into his arms. 'I don't like dwelling on it. But you've shown me that ignoring it doesn't work either. What I want is to learn from it and move forward. I love you, Ava—heart and soul. I want to be with you always. I want to protect you. I want to be the man you turn to when you're busy and… Aw, hell.' He swiped an unsteady hand through his hair. 'When you walked off my plane the other day you took my dead heart with you and made me realise that not only couldn't I live without it, but I didn't want to.'

Ava felt her love for him swell up to the point of overpowering her. 'Oh, Wolfe, I think I've loved you for ever.'

'Thank God.' Wolfe released a pent-up breath and bent to kiss her. 'I think you just made me the happiest man on earth, and there's only one way you could possibly eclipse that.' He reached inside his breast pocket and withdrew a square box. 'It probably doesn't compare to the Crown Jewels in your vault, but I hope you will accept it, baby, as a declaration of just how much you mean to me.'

Ava gasped as she shakily opened the box and saw a ring— a huge navy blue sapphire with two sparkling diamonds on either side.

Wolfe removed it and steadied her hand before slipping it onto her finger. 'Perfect. I knew the colour would match your eyes.'

'Oh, Wolfe.' Ava hugged him tightly, huge shiny tears blurring her vision. 'It's beautiful, and of course I'll accept it, but…' She stopped, suddenly realising the enormity of what he was setting himself up for.

'But what?' His eyes scanned her face. 'If you have a problem I'll fix it.'

'It's not me, Wolfe, it's you.' She gazed at the huge rock on her finger before forcing herself to meet his eyes. 'You probably don't know this yet, but my father has just announced that he'll be abdicating in a month and—oh, *non*!' She squirmed in his arms until he released her enough for her feet to touch the ground once again. 'My father is waiting for me!'

Wolfe buried his face in her hair. 'Wriggling around in my arms like that isn't exactly the quickest way to get back to him. I've missed you,' he admitted huskily.

'And I've missed you. But I have to go to him. You know what he's like. If I don't he'll most likely announce my engagement to Lorenzo without me!'

'He won't.'

'How do you know that? Everyone must be talking. Wondering what is going on.'

'Any fool back there who saw my face knows exactly what's going on. And your father is no fool.'

Talking about her father reminded Ava of her earlier concern and she stilled. 'Wolfe, if you take me on you have to know that your life will change dramatically. You'll have to become a citizen of Anders. You'll have to—'

'Be your back-up person. I get it, Ava. I know what marrying you entails and, frankly, I'd want to marry you if we had to build mud brick houses in the middle of the desert for a living.'

Still she hesitated. 'But what about your business? Your travel? I know if you curb your passions you'll end up unhappy, and I couldn't bear for that to happen.'

'Ava.' He cupped her face in his hands. 'You're not listening—which isn't all that surprising—but…' He laughed as she took a playful swipe at him. 'But you should know by now that I don't do anything without working everything out in advance.'

'So what have you worked out, Monsieur General?'

He gave her the lazy smile of a man who had everything he wanted in life. 'My brother loves running Wolfe Inc far more than I ever did, and I only ever travelled to stop myself from having to think about my life. I don't want to do that any more. And you'll need someone by your side. Just as your father wants.'

Ava finally allowed the smile she'd been holding back to beam up at him, so happy she felt as if her heart was aching with joy. She tightened her arms around his neck. 'You know, in my wildest dreams I imagined love could be just like this.'

Wolfe shook his head. 'My wildest dreams never even gave me a glimpse of this level of happiness. You did that, Ava. You filled a gap in my heart I never even knew existed, and I want you to know that I will be yours for ever.'

Ava gave him a watery smile. She caught the serious undertone to his words and knew that she could trust this man not only with her life but with her heart. Knew that now he had opened himself fully to her he would never let her down. That he would never leave her.

'Good. Because I love you to pieces, James Wolfe, and I will never leave you.'

Wolfe's hungry gaze burned into hers, but just when she thought for sure he was going to lose some of that inimitable control of his he removed his arms from around her waist and clasped her hand with his.

'We need to hurry up and break the news to your father,' he said roughly. 'I've never been a patient man and, as lovely as you look in that dress, it's time you were wearing something else.'

Ava smiled slowly, basking in the glow of Wolfe's unguarded love. 'And do you have something specific in mind?'

'Oh, yeah.' He tugged on her hand and brought her up against him for one brief, soul-deep kiss. 'Me.'

* * * * *

THE THRONE HE
MUST TAKE

CHANTELLE SHAW

CHAPTER ONE

What did *happen to Vostov's royal children?*

THE NEWSPAPER HEADLINE caught Holly Maitland's eye when she walked into the reception lounge of the Frieden Clinic to await the arrival of her new client.

The exclusive private psychiatric practice catered for an international clientele, and like most of the clinic's staff Holly was fluent in several languages. She noted that the French, Italian and German newspapers all bore similar headlines to the English papers. But until the recent media interest in Vostov she—and, she suspected, many other people—had never heard of the tiny principality in the Balkans.

She turned her attention away from the newspapers, which were neatly arranged on a coffee table in front of an elegant brocade sofa. Large windows on three sides of the room offered spectacular views of the Austrian Alps. The gentle tick of an antique wall clock barely intruded on the cloistered quiet of the lounge, and the general ambience was one of discreet luxury.

Outside, the mountains stood guard like a craggy fortress, with their sharp peaks pointing towards a topaz-blue sky. Last night's fresh snowfall glistened in the winter sunshine.

Holly scrutinised the road that snaked its way up from Salzburg. The snow-clearing machines had already done their job, but there were no cars on the road and her client was late.

She felt a flicker of irritation as she wondered why he had declined to be collected from the airport by a chauffeur and driven to the Frieden Clinic which was the usual arrangement. She hoped he was not going to be difficult, but all the indications suggested that Jarek Dvorska Saunderson was likely to be a pain in someone's backside. *Hers*.

Jarek was a high-flier in the City of London, often described as 'the man with the Midas touch' after his success on the stockmarket which had earned him a personal multi-million-pound fortune. But a couple of years ago there had been problems at Saunderson's Bank—one of the UK's most prestigious private banks—where Jarek had held a senior position. He had been fired by the bank's new chairman, who also happened to be his brother-in-law: Spanish business tycoon Cortez Ramos.

The blip in his career had evidently not impacted on Jarek's jet-set lifestyle. He was pursued relentlessly by the paparazzi, and rarely did a week pass without another exposé in the tabloids of his outrageous exploits—usually accompanied by a photo of him with a blonde bimbo draped around him.

Stories of his heavy drinking, partying and womanising were legendary—as was his passion for the risky sport of motorbike racing. There had been intense news coverage recently, when he had crashed his bike during a race and afterwards assaulted a journalist who had tried to interview him. It was that event which had apparently prompted Jarek to seek help for his 'issues', Professor Franz Heppel, the medical director of the Frieden Clinic, had explained to Holly during a briefing about her new patient.

She glanced at the clock. Maybe he wasn't coming? She knew only too well how hard it was to face up to personal demons, and from the sound of it Jarek Saunderson had his fair share of those.

A rumbling noise jolted her from her thoughts and she instinctively looked up at the higher slopes of the mountains. During the winter months the avalanche risk in the Alps was high, particularly after heavy snowfall. But there was no sign of the kind of fast-moving white mass that struck fear into the hearts of skiers and climbers. She looked back at the road as the throaty, roaring noise grew louder and saw a motorbike hurtling around the bends.

Minutes later Holly watched the bike turn onto the private road leading to the Frieden Clinic and wondered if the rider was her client. It would be typical of everything she'd heard about Jarek for him to ride a motorbike into the mountains in January, when there was the threat of treacherous black ice on the roads. A sports commentator who had watched him compete in the notoriously dangerous Isle of Man TT superbike race had suggested that either Jarek had a death wish or a massive ego which made him believe he was indestructible.

Her first assignment at the Frieden Clinic promised to be interesting, possibly challenging, and ultimately—she hoped—successful, Holly mused. She was keen to make a good impression with Professor Heppel during the three-month probation period of her new job. His world-renowned clinic employed the very best international experts, and her appointment as a psychotherapist was a huge boost to her career.

The noise of the motorbike stopped, and from her vantage point at the window she watched the rider dismount. As she passed the mirror in the entrance hall she glanced at her reflection, to check that her hair was neatly secured in its chignon. Her crisp white blouse, navy skirt and low-heeled black shoes were businesslike, although she noted with a grimace that the blouse gaped slightly across her bust. A result of too many helpings of the chef's *apfelstrudel*, she thought ruefully.

It occurred to her that Stuart would not have approved of her more voluptuous shape. When she had shown him pictures of herself as a nineteen-year-old photographic model he had raved about her slim figure, even though she had clearly been unhealthily thin.

'My modelling career was ten years ago and I survived on a diet of apples and black coffee,' she'd told him when he'd nagged her to go to the gym. 'Women were designed to have breasts and hips, and I have no intention of starving myself to conform to the fashion industry's unrealistic ideal of how women should look.'

A few months after that conversation Stuart had dumped her and announced his engagement to willowy blonde Leanne, who was now pregnant with his baby.

Holly swiftly shut off the painful thought as she opened the door and stepped outside to the porch to welcome her patient. She had moved from London to Austria two weeks ago, and loved living in the mountains where the air was fresh and clean. But the smell of cigarette smoke drifting towards her now made her wrinkle her nose in disgust.

'Mr Saunderson?' The man had his back to her, but she was sure it was him. He had removed his crash helmet and the streaked blond hair spilling over the collar of his black leather jacket was recognisable from his too-numerous-to-count appearances in the tabloids. 'May I remind you that there is a strict no smoking policy at the Frieden Clinic? The house rules *are* listed in the brochure.'

The broad leather-clad shoulders lifted in a nonchalant shrug. 'I didn't read the brochure.'

Holly stifled the urge to knock the cigarette from his fingers and said tartly, 'What a pity. If you had, you would have seen that the Frieden Clinic takes a holistic approach to treating nicotine addiction and has an excellent success rate for helping to break a dependency on cigarettes.'

'I don't have a nicotine addiction.' He turned around then, and took another drag on his cigarette. 'You wouldn't begrudge the condemned prisoner a final cigarette, would you?'

He spoke in a lazy drawl and his mouth crooked into a careless smile as if he was well aware of his devastating effect on susceptible females.

'Smoking is a filthy habit,' Holly snapped, forgetting that she should take care not to reveal her personal prejudices. But her first sight of Jarek in the flesh, rather than in a photo in a newspaper, had made her forget everything. If he asked her name she would be unable to tell him, because the single thought in her head was that he was lethally attractive.

'Not as filthy as some of my other habits,' he murmured.

There was amusement in his voice, and a mocking gleam in eyes that even from a distance of a few feet away were like brilliant blue laser beams directed straight at Holly. She watched him grind the cigarette out against the sole of his boot and drop the stub into his pocket before he walked up the steps to join her on the porch.

While she groped for her sanity, and for something—anything—to say, his smile faded and there was a hard edge to his voice when he spoke again. 'And I no longer use my English adoptive parents' name: Saunderson. I prefer to be known by the name I was given at bir—' He stopped abruptly and then said, 'By my Bosnian name: Dvorska.'

'Right... Mr Dvorska. Um...' God, was that breathless voice really hers? Holly cleared her throat. 'Welcome to the Frieden Clinic.' She frowned as she recalled his comment. 'Why did you call yourself a condemned prisoner? Frieden is the German word for peace, and the Frieden Clinic is a place of sanctuary—not a prison. I hope you will find a sense of peace and tranquillity here, while I endeavour to help you on your journey to a lasting recovery from the emotional issues that have created a negative impact on your life.'

'Peace?' His laugh was an oddly grim sound. 'I sincerely doubt I'll ever find *that*. You say that *you* will be helping me on this wondrous journey to enlightenment?' His tone was sardonic. 'I'd assumed you are the receptionist. When I met Professor Heppel in London he told me I had been assigned a psychotherapist called Dr Maitland.'

'Forgive me. I should have introduced myself.' Feeling flustered, Holly extended her hand towards him. 'I'm Dr Holly Maitland.'

Almost imperceptibly Jarek Dvorska's demeanour changed. He still spoke in that lazy drawl, as if he was bored with his life—which, according to the gossip columns, was an endless round of parties with his similarly louche millionaire friends—but his ice-blue eyes were sharply intelligent and his intent gaze gave Holly the unsettling idea that he could see inside her head.

'You are *not* what I was expecting,' he murmured after a lengthy pause.

She swallowed as he enclosed her hand in a firm grasp. Heat shot up her arm, as if she'd stuck her fingers into an electrical socket, causing the tiny hairs on her skin to prickle. Far more embarrassingly, she felt her nipples tighten. Jarek dropped his gaze to her breasts and the eyes that had reminded Holly of glacial pools now gleamed hotly with a wicked promise that she assured herself had no effect on her.

'It's quite common to form ideas about another person before actually meeting them.' She ignored the frantic thud of her heart and gave him a cool smile. 'What were your expectations of me?'

'I assumed you would be older,' he said bluntly. 'Frankly I'm not interested in unburdening my soul to a psychologist. I'm only here because my sister believes I need to learn to control my temper, and my brother-in-law threatened to kill me if I do anything to upset Elin in the final weeks of her pregnancy.'

He did not sound as if he was joking.

Holly felt a pang of envy for Jarek's sister. She'd had many years to come to terms with her infertility, but there was still a little ache inside her when she heard of other women who were on the magical journey to motherhood.

She switched her thoughts to Jarek. There had been deep affection in his voice when he'd mentioned his sister, which belied his image in the tabloids of a reckless playboy who cared only about his personal gratification with an endless supply of pretty women.

'I suppose your reference to my age means you think I lack experience? But I can assure you I have a Doctorate in Counselling Psychology and Psychotherapy and I have experience working as a psychotherapist in both the private health sector and the NHS in England.'

The leather-clad shoulders lifted in another shrug that made Holly appreciate Jarek's formidable physique. She was slightly below average height, which was why she had never made it onto the catwalk during her brief modelling career, and he towered over her. She estimated he must be two or three inches over six feet tall.

'I don't doubt you are highly qualified,' he murmured. 'Professor Heppel spoke very highly of you. But he failed to mention that you are beautiful, Dr Maitland.'

It was not difficult to understand why women fell for him in droves. He could turn on his charm as easily as flicking a switch. His husky voice smouldered with a sensual heat that made her insides melt and it took all her willpower to meet his gaze calmly.

'Professor Heppel offered me a job at his clinic based on my reputation as a dedicated psychotherapist,' she said crisply. 'Please—call me Holly,' she continued. 'We are going to be spending a lot of time together over the next few weeks and we need to feel comfortable around each other. It is important to establish trust and respect between a patient and his therapist.'

'Comfortable…' Jarek rolled the word off his tongue in a smoky, sexy voice that lit a flame in the pit of Holly's stomach. 'Women don't usually feel *comfortable* around me. My talents are considerable…' he grinned at her startled expression '…but offering comfort is not one of them.'

'I don't suppose it is,' she said drily. 'I'm sure your legions of female devotees are attracted to your dangerous image. But presumably your numerous shallow affairs fail to make you happy? Which is why you have sought the help of a psychotherapist to enable you to make changes in your lifestyle that will allow you to have more fulfilling relationships.'

'I told you—I've only agreed to undergo therapy to please my sister.'

His lazy smile did not change but the warmth had gone from his eyes, leaving them as cold and hard as ice. Holly gave a little shiver. There was something predatory about him that was at variance with his reputation of a dissolute playboy. She had a feeling that people saw in Jarek exactly what he wanted them to see. But if the life that he played out in the full glare of the media was a lie, who was the *real* Jarek Dvorska?

'Why do women think that men can only feel fulfilled if they are in a relationship?' he drawled. 'I'm perfectly content to have shallow affairs—in fact the shallower the better. The truth is that the ultimate male fantasy is for hot, hard sex without strings. Emotional strings, I mean. *Real* strings add an interesting element to sex play, but personally I prefer to use silk cords for bondage games.'

Holly was furious with herself for blushing—and furious with him for being an arrogant jerk. To think she'd wasted thirty seconds of her life wondering if he had hidden depths! But, like it or not—like *him* or not—Jarek was her client and it was vital that she established a rapport with him. At the end of his six-week stay at the clinic he would discuss with Professor Heppel if her treatment had been successful for him. A bad report would jeopardise her job at the Frieden Clinic—but, more than that, psychotherapy was her vocation, and she had a genuine desire to help every patient she worked with.

She made herself smile at Jarek. 'We can explore your theories about relationships and the possible reasons for your fear of commitment during our sessions. It's good that you can speak openly and honestly regarding your feelings about casual sex. You can be confident that I will do my best to help you with your issues.'

He threw back his head and laughed—low and husky and outrageously sensual. 'I promise you I don't need any help with sex, angel-face.'

Holly knew she was blushing again, and felt even more mortified when she saw Jarek's eyes flick down to her breasts again. He could hardly fail to notice the hard peaks of her nipples outlined beneath her blouse. 'Let's go inside, where it's warm,' she said tightly. 'I should have put my coat on before I came out to meet you and I'm cold,' she added, keen to emphasise that her body's involuntary reaction was to the icy temperature, and she was *not* affected by his potent masculinity.

Avoiding the speculative gleam in his eyes, she ushered him into the clinic and indicated a door leading off the entrance hall.

'Through there is a boot room, where ski equipment is kept and where you can leave your bike gear. Your luggage arrived this morning, and one of the support staff will take your cases to your private residential retreat later. I'll wait for you in the lounge. Would you like a cup of coffee?'

'I'd love one. I'm glad you don't disapprove of *all* stimulants. I was worried I'd have to give up every source of pleasure during my stay.'

His wicked grin did peculiar things to Holly's insides. She waited until he had closed the boot room door behind him before she released her breath. While she switched on the coffee percolator and arranged the cups on a tray she tried to rationalise why she had reacted to Jarek the way she had. Her heart was still beating too fast and every nerve-ending in her body felt acutely sensitive, so that she was aware of the scrape of her lace-edged bra against her breasts.

She hadn't expected him to be so *overwhelming*, she thought ruefully. Dressed in all that black leather, he'd exuded a primitive sensuality that had made her want... She bit her lip as a shocking image flashed into her mind of her lying naked on a bed, with her wrists secured to the headboard by silken cords. In her fantasy Jarek stroked his hands over her breasts and hips before he pushed her legs apart and bent his head to flick his tongue over the inside of her thighs.

'Careful.'

The smoky voice close to her ear jerked her from her

erotic daydream and she looked down and saw that she had overfilled a cup and coffee was pouring over the rim into the saucer.

'Oh.' She hadn't heard him walk across the lounge and she dared not look at him, terrified that his laser-bright gaze might see inside her head. 'I'm terribly clumsy,' she gabbled as she grabbed a handful of napkins and mopped up the spillage. 'How do you take your coffee?'

'Black and bitter—like my heart.'

Beneath his light tone there was something darker that made her wonder again who was the *real* Jarek? The jester, or the man with secrets that he seemed determined to keep hidden?

She handed him his coffee before adding cream and sugar to her own cup, craving a sweet fix to calm her nervous tension. Jarek sat down on the sofa. The empty space next to him was the obvious place for Holly to sit, but instead she chose an armchair. Only when she was at a safe distance from him did she look directly at him, and her heart gave an annoying jolt.

So much for her hope that without his biker leathers he would be less impressive. Superbly tailored black trousers drew her attention to his lean hips and the long legs that he thrust out in front of him. A charcoal-grey fine wool sweater moulded the hard ridges of his pectoral and abdominal muscles. His eyes were that astonishing bright blue, set in an angular face that was cruelly beautiful. He reminded her of a wolf—especially when he flashed a wide grin that revealed his white teeth.

Holly forced herself to study him objectively. His cheekbones were too sharp and his mouth too wide for him to be conventionally handsome. She estimated that there was at least two days' growth of stubble on his square jaw, and his rakish appearance was accentuated by the streaked blond hair that hung down on either side of his face. He pushed it back with a careless sweep of his hand.

Needing an excuse to avoid looking at him, she jumped up and walked over to the sideboard where the clinic's presentation packs were kept.

'I'll explain a little bit about the aims of the Frieden Clinic and give you another brochure so that you can read our mission statement in full.'

She spoke to him over her shoulder.

'In a nutshell, our ethos is to identify and treat the root cause of each patient's problems. The problems which may have led them to become reliant on potentially harmful substances or exhibit particular behaviour traits. At the Frieden Clinic we understand that every patient is unique, and we tailor an individual programme of treatment and support, matching the patient with a psychologist who will live at an Alpine retreat with them and provide therapy whenever the patient requires it, twenty-four hours a day. As well as clinical therapy, patients are encouraged to experience the wide range of complementary therapies which are available, such as massage and yoga. Leisure time is another important aspect of your stay with us, and there will be opportunities for you to ski and to enjoy many other activities in the beautiful surroundings of the Austrian Alps.'

Having located the brochures in the last drawer she looked in, Holly turned to face Jarek and discovered that he had picked up a newspaper and was reading it. Evidently he was more interested in the story on the front page than what she had to say, she thought, annoyed by his rudeness.

'Would you like me to repeat any of what I've just told you?' she asked, in a painfully polite voice that failed to disguise the bite in her tone.

He dropped the newspaper onto the table and for a

split second she glimpsed a…a *tortured* expression in his eyes. There was no other word to describe it. But then he blinked and Holly told herself she must have been imagining things, for his ice-blue gaze was indefinable.

'It all seems clear enough. If I'm a good boy I'll be allowed to go skiing,' he drawled.

He was her patient, and she would do her best to build a rapport with him even if it killed her, Holly told herself.

Through the window she saw a car draw up in front of the clinic.

'Your personal chauffeur, Gunther, is here to take you to Chalet Soline. You have also been assigned a gourmet chef, and a maid who will take care of you during your stay. Professor Heppel will visit you this evening, after you have had a chance to settle in. Several social events have been arranged for your enjoyment, including an evening in Salzburg which will be an opportunity for you to meet the rest of the medical team and other patients who are receiving treatment. Part of the evening's entertainment will be a chamber concert at the famous Marble Hall at the Mirabell Palace.'

'I'm not sure I'll be able to handle that amount of excitement,' he said drily. 'I hope there will be a well-stocked bar.'

'Clients are asked to abstain from alcohol whilst they are on a treatment programme,' Holly reminded him. 'But don't worry—I will be with you to support and encourage you on your journey to sobriety.'

Jarek got up from the sofa and the lounge suddenly seemed to shrink. It wasn't just his height that made him dominate the room. He exuded a raw magnetism that sent heat coursing through Holly's veins when he raked his bright blue eyes over her, from her head down to her toes, lingering a fraction longer than was appropriate on the firm swell of her breasts.

'I should have guessed from your schoolmarm appearance that you are a fan of chamber music. I bet your idea of an exciting night is to go to bed early with a milky drink,' he said, in that lazy, mocking way that made her want to slap him. *Hard*.

'My bedtime habits are not up for discussion,' she snapped, stung by his unflattering description of her. 'Schoolmarm' made her sound like a frump.

He was testing her professionalism to its limits. She had never met such an *infuriating* man. She watched the corners of his mouth lift in a slow smile, as if he could not be bothered to exert more than the minimum of effort.

'We could discuss *my* bedtime habits instead, if you like? I guarantee they are more interesting and…energetic than yours.'

'I'm well aware of that. Anyone who reads the gutter press is regularly treated to intimate details about your love affairs.'

His grin widened, and his eyes had a wicked glint that made Holly's heart beat faster. How could his eyes be as cold as ice one minute and in the next instant burn with blue flames that made her feel hot all over?

'Presumably *you* read the tabloids, as you seem to know so much about me,' he said softly. 'The intimate details you mention are fifty per cent true and fifty per cent the product of an editor's fevered imagination. But I don't have *love* affairs.' His tone hardened. '*Love* plays no part in my sexual adventures. As long as you remember that, we should get on fine.'

'Why do I need to remember it? I'm not interested in your sex-life except in my professional capacity as your therapist.'

'Of *course* you're interested in me, angel-face. Those big brown eyes of yours soften like molten chocolate every time you look at me. Do you think I haven't noticed the hungry glances you've been darting at me when you think my attention's not on you?'

His smoky, sensual voice sent a shiver of unwanted re-action the length of Holly's spine. It was imperative that she took back control of the situation and of herself. Her reaction to Jarek was utterly inexplicable. He was an arrogant, over-sexed playboy and the absolute anathema of the intellectual men she had dated in the past.

Before she'd left London she'd had dinner a couple of times with Malcom, who was an art historian, and he had told her some really quite interesting facts about Islamic art. Although admittedly after three hours of listening to him talking about his favourite topic her attention *had* started to wander.

'You're wrong, I'm afraid.' She was pleased that she sounded cool and collected—the opposite of how she felt. 'All I care about is doing my job to the best of my ability, and my interest in you is purely from the perspective of my role as your psychotherapist. I'm determined to dis-cover how you tick, Jarek. You've described yourself as a prisoner,' she said gently, 'but perhaps the prison bars are inside your head.'

Jarek sprawled in the back of the limousine and considered telling the driver to turn the car around and take him back to the Frieden Clinic, so that he could jump on his motor-bike and get the hell out of Dodge. But he had given his word to his brother-in-law that, for Elin's sake, he would spend six weeks undergoing psychotherapy. And, because his sister was the only person in the world whom he loved, he would stick it out even though it promised to be the most boring few weeks of his life.

Although perhaps it wouldn't be as tedious as he'd first feared, he mused, visualising the delectable Dr Maitland.

He had told her the truth—the only time he intended to do so—when he'd admitted that she was different from his expectations of her. Holly was a stunning brunette, but he had imagined her as a matronly figure, possibly wearing a tweed suit—rather like the vicar's wife in Little Bardley, who had always been kind to him when he'd been an angry teenager and constantly at loggerheads with Ralph Saunderson, his adoptive father.

But Holly looked nothing like a vicar's wife, and even her uninspiring clothes couldn't hide her gorgeous curvaceous figure. The sight of her too-tight blouse straining across her breasts, affording him a tantalising glimpse of creamy flesh where the material gaped around the buttonholes, had sent a rush of heat straight to his groin.

Frankly, she had rendered him speechless—which was not a condition Jarek often suffered from. He was clever with words, and always knew the right things to say—to women especially. That was why he could not understand why he had blurted out to Holly that she was beautiful. He'd sounded like an adolescent on a first date. Usually he was the king of cool, and the funny thing was that the more he acted as if he didn't care the more interested women were in him.

The truth was he really *didn't* care about anything or anyone apart from his sister, whom he had protected since she was a baby. But Elin was married to Cortez now, and they had a son, Harry. Soon their second child would be born. Jarek had accepted that Elin's life had moved on and, although they would always share a close bond, that her priorities were her husband and family. Hell, he'd even accepted that Cortez, who was actually Ralph Saunderson's secret son and heir, was a decent guy.

But, while his sister deserved to be happy, Jarek knew he would never come to terms with what he had done, and the grief he had caused to both Elin and Ralph Saunderson. It was his fault that Lorna Saunderson had died, and the raw pain inside him was his punishment—it was what he deserved.

He steered his mind away from the dark path of memory, which inevitably led to the self-destructive behaviour his sister had begged him to seek help for. The truth was *no one* could help him. He pictured Dr Maitland's doe eyes and her serenely lovely face. He'd nicknamed her 'angelface' but there was nothing angelic about her sinfully sexy mouth. He'd found himself longing to taste and explore it with his tongue.

At another time—even a month ago—he would have viewed Holly as an enjoyable distraction, and nothing would have stopped him from taking advantage of the awareness of him that she had unsuccessfully tried to hide.

But the letter he had received three weeks ago had made him question everything he'd believed he knew about himself. It had even made him wonder...who *was* Jarek Dvorska?

CHAPTER TWO

JAREK STARED OUT of the car window at the stunning Alpine landscape. All around him majestic snow-white mountains touched the sky and were reflected in a gentian-blue lake. The pine trees growing on the slopes looked as if they had been dusted with icing sugar, and here and there quaint Hansel and Gretel chalets peeped out from beneath snow-covered roofs.

The mountainous scene was exquisite, but there was also an inexplicable familiarity about it that he found puzzling. Ever since his adoptive parents had taken him on a skiing holiday in Chamonix, when he was twelve, Jarek had felt 'at home' in the mountains. But that did not make sense, because he had spent the first nine years of his life in the Bosnian capital Sarajevo. He had no recollection of his family's home in the city, but he remembered the grim grey orphanage where he and Elin had lived after their parents had died.

Why did he feel a sense of recognition when he skied down a mountain? he had once asked Lorna Saunderson, when he'd been trying to make sense of the images inside his head that he thought must be snatches of dreams—because how could they be real memories? For that matter, how had he known instinctively how to ski, without any help from an instructor, on that trip to Chamonix?

His adoptive mother—the only woman he had ever called Mama, since he had no idea who his real mother was—had reminded him that Sarajevo was surrounded by mountains. She'd suggested that perhaps staff at the orphanage had taken the children on a trip to the mountains and he had forgotten it.

Jarek thought it was unlikely. His memories of early childhood were of fear and hunger and regular beatings from the staff—although he had no idea what he might have done to merit such severe punishment. He certainly did not remember being taken out of the orphanage, and his recollections of Bosnia were only of the war that had taken place there in the nineteen-nineties, when Sarajevo had been besieged by Serbian soldiers.

His boyhood memories were of the sound of machine gun fire and the loud explosions when bombs had fallen into the compound outside the orphanage, where the children had played. He and the other orphaned children had huddled together in a damp cellar while Sarajevo had been under fire. Sometimes the few staff who had not deserted the orphanage or been killed had been in such a rush to get down to the cellar that they'd left the babies upstairs in their cots when the bombing started.

But Jarek had always refused to abandon his little sister, and had constantly risked his life to take her down to the cellar, where she would be safe. Elin had been about a year old when the war had begun, and even then she had been remarkably pretty. When a wealthy English couple—Ralph and Lorna Saunderson—had decided to adopt a Bosnian orphan they had chosen a golden-haired angelic little girl. But Elin had become so distressed when they'd tried to separate her from her older brother that Lorna had insisted on rescuing Jarek too, and so the children had escaped hell and gone to live at stately Cuckmere Hall on the Sussex Downs.

For years Jarek had not thought too deeply about his strange affinity with mountains. He did not take *anything* too seriously, because he was afraid that if he did the darkness in his soul might devour him. But that god-damned letter—from a man who had allegedly worked for Vostov's royal family over two decades ago—had unlocked Pandora's Box. The only way he could prevent the nightmares which had plagued him recently was to drink enough vodka so that he did not so much sleep as sink into oblivion for a few hours, if he was lucky.

He had convinced himself that the letter was a hoax and ignored it. But when he'd arrived at the Frieden Clinic and seen that newspaper headline about Vostov something had flashed into his mind that he might have believed was a deeply buried memory—if it hadn't been so crazy. Unthinkable. He didn't want to think, and he certainly wasn't going to allow Dr Holly Maitland access to the innermost secrets that his instincts warned him were best kept hidden.

'Hey, Gunther.' Jarek leaned forward to speak to the driver. 'How far is it to the chalet where I will be staying?'

'We should be there in approximately ten minutes, sir,' Gunther replied in perfect English. 'We will soon come to a town and ski resort called Arlenwald. Chalet Soline is on the other side of the town, a little higher up the mountain.'

'Does Arlenwald have any good bars?'

'Bibiana's Bar is a popular place with young people who like to drink Schnapps and watch the dancing girls. Or the Oberant Hotel is very charming. I believe they have a string quartet who play music while guests enjoy afternoon tea.'

'Hmm…tea or Schnapps—what is your preference, Gunther?'

'I am not fond of tea, sir.'

'Nor me. How about we stop at Bibiana's Bar so I can buy you a drink?'

'Dr Maitland instructed me to take you straight to the chalet,' Gunther said doubtfully.

Jarek smiled. 'There is no need to tell her that we took a short detour, is there?'

'What do you mean, he's not here?' Holly stared at Karl, the chef and butler at Chalet Soline. 'The chauffeur left the Frieden Clinic with Mr Dvorska two hours ago, to make a journey that has taken me twenty minutes.'

Admittedly the four-by-four she had used to drive herself to the chalet was better suited to the mountain roads than a limousine, but it should have taken the chauffeur no more than half an hour to deliver Jarek to the luxury alpine lodge where he would stay while he underwent a course of psychological treatment.

'I understand that Mr Dvorska wished to spend some time in Arlenwald,' Karl told her. 'Gunther telephoned to say he had left the patient in the town, because he had to attend another appointment, and that Mr Dvorska intended to walk the last part of the journey to Chalet Soline.'

Holly frowned. 'I know Gunther had to go to Salzburg today, but I expected him to follow my instructions and bring the patient here first. Goodness knows what Mr Dvorska has found to do in Arlenwald. There are only a few ski shops and hotels—and that dreadful bar where the waitresses dress up in supposedly Austrian folk costumes. I doubt the traditional dirndl was as low-cut as the dresses worn by the girls at Bibiana's Bar,' she said drily.

The lively bar, which was a popular venue for the après-ski crowd, was just the kind of place that Jarek would head for, she thought grimly. She shouldn't have let him out of her sight. Jarek's fondness for alcohol had been extensively documented in the tabloids, and she should have stuck to him like glue and escorted him to Chalet Soline herself. Instead she had sent him off with the chauffeur to give herself time to try and understand why *he*, of all men, had made her aware of her sensuality in a way she had never felt before.

Just thinking about his too-handsome face and his sexy grin that was both an invitation and a promise caused heat to unfurl in the pit of her stomach. She grimaced. Sexual alchemy was an enigma, and scientific research had yet to fully explain the complex biological and psychological reasons why one person was attracted to another. At a basic level her awareness of Jarek was the purely primal reaction of a female searching for an alpha-male, Holly reminded herself. But she was an intelligent, educated woman of the twenty-first century and she was *not* at the mercy of her hormones. She would simply have to ignore the thunder of her pulse when Jarek looked at her with that wicked glint in his eyes that made her want to respond to his unspoken challenge.

Her conscience queried whether she should ask Professor Heppel to assign a different psychotherapist to work with Jarek—except that she could not think of a good reason to request being taken off his case. She certainly could not admit that she was attracted to her patient. It would be tantamount to professional suicide.

Besides, she thought as she climbed into the four-by-four and headed towards the town that she had driven through five minutes earlier, right at this moment her feelings for Jarek Dvorska were murderous rather than amorous.

Bibiana's Bar was at the far end of Arlenwald's pretty main street. Popular with skiers and snowboarders, even at five o'clock in the afternoon the place was packed with people clutching huge steins of beer, and Holly struggled to thread her way through the crowd over to the bar. Rock music pumped out from enormous speakers and the heavy bass reverberated through her body and exacerbated her tension headache. It seemed impossible that she would be able to find Jarek in this crowd, and she didn't even know for certain that he was here.

After a fruitless search, with her head pounding in competition with the music, she was about to give up. Then her attention was drawn to two girls wearing micro miniskirts and cropped blouses that revealed their lithe figures, who were dancing on top of a table.

Following her instincts, she made her way across the room and felt a mixture of relief and anger when she spotted Jarek sitting in an alcove. Another girl was perched on his knee, and as Holly watched him slide his hand over the girl's bare thigh her temper simmered.

Trust him to find a dark corner to commit dark deeds, she fumed. She would have loved to walk away and leave him to get on with his sordid lifestyle of booze and bimbos, but she did not relish having to confess to Professor Heppel that she had failed in her first assignment.

She became aware that Jarek was not watching the girls who were dancing so frenetically in front of him. His brilliant blue eyes were focused on her. Once again her body responded to the challenge in his bold stare and she felt her nipples pull tight. He was unfairly gorgeous, and she was helpless to prevent her body's treacherous reaction to him. The cruel beauty of his angular face and that too-long dark blond hair that he pushed off his brow with a careless flick of his hand were a killer combination. Few women would be able to resist his rampant sensuality and the devil-may-care attitude that warned he was untameable.

The girl sitting on his lap clearly found him irresistible. Holly was irritated as she watched Jarek lower his head and murmur something to the girl, who giggled as she slid off his knee and glanced over at her.

The other girls jumped down from the table and blew extravagant kisses to Jarek as they sauntered away but he ignored them, and the smouldering gaze he directed at Holly made her feel as if she was the only woman in the room. It was what he *did*, she reminded herself. He was a master of seduction. But she was not about to climb onto the table and perform a sexy dance for him. She was his therapist, for heaven's sake!

'You were expected at Chalet Soline two hours ago, but it's my fault entirely that you didn't make it,' she said breezily, to hide the fact that she wanted to strangle him. 'I should have realised I would need to babysit you to keep you out of trouble.'

His grin made her heart give an annoying flip. 'Ada, Dagna and Halfrida were no *trouble*,' he drawled. 'Especially Halfrida. She wanted to know if you are my wife, come to nag me.'

'It's a pity she didn't ask *me*. I would have told her that if I was ever interested in marrying you would be the last person I'd choose for my husband,' she said tartly, goaded by the memory of how the pretty blonde had cuddled up to him.

'Really? I'm considered quite a catch.' He sounded highly amused. 'In fact a few of the tabloids have described me as "Europe's most eligible bachelor".'

'The fact that you are a multi-millionaire no doubt goes a long way to explaining your eligibility.'

He laughed, and a gleam of admiration flickered in his eyes. 'Your name suits your prickly nature, Holly. So, would you marry for money?'

'Of course not. And as I have already said, I'm not looking for a husband.'

His brows lifted. 'I'm surprised. I had you down as the type of woman who dreams of a cottage with roses round the door, marriage to a dependable guy and a couple of babies.'

She masked the sharp stab of pain in her heart with a brisk smile. 'I grew up in the English countryside, and my experience of quaint old cottages is that they are damp and expensive to heat. I'm too busy with my career to think about marriage. Being a psychotherapist isn't a nine-to-five job—which is why I am here at...' she glanced at her watch '...ten to six in the evening to save you from yourself.'

'Maybe I don't want to be saved.' There was steel beneath his soft tone.

Holly looked pointedly at the three-quarters empty bottle of vodka on the table in front of him. 'Your notoriety with the press means you are very recognisable. For all you know, someone here in the bar might have taken a photo of you drinking and partying and posted it on social media. How do you think your sister will feel if she hears that you've wimped out of having treatment?'

His expression turned wintry. 'I have never *wimped out* of anything in my life!'

'Acknowledging and dealing with emotional baggage takes courage. It would be far easier to carry on with your selfish lifestyle, even though your drinking and wild behaviour hurts the people who love you.'

'No one loves me,' he said lightly, as if his flash of temper moments earlier hadn't happened—as if he didn't care.

Holly frowned. It was her job to understand people, but she could not read Jarek and she wasn't sure if she had heard something raw in his voice or if she had imagined it.

'Your sister must love you or she wouldn't be concerned about you,' she murmured.

His bland smile gave nothing away. 'Elin has her own family—and good luck to her. I'm glad she is happy again. I was afraid I had ruined...' He stopped speaking and his jaw clenched.

'You had ruined what?' Holly held her breath, hoping he would continue. She sensed that what he had been about to say was an important clue that might help her to fathom him out.

'It doesn't matter.'

She couldn't force him to talk to her. Patience was a therapist's most valuable tool, she reminded herself. And nor could she drag him out of the bar. So she stood there, wondering with a growing sense of panic what her plan of action would be if he refused to leave.

To her relief he stood up and raised his arms above his head, giving an indolent stretch that caused the bottom of his sweater to rise up a little and reveal golden skin above the waistband of his trousers.

Her eyes were drawn to that strip of bare torso, covered with a fuzz of dark blond hair that disappeared beneath his trousers, and heat swept through her as her wayward imagination pictured where the hairs grew more thickly... around the base of his manhood.

His voice jolted her from her thoughts, and she flushed, praying he had not guessed her wanton imaginings.

'While I am touched by your desire to save me,' he drawled, 'I can't help wondering if your concern is more about proving to Professor Heppel that he was justified in offering you a job at his clinic. Gunther mentioned that you were only recently appointed at the Frieden Clinic.'

'Believe it or not, I care about doing a good job and I

genuinely want to help you.' She tried to ignore her guilt that there was an element of truth in his words.

To her relief he said no more as he picked up his jacket and followed her out of the bar. A tense silence filled the four-by-four while she drove them to Chalet Soline, and she could think of nothing to say to lighten his mood—which had become grimmer still when they arrived at the alpine lodge and were greeted by Karl.

The chef-butler ushered them into the wood-panelled sitting room, where a fire was blazing in the hearth and deep leather sofas piled with colourful cushions created a sense of stylish informality. Jarek gave a cursory glance at his surroundings as he crossed to one of the tall windows and stared out at the dark winter's night.

'It goes without saying that I will hold everything you choose to tell me during our sessions in absolute confidence,' Holly said quietly as she watched him prowl around the room.

He was like a caged wolf, simmering with silent fury. She was surprised he wasn't showing any obvious signs of being drunk, even though he had consumed enough vodka to render him unconscious. Thankfully he hadn't staggered out of Bibiana's Bar—or, worse, needed to be carried out to the car by burly security staff. She did not want Professor Heppel to find out that her client had been caught drinking in a bar within an hour of checking into the Frieden Clinic.

'I hope you will be comfortable at Chalet Soline. Karl is an excellent chef, and the maid, Beatrice, will take care of the house. I'll show you up to the master suite. You'll probably want to take some time to settle in and freshen up before you meet Professor Heppel this evening.'

She dared not suggest that he might need to sober up,

but the hard gleam in his eyes told her he had understood perfectly well what she'd meant.

'I don't need a nursemaid or a babysitter.'

He crossed the room in long strides and halted in front of her, so close that she breathed in the spicy scent of his aftershave and her senses went haywire.

'And I definitely do not need a prissy, much too pretty psychologist to patronise me.'

Holly was disgusted with herself for the way her heart leapt at his offhand compliment. Flirting was second nature to him, she reminded herself. He hadn't singled her out specially, and she would *not* respond to the blazing heat in his eyes.

'I know what *you* need,' he drawled, his voice lowering so that it became wickedly suggestive and sent a shiver of reaction down her spine.

She arched her brows. 'Enlighten me.'

He gave a wolfish smile. 'You need to buy a bigger blouse.'

Holly followed his gaze down her body and was mortified to see that a button on her blouse had popped open and her lacy bra was showing. Blushing hotly, she attempted to refasten the blouse, but Jarek moved faster and his knuckles brushed the upper slopes of her breasts as he slid the button into the buttonhole.

The brief touch of his skin on hers made her tremble. Goosebumps rose on her flesh and her nipples jerked to attention. The mocking gleam in Jarek's eyes dared her to make the excuse again that she was cold, now they were inside the warm chalet.

She was tempted to wipe the smug smile off his face with the sharp impact of her palm against his jaw, but managed to restrain herself from behaving so unprofessionally.

He swung away from her and raked a hand though his

hair, almost as if he had been as shocked by the bolt of electricity that had shot between them as she had.

His manner changed and he said abruptly, 'Is there a room that I can use for an office? I want to get on with some work.'

'There's a small study along the hall. But you are supposed to be using your stay at the Frieden Clinic as a retreat from the stresses of your everyday life—and that includes taking a break from work so that you can focus on exploring your emotions.'

Jarek gave her a sardonic look. 'My company, Dvorska Holdings, employs several hundred people. I am also the executive director of a charity, and take an active role in the day-to-day running of the organisation. I can't abandon my responsibilities to my staff—or to the great number of volunteers who give up their time to support Lorna's Gift.'

He laughed softly.

'As for exploring my emotions… 'I'll quote a famous female American journalist and advice columnist called Dorothy Dix, who said, *"Confession is always weakness. The grave soul keeps its own secrets, and takes its own punishment in silence."*'

What had he meant by that? Holly wondered as she watched Jarek stride out of the room. She couldn't keep pace with his mercurial changes of mood. Just when she had been convinced that he was the disreputable playboy portrayed by the tabloids, and a shameless flirt with a ready line of sexual innuendo, he had surprised her by sounding as if he genuinely cared about his role with a charity.

She knew that he was co-director with his sister of Lorna's Gift—a charitable organisation that raised money to support children living in orphanages around the world. But she had assumed that Jarek was simply a figurehead for the charity, and it was disconcerting to discover that he took some things seriously.

It would be easier if he *was* nothing more than fodder for the celebrity-obsessed paparazzi, she thought, because then she could dismiss her reaction to his potent sensuality as a temporary aberration.

Holly rubbed her hand across her brow to try to ease her tension headache and glanced at the clock. Professor Heppel was due to arrive for dinner at Chalet Soline in two hours, which gave her time for a soak in the hot tub and a chance to get a grip on her wayward emotions.

The next time she met Jarek she was determined to be coolly professional.

Jarek switched off his laptop, having finalised another successful business deal. The one thing he could rely on in the grim mess that was his life was his ability to make money, he thought cynically. Although he had not always been lucky.

Over the past two years his instinct for correctly guessing how global markets would perform had catapulted him onto the list of the world's top ten most successful traders, and enabled him to recoup the huge losses he'd made at Saunderson's Bank.

That embarrassing episode had resulted from an unfortunate combination of events. He had taken a particularly risky gamble on the Asian stockmarkets, and an earthquake in Japan had led to a temporary suspension of trading on the Nikkei—with disastrous consequences for his investments and the near-collapse of one of England's oldest and most prestigious private banks.

Ralph Saunderson had probably turned in his grave, Jarek thought sardonically. He had been a feral boy of nearly ten when he had been taken from war-ravaged

Sarajevo to live at Cuckmere Hall, and his resistance to authority had meant that there had been no love lost between him and Ralph. Following his adoptive father's death, he had been shocked to discover that he had been excluded from Ralph's will, and that Cortez Ramos—Ralph's biological son—had inherited Cuckmere Hall and the chairmanship of Saunderson's Bank.

He knew why Ralph had chosen Cortez to be his heir. Ralph had blamed him, Jarek, for Lorna Saunderson's death, and Jarek had for once agreed with his adoptive father.

He was haunted by memories of when his adoptive mother had been fatally shot by an armed raider during a robbery at a jeweller's. The four years that had passed since that terrible day had not dimmed the images in his mind of Lorna lying crumpled on the floor, and Elin kneeling beside her sobbing hysterically. The keening cry his sister had given when she'd realised that her adored mama was dead would echo in his head for ever.

In Sarajevo, Jarek had seen the bodies of dead soldiers and heard the rattling last breaths of young men—some of whom had been teenagers, only a few years older than him. He'd thought that nothing could be worse than the atrocities he'd seen in that bloody and brutal civil war, but the knowledge that Mama had died because of *his* reckless attempt to overpower the gunman was an agony that would be with him for ever.

He would never forgive himself, even though Elin loyally insisted that he wasn't to blame.

It had been his idea to set up a charity to support orphans in honour of Lorna Saunderson and, ironically, his willingness to take risks on the stockmarket meant he had earned a fortune for Lorna's Gift. It was some kind of reparation for what he had done, but nothing would ever ease his guilt.

God knew what a psychologist would make of him if he ever revealed the dark torment in his soul, Jarek thought grimly. But he had no intention of *exploring his emotions* with the deliciously sexy Dr Maitland.

Some things were best left alone—which was why he had decided not to respond to the request he had received from the head of the National Council of Vostov, asking him to have a DNA test which might prove that he was related to Vostov's royal family, who had all perished in a car accident twenty years ago.

There was no possibility that it could be true, he assured himself. The idea was ridiculous. But what if his night-mares were *not* simply horrific figments of his imagina-tion? his conscience whispered. It would mean that the images in his mind were of real events, real people...*his parents*.

At the orphanage he had been told that his mother and father had been killed early in the war, when the apart-ment block where they'd lived had been destroyed by a bomb. Jarek and his baby sister had been pulled from the rubble and the trauma had wiped out all his memories of his life before that day.

He'd accepted the explanation eventually—after he had been beaten by the orphanage staff whenever he'd talked about his strange dreams. But now his nightmares had re-turned, more vivid and terrible than when he was a boy. And if the scenes that played out in his subconscious mind *were* real events then he had something even more devas-tating than his adoptive mother's death on his conscience.

Jarek pushed his hair off his brow and acknowledged that if he had not been stuck halfway up a mountain he would have headed to the nearest bar and sought to escape the demons inside him with another bottle of vodka and an attractive blonde—or two. He remembered the girls at Bibiana's Bar and for a moment was tempted to take the four-by-four parked outside the chalet and drive himself to Arlenwald, to hook up with Halfrida and her friends.

It would be worth it just to ruffle Dr Maitland's feathers.

His lips twitched as he remembered Holly's outraged expression when she'd discovered him in the bar. The truth was he would like to do more than *ruffle* her, he brooded. His body stirred as he pictured her delectable curves. She was an intriguing mix of uptight schoolmistress and sensual siren, and Jarek couldn't remember the last time he had been intrigued by a woman.

If she had been someone other than his psychologist... Hell, if *he* had been someone else—someone better than the man he knew he was—he would have enjoyed allowing their mutual sexual attraction to reach its logical conclusion and taken her to bed.

But Holly had stated that she wanted to find out what made him tick, and he was utterly determined to prevent her from uncovering the secrets buried deep in his soul.

CHAPTER THREE

JAREK FOUND AN outlet for his restless energy in the chalet's gym. He could think of other, more enjoyable ways to get hot and sweaty than pounding his fists into a punch-bag. But he had promised his brother-in-law there would be no more scandalous stories about his personal life in the tabloids—which meant that until Elin's baby was born he had to keep away from bars and airhead blondes who were attracted to his multi-millionaire status and bad-boy image.

The truth was he'd never cared about what was printed about him—which was mostly lies. Any publicity, good or bad, was publicity for Lorna's Gift, and he seized every opportunity to promote the vital work of the charity.

But Elin's husband Cortez took a different view.

'Elin gets upset when she sees your name in newspaper headlines or on the pages of gossip magazines, invariably with intimate details of your sex-life,' Cortez had warned him. 'She has gestational high blood pressure, which could lead to more serious complications with her pregnancy, and her obstetrician says it is crucial she doesn't suffer any stress that could cause her blood pressure to rise even higher.'

Jarek shared his brother-in-law's concern. Elin and Cortez had not been together when Elin had nearly died giving birth to their first child, and it had been Jarek who had sat by her bed in ITU, willing her to pull through for the sake of her baby son in the hospital nursery.

There were worse places to spend the next few weeks than the spectacular Austrian Alps, he mused. Chalet Soline offered six-star luxury, and next to the well-equipped gym there was a sauna room while outside on the decked area stood a hot tub. He *would* find it relaxing after his punishing workout to lie in a bubbling hot tub and look up at the snow-covered mountains, or count the stars that glittered diamond-bright in the night sky.

But when he glanced at his watch he realised he did not have time before Professor Heppel arrived.

About to head back to his room, to shower before dinner, he glanced out of a window and noticed that the lights had been switched on around the hot tub. Steam was curling up from the surface of the water, forming wispy white clouds against the black night sky.

Jarek stopped dead and stared at the figure of a woman rising out of the steam like a mystical goddess. And what a figure! He swallowed as he watched Holly wade across to the edge of the pool. It was no exaggeration to say that she was a goddess, with an hourglass figure that was reminiscent of the silver screen sirens from a previous era, like Sophia Loren and Elizabeth Taylor.

She was wearing a one-piece swimsuit with cut-out sections at the sides that drew attention to her slender waist. Jarek wanted to explore the tantalising areas of her bare skin on display with his hands. He lifted his eyes higher to her voluptuous breasts, barely contained within the tiny triangles of gold material that formed the bra cups of the swimsuit, and felt himself harden. He was fascinated by her daring choice of swimwear, which was such a contrast to the unexciting clothes she'd worn earlier.

Moving his gaze lower, he followed the rounded curves

of her hips and her toned thighs, exposed by the swim-suit's high-cut legs.

Who was the real Holly? he wondered. The serious psy-chologist, or the sizzling sex bomb who made the blood thunder in his veins? His body felt taut and energised after his gym workout and he wanted—quite possibly more than he'd ever wanted anything in his life, he discovered—to pull Holly beneath him and ease her stretchy swimsuit aside so that he could thrust his rock-solid erection home.

It was lucky he had worn loose sweatpants for his ses-sion in the gym, Jarek thought derisively. He was so turned on by the sight of Holly in her barely there swimsuit that he felt he might explode.

His common sense told him to head back to his room. But he rarely heeded good advice.

The temperature outside the chalet was way below zero, and as the icy air hit his heated skin every nerve-ending in his body tingled.

Jarek allowed the door to thud closed behind him as he stepped outside onto the wooden decking. The sound caused Holly to jerk her head round, and she gave a star-tled cry when she saw him, followed by a curse when she dropped the towel that she had just picked up from the deck into the water.

'You startled me. I thought you were working in the study,' she muttered in an embarrassed voice, as if he had caught her naked—which she very nearly was, Jarek mused as he roamed his eyes over her insubstantial swim-suit and felt the ache in his groin clamour to be appeased.

He did not reply, for the simple reason that he could not think of anything to say—couldn't think of anything at all but how utterly perfect she was with her skin flushed pink from the heat of the hot tub and a deeper flush on her pretty face.

Her hair was piled on top of her head and loose tendrils curled about her cheeks. She was a luscious goddess, and he wanted nothing more than to drop to his knees in front of her to worship her bounteous beauty with his mouth and explore every secret place on her body with his tongue.

He was jolted from his sexual haze by the sound of her clipped voice.

'Would you please pass me another towel? There's a pile of clean towels on the shelf outside the sauna room,' she said when he didn't move, just stared at her while he tried to control the conflagration of lust that burned down to his bones.

'Jarek, for heaven's sake—I'm freezing.'

He couldn't tear his gaze from the prominent points of her nipples, clearly outlined beneath her clingy swimsuit. His mouth went dry as he imagined peeling the swimsuit from her breasts to feast his eyes and then his lips on those provocative peaks.

Somehow he forced himself to turn and walk into the house, and he grabbed a towel before retracing his steps back across the decking.

Holly held out her hand for the towel, but Jarek did not pass it to her immediately. 'First let your hair down,' he growled.

'Are you kidding?' Her brown eyes widened.

There was shock, anger and something else that was harder to define but made him ache even more, in her expression.

'Do you want me to catch pneumonia?'

She didn't wait for him to reply—which was probably a good thing, he acknowledged, because he would have to admit that what he *wanted* was her legs wrapped around his back.

Throwing him a look of sheer irritation, she lifted her

hands up and released the clip on top of her head so that her hair tumbled down around her shoulders in glossy waves of rich chocolate-brown. 'Satisfied?'

He doubted he would ever be satisfied again with the too thin, too blonde, brittle women who came and went from his bed in an endless stream of unmemorable sexual encounters. They *always* came, he thought sardonically. He was as good at sex as he was at making money, yet neither activity ever filled the emptiness inside him.

Finally he heeded his common sense, aware that indulging his sexual desire for Holly might satisfy him temporarily but that he would soon grow bored of her. It was just how he was: 'a restless soul', Mama had once described him, while his adoptive father had accused him of being reckless. Ralph had been proved right.

He gave Holly the towel and she immediately dragged it around her shoulders to hide her gorgeous body from him before she stepped out of the hot tub and stalked back to the chalet.

Jarek caught up with her in a few long strides. 'Why are you here?' he demanded, placing his hand on her arm to prevent her walking through the door that led from the gym annexe into the main part of the house.

'Where else would I be?' She tensed beneath his hand and with obvious reluctance raised her eyes to his face.

'I assumed you had gone to wherever you live. Do you rent a place in Salzburg? Or is there staff accommodation at the Frieden Clinic, where we met earlier?'

She frowned. 'I live here—at Chalet Soline. When I'm in London I share a flat with a friend, but for my job with the Frieden Clinic I am required to live at one of the clinic's residences so that I can provide psychological support around the clock. Every member of the clinical team is assigned to a chalet, where they treat patients on an individual basis. Professor Heppel came up with the radical approach of providing access to twenty-four-seven treatment, rather than sessions which last for an hour once or twice a week. His highly successful method is explained in the brochure that you didn't bother to read—and I also explained the set-up when I met you at the clinic's reception centre earlier today. But you seemed more interested in reading a story in the newspaper than listening to me.'

Holly's disapproving tone reminded Jarek of the headmistress who had expelled him from his exclusive private school at the age of fifteen, after he had been caught smuggling alcohol into the school and selling it to the other boys. He had argued that his business venture had shown entrepreneurial spirit, but the headmistress had warned that his rebellious nature would ultimately be his ruin.

He thought of the newspaper headline that had seized his attention when he had arrived at the Frieden Clinic.

What did happen to Vostov's royal children?

Jarek feared the answer was buried in his subconscious mind, and that his nightmares might reveal a truth that was too shocking for him to contemplate. Certainly he could not risk Holly hearing him shout out in his sleep, as had happened on one of the rare occasions when he had spent a whole night with a woman he had picked up in a bar.

The next morning Tara… Tyra—he hadn't taken much heed of her name—had said he'd kept her awake with his shouting and maybe he should talk to a psychiatrist or something about the crazy stuff in his head.

Jarek's chosen method of preventing his bad dreams was to drink enough vodka until he was unconscious. But without access to alcohol God knew what his nightmares might reveal.

He realised that Holly was speaking again. 'I believe you will find it beneficial to be able to discuss issues with your therapist whenever you need to, instead of having to wait for an allotted time for treatment sessions. If you want to talk to me in the middle of the night you can ring through to my room and wake me up. Part of my job is to be available whenever you want me.'

'Is that so…?'

Jarek felt the hard thud of his pulse and knew he had to resist it—had to resist *her*. There was a curious innocence about Holly that made him want to protect her from himself.

'There is only *one* reason why I would wake you in the middle of the night, angel-face,' he drawled, 'and it wouldn't be because I want to talk.'

He watched a scarlet stain spread over her face and wondered when he had last seen a woman blush. For a few seconds he felt a tug of regret, because he could not allow this shimmering, ephemeral thing between them that was something other than sexual attraction—something *more*—to flourish. He was who he was: reckless, rebellious, with a knack of destroying everything that was good in his life.

'There you go again with the sexual innuendo.' She put her head on one side and studied him intently. 'Are you trying to frighten me? Because I have to tell you that you aren't succeeding.'

'You *should* be afraid of me,' he said roughly. 'I am everything you have read about me and worse.' He wanted to shout at her that he didn't deserve the sympathy he could see in her velvet brown eyes. His jaw clenched. 'This is a complication I don't need right now.'

She wrinkled her nose and Jarek swore silently. He didn't *do* cute, his brain insisted, but his body paid no attention.

'What do you mean by "this"? she asked, looking puzzled.

He stretched out his hand and jerked the edges of the towel she was clutching around her from her fingers. With a cry of protest she tried to snatch it back, but he whipped it away from her body and trailed his eyes with slow deliberation over her skimpy swimsuit. Desire kicked hard in his gut as he stared at her lush breasts, half-spilling over the top of the swimsuit, and the hard points of her nipples that betrayed her so sweetly.

'This,' he growled, moving his hand over her body from her throat to her hips, but not actually touching her. Not quite.

He heard her catch her breath and it took all his will power to resist stroking his fingertips across her skin.

'You can deny the sexual attraction between us all you like,' he taunted, 'but your body is sending out a different message.'

He dropped his gaze to where the sides of her swimsuit were cut away and decided he would happily give away his entire fortune if he could trace his hands over the tantalising areas of bare skin. But if he touched her he did not trust himself to be able to stop. He couldn't remember ever feeling so hungry for a woman, but no doubt the restless ache inside him was because he hadn't had sex for almost a month.

He wanted Holly so badly simply because she was there in front of him, wearing a sexy swimsuit, and because he'd never had to deny himself a woman before.

It was an inconvenient time to discover that he had scruples, he thought sardonically. Delectable Dr Maitland was off-limits, and he had to content himself with stepping closer to her.

He noticed the pulse at the base of her throat beating erratically. 'Believe me, I'm tempted to accept the invitation you are sending out, angel-face,' he told her softly. 'But it will cause a lot less trouble for both of us if I cancel my booking with the clinic before we do something that *you* might regret and *I* will forget far too easily.'

Anger flashed in her eyes. 'Any invitation is purely in your imagination,' she said tightly. And then a note of panic edged into her voice. 'You *can't* be thinking of leaving the Frieden Clinic? You told me that you had assured your brother-in-law you would undergo psychotherapy to deal with your anger issues and allay your sister's concerns about you.'

He shrugged. 'I told Cortez I would keep off the paparazzi's radar until Elin has the baby. As long as I keep out of trouble there is no reason for my sister to find out that I decided not to remain at the clinic.'

'She will find out when she asks me for an update on how you are responding to treatment.'

Jarek stiffened. 'Are you intending to make weekly reports on my progress? Perhaps I'll earn a gold star if I'm a good boy,' he said with icy sarcasm. He shook his head. 'I can't *believe* my sister asked you to *spy* on me. Or that you agreed. What happened to your promise to respect my confidentiality?'

'Not spy on you,' she denied quickly. 'Elin phoned me before you arrived, and it's obvious that she cares about you and is concerned about your emotional health.' Holly's voice faltered when he swore. 'Your sister asked me to call her if you refused to stay. I won't lie to her and pretend you are receiving treatment.'

'So the Frieden Clinic *is* my prison and *you* are my gaoler—albeit a very beautiful one,' Jarek drawled, in the lazy tone he had perfected over many years in order to hide his true thoughts.

He acknowledged that he could not leave the clinic and

risk upsetting Elin, but that meant he was trapped at Chalet Soline with Holly.

There might be *some* benefits to his enforced captivity, he mused. The Frieden Clinic prided itself on its exclusivity, and guarded the privacy and anonymity of its wealthy clientele. Nobody, apart from Elin and Cortez, knew of his whereabouts, and he hoped 'the Vostov problem' would disappear when the principality's National Council could not find him to repeat their request for him to have a DNA test.

He was no *prince*, he brooded. He was plain Jarek Dvorska. And his parents—if only he could remember them, God rest their souls—had been poor peasants. That was what the staff at the orphanage had told him. His parents had definitely *not* been Prince Goran and his consort Princess Isidora who, with their young son and baby daughter, had died in a car accident on a mountain pass as the family had attempted to escape from Vostov into neighbouring Croatia during the Balkan conflict.

Jarek pulled his thoughts back to the present. He guessed Holly was looking tense because she was worried that her first patient at the Frieden Clinic was about to walk out and that would *not* be a good start in her new job.

He let his eyes roam over her, noting the rich coffee and chocolate tones of her silky hair and those huge Bambi eyes fringed by impossibly long lashes. Her sensual mouth would tempt a saint, let alone the sinner he knew he was.

He shrugged. For once in his life he had tried to do the right thing, but fate had decided to throw him and Holly together and he wasn't about to complain. She would be an entertaining distraction. He had promised Cortez he would keep his private life out of the media's spotlight, but he hadn't taken a vow of celibacy.

He let go of Holly's arm and she immediately bolted

away, without pausing to cover herself with the towel. Jarek felt anticipation jolt through him, hot and fierce, as he watched her race down the hallway. His eyes were drawn to the delightful curves of her derriere that were barely covered by her tiny swimsuit.

The next few weeks promised to be interesting.

CHAPTER FOUR

THE MINUTE HOLLY reached her bedroom she pulled off her swimsuit and kicked it across the floor in an uncharacteristic display of temper. But *really*! Jarek's arrogant belief that he was God's gift to womankind was *infuriating*.

She was annoyed with herself for the way she had responded to him. Her swimsuit revealed a lot more of her body than she was comfortable with, and it must have given the wrong impression about her. She'd looked more like a porn star rather than a doctor of psychology, she thought, hot with embarrassment. If she had been wearing her functional navy blue one-piece it was doubtful that Jarek would have given her a second look, let alone stared at her with the undisguised hunger in his eyes that had evoked a shocking throb of need low in her pelvis.

She blamed Kate, her flatmate in London. Holly hadn't packed any swimwear when she'd come to Austria to work at the Frieden Clinic, but then Professor Heppel had told her she could use the sauna and hot tub at Chalet Soline, and she had asked Kate to post her swimsuit to her. Unfortunately her friend had sent the frivolous gold swimsuit that she'd bought on an impulse for that disastrous—as it had turned out—holiday to Barbados with Stuart.

A glance at the clock warned Holly that there was only twenty minutes before the clinic's medical director was due to arrive at the chalet for dinner. After bundling her hair into a waterproof cap she hurried into the shower, and while she stood beneath the spray her mind flew back to the time when she had told Stuart that she was unable to have children.

It was not a conversation she had expected to have with him, when they had only been dating for eight months. But Stuart had surprised her on the second evening of their holiday by talking about the future.

'My father is considering making me a partner in the family law firm and he has made it clear that he would like me to settle down. I feel that it's time for me to think about getting married and raising a family of my own.'

They had been strolling along the beach when he had stopped and taken hold of Holly's hand.

'I would like you to be my wife, Holly. We share the same values and we both have successful careers. I can't think of anyone else I'd rather have as the mother of my children.'

Stuart had not sworn undying love for her, but that hadn't made it any easier for Holly to tell him she could not give him a child because she had a rare syndrome which meant she had been born without a womb.

Finding out when she was fifteen that she had Mayer Rokitansky Kuster Hauser syndrome—commonly shortened to MRKH—had been devastating, but at the time of her diagnosis her infertility had not been as much of an issue as her feeling that she was not 'normal'.

The syndrome meant that she had been born with a shortened vagina, and she would need surgery to enable her to have sex. As a teenager she had found it excruciatingly embarrassing to discuss intimate details about her body with her doctors, and it had been frankly impossible to talk about her condition with her parents. She had felt too self-conscious to go on dates until she was at university, and her few sexual experiences had been uncomfortable—probably because she had been so tense, she acknowledged.

Deciding when to bring up the subject of her condition and her infertility with men she dated had always been difficult. If she mentioned it on a first date it seemed pushy, and gave the impression that she was hoping for a physical long-term relationship. But if she waited weeks or months it seemed dishonest.

'I wish you had told me earlier in our relationship,' had been Stuart's response after she had broken the news that she was infertile. 'Having a child is important to me.'

Holly had refrained from pointing out that something like one in seven couples experienced problems conceiving, and that having children was not an automatic right. But Stuart's reaction had re-awoken the feeling of inadequacy that she had struggled with since she had been diagnosed with MRKH syndrome. It was true she hadn't been madly in love with Stuart, but his rejection had still hurt—especially when she'd heard a few months after they had broken up that his new girlfriend was pregnant.

She dragged her mind back to the present and stepped out of the shower to dry herself before hurrying into the bedroom to get dressed. Her dusky-pink cashmere dress had been an extravagant purchase, but its simple elegance was worth the price tag. She accessorised it with a wide belt and matching grey kitten-heel shoes.

It was an outfit she had worn several times before, and always felt comfortable in, but tonight when she looked in the mirror she decided that the dress moulded her curvaceous figure a little too lovingly. But it was five minutes to eight, and she only had time to pull a comb through her hair before she hurried downstairs.

She found Karl in the dining room, rearranging the table settings. 'Professor Heppel telephoned a few minutes ago and apologised. He cannot come for dinner this evening because his mother is unwell and he must go to Vienna to visit her,' the chef told her. 'The professor also asked me to tell you that he has booked tickets for you and Mr Dvorska to attend the masquerade ball which will take place in Salzburg next weekend.'

Holly's heart sank at the prospect of having dinner alone with Jarek while her mind still insisted on replaying those moments by the hot tub, when sexual chemistry had sizzled between them.

She watched Karl light the candles in the centre of the table. A fire was crackling in the hearth and the lamps had been turned down low, creating a dangerously intimate feel to the dining room. 'Perhaps Mr Dvorska would prefer to have his dinner served in the lounge in front of the television,' she murmured. 'I'm happy to eat in the kitchen.'

'It's bad for the digestion to eat at the same time as doing another activity.'

The lazy drawl sounded from behind her and Holly's stomach tied itself into a knot as she swung round and saw Jarek stroll through the door.

Undoubtedly *he* would unsettle her digestive system, she thought. Butterflies had leapt in her stomach when he had appeared by the hot tub, wearing a pair of sweatpants that sat low on his hips and a black gym vest that had revealed too much of his sleek, golden-skinned body. Her blood had run hot in her veins when he'd stared at her with a hard glitter in his eyes that had made her wish she could respond to his unspoken challenge.

At least now they were both dressed—but Jarek looked no less devastating in close-fitting black trousers and a black silk shirt unbuttoned at the throat to reveal a sprinkling of dark blond chest hair. Holly shivered, despite the heat from the roaring fire. There was something elemental and sensual about a real fire, and her wayward imagination pictured her and Jarek lying on the fur rug in front of the hearth, their naked limbs entwined.

She did not dare look at him for fear that he would somehow guess her thoughts. What was *wrong* with her? she asked herself in silent despair. The truth was that Jarek's rampant sex appeal made her aware of her sensuality in a way she had never felt before.

'Dr Maitland and I will have dinner in here,' Jarek said to Karl.

He pulled out a chair for Holly, leaving her no option but to sit down at the table, and as she inhaled the spicy scent of his aftershave something visceral tugged in the pit of her stomach.

'Don't look so tense.' He sounded amused. 'I don't bite.'

His wide grin revealed his white teeth and once again he reminded Holly of a wolf.

'Unless you would *like* me to bite you,' he said softly. 'Pleasure can be enhanced by a little pain, don't you find?'

She swallowed and forced herself to look at him calmly across the table, where he had taken his place opposite her. 'You have to stop this. I'm sure you automatically flirt with every woman you meet, but I suspect that your sexually suggestive remarks are designed to distract me from doing my job.'

Fortunately Karl reappeared then, to serve the first course. Holly picked up her glass and took a sip of elderflower water, wishing she could have a glass of wine—or preferably a *vat* of wine, she thought ruefully. She needed something to render her unconscious, so she did not have to cope with Jarek's teasing remarks that made her feel crazily out of control and in danger of doing something very stupid…like walk around the table and kiss his too sexy mouth to shut him up.

She stared down at her bowl of potato soup with little dumplings. It was an Austrian speciality and one of her favourites, but she found that her appetite had disappeared.

It was her professional duty to help Jarek feel at ease, she reminded herself. Patients were often reluctant to talk about their problems and she was trained to break down barriers gently.

Once Karl had left the room she murmured, 'I have read through your notes, but it would help me to gain a better understanding of you if you could tell me about the issues that led to your decision to seek psychotherapy.'

'I agreed to try therapy because other people believe I have issues,' he said sardonically. 'And before I allow you to dig around in my emotions, it only seems fair for you to tell me about yourself. You *did* say it is important for therapist and patient to establish a bond of trust,' he reminded her.

'That's true,' Holly acknowledged. 'But I assumed that Professor Heppel had showed you my CV, which gives details of all my professional qualifications.'

'I meant that I want to get to know you on a *personal* level.'

He trapped her gaze with his, and even though the table was between them it wasn't nearly wide enough for Holly's liking. She had a sense that his piercing blue eyes could see inside her head and that he *knew* she was helpless to control the way he affected her.

It struck her then that Jarek had no intention of revealing his thoughts—or, as he put it, allowing her *to dig around in his emotions*. His scathing opinion of psychotherapy would make her job even harder.

'Who *is* Holly Maitland?' he said softly, as if he was

genuinely interested and his question *wasn't* simply another diversionary tactic.

She shrugged. 'What do you want to know?'

'You mentioned that you lived in the countryside. Where *was* that, exactly?'

'I grew up on my parents' farm in Cumbria. It's a beautiful part of the world, but the farm is in a remote area of the fells, seven miles from the nearest village. It sounds romantic to live on a desolate, windswept moor,' she said with a faint smile, 'but when I was a child I felt very isolated.'

'Do you have brothers and sisters?'

'A brother—Callum. He's five years older than me, and when we were children he was always helping my father. Cal will inherit the farm one day, and now that he and his wife have a little boy it means that Maitland Farm will remain in the family, as it has done for five generations.'

Holly hoped Jarek had not noticed the slight tremor in her voice when she had mentioned her nephew. Daniel was six months old, and when she'd held him soon after he was born she had felt sad, knowing she would never hold her own baby. But just as bad had been her guilt that she was a disappointment to her mother.

She supposed it was natural that her mum had grown close to Callum's wife. After all, Brenna had given Ann Maitland a longed-for grandchild, which was something her daughter could never do. It was immature to feel envious of the bond between her mother and sister-in-law, Holly reminded herself.

'So why did a farmer's daughter decide to become a psychologist?' Jarek asked.

'I didn't know I wanted to study psychology when I left school.' She sighed. 'To be honest, all I wanted was to live somewhere with a population greater than fifty. When

I was offered a place at a university in London to study modern languages I couldn't wait to experience city life.'

'Did your parents understand why you wanted to leave the farm?'

Holly felt a familiar stab of guilt. It was not an exaggeration to say that her moving away from home had felt like a betrayal of her family's long history of farming the desolate Cumbrian fells. She glanced at Jarek, surprised that a man who actively encouraged the press's portrayal of him as shallow and only interested in the pursuit of pleasure had asked such an unexpectedly intuitive question.

'I'm not sure that either of my parents have ever understood me,' she admitted. 'The farm is their life, but even as a child I knew I wanted to do something else. Mum wanted to pass on to me the traditions she had learned from her mother and grandmother, and she was disappointed that I had no interest in learning how to make jam or spin wool. I've always felt that I fall short of being the kind of daughter my mother hoped for…especially when I found out that I—'

Holly broke off abruptly, shocked that she had opened up so much to Jarek. There was no reason to tell him that she had a rare syndrome which meant she was infertile.

'That you…what?' he prompted.

A look of impatience flashed on his face when the door opened to admit Karl bringing the main course, but Holly was grateful for the interruption.

'What were you about to say?' Jarek asked, as soon the chef had finished serving the meal and departed from the room.

'Oh…' She pretended to look vague. 'I don't remember.'

His eyes narrowed on her flushed face, but to her relief he did not pursue the subject. 'What did you think of city life when you moved to London?'

'Truthfully, I found it a little overwhelming. But I was spotted by a model agency scout in my first term at university and thought I could do a bit of modelling to earn some money. Quite unexpectedly I became a successful photographic model. It seemed glamorous at first, but trying to juggle my studies with photo shoots and the frenetic social life that was part of the modelling scene affected my health—both physically and emotionally.'

Holly put down her knife and fork, unable to eat any more of the rich pork dish.

'On the surface I appeared to have a fantastic life,' she told Jarek, 'but I put on an act to hide the fact that I was finding the pressure hard to deal with. Luckily the university arranged for me to see a wonderful counsellor, who helped me through that difficult period in my life. Having personal experience of the benefits of counselling was the reason I switched to a combined psychology and psychotherapy degree.'

Counselling had helped her to accept that she had been born with MRKH syndrome, Holly thought to herself. With her counsellor's support she had worked through her grief that she was infertile, and she had even stopped believing—mostly—that she was a disappointment to her parents. But she had not completely overcome the body image issues that had worsened when she'd started modelling.

Men had desired her for the way she looked, but she had felt a fraud because, in her mind, she wasn't a *normal* woman. She had been ashamed of her body, and counselling had not completely banished her insecurities. What man would want to make love to a woman who had to use dilators before she could have sex?

She glanced at Jarek, the infamous playboy whose list of lovers was reputedly longer than a telephone directory, and a cold dose of reality washed over her. He was flirting with her because he couldn't help himself, but she was sure the smouldering desire in his eyes would quickly disappear if he discovered that he would need patience to arouse her fully before he could make love to her.

She remembered reading a tabloid story in which a well-known stage actress had claimed she'd had sex with Jarek in her dressing room during the ten-minute interval of a West End play. Maybe there was an added thrill to spontaneous sex, Holly brooded, but for her a quickie was out of the question.

She bit her lip. Why was she imagining having sex with Jarek? There was no chance of it happening. Firstly because it would be ethically and morally wrong for her to have an affair with a client, and secondly because the pretty girls at Bibiana's Bar were more his type than an unexciting psychologist who had a hang-up about sex.

Knowing those things made it easier to resist his sexy charm when he suggested they sit by the fire to drink their coffee. She gave him a cool smile and felt a spurt of satisfaction when he looked surprised. No doubt he was used to women falling at his feet, but *she* was immune to his potency she told herself firmly.

Jarek lowered his long frame onto the sofa in front of the fire and patted the empty place next to him. But Holly walked straight past and sat down in the armchair furthest away.

His phone rang and his hard features softened when he looked at the screen. 'Do you mind if I answer this?'

'Be my guest,' she murmured.

She guessed the caller was a woman when he stood up and strolled over to the window, speaking into the phone in a low tone. Once or twice he laughed softly, and Holly felt an inexplicable ache beneath her breastbone.

She wasn't lonely, she assured herself. She had plenty of friends.

But recently several of her close friends had got married, and at dinner parties the conversation tended to be about pregnancy and childcare. It would be nice to have someone special to share laughs with, to share her life with, she acknowledged, but she hadn't dated anyone since Stuart.

She had a good career, Holly reminded herself. Staying at a luxury chalet in the Alps was a wonderful perk of her job. She took a chocolate from the dish on the coffee table and bit into it. The creamy truffle tasted divine, and she closed her eyes while she focused her senses on the sensual pleasure of the chocolate melting on her tongue.

'At least my sister is happy that I have decided to remain at the Frieden Clinic for the next few weeks.'

Holly's eyes flew open and she saw Jarek slip his phone into his pocket before he strolled over and sat down on the footstool close to her chair. Too close for her comfort, she thought, watching the firelight dance over his hair and throw the hard angles of his face into sharp relief. Her fingers literally *ached* to discover if the blond stubble shading his jaw felt prickly to the touch.

'Elin sounded nice when I spoke to her before you arrived...' she murmured, annoyed with herself for feeling pleased that his phone call had been from his sister. 'She told me that the orphanage where you lived in Sarajevo was partially destroyed when it was hit by mortar shells. Elin said she was too young for her to remember much about the war, but she knows that you took care of her and undoubtedly saved her life many times.'

He shrugged. 'I am six years older than my sister. There was no one else to look after her because many of the staff were killed. The kids who survived were the forgotten children of a brutal war,' he said grimly. 'When there was a lull in the machine gun fire I used to go out with a couple of other boys to steal food from the few shops that still operated. We'd take provisions back to the younger children in the orphanage.'

'It sounds horrific. What happened to your parents?'

'They died in a bomb explosion.' Jarek's voice was emotionless. 'Apparently it was a miracle that Elin and I were pulled from the rubble alive.'

'It must have been devastating to lose your parents when you were so young,' Holly said softly. 'Do you remember much about them?'

'I don't have any memories of them.' His jaw clenched. 'I was told by the orphanage staff that the trauma of the explosion had somehow wiped out all my memories of my parents.' He stared at her with an odd intensity in his bright blue eyes. 'Is that possible? As far as I'm aware I did not suffer any head injury which could have caused memory loss.'

'Well, post-traumatic stress can be responsible for memory loss, but it is more likely to manifest with a person having flashbacks and nightmares of a traumatic experience,' Holly said thoughtfully. 'There is a form of memory loss called dissociative amnesia, in which information is lost from the conscious mind as a result of emotional trauma. In such cases a person's behaviour can be influenced by a past trauma, even though their conscious mind doesn't remember what happened. For instance, if a young girl was dragged into some bushes and raped, she might, as an adult, be terrified to walk through woodland. But because her mind has blocked out the rape she doesn't understand the reason for her fear.'

'Do you mean that the brain blocks out bad memories?

I have sometimes wondered if I had an unhappy life with my parents, which is why I can't remember them.'

'I suppose that's possible. Another explanation might be that you had a loving relationship with your parents and losing them suddenly was so traumatic that you developed what can be described as emotional amnesia—meaning that you are unable to remember events which occurred in a specific period of time. That would explain why you have no memories of your life before your parents were killed. How much do you remember of living at the orphanage?'

'I remember *everything* about that hellhole.'

The harsh scrape of Jarek's voice sent a shiver through Holly.

'I'm thankful that my sister was too young to remember much.' He pushed his hair off his face. 'I can only think that whatever happened when I was very young must have been unimaginably horrific for my mind to have blocked out all early memories of my childhood, and yet I am able to recall vividly the terrible things I witnessed in Sarajevo.'

'I read in your notes that you have had an MRI scan which reveals no indication of any structural brain injury. That suggests that we should focus on psychological testing to try to get to the root of your memory loss. Psychotherapy and CBT—cognitive behaviour therapy—have both proved to be highly successful in helping patients to recover memory.'

'You must have heard the saying "Let sleeping dogs lie"? I can't help but think I should do the same,' Jarek murmured.

His lazy tone took Holly by surprise after the rawness she'd heard in his voice moments earlier. He smiled, but there was a bleakness in his eyes that tugged on her tender heart as she pictured him as a young orphaned boy,

trapped in a besieged city during one of Europe's bloodi-
est civil wars.

'I believe your fear of what lies in the past will prevent
you from finding happiness in the future. I want to help
you unlock your memories,' she told him softly.

His sharp gaze searched her face. 'Why?'

'I know what it's like at the bottom of the well…what
it's like to be in a place so deep and dark that you can't
imagine the light, let alone see it.' She swallowed, wondering why she had revealed her vulnerable side to Jarek.
'Besides, you're paying me a lot of money to be your psychotherapist,' she said briskly. 'And, actually, I am very
good at what I do.'

'I'm sure you are.'

His voice turned smoky and curled around her, making
her fiercely aware of him.

'Actually,' he mimicked gently, *'I* am very good at what
I do, too.'

Holly flushed as she guessed he wasn't referring to
his skill at studying the financial markets and making
money. She hadn't noticed him move closer, but he was
right there in front of her. The footstool he was sitting on
was slightly lower than her chair, and his eyes were level
with hers when he leaned forward and rested his forearms
on the arms of the chair, caging her in. She felt her heart
collide painfully with her ribs as he stretched out his hand
and brushed his thumb over her lips.

The effect on her was dizzying. Scalding heat swept
through her veins and pooled, molten and shockingly
needy, between her legs. Somehow she resisted the temptation to part her lips and draw his thumb into her mouth.
She wanted him inside her—in every way.

The startling realisation acted as a reminder that her

body would fail her, as it had done so humiliatingly in the past.

She jerked her head away from him. 'What are you doing?'

'You had chocolate on your mouth.' He lifted his thumb to his own mouth and licked off the smear of chocolate that he had removed from her lips.

Heat rolled through her again and a curious heaviness filled her breasts and unfurled in the pit of her stomach. *This has to stop right now*, a sane voice in her head demanded. Amusement gleamed in Jarek's eyes, but there was also something darker and more intent that stole her breath. He was a notorious womaniser, she reminded herself, and she was way out of her depth.

But she could not seem to move...could not tear her eyes from his mouth as he leaned forward, bringing his face so near to hers that his warm breath grazed her lips.

He was going to kiss her.

Holly trembled, wanting to feel his mouth on hers more than she had ever wanted anything in her life. She swayed towards him, bringing their bodies so close that she could see the tiny lines around his eyes and the faintly calculating expression in his ice-blue gaze.

Unease rippled down her spine.

He was her *patient.*

The cool voice of her sanity spoke again, forcing her to acknowledge that she was in danger of throwing away everything she had worked so hard for. It was not just her professionalism she was risking but her dignity and self-respect. Had she been tempted to sacrifice all that? For what? A five-minute fumble with the tabloids' favourite bad-boy, she silently answered her own question.

'I think I'll go to bed,' she said jerkily, and silently

cursed herself for sounding so gauche. She managed to restrain herself from adding the clarification *alone*.

Jarek lifted his brows as if he knew—damn him—the shockingly erotic images that flashed into her mind of them in bed together.

She swallowed. 'It's late.'

Following his gaze over to the clock, she steeled herself for him to point out in his lazy drawl that nine-thirty was hardly 'late'.

To her relief, he made no comment and did not try to stop her when she jumped up from her chair.

'Goodnight,' she choked. 'We'll start proper therapy tomorrow.'

His dry rejoinder, 'I'll look forward to it,' mocked her as she fled from the room.

CHAPTER FIVE

A LINE OF black limousines queued outside Salzburg's grandest hotel, waiting to deliver guests to the masquerade ball. Jarek tried to curb his impatience as Gunther inched the car slowly forward. He was not in any hurry to get to the ball—which he expected would be as tedious as such events usually were—but from as far back as he could remember he had felt an inexplicable sense of claustrophobia when he was in a car.

It was why he preferred to ride a motorbike.

He wondered if his irrational fear of travelling in cars was connected to his nightmares. Something Holly had said about it being possible for a forgotten trauma from the past to influence behaviour in adulthood had resonated with him.

This evening, when the chauffeur had opened the door for him to climb into the back of the car, he'd felt a sense of terror as a wisp of real memory or a bad dream—he did not know which—had flashed into his head. It had faded before he could assimilate what he had seen, but it had shaken him.

He stared out of the window, watching the flurry of snowflakes drifting down from the night sky. If he had been on his own he would have jumped out onto the pavement and walked the last few hundred yards to the hotel's entrance. But the temperature outside was below zero and Holly would freeze in her strapless ballgown.

He could do with a blast of cold air to bring his temperature down, Jarek thought as he glanced at her sitting beside him. Desire kicked hard in his groin as he allowed his eyes to linger on the creamy upper slopes of her breasts, rising above the low-cut neckline of her dress.

'Explain to me why we are attending a masked ball,' he murmured, in an attempt to divert his mind from the erotic fantasies about her that had made him uncomfortably hard ever since she'd walked into the lounge at Chalet Soline, looking as if she belonged in an adults-only fairy tale, wearing a dramatic creation of burgundy silk and lace.

The dress's full skirt emphasised Holly's tiny waist, and Jarek was sorely tempted to press his mouth against the smooth skin of her bare shoulder and kiss his way down to the deep valley between her breasts.

'Austria is famed for its ball season, which lasts from just before Christmas right through until early summer,' she told him. 'And Professor Heppel believes it is important for patients to attend social functions accompanied by their therapists, so that they can address any issues which might stem from social anxiety. For example, a person might drink heavily to boost their self-confidence. Although I very much doubt that a lack of confidence is the reason why *you* drink,' she said drily.

Jarek's mouth twitched. He was frequently amused by her acerbic wit, and greatly entertained by the way she bristled when he teased her. Holly's nature was as prickly as her name suggested, and he found her disapproval of him a novelty when other women invariably fawned on him.

He stretched his arm along the back of the car seat and

was delighted when she stiffened. 'Are you saying that alcohol will be served at the ball? Suddenly the evening promises to be more entertaining.'

She jerked her head round, and even in the dark interior of the car he felt the force of the glare she directed at him. 'Obviously you are expected to stay away from the bar. The point of the exercise is for you to understand that you do not need to get drunk in order to have a good time. I'll be keeping a close eye on you the entire evening,' she warned. 'In case you get any ideas.'

'Oh, I have *lots* of ideas.' He couldn't resist lowering his head so he could whisper in her ear. 'I am *very* inventive.'

He was fascinated by the scarlet stain that bloomed on her pretty face. Her blush spread down her throat and across the slopes of her magnificent breasts, which reminded him of ripe peaches that he longed to taste.

'You have to stop this,' she snapped. 'It is completely inappropriate for you to flirt with your psychologist. Or at least I'm *supposed* to be giving you therapy,' she muttered, her frustration evident in her voice. 'But you have been at Chalet Soline for a week and we have only managed one half-hour session.'

'I don't know *where* the week has gone,' he said blandly.

'You seem to have spent most of it sleeping.' The bite in her tone was even sharper. 'I've never known a man to lounge around in bed like you do.'

'Have you known *many* men?'

Behind his teasing he realised that he really wanted to know—which was curious, because he had never been mildly interested in his mistresses' tally of lovers. But, despite the simmering sexual chemistry between him and Holly, he could *not* risk making her his mistress, Jarek brooded.

The realisation that he liked her as well as desired her

made him even more determined to resist her. Nothing good ever came to the people he cared about. Holly wanted him to confide his darkest secrets to her, but if he did that she would run as fast and as far from him as she could get—if she had any sense.

'My love-life is none of your business.'

She tightened her fingers around her evening purse, and Jarek had an idea that she was imagining she had her hands around his throat.

'Seriously, every day last week you only emerged from your bedroom at lunchtime, and every afternoon you took yourself off to the Frieden Clinic's treatment centre for a massage. I don't suppose it has anything to do with the fact that the Swedish masseuse, Inga, is a very attractive blonde?' she suggested sarcastically.

Her voice softened.

'Don't think I haven't realised that you are avoiding me, Jarek. It's not unusual for people embarking on psychological treatment to find talking about their problems difficult to begin with.'

The way she spoke his name felt like a kick in his gut. He wanted to pull the pins from her elegant chignon and thread his fingers through her mass of silky brown hair. Worse, he wanted to tell her things he had never told anyone else—not even his sister.

He could not risk upsetting Elin with his crazy idea that their parents *hadn't* died in a bomb blast in Sarajevo, as they had always believed.

In the past week there had been further media reports on the rumour circulating in the Principality of Vostov that the royal family had been assassinated two decades ago, on the orders of a military commander. Ordinarily Jarek would not have taken much interest in the story, but the letter he'd received a few weeks ago, and the request for him to have a DNA test, were preying on his mind.

'Who is Tarik?' Holly asked quietly, jolting him from his thoughts. 'I heard you shout out the name in the middle of the night. Your bedroom is at the opposite end of the chalet from mine, so you must have been shouting loudly to have woken me. Did you have a nightmare?'

'If I did I don't remember it,' he lied.

The dream was one he'd had many times before: a car standing on a driveway with its engine running, bright headlamps cutting white circles in the dark night. People talking in frantic voices. He sensed their fear, but in his dream he could not see their faces. Someone was trying to bundle him into the car but he didn't want to go, and he was crying, shouting out a name.

Tarik...

'You have no idea who Tarik is?' she persisted. 'He might be the key to unlocking your lost memories.'

He looked away from her searching gaze. 'Actually, I remember that Tarik was a boy I knew at the orphanage. We used to play football when the bombing stopped for a while.'

His answer seemed to satisfy Holly. But Jarek knew that the boy in the orphanage had been called Ivan. Years after he had been adopted by the Saundersons he had returned to Sarajevo, to see if any of his friends had survived. He'd found Ivan living rough on the streets—a drug addict and as much a victim of the war as the thousands of people who had perished at the time.

Jarek knew that *he* could have been Ivan, but by a twist of fate he had been taken to live at a stately home— Cuckmere Hall in England. His sense of guilt that he had escaped the hell of war when so many like Ivan had not added to the weight of guilt on his shoulders. Lorna Saunderson had rescued him from the orphanage and been a mother to him. But he had repaid her kindness with reckless behaviour that had cost Mama her life.

He was glad to escape his thoughts as the car came to a halt in front of the entrance to the hotel. But his relief was short-lived when he noticed the bright glare of a camera flashbulb.

'You didn't mention that the goddamned press would be here,' he accused Holly.

A picture in the newspapers of him arriving at the ball would alert Vostov's National Council that he was in Austria.

'The photographer doesn't work for the press. He is simply taking photos of people as they arrive. The guests will be able to buy the pictures to raise funds for the children's charity the ball is in aid of. I know you promised your brother-in-law that you would keep a low profile until your sister has her baby, but I doubt the paparazzi will be interested in a charity ball in Salzburg,' Holly murmured. 'Anyway, your mask will hide your identity.'

She handed him a black eye mask before affixing her own over her face. Her mask was an elaborate affair, decorated with sparkling diamante and feathers which drew attention to her big brown eyes. A man could drown in those velvet-soft eyes if he wasn't careful, Jarek brooded as he stepped out of the car.

He offered her his arm to escort her into the hotel and noted how she hesitated and took a deep breath that caused her breasts to rise and fall before she placed her hand on his arm.

The hotel's foyer was crowded with guests: the women were wearing elaborate ballgowns and the men resplendent in tuxedos. Double doors opened onto the ballroom, which was ablaze with lights from crystal chandeliers.

'We don't have to stay here.' Holly spoke in an under-tone as they walked into the ballroom. 'In the car I felt that you were finally starting to open up when you spoke about your childhood friend Tarik, from the orphanage. I think we should go back to Chalet Soline to discuss the parts of your childhood that you do remember. There may be something that triggers memories of your parents.'

Jarek kept his expression bland. He had deliberately made himself unavailable for therapy sessions all week—which was undoubtedly the act of a coward, he acknowl-edged grimly. But his strategy of avoiding being alone with Holly was under threat. At least while they were at the ball there would be no chance of the soul-searching conversation she was so keen on.

And so he gave her one of the easy smiles that he'd learned as a teenager never failed to win women over. De-sire jack-knifed inside him as he watched her pupils di-late, so that the eyes staring at him from behind her mask darkened with a sultry promise he knew he would ulti-mately have to resist.

'It would be a pity to leave now that we are here—es-pecially when you are the belle of the ball. You look stun-ning in your ballgown,' he murmured.

It was not an idle compliment. Her lovely face and gor-geous figure evoked an odd tightness in his chest, and a rather more predictable tightening in his groin.

'Working on uncovering my past can wait until an-other day.' *Preferably another millennium*, Jarek thought to himself. 'Tonight I'd much rather focus on the present.'

The orchestra struck up a waltz and he swept her into his arms before she could argue.

As he steered Holly around the dance floor Jarek was grateful to his adoptive mother for teaching him the social graces that had allowed him to fit in with high society. He had been a feral boy who had lived off his wits to survive in a war when Lorna Saunderson had persuaded her husband to adopt him. Now, at this grand ball, he suddenly felt an odd sense of recognition.

A memory flashed into his mind. He saw himself as a child, sitting at the top of a wide staircase and peering down through the banisters on a huge room below. There was a crowd of people dressed in ornate clothes, and he could hear music and the indistinct buzz of chatter and laughter. It must have been a party, but Jarek sensed it had not taken place in Sarajevo. Where could he have been when he had observed such revelry from his secret hiding place? And where had his parents been?

Holly had suggested that thinking about his childhood might trigger memories of his parents, but Jarek could not picture them. It was as if a curtain had been pulled across his past and he feared what he might discover if he tried to see behind it.

He needed a distraction, and previously vodka had provided a welcome escape from his demons. But if he went anywhere near the bar tonight his personal gaoler would be right beside him to give him one of her pithy lectures.

That left him with only one option, he brooded as he tightened his arm around Holly's waist and pulled her hard up against his body. He would have to distract himself with his beautiful psychotherapist.

Holly ran the zip of her dress down her spine and dragged in a deep breath, relieved finally to be able to fill her lungs with oxygen. The ballgown's boned bodice emphasised her narrow waist and pushed her breasts high, but after several hours of having her ribcage constricted she was glad to change into comfortable cotton pyjamas.

Not that she felt like sleeping. It was past midnight, and

she should be tired after she'd danced the night away with Jarek at the ball. But her heart was still racing as fast as it had been when he'd whisked her around the ballroom. She had felt giddy as he'd held her—so close to him that she'd felt his powerful thighs pressed up against her. At some point she had given up trying to hold herself stiffly and had melted into him, unable to resist the sexual chemistry that had burned like a white-hot flame between them.

It had been a magical evening. But reality had caught up with her when Gunther had driven them back to Chalet Soline after the ball had finished. In the car Jarek had seemed tense and uncommunicative—in marked contrast to his behaviour throughout the evening, when he had been so charming and attentive that Holly admitted she had fallen under his spell.

Back at the chalet, the chef had left a tray of coffee in the sitting room, where the embers of the fire had emitted a welcoming glow. She had half-expected Jarek to suggest they drink their coffee together, but he had bade her a curt goodnight and gone straight up to his bedroom, leaving her feeling deflated and rather stupid.

What had she hoped might happen if they'd sat in the cosy sitting room with the lights turned down low? she angrily asked her reflection as she pulled the pins out of her chignon and dug her fingers into her hair to massage her scalp. The evening could not have ended any differently even if Jarek *hadn't* been her patient.

She opened her bedside drawer and took out the purse that contained her set of dilators. The surgery she'd had as a teenager had been successful in lengthening her vagina, but her gynaecologist had advised her to use the dilators a few times a month if she wasn't having sex regularly. After Stuart had ended their relationship a year ago Holly had not dated anyone seriously. She'd continued to use her dilators, but not as often as she knew she should—because there didn't seem much point when she seemed destined to remain single.

Logically, she knew she shouldn't feel ashamed or embarrassed about her body, but a little voice inside her head whispered that Jarek could have any woman he wanted, and was unlikely to want *her* if he found out that she was a freak.

She shoved the dilators back in the drawer before she climbed into bed and then opened her notebook to write up Jarek's notes. She had a job to do, she reminded herself fiercely. She'd been an idiot to fall for his seduction routine at the ball—which, quite clearly, had been a calculated ploy to stop her from delving into his emotions. But behind Jarek's image of indolent playboy—an image she was beginning to realise he cultivated deliberately— she'd glimpsed the damaged soul of a boy who had witnessed the horrors of war and risked his life to protect his younger sister when he had been only a child.

Holly knew that severe childhood trauma could have a lasting and devastating effect throughout a person's life, and even though Jarek did not want her help she would nevertheless do her best to persuade him to start a programme of counselling sessions. Tomorrow she would not let him out of her sight, she resolved as she curled up beneath the duvet and turned off the bedside lamp.

She woke with a start and felt disorientated to find herself in darkness. She had been dreaming that she was in a brightly lit ballroom. Her brain caught up and remembered that she was in her bedroom at Chalet Soline, and when she switched on the lamp she saw on the clock that it was four in the morning. Dawn was still three hours or so away, and while she was wondering what had woken her she heard Jarek's voice.

He was shouting, as he had done the previous night—harsh, incomprehensible words. Dear God, the fear in his voice tore on Holly's heart. What terrors stalked his nightmares?

She threw back the covers and leapt out of bed, driven by an instinctive desire to help him. She did not even pause to grab her robe before she ran down the corridor to his room.

The first thing she noticed when she opened his bedroom door was a table by the window, upon which three brightly lit computer monitors displayed columns of red and green numbers.

'Jarek?' she called softly.

He did not reply, and while she hovered in the doorway, wondering if she should return to her room, he cried out again, and the tortured sound sent a shiver through her. The glow from the computer screens allowed her to make out his shape on the bed. She walked over to him and, after hesitating for a second, switched on the bedside lamp and saw that he was sprawled on top of the bedspread.

His tuxedo jacket, she noticed, was draped over the back of a chair. He was still wearing his trousers, and his white silk shirt was unbuttoned so that it hung open to reveal a muscular chest covered with whorls of dark blond hair. Holly dared not allow her eyes to travel over his flat abdomen and lower, to where the path of body hair disappeared beneath his waistband. Instead she forced her gaze up to his face, and was struck anew by the stark beauty of his hard-boned features.

One arm was lying across his eyes. Holly's heart twisted when she saw a single tear slide down his cheek.

'Jarek!' she said more loudly, desperate to rouse him from his nightmare.

She leaned over the bed and gave a startled cry when

his eyes flew open and he snapped his fingers around her wrist. He gave a hard tug, so that without quite knowing how she ended up sitting on the edge of the bed, next to where he lay.

'Is this an example of your bedside manner, Dr Maitland?' he drawled. 'I usually wear nothing in bed… There could have been an interesting development in our patient/ psychologist relationship if you'd sneaked into my bedroom and found me stark naked.'

Amusement gleamed in his bright blue eyes when she blushed, and Holly's sympathy for him was replaced by a desire to slap the smug grin off his face.

'I did *not* sneak into your room,' she said tightly. 'You must have been having a nightmare—you were shouting. You woke me up.' She tried to no avail to tug her wrist out of his grasp. 'I came to see if I could help. You said the name Tarik again, but I couldn't understand anything else because you were speaking in a language I didn't recognise.'

'My first language is Bosnian,' Jarek said slowly. He sat up and leaned against the headboard of the bed, still retaining his hold on her wrist. The teasing smile that had played on his lips a few seconds earlier had disappeared. 'I rarely spoke it after I was adopted and learned to speak English. My sister was too young to remember any of the Bosnian language.'

'The fact that you called out in your first language suggests you were dreaming about an incident in your childhood. Can you remember anything about the dream?' Holly pressed.

'No. But the recent volatility of the financial markets is enough to give *anyone* nightmares,' he quipped.

'I don't think your dream was about tumbling share prices on the stockmarket.' She swallowed her frustration and looked over at the blinking computer monitors. 'Why is your computer system active at this time of night? Well, technically it's four-thirty in the morning, but it feels like the middle of the night to *me*.'

Jarek pushed his untidy blond hair off his face. 'I had been working before I sat on the bed for a couple of minutes. I must have fallen asleep.'

'Working?' Holly could not hide her surprise. 'I know you said you wanted to use the study downstairs as your office, but every time I've walked passed that room you haven't been there, and I've never actually seen you do any work.'

'I don't make vast amounts of money by sitting around and twiddling my thumbs,' he said drily. 'Of *course* I work. Mainly at night, because most of my trading is on the financial markets in the Far East, which is on a different time zone to Europe. One a.m. here is nine a.m. in places like Hong Kong and Shanghai, when the Asian stock exchanges are open for trading.'

'So you have to catch up on sleep in the daytime to make up for the fact that you stay awake working most of the night...' Holly stared at him. 'Why do you encourage the media to portray you as a feckless playboy?'

He gave another shrug. 'How do you know that I'm not *exactly* as I'm perceived by the press?'

'I looked you up on the internet,' she admitted. 'Amid the countless stories of your wild womanising and partying, which seem to confirm your bad-boy reputation, I discovered just how much money you have raised for the charity Lorna's Gift. Another little-known fact overlooked by the press is that you spend several months every year visiting orphanages around the world. You are the driving force behind a scheme in some of the world's poorer countries to promote the idea that it is better for children who have no families of their own to be fostered rather than grow up in institutions.'

'Don't make me out as some kind of saint,' Jarek told her harshly. 'The truth is that there's not much difference between financial trading and gambling. I take big risks, and I've been lucky so far that most have paid off. But that wasn't the case two years ago, when I caused the near-collapse of Saunderson's Bank.' He gave a bitter laugh. 'My adoptive father was right when he said I have a destructive streak in my nature.'

'I don't believe that is true.' Holly looked away from him and quickly blinked away the tears that welled in her eyes. Jarek sounded so *raw*. 'I wish you would allow me to try and help you,' she said in a low tone. 'Regression therapy might enable you to relive a traumatic event from your past, so that you can come to terms with whatever happened to you when you were a child.'

'You have a soft heart, don't you, angel-face?'

His voice was deeper than Holly had ever heard it, and if her heart hadn't already melted it would have done then.

'You should have told me to leave Chalet Soline when you had the chance—and when I stood a chance of resisting you,' he told her. 'But now it's too late.'

She swallowed as he picked up a lock of her long hair and wound it around his fingers. The intent expression in his eyes caused her heart to slam into her ribs, and she knew he must be able to feel the erratic thud of her pulse as he stroked his thumb-pad over her wrist.

'I'm not a fool,' she told him stiffly. 'At the ball tonight you pretended to be attracted to me to distract me from asking awkward questions which might reveal something about your past.'

'Is that what you think I was doing?'

'I *know* it was. When we returned to the chalet you couldn't wait to get away from me.'

'What do you think would have happened, Holly?' he murmured. 'If we had been alone in the sitting room, with the flames crackling in the hearth and both of us imagining making love on the fur rug in front of the fire?'

Betraying colour flooded her face as she recalled her erotic fantasy. It had been exactly as Jarek had described. 'I wasn't imagining anything of the sort,' she denied jerkily.

'Liar!'

His laughter was a soft rumble that tugged at something deep inside her. Her breath caught in her throat when he gave a little tug on her hair to pull her head nearer to his. Like a fish caught on a hook, she thought, except that she didn't try to escape as he reeled her in.

She licked her dry lips, unable to look away from his glittering blue gaze as he drew her closer to him, closer to the wickedly sensual mouth that crooked in a knowing smile.

'What are you doing?' she demanded in a husky voice she did not recognise as her own.

'What you want me to do,' he promised.

His arrogance should have appalled her. But Holly was beyond caring about anything other than her desperate need for him to kiss her. Time was suspended, and she had the crazy feeling that she had been waiting for this moment and for this man her whole life. She could feel her heart trying to claw its way out of her chest as Jarek's breath whispered across her lips. He angled his mouth over hers. And then he simply claimed her—as if he was her master and she belonged utterly and entirely to him.

His kiss was everything she had imagined it would be. Hot, hungry, demanding her response. And she was powerless to deny him. She went up in flames instantly, and in a distant recess of her mind she recognised that she had never been kissed so expertly before.

Jarek was the Viking invader of her fantasies about him, and his kiss was no gentle seduction but a passionate plundering of her senses. He used his tongue with consummate skill to explore her mouth and thrust his hand into her hair to hold her prisoner while he kissed her with a stunning eroticism that made her tremble.

He finally let go of her wrist—but only so that he could wrap his arms around her and haul her against his bare chest. Her hands flailed wildly for a second, before she succumbed to temptation and placed them flat on his chest, running her fingers over the whorls of blond hair that grew thickly over his torso. She pushed his unbuttoned shirt off his shoulders and revelled in the feel of his satin-smooth skin beneath her palms. His body was a masterpiece of masculine beauty and she traced her fingers over the hard ridges of his abdominal muscles, fascinated by his toned hardness in contrast to her soft, feminine curves.

In a seamless movement he rolled her over, so that she found herself lying on her back on the bed. He stretched out beside her and propped himself up on his elbow, cradling her chin in his other hand while he kissed her again, slow and leisurely this time, but no less heart-shaking.

Holly ran her fingers through his hair. Her senses were inflamed by the heat of his body, the musky fragrance of his aftershave and the skilful flick of his tongue inside her mouth. She sank deeper into the soft mattress as he smoothed his hand down her body, over the firm mounds of her breasts covered by the stretchy material of her pyjama top. Her heart thudded when he gripped the hem of her top and in one fluid movement pushed it up to her neck, baring her breasts. The cool air on her heated skin caused her nipples to pucker, and the feral growl Jarek gave sent a shudder of response through her.

'Your breasts are even more beautiful than I had imagined them,' he said thickly. 'I wish that I had followed my instincts when we returned from the ball, and undressed you in the firelight before making love to you in front of the fire.'

The sound of his voice jolted Holly from the sexual haze that had clouded her brain. The inherent arrogance of his statement sent a chill through her.

'Assuming I would have *allowed* you to undress me,' she muttered.

'Of course you would.'

He laughed, and it felt like a knife through her heart.

'Why *else* did you come to my room tonight?'

'You were having a nightmare.' She yanked her pyjama top down and sat up. 'You *can't* think I came for any other reason?' Her face flamed when he looked amused. 'I am your psychotherapist and I rushed to your room after I heard you call out to see if I could help you.' She gave a ragged sigh of frustration. 'The truth is that we can't start a relationship while you are my client.'

'Relationship?' His brows rose. 'I thought we were going to spend what's left of the night together—not align our diaries for the next few months.'

Holly welcomed the burst of temper that exploded inside her and which—for now, at least—stopped her feeling as if she wanted to cry. What a fool she was, she thought grimly.

'I suppose the thought of being with a woman for even one month must seem like an eternity to the world's most prolific playboy,' she said furiously. 'You shouldn't have kissed me, and I admit I should not have responded. It was a moment of madness and I assure you it won't happen again.'

She swung her legs over the side of the bed and stood

up, telling herself she was relieved that he did not try to stop her. To her utter shame she smelled the betraying musky scent of her arousal, and was sure Jarek must be able to smell it too. It was no wonder that he had assumed she was his for the taking.

But if he had attempted to have sex with her he would have found her body unyielding, and she would have felt even more humiliated than she did right now.

Feeling sick with self-loathing, she hurried over to the door. But she hesitated on her way out of his room and turned to face him. He was still sprawled on the bed, like an indolent sultan deciding which of the concubines in his harem he would summon to pleasure him.

For a mad moment Holly wondered what would happen if she forgot her principles and walked back over to him, peeling off her pyjamas on her way to his bed. Her breasts ached for his touch, and there was a slick, molten heat between her legs. But the fantasy was ruined by the reality that it took time for her body to become fully aroused, and that if she rushed sex would be uncomfortable for her.

'When I heard you shouting you sounded terrified—as if someone was trying to murder you,' she told Jarek. 'You are going to have to confront your past some time—and, although I feel horribly embarrassed about my unprofessional behaviour tonight, I want you to know that my only desire is to help you tackle your demons.'

For a split second an expression flashed across his face that startled Holly. He looked *lost*—and vulnerable, as he must have been when he was an orphaned boy struggling to survive in war-torn Sarajevo.

Her heart ached for him, but he wasn't interested in her heart, she reminded herself as she stepped into the corridor and quietly closed the door behind her.

CHAPTER SIX

'I'M GLAD TO see you've made it down to breakfast for once,' Holly said, coming to an abrupt halt in the doorway of the dining room when she saw Jarek sitting at the table, drinking a cup of coffee.

She did not sound gladdened by the sight of him, he thought. Her usually melodious voice was at least two octaves higher, and the pink stain on her cheeks reminded him of when he had shoved her pyjama top out of the way and watched warm colour spread down her throat and over her perfect round breasts with their rosy tips that he had ached to taste.

He still ached, he acknowledged. Sleepless nights were nothing new to him, but since Holly had left him last night he'd felt restless and dangerously out of control. Unexpectedly he'd found he wanted something more than the litany of meaningless liaisons that defined his life. But he should know better. He knew himself too well, and none of what he knew was any good.

The headlines on many of the morning's newspapers did not help to lighten Jarek's mood.

In Vostov, Asmir Sunjic had gone public with his story that he had been in the car with Prince Goran and his wife and children on the night of the fatal crash that had supposedly taken the lives of every member of the royal family.

Asmir insisted that the crash had not been the result of a tyre blow-out, as had been reported at the time, but that in fact the car had been hit by gunfire. Even more astonishing was Asmir's claim that when the car had spun off the road and crashed into dense woodland he had managed to smuggle the royal children away to safety. Moments later the car had exploded in a fireball, with the Prince and Princess inside.

If the old Vostovian man's story was true, the papers suggested, the royal children—who would now be adults— might be alive.

It was a big *if*, Jarek brooded. He welcomed the distraction of watching Holly walk across the room and take her place opposite him at the table. Her colour was still high, and he was intrigued when she refused to meet his gaze and seemed to be fascinated with the toast rack.

'I've drawn up a schedule of counselling sessions for you,' she said, in a brisk tone that warned him she would not be distracted from her determination to persuade him to spill his guts. She was dressed as if she meant business, but he knew that her calf-length skirt and crisp blouse— buttoned all the way up to her neck this morning—concealed a voluptuous body. He felt himself harden as he recalled how soft her sweet curves had felt when he'd held her in his arms.

'How very efficient of you,' he drawled.

He was tempted to reach across the table and remove the clasp that secured her hair in a knot on top of her head, so that the heavy mass of gleaming brown silk spilled around her shoulders. But if he did that he knew he would have to walk around the table and sink his fingers into her hair, so he contented himself with brushing his fingertips over the faint grazes on her cheek.

'I left my mark on you last night,' he said ruefully, rubbing his hand across the stubble on his jaw. 'Perhaps it's as well that things did not progress between us. Your skin is so fine that if I had put my mouth on your breasts I would have scraped you with my beard.'

She stiffened, and he waited for her to slap him down with one of her sharp retorts. Instead her silence trembled with tension, and Jarek felt an odd sensation as if his heart was being squeezed in a vice when he saw her lower lip wobble before she caught it between her teeth.

'You don't need to remind me of my shameful behaviour last night.' Her voice shook. 'I will understand if you wish to make a complaint about my unprofessional conduct to Professor Heppel.'

Even worse than the painful emotion in her voice was the dark luminosity of her eyes. 'For God's sake, Holly,' he said roughly, 'there is no reason for you to feel ashamed. Believe me, I should know. Shame is my middle name.'

'I wonder why you think that. It will be a good starting point for your first counselling session.' The determined look was back in her eyes. 'I thought we could make a start straight after breakfast.'

For twenty seconds Jarek considered telling Holly of his crazy suspicion that his amnesia about the early years of his life was somehow connected with events that had taken place in the Principality of Vostov more than two decades ago. But he was sure she would not believe him— and he did not really believe himself that Asmir Sunjic's story could be true. If his parents had been a prince and princess, it seemed inconceivable that he had no memory of them—or of spending the first years of his childhood living in a royal palace.

How, then, had he ended up in an orphanage in Sarajevo? There were so many unanswered questions. It was more likely that the old man in Vostov was a fantasist, or an opportunist hoping to make money by selling his bizarre story to the media, Jarek assured himself.

He glanced at Holly and found her watching him with big dark eyes that reminded him of molten chocolate: soft and sweet and so very tempting.

'I've decided to go skiing this morning,' he said abruptly. 'Heavy snowfall is forecast for the next few days, which means that today might be the only opportunity to hit the slopes.'

She looked as if she wanted to argue, but perhaps she guessed it would be pointless because she murmured, 'All right. I'll come with you. Maybe spending the day outside in the fresh air will help you to relax and you'll feel able to talk about your childhood.'

'How can I talk about it when a chunk of my memory is missing?' he growled irritably. 'You make it sound simple, but presumably the reason my mind has blocked out certain memories is because they are disturbing.'

She nodded. 'But your lost memories surface in your nightmares. Whatever happened to you as a child is stored in your subconscious mind.'

'What the hell is wrong with leaving those memories buried, instead of digging them up so that you can psychoanalyse them?' he demanded, feeling that restless ache inside him when she smiled gently.

'I hope I can help you to uncover your past so that you will be freed from the horrors that stalk your dreams.'

'What if *I* am the horror?' he muttered. 'What if I am afraid to remember my early childhood because I did something terrible?'

He saw her shocked expression before she quickly masked it. What had made him blurt out his secret fear to Holly, Jarek wondered grimly.

She shook her head. 'How old were you when you went

to live at the orphanage and were told that your parents had died?

'Six. But I have no memories of my life up until then.'

'You were a *child*, Jarek,' she said softly. 'What can a six-year-old boy have done?'

Killed his parents.

The thought flashed into Jarek's mind, along with that wisp of a memory he had seen before in his nightmares. He visualised a car with its engine running, heard a man's voice speaking urgently.

'Put the boy in the car, Dora. There is no time to search for Tarik. If we do not leave now we will all be killed.'

Who were Dora and Tarik? Jarek wondered. And why did he feel that he had somehow been responsible for his parents' death if they had been killed in a bomb explosion in Sarajevo?

Frustration surged through him when a curtain fell across his mind once more and hid his memories. His inability to recall his childhood was something he'd had to live with all his adult life, but he realised that Holly had been right when she'd said he could not look to the future until he had dealt with his past. Before he'd arrived at the Frieden Clinic and met his beautiful psychotherapist he had been uninterested in what his future held. So why did it suddenly matter now?

He glanced at Holly and his jaw clenched. He shouldn't have kissed her, but now that he had he found himself wanting things he could never have. After his adoptive mother's death four years ago he had vowed that no one else would suffer as a result of his destructive nature.

Too restless to remain inactive, he scraped his chair back and rose to his feet. The gentle expression in Holly's eyes felt like a knife in his heart. He did not need her sympathy and he was certain he did not deserve it.

'How well can you ski?' he asked tersely. 'There are a couple of black runs at Arlenwald that I want to try, but if you are a novice you won't manage them. I'll leave you on the easier slopes.'

'As a matter of fact I'm an experienced skier. I was taught by an ex-boyfriend who was a skiing champion. Brett had an *amazing* technique,' she murmured, a smile playing on her lips.

He must be losing his mind, Jarek decided. What other reason could there be other than madness for the acid burn of jealousy in the pit of his stomach when he pictured Holly with another man?

'You said your skiing instructor was an ex-boyfriend… Was the break-up a recent event?'

She shook her head. 'No, I dated Brett years ago—while I was at university and working part-time as a model. We met at a party and he invited me to his home in Colorado, which is where I learned to ski. The romance fizzled out after a few months, but I've continued to ski regularly— mainly in Europe.'

'Why don't you have a man in your life currently?' Jarek hoped his idle tone disguised his curiosity.

'What makes you think I'm not in a relationship?' she countered.

'You wouldn't have kissed me if you were involved with another guy.'

He did not know why he was so certain that Holly was a one-man woman, but it was a reminder that she was off-limits to him. He sensed that he could hurt her. What was surprising was that he *cared*.

He watched her eyes darken and knew she was remembering the heat that had burned hotter than the fiercest flame between them when he had kissed her, and when she had responded with a sweet ardency that made his gut clench just thinking about it.

'I thought we had agreed that what happened last night was a mistake best forgotten,' she said tautly.

'I don't remember agreeing to forget it,' he drawled. 'Seriously, not only are you beautiful, but you are clever and compassionate—you must have to fight men off. I don't understand why you're not married.'

'That's rich, coming from a notorious playboy,' she murmured, in that dry way of hers that so amused Jarek.

He shrugged. 'I'm shallow and easily bored. What's your excuse?'

She was silent for a moment, and when she finally spoke the huskiness in her voice scraped on something raw inside him that he hadn't known existed until then.

'The truth is that I have never met anyone who was prepared to love me for the way I am,' she said quietly.

He frowned. 'And how *are* you?'

'Flawed.' She smiled faintly. 'You are not the only one with secrets, Jarek.'

'I'll tell you mine if you tell me yours.' He meant it, and it was then that he realised he was in grave danger of losing his sanity around Holly.

'I'm afraid that's not how psychotherapy works.' Her tone became brisk once more. 'It's only fair that if we spend today skiing you agree to give counselling a fair chance tomorrow.'

He couldn't help but smile at her earnest expression, and his smile widened as he walked around the table and bent his head down to hers. She immediately stiffened, and the pulse at the base of the throat leapt frantically beneath her skin.

'You're forgetting something, angel-face,' he said softly as he angled his mouth over hers.

The kiss was hard and fierce and unsatisfactorily brief. Desire delivered a sharp kick to his gut when he felt her lips part beneath his, and it took all his will power to lift his head and step away from her.

'I've never claimed to play fair.'

His voice was harsher than he'd intended: a warning to himself as much as to Holly, Jarek acknowledged as he spun round and strode out of the room.

The view down the mountainside was spectacular and terrifying. Holly felt a trickle of fear run the length of her spine as she stared at what appeared to be an almost vertical expanse of white snow, glistening in the late-afternoon sunshine. She had never attempted to ski down such a steep run before—although technically it wasn't a proper ski run.

Jarek had decided to ski off-piste, and she had felt that it was her duty to accompany him. The snow here, away from the main ski runs, had not been compacted by snow-cat machines to flatten out the surface, and there were no coloured marker flags. More importantly there were no other skiers in sight—probably because no one else was crazy enough to want to ski on such challenging terrain.

She must be out of her mind, Holly thought, conscious of her heart hammering in her chest. Although she had told Jarek the truth when she'd said she was an experienced skier, she had omitted to mention that prior to arriving in Austria she had not skied for more than a year. The two black runs at Arlenwald were notoriously difficult, and her nerve and skill had been tested when she had followed Jarek down the slopes.

She had been feeling rather pleased with herself, and looking forward to a soak in the hot tub, knowing her muscles were going to ache like mad tomorrow— But…

'I'm not ready to finish yet,' Jarek had said when she'd suggested they return to Chalet Soline. 'You go back if you want to. I'll meet you later.'

'The daylight will fade soon,' she'd pointed out, but he had dismissed her argument and joined the queue for the ski lift, insisting there was enough time left for a final turn on the slopes.

'Call Gunther and ask him to drive you back to the chalet. I don't need a nursemaid.'

He had not hidden his irritation when she'd voiced her concern that it was dangerous to ski off-piste alone.

In fact Holly had not been worried about his physical safety. She'd quickly discovered that he was brilliant on skis—although he took too many risks, in her opinion. She was more concerned that if she left Jarek on the slopes he would be tempted to visit a bar back at the ski resort in order to enjoy the lively après-ski scene, thereby avoiding any in-depth conversation with her, as he had successfully been doing all day.

Her hope that when they took a break from skiing for lunch she would be able to encourage Jarek to talk about his childhood had been thwarted when he'd turned on his effortless charm. The memory of when he had kissed her at breakfast had weakened her resistance to him, and she had found herself responding to his outrageously sexy smile and entertaining conversation—even though she had known his deliberate seduction was a ploy to distract her from asking him questions about his past.

She was getting nowhere with Jarek's treatment, and Holly felt half inclined to give up with him. It was *not* part of her remit to chase him down a mountain, and she could not force him to have psychotherapy. But she couldn't forget the raw pain she had heard in his voice when she'd heard him shouting out in the night.

Clearly Jarek was haunted by the horrors of war that he had witnessed as a child, and he could not run from his past for ever, however much he tried, she brooded as she glanced at him, standing beside her at the top of the ski run. He had told her that he loved the mountains, but admitted that he did not remember where he had learned to ski. It was yet another mystery that she wanted to help him solve, if only he would let her.

She consoled herself with the thought that once they reached the bottom of the slope dusk would not be far off and they would not be able to ski any more that day. All she had to do was keep upright on her skis and pray that her nerve held on this final run.

'Are you sure you want to do this?' Jarek lifted up his goggles and scrutinised her face. 'You look nervous. It's fine if you want to chicken out.'

Her chin came up. His arrogance infuriated her, but she smiled sweetly and imagined him skiing over the edge of a ravine. 'I'm ready when you are.'

'Good.' He pulled his goggles back down over his eyes. 'Let's go.'

Jarek pushed off on his skis and was almost instantly engulfed by a cloud of powdery snow. Holly took a deep breath as she prepared to follow him.

The snow was deeper than she'd expected, and every time she turned snow flew up around her so that she could barely see ahead through the white cloud. She knew that on powder snow it was better to ski fast and establish a rhythm of short, even turns. It was exhilarating, and exhausting, but she dared not slow her pace because she could just see Jarek ahead, speeding away from her.

She concentrated on trying to catch up with him, and did not pay much attention when she heard an odd muffled sound. But moments later she noticed the snow around her starting to break away, and she knew—although she had never experienced it before—that a moving slab of snow was the first sign of an avalanche.

Terrified, Holly pointed her skis straight, desperately hoping she could outrun the avalanche, but then she heard a loud noise and saw a fracture line run across the snow slab as it shattered. Blocks of snow immediately started to slide down the mountain at an incredible speed. It felt as if a rug had been pulled from beneath her, and when she turned her head she saw that the entire side of the mountain had broken away and was hurtling down, ready to take her with it.

'Jarek!'

Through the cloud of white snow surrounding her she glimpsed his helmet, but she did not know if he had heard her voice. Her heart was pounding with fear as she fought to stay upright on her skis, aware that if she fell she would be swept down the mountainside and buried beneath tons of snow. She saw Jarek look over his shoulder and then point his ski stick over to a group of pine trees.

Holly turned her skis in the direction of the trees, adrenalin and a fierce instinct to survive sharpening her sense of balance as the snow slab beneath her skis swept her relentlessly down the mountain.

Somehow she managed to stay ahead of the line of fast-moving snow until she reached the trees, and she grabbed hold of a branch just as the avalanche slammed into her. The snow still looked pretty and powdery, but it felt like a concrete wall hitting her. And it kept on coming—great slabs of snow crashing down, so that she had to cling to the branch with all her strength and pray that the tree would not be swept away by the tidal wave of snow, taking her with it to almost certain death.

Holly had no idea what had happened to Jarek, and before she could call out to him again a huge slab of snow smashed into her with such force that it felt as if her shoulder had been ripped out of its socket. The pain was indescribable, but she knew that if she fainted she would die, so somehow clung on to the tree branch for what seemed like a lifetime. Until miraculously the roaring noise that filled her ears abated and she realised the avalanche had stopped.

The sudden silence was eerie. Gradually she became aware of a ragged, uneven sound that she realised was her own shallow breathing. So she was alive. But she was unable to move because she discovered that she was buried up to her waist in snow, which was already setting like concrete. If she hadn't clung on to the branch of the tree Holly knew that she would have been completely engulfed by the avalanche.

The realisation of how close to death she had come wasn't something she could deal with right now.

She heard cracks and creaks as tree branches began to break under the weight of snow on them. And then a voice, harsh with urgency.

'*Holly!* Thank God!'

Jarek appeared from where the pine trees grew more densely and made his way over to where Holly was trapped against a tree trunk by the snow that had piled high around her like an icy straitjacket.

'I was afraid you'd been swept down the mountain,' he said unsteadily. 'But you're all right, angel-face, you're alive.'

He pulled a snow shovel from his backpack and started to dig away the snow around her.

'It's okay, baby. I'll get you out and back down the mountain in no time. You're safe. I'll take care of you.'

Despite being numb from shock, and the cold that seemed to have turned the blood in her veins to ice, Holly was startled by the raw emotion in Jarek's voice. He brushed the snow away from her face and his blue eyes glittered with an odd intensity before he bent his head and claimed her mouth in a fierce kiss that stole what was left of her breath.

'I thought I'd lost you,' he muttered.

And then she knew she must be suffering from shock because he sounded as though it mattered— *she* mattered—to him.

It took several more minutes before he finally cleared the snow away from her legs and feet. 'Luckily you didn't lose your skis. Do you think you can ski the rest of the way down the mountain?'

'I'll have to. How else can we get down?'

Her numb sense of shock was fading, and feeling had returned to her body. She moved her arm and pain shot down from her shoulder all the way to her fingertips. The burning sensation was so agonising that she let out a scream.

'What's the matter?'

Jarek swore as her knees gave way and she almost blacked out. He caught her as her legs crumpled beneath her.

'Holly, are you hurt?'

'I've done something to my shoulder,' she told him through gritted teeth, trying desperately not to be sick.

The pain was so severe that she wondered how she could possibly ski when every slight movement was excruciating. She began to shiver uncontrollably, and was only partly aware of Jarek removing her skis.

When he took off his own skis, and fitted them into the carry-straps on his backpack, she stared at him. 'What are you doing?'

'There is an emergency shelter not far from here. We should be able to find it using the GPS on my phone. Once

I've got you somewhere safe and warm I'll call the ski patrol and tell them you need to be airlifted off the mountain.'

'I'm sure that won't be necessary.' Holly hated making a fuss. 'I've probably just pulled a muscle in my shoulder and it will stop hurting soon—at least enough for me to ski down.'

She moved her arm gingerly and could not restrain a gasp of agony.

Jarek was studying a map on his phone's screen. 'The shelter is on the other side of the trees and over the next ridge. It should take approximately twenty minutes to walk to it from here.' He slipped his arm around her waist and leaned down to her. 'Put your arm round my neck.'

She shook her head when she realised his intention. 'You can't carry me. There's nothing wrong with my legs. I can walk.'

She took a step forward to prove her point, and discovered that the slightest movement made her shoulder hurt even more.

'Don't argue, Holly,' he said implacably. 'You're injured and shocked. The temperature will drop quickly, now that dusk is falling, and you're in danger of developing hypothermia.'

Holly didn't have the strength to disagree, and in truth she doubted she had the energy to walk any distance. She was colder than she had ever been in her life, and every shiver that juddered through her body sent a throb of searing pain to her shoulder.

Jarek carefully lifted her into his arms and she bit down hard on her lip to hold back a cry. He carried her through the snow, and Holly was amazed by his strength and physical fitness. Several times she urged him to let her try to walk, but he refused. He did not even seem out of breath when they eventually arrived at a small wooden hut perched on a rocky outcrop and dwarfed by the towering Alps.

As soon as Jarek had opened the door and gently set her on her feet he pulled his phone out of his backpack. While he called the emergency services Holly looked around the hut. The furniture was basic—a narrow bed, a table and a couple of chairs—and at the far end of the hut was a small kitchen area with a wood-burner stove. She opened a door and found a toilet and a sink. At least the hut was safe and dry, but it felt no less cold inside than outside in the sub-zero temperature.

'It was lucky that we happened to ski fairly near to this emergency shelter,' she said to Jarek through her chattering teeth when he'd finished his phone call.

'Luck played no part in my decision of where to ski. Before we set out this morning I did some research and found out about this shelter—which is funded by donations and managed by the ski club in Arlenwald. I also checked the weather forecast and avalanche risk report—which was low. I certainly wouldn't have suggested skiing off-piste and putting our lives in danger if I'd thought there was any chance of an avalanche,' he said grimly.

He frowned as he watched her struggle to unfasten the chin-strap of her ski helmet while her body shook with uncontrollable shivers.

'Let me help you.' He came closer to help remove her helmet and swore softly. 'Your lips are turning blue—which is a sign you're developing hypothermia.'

'I think snow got into the top of my ski suit when I was caught in the avalanche. The lining of my jacket is wet,' Holly mumbled. She was finding it hard to talk coherently, and all she wanted to do was go to sleep.

Jarek moved over to the fireplace, where a pile of logs was stacked against the wall. 'I'm going to light a fire, and once the hut has warmed up I'll help you out of your ski gear. I brought some spare clothes in my pack, as well as emergency food supplies. We're going to have to spend the night in this hut,' he told her. 'The ski patrol can't get to us because they're dealing with a major incident further down the mountain. The avalanche swept away a group of skiers, and two people are still missing.'

Holly knew that if it had not been for Jarek's quick thinking she could have been swept away by the avalanche and buried beneath the snow too. She prayed the rescue services would find the missing skiers in time—but it was now dark, and the chances of locating the skiers alive would lessen with every minute they remained buried.

She felt she should offer to help build the fire, but she was so cold that she had lost all sensation in her fingers and toes and she felt sick from the throbbing pain in her shoulder. *Snap out of it*, she ordered herself when she felt an inexplicable urge to burst into tears. She guessed it was shock that had made her feel helpless and unable to do anything other than slump on a chair.

Within a few minutes Jarek had got a fire going, and the orange flames threw out a cheery glow in the dark hut. He lit the kerosene lamp that was on the table and light flickered over the hard angles of his face as he drew Holly to her feet and tugged the zip of her jacket down.

Pain ricocheted through her shoulder when he began to pull her jacket off. '*Ow!* I'll have to leave my jacket on. It hurts too much to take it off.'

'Your body won't warm up while you're wearing wet clothes,' he said firmly. 'Let's get this over with. And then I've got some painkillers in my pack that you can take.'

He tugged off her boots and socks, and before Holly could argue had pulled down her salopettes and helped her to step out of them. Next he unzipped the thermal fleece she wore beneath her jacket. Her base layer was a sports vest which had an inbuilt support bra, and that too was damp from the snow that had got into her jacket and seeped through the layers of clothes to her skin.

Jarek hooked his fingers into the waistband of her thermal leggings and tugged them over her hips and down her legs.

'I'll keep my top on,' Holly said quickly when he moved his hands to the hem of her vest. She felt self-conscious as it was, standing in front of him in her knickers. And the knowledge that she was not wearing a bra brought a flush to her cheeks that had nothing to do with the heat from the fire.

'It's wet, so it comes off.'

He ignored her attempt to slap his hands away and tugged her top up and over her head.

'I don't know why you are acting so shy,' he said when she crossed her arms over her bare breasts and tried to stifle the gasp of pain caused by sudden movement.

Holly reassured herself that her nipples were as hard as pebbles because she was *cold*, and not because of the hot gleam in Jarek's eyes.

'I saw your breasts when you came to my room last night, and very pretty they are, too,' he drawled. 'But you can put this on to protect your modesty.' He handed her a shirt that he had taken out of his backpack. 'Do you want me to help you put it on?'

'I want you to go to hell,' she told him, anger and embarrassment overriding the pain in her shoulder for a moment as she turned away from him and pulled the shirt on, before fastening the buttons over her breasts.

Jarek's shirt was much too big for her, and came down to her mid-thighs, but although her body was mostly covered Holly was very aware that she was nearly naked beneath the shirt, and trapped in an isolated mountain shelter with the sexiest man on the planet.

His mocking grin infuriated her even more. 'Your temper is back so you must be feeling better, angel-face.'

'I wish you wouldn't call me that,' she snapped, hating the way her heart flipped when he pushed his hair back from his face, drawing her attention to the chiselled beauty of his hard features.

He was so tall that his head almost brushed against the roof of the hut, and his mane of thick blond hair and the darker blond stubble on his jaw added to Holly's impression of him as a Viking invader who was a dangerous threat to her heart.

'But it's true…' His tone was suddenly serious. 'You have the face of an angel.' He moved away to the far end of the hut and murmured, just loud enough for Holly to hear him, 'Not to mention a body that would tempt a saint.'

CHAPTER SEVEN

HOLLY JERKED HER eyes away from Jarek as he began to strip off his ski jacket and salopettes. She knelt in front of the fire, and when he joined her a few minutes later she silently cursed her accelerated heart-rate when she saw he had changed into a pair of sweatpants that sat low on his hips. She guessed he had only brought one spare shirt, which she was wearing. In the firelight the whorls of hair that covered his chest and arrowed down over his flat stomach were pure gold.

He dumped a pile of blankets on the floor. 'I found these in a storage box. We'll stay close to the fire and keep it burning through the night. You'll soon warm up,' he assured her, wrapping a blanket around her.'

He moved away to the kitchen and a short while later came back and handed her a steaming mug of hot chocolate.

Holly stared at him. 'How on earth…?'

'I brought packets of instant chocolate powder in my backpack, as well as bottled water which I boiled on the stove,' he explained. He gave her a foil blister-pack of pills. 'These are just non-prescription painkillers, but they might help dull the pain in your shoulder. As soon as we get off the mountain tomorrow you'll need to have it X-rayed.'

Jarek dropped down to sit on the floor beside her and

put another log on the fire. They sipped their drinks in an oddly companionable silence. Holly felt relieved, and grateful to be safe after her terror in the avalanche. The overly sweet hot chocolate tasted better than anything she had ever drunk, and sitting in front of the fire, she was finally starting to feel warm again.

It was a novelty to have someone take care of her, she mused. She had moved away from her family when she was eighteen and she valued her independence—especially since Stuart had ended his relationship with her when she'd told him she could not give him a child. She'd had to accept that she might always be alone and had told herself she was fine with that. Today on the mountain she had felt more vulnerable than she had ever felt in her life, but she hadn't doubted that she could rely on Jarek to save her. Once again he had shown her a different side to him than the careless playboy image portrayed by the tabloids.

He had been her client for a week, but she was still no closer to working out who was the real Jarek, she though ruefully. She glanced at him and her heart gave a jolt when she found him watching her, with an unholy gleam in his bright blue eyes that evoked a different kind of heat deep inside her. The firelight danced over his naked torso, high-lighting his taut abdominal muscles and gilding his broad shoulders.

Their eyes met…held…and the atmosphere inside the hut altered subtly from cosy to something far more dangerous.

Holly heard herself swallow and quickly looked away from him. 'You make a good fire,' she murmured, searching for something to say. 'Were you a boy scout? I can't imagine where else you would have learned your impressive survival skills.'

'No, I don't suppose you, or anyone who has not lived

through a war, can imagine what it's like to hear the constant noise of mortar fire and wonder if the next bombardment will strike what is left of the building you're sheltering in,' he said, somewhat drily.

She bit her lip. 'That was thoughtless of me. Of course you weren't a boy scout. You didn't have a chance to enjoy normal childhood activities growing up in Sarajevo.'

Jarek raked his hand through his hair and stared at the flames leaping around the logs. 'I was taught how to build a fire by the soldiers who were defending the city. I got friendly with some of them, and I would run messages along the frontline because I was small enough to avoid being noticed by the attacking troops.' He shrugged. 'The enemy snipers took no notice of a half-starved nine-year-old boy. When the orphanage was bombed I used whatever I could find—chair legs and bits of broken door—to make a fire to keep the younger children warm. My survival skills were learned out of necessity.'

'I'm sorry I said I wanted you to go to hell,' Holly said in a low tone. 'You spent your childhood there, didn't you?'

She pictured Jarek as a young boy, struggling to survive and take care of his baby sister and the other orphaned children who had been innocent victims of a brutal war.

'I haven't thanked you for saving my life,' she whispered. 'I dread to think what would have happened to me if I had been on my own when the avalanche struck.'

She flinched when he swore.

'You wouldn't have been on that part of the mountain if it wasn't for my bloody irresponsible decision to take you skiing off-piste,' he said savagely. 'It is entirely my fault that you are hurt and having to spend the night in an emergency shelter.'

'It was my *choice* to ski off-piste,' Holly insisted. 'Far from being irresponsible, you knew the location of the hut before we set out and you were well prepared for an emergency.'

He gave a bitter laugh. 'Don't try and make me out as a hero. Ralph was right when he accused me of having a destructive streak. I ruin lives and I destroy everything that is good—including Lorna.' His voice dropped to a raw growl, as if he was in pain. 'Especially Mama...'

'Who is Ralph?' Holly asked quietly.

'Ralph Saunderson was my adoptive father. He and his wife Lorna rescued my sister and me from the orphanage in Sarajevo.' He grimaced. 'I don't think Ralph particularly enjoyed fatherhood. He didn't care for his own son, much less me—a feral boy with a chip on his shoulder and an aversion to authority. But Lorna was a wonderful mother to Elin and me. It broke my sister's heart when Mama died.'

Jarek dropped his head into his hands.

'It was my fault. I was responsible for my adoptive mother's death as much as if I had fired the shot that killed her. I didn't need that bloody journalist to point out the fact to me,' he muttered.'

Holly frowned. 'Are you referring to the journalist you assaulted at a press conference, after you were involved in that crash during a motorbike race?'

'The journalist accused me of riding recklessly and endangering the safety of the other competitors in the race—which wasn't true...the race stewards had no concerns about how I'd ridden. But the press love to stir up trouble, and that journalist dug up the story from four years ago about Lorna's death. I lost my temper because I couldn't bear to be reminded of what I'd done,' he admitted heavily.

'What did you do?' she asked softly.

She wanted to reach out and put her hand on Jarek's hunched shoulders, somehow magic away the pain that she had heard in his voice. He seemed so alone, and with a flash of insight she realised that his party-loving play-boy image in the press was a façade he used to hide his tormented soul.

He gave a heavy sigh, as if he was worn down by the burden he had carried for so long. 'It was Mama's birth-day, and Elin and I had taken her to a jeweller's so that she could choose a gift.' His voice was a harsh scrape of sound. 'We were the only customers in the shop when a man walked in and pulled out a pistol. He ordered me, my sister and the shop assistant to lie down on the floor, and he aimed the gun at Lorna while he grabbed jewellery from the display cases.'

Jarek's jaw clenched.

'I could tell the guy was nervous. When he dragged Lorna towards the door I guessed he intended to take her with him as a hostage. She was terrified, and crying, and the gunman was shouting at her to shut up. In the confu-sion I seized my chance and managed to rugby tackle him to the floor. But before I could grab the gun he pulled the trigger. The bullet went straight through Mama's heart, killing her instantly.'

'Jarek, it wasn't your fault.'

Holly's heart splintered when she saw a tear slip down his cheek. The firelight flickered over the angles and planes of his face, where the skin was stretched taut and his mouth was so grim that it was hard to imagine his trademark sexy grin. He never smiled with his eyes, she realised.

He did not seem to have heard her. 'My recklessness killed her,' he rasped, as if he had swallowed glass. 'The soldiers in Sarajevo had a motto: *Shoot first or be shot*. But I didn't have a gun, and my decision to tackle an armed robber was crassly irresponsible.'

'I believe you acted instinctively to protect your adoptive mother.' she said gently. 'As a young boy you had protected your sister from the dangers of war. Childhood experiences frequently affect our behaviour as adults, and your determination to take care of people in need of help was programmed into you when you were nine years old.'

He turned his head towards her and she wanted to weep when she saw the torment that dulled his blue eyes, and the flash of vulnerability that flickered on his face before he let his hair fall forward to hide his expression.

'Lorna died as a result of an unforgivable act, but *you* did not fire the gun that ended her life and *you* were in no way to blame,' Holly told him fiercely.

She reached out and placed her hand on his forearm, hoping the physical contact would in some small way ease the loneliness that she sensed never left him. She guessed that this was the first time he had ever spoken about his guilty feelings over his adoptive mother's death.

'The only life you are careless with is your own. You must have known that the armed man who robbed the jewellery shop could have aimed his gun at you, but that didn't stop you trying your best to protect Lorna.' She bit her lip. 'I wish you could see what I see. You are a brave and good man, Jarek.'

'If that is really what you see then I suggest you need your eyesight tested,' he said mockingly, but there was a note almost of desperation in his voice as he picked up her hand and threaded his fingers through hers.

Holly sensed that he wanted to believe her, but he couldn't allow himself to do so because he was convinced there could be no redemption for him.

'I wish I had followed my instincts when I arrived at the Frieden Clinic. You knocked me senseless with your beautiful smile, before announcing that you were my psychotherapist and we would be living together for six weeks,' he said harshly. 'For your safety and my sanity I should have jumped back onto my motorbike and ridden far away from you.'

'I'm glad you didn't,' she whispered.

In a distant corner of her mind Holly was aware that the painkillers had done their job, and when she moved she felt only a twinge instead of the agonising sensation of a red-hot poker being thrust into her shoulder.

She assured herself that all she wanted to do was offer Jarek comfort as she knelt in front of him and placed her hands on either side of his face. But even that small contact between their bodies created an electrical current that shot through her, and she could not restrain a soft gasp as heat unfurled low in her belly.

His bright blue eyes glittered as hard as diamonds. 'You're playing with fire, angel-face,' he said, in an oddly thick voice. 'You would be safer outside on the mountain than in here with me. There are things you don't know about me. Secrets I don't even know about myself.'

His beautiful mouth twisted.

'A long time ago I think I did something so terrible that my mind has blocked out my memories. You told me that *is* possible,' he growled, when she traced her fingertips over the rough stubble on his jaw. 'For all either of us know I could be a monster...I don't know...a murderer.' He glared at her when she didn't cower away from him. 'I don't know *what* I am,' he said grimly, 'but I do know that I'm no good for you.'

It occurred to Holly then that Jarek was trying to protect her from himself, as if he really *did* believe he was a monster, and her heart ached for him.

'I do think something bad happened to you when you were a child, but I don't believe for one second that you are a bad person. Besides,' she murmured in a deliberately lighter voice, 'I'm not suggesting that we align our diaries for the next few months.'

His eyes narrowed when she quoted the exact same words he had said to her after that explosive kiss in his bedroom at Chalet Soline. She sensed that some of his fierce tension had left him, and his mouth crooked in a lazy smile that made her tremble almost as much as the feral gleam in his eyes.

'What are you suggesting, then?' he drawled, all arrogant male confidence once more.

On one level Holly wondered what on earth she was doing. Perhaps her close brush with death on the mountain was the reason for the wildness that filled her, and made her wonder how she had resisted him until now.

'This,' she whispered against his lips, before she covered his mouth with hers.

He went very still, and her stomach plummeted when she thought he was going to push her away. But then he made a noise in his throat—a low growl of hunger that connected directly to the molten core of her femininity. His arms closed around her like steel bars and he sank his fingers into her hair at the same time as he thrust his tongue into her mouth and took command of a kiss that quickly became a ravishment of her senses.

He should bring an end to this right now, Jarek told himself. Before the feel of Holly's lips pressed against his became an addiction he would never be able to break. But the sweet ardency of her kiss and—dear God—her *generosity* evoked something inside him that he had never felt with any other woman. *'I don't believe you are a bad person,'* she had said, in stark contrast to everyone else throughout his life, who had said the opposite. Not his sister, of course, but Elin's loyalty made her blind to his faults. Even

Mama had been fond of him *despite* his flaws, as if he was a challenge or a penance.

No one apart from Holly had ever suggested that he might be any good. But unfortunately she was wrong. If there was any shred of goodness in him then he would *not* tumble her down onto the pile of blankets in front of the fire and stretch out beside her. He would *not* cradle her jaw in his palm and kiss her with unrestrained hunger. And he would *not* take such delight in her soft sigh of surrender when he unbuttoned the shirt he had lent her and played with her breasts.

Her nipples puckered in anticipation of his touch, and she gave a thin cry when he traced moist circles around one aureole with his tongue before drawing the hard nub at its centre into his mouth and sucking—hard. The greedy sounds she made became ever more frantic when he transferred his mouth to her other breast, and because he was bad he took fierce pleasure in the way her hips jerked off the floor in an invitation he had no intention of declining.

The firelight flickered over her body and Jarek followed the path of the flames with his tongue to explore every delicious dip and curve...the smooth slopes of her breasts, the indentation of her waist, and down, down to taste the silken skin of her inner thighs. He laughed softly at the muffled sound she made—half-protest, half-plea— when he hooked his fingers into her panties and tugged them down her legs.

She was so sweetly responsive that it made him ache deep in his gut. And he was so hard. *Sweet heaven*, he was more turned on than he could ever remember being. He wanted to pull her beneath him and sink between her milky-white thighs, drive his rock-solid shaft into her slick heat and glory in the fiery passion that had simmered between them for what seemed like an eternity, but in fact was only one week. Six weeks with this woman would kill him, Jarek thought wryly. Worse still, he might be tempted to tell Holly what he saw in his nightmares, and then she would know for sure that there was nothing good about him.

But he would not have months or weeks or even any more days with her. She could not save him, however much she believed that therapy would help him. Jarek knew he must walk away from her before he destroyed her, as he had almost done today on the mountain, and just as he had destroyed Mama. There was only this one night, and he was arrogant enough to want her, even as mindless with desire as he was.

But this wasn't about him. Tonight was all about Holly.

He felt a tremor run through her when he dipped his tongue into her navel and then pressed soft kisses over her stomach. But when he pushed her legs apart and knelt between her thighs she stiffened.

'You can't…'

Her shocked whisper was barely audible, and he grinned at her before he bent his head.

'Oh, yes, I can, angel-face,' he assured her thickly.

His nostrils flared as he caught the sweet scent of her arousal and he could not wait any longer. He slid his hands beneath her bottom and lifted her towards him, holding her at just the right angle. He had never seen a more beautiful sight than her splayed open before him. With a growl of satisfaction he set about his appointed task, and with his tongue bestowed the most intimate caress of all.

She made a startled sound, as if what he was doing to her was new, and her fingers gripped his hair. When he placed his mouth over the tight little nub of her clitoris she gave a sharp cry as she shattered around him.

Jarek didn't know how he found the strength of will to

ignore the thunderous drumbeat of his own desire—especially when Holly tried to slide her hand beneath the waistband of his sweatpants. But she had been shocked and scared in the aftermath of the avalanche, and he knew that if he took advantage of her vulnerability he would hate himself even more than he already did.

He hadn't finished with her yet, though, and while she was still panting and gasping from her first orgasm he pressed his mouth against her riotous heat once more and took possession of her with a mastery that had her sobbing his name as she climaxed again.

Afterwards he drew her trembling body against him and held her against his chest—against the heart that ached dully as she fell asleep in his arms and he watched over her for the rest of the night to keep her safe.

The cold woke her. Holly opened her eyes and felt disorientated for a few seconds, before she remembered that she had spent the night in an emergency shelter halfway up a mountain. A shaft of bright light came into the hut through the one small window, and she registered that the fire had gone out and there was no sign of Jarek.

Memories rushed into her mind, followed swiftly by self-recrimination.

What had she done?

More pertinently, what had she allowed *Jarek* to do?

She turned her head slowly, expecting to see him at the far end of the hut. The sight of her knickers on the floor next to her was a reminder of just how bad the situation was, but in case she was in any doubt images flashed into her head of her sprawled on the floor, with her legs wide apart and Jarek on his knees, holding her thighs firmly open with his hands as he leaned forward and put his mouth *there*, right at her feminine core.

Worse than the erotic images in her mind was the accompanying soundtrack: her pants and gasps culminating in the keening cry that had been torn from her when he'd made her come—*twice*. And his laughter…deep and husky…the memory of it even now brought her skin out in goosebumps that had nothing to do with the bitterly cold temperature inside the hut.

She briefly debated if it would have been preferable to have been swept to her doom by the avalanche than to be lying here facing humiliation and dismissal from her job. The knowledge that her behaviour had been unprofessional, to say the least, prompted her to get up from the floor—but she quickly discovered that the effects of the painkillers had worn off and a sickening bolt of pain throbbed in her shoulder.

It was imperative for what remained of her dignity that she put her knickers back on before she faced Jarek and so, gritting her teeth, she forced herself to bend down and pick them up. She had just managed to pull them on and struggle into her salopettes when the door of the hut opened and he walked in.

'Good—you're awake,' he said coolly, with no hint in his voice of the sensual lover from the previous night.

Holly's fragile hope that he would sweep her into his arms withered and died. He was dressed in his ski clothes and his eyes were hidden behind designer shades. With his just-got-out-of-bed blond hair falling over his collar he looked like one of the beautiful people who flocked to St Moritz or Klosters.

A sense of hopelessness swept over Holly as she acknowledged that she was not a glamorous socialite or an A-list female celebrity, like the women Jarek was used to. His cavalier attitude this morning made her think he had made love to her simply because they had been stranded on the mountain and he'd probably been bored.

But their enforced proximity had not been the only reason, a nasty little voice in her head taunted her. She had thrown herself at him with all the finesse of a gauche teenager. It was likely that he had kissed her out of politeness, because he hadn't wanted to embarrass her by rejecting her clumsy overtures. If he had really desired her then surely he would have wanted to have full-blown sex with her?

Thank heaven he hadn't tried to, she thought, going hot and then cold as she imagined how humiliating it would have been if she'd had to explain that she was different from other women. Flawed.

'The helicopter is on its way.'

His brisk voice jerked her from her painful thoughts.

'Can you manage to put your jacket on if I help you?'

She remembered how tenderly he had taken care of her when he had carried her to the shelter. Clearly she had misconstrued his attentiveness and taken it as a sign that he felt something for her.

'I think you've done enough,' she said curtly, glad of the hot flare of temper to replace the mortification that bit deep into her soul.

'I didn't hear you object last night,' he drawled, and his softly mocking tone made her long to sink through the floor.

She wished she could see the expression in his eyes, which were hidden behind his sunglasses. She felt exposed and, worse, she felt foolish for wanting him to claim her mouth with his and brand her with the hungry passion that had devoured them both—or so she had believed.

She had made a fool of herself, Holly thought miserably.

The *whump, whump* of a helicopter's rotor blades was a welcome distraction. Jarek moved towards her and seemed about to say something, but just then a paramedic walked into the hut and started questioning Holly about the injury she had received. While she explained about the pain in her shoulder, and then insisted that she could walk and did not need to be carried on a stretcher, Jarek stepped outside.

The paramedic wrapped a foil blanket around her to raise her body temperature and helped her walk across the snow to the waiting helicopter. It was only when she was strapped into a seat and the helicopter was about to take off that she panicked, realising Jarek was not on board.

'Your friend decided to ski down the mountain,' the paramedic explained. 'We'll fly you straight to the hospital. Try not to worry—you are safe now.'

Holly wasn't worried for herself, but she *was* concerned about Jarek. Last night had been the first time he had opened up to her and revealed his guilt over his adoptive mother's death. She was convinced he would find counselling beneficial, but *she* could no longer be his psychotherapist. Not after she had behaved like a slut and allowed him to take shocking liberties with her body.

She winced as she pictured herself naked in front of the fire, her principles abandoned and her legs spread wide. Her sense of honour demanded she must tell Professor Heppel that she could not continue in her role as Jarek's counsellor because of a conflict of interest.

Several hours later a hospital doctor studied an X-ray of Holly's shoulder and confirmed that it wasn't broken, merely sprained and badly bruised from the impact of the avalanche. She was given strong painkillers and advised to rest her shoulder as much as possible for the next few days.

She knew she had escaped lightly, and Professor Heppel expressed the same opinion after Gunther had collected her from the hospital and driven her to Chalet Soline.

Holly had expected Jarek to be at the chalet, and her heart sank when Professor Heppel told her that he had checked out of the Frieden Clinic.

'Obviously I will resign immediately,' she said stiffly, thinking it would be marginally less embarrassing to leave of her own accord than to be fired for professional mis-conduct.

The clinic's director looked puzzled. 'Why do you wish to resign? Mr Dvorska gave an excellent report on how you had helped him in the brief time he was here. He has cut short his stay at the clinic because he heard this morning that his sister has given birth to her baby—several weeks early. I understand that there were complications with the birth and Jarek has gone to England to be with his sister.'

Holly's relief that Jarek had not made a complaint about her inappropriate conduct was short-lived as she prayed that Elin and her baby were both all right. His concern for his sister might explain why he had been so off-hand with her at the hut, she brooded. He would have been impatient to get off the mountain, and understandably his thoughts would have been focused on Elin.

For the next few days she was virtually housebound, while her injured shoulder gradually healed, and with time on her hands she found her thoughts centred on Jarek, and the notion that he had been distracted by worry for his sister rather than deliberately dismissive of the scorching passion they had shared. When she had knelt in front of him and kissed him he might have rejected her. But he had kissed her with a fierce intensity, as if he had been lost in a desert and had suddenly stumbled on an oasis where he could assuage his thirst.

The idea that he had responded to her out of a gentle-manly desire to save her from embarrassment just didn't fit. She was thirty-one, and although she did not have a long list of previous lovers she was experienced enough to recognise white-hot lust. Jarek's erection had been as hard as a spike beneath his sweatpants, so he couldn't have been pretending to desire her. It had been the real thing.

His mobile phone number was in his file. Holly reminded herself that it was not unusual for a therapist to call an ex-patient for a follow-up report after they had left the clinic, but her hands shook as she entered his number on her phone.

He answered on the third ring, and his sexy, smoky voice curled around her like a caress. She grimaced when she felt her nipples tighten. If he could have such a strong effect on her when he was a thousand miles away, God help her if he asked to see her again.

'Hi, Jarek, it's me…um…' She flushed, 'I mean Dr Maitland…from the Frieden Clinic.'

'I'm perfectly aware of who you are, Holly,' he drawled, sounding amused, and she just *knew* that he knew that her face was scarlet.

She cleared her throat. 'I called to ask how your sister and her baby are. I mean… I hope they are okay.'

She sensed his surprise and wished she'd listened to her common sense, which had urged her not to phone him.

'Mother and baby are both fine now. Elin had a health scare in the late stages of her pregnancy and her daughter had to be delivered by Caesarean section a month early. Rosalie is tiny but healthy, my sister is over the moon and my brother-in-law is besotted with the two females in his life,' Jarek said drily.

'I'm glad.' She hesitated. 'I want to apologise for snapping at you in the morning…after we had spent the night in the emergency shelter. I thought you regretted what had happened between us. But then I heard from Professor Heppel that you had rushed away to be with your sister.'

Jarek's silence on the other end of the line wasn't encouraging, but Holly ploughed on.

'I was hoping to persuade you to continue your course of treatment with another psychotherapist. Clearly I cannot be your therapist due to our personal relationship—'

'I hardly think that one night together constitutes a *relationship*,' he interrupted curtly. 'I told you—I don't have relationships. What happened between us in the hut was a mistake brought about by an excess of adrenalin after we had survived the avalanche.'

Ow!

Holly gripped her phone tighter and told herself to end the call now—this second. But she must have a masochistic streak, because she muttered, 'An excess of adrenalin? Really? Most people would call what we both felt...*feel*... desire.'

'Look, Holly—' he sounded impatient '—we had a good time together but it wasn't memorable—at least not for me. I suggest you forget me. You're a nice girl, and you deserve to meet a great guy who will fall in love with you.'

This was worse than *ow*! It was excruciatingly embarrassing. Holly wanted to die a thousand deaths, but pride forced her to say lightly, 'I'm thirty-one. By no stretch of the imagination could I be described as a "girl". I'm sorry I made the mistake of believing that beneath your playboy image there was a man of substance.' And then, because she was innately truthful, she said quietly, 'As a matter of fact I *still* believe you are a better man than you think, and I urge you to engage a counsellor to help you face up to your past.'

She ended the call before he could say anything else she did not want to hear. The knowledge that her humiliation was self-induced, because against her better judgement she had phoned him, only made her feel worse. She wanted to burst into tears. Instead she gave in to the childish urge to throw her phone across the room and heard a satisfying thud as it hit the wall.

CHAPTER EIGHT

JAREK CRADLED HIS phone in his hand long after it had gone silent, as if holding it would somehow prolong his contact with Holly. He knew he would not hear from her again—which had been his intention when he'd rejected her so cruelly. Right from the start he had wanted to protect her from his destructive nature, but he'd been able to tell from the huskiness in her voice that he had hurt her—and not only her pride.

Yet despite her obvious embarrassment she had told him she still believed in him, thought that he was a better man than he knew himself to be. He wished it was true, but he was afraid that the dark shadows in his mind hid even darker secrets.

It was why he had left Austria and flown to London immediately after he'd skied down the mountain where he had so nearly been responsible for another tragic death. He went cold when he thought of how easily Holly could have been swept away by the avalanche. He'd checked out of the Frieden Clinic because he did not want her to discover that her faith in him had been misplaced.

He turned away from the window and the uninspiring view of a bleak winter sky and the bare skeletons of the trees. February in England was his least favourite time of the year. In another month or two the Cuckmere Hall estate on the South Downs would begin to look green, rather than grey and dead, and Elin would no longer be fretting about frost damaging the new shoots in the estate's vineyards.

Although at the moment his sister was too enamoured of her brand-new baby daughter to have time to worry about Saunderson's Wines, Jarek mused.

He had never shared Elin's interest in the winery that Lorna Saunderson had established. But Elin's husband Cortez was a world-renowned vintner, and the sparkling wine now produced on the estate had won several prestigious awards.

Jarek looked across the room to where his sister and brother-in-law were sitting close together on the sofa. Elin was cradling baby Rosalie and Cortez was bouncing their two-year-old son Harry on his knee. They were the perfect family, and Jarek certainly did not begrudge them their obvious happiness. Despite a rocky start he and Cortez had become friends, and he was always made to feel welcome at Cuckmere Hall. But he had never felt that he belonged at the gothic mansion he had once expected to inherit from Ralph Saunderson. And anyway Ralph had chosen his illegitimate son to be his heir, rather than the adopted son he had accused of being reckless.

Moodily, Jarek walked over to the fireplace, where a cheery fire burned in the grate. Under Cortez's supervision Cuckmere Hall had been transformed from a draughty old house to a stylish and comfortable home. But it wasn't Jarek's home any more than his starkly minimalist penthouse in London or the various other properties he owned around the world felt like home.

An image flashed into his mind of a big, bright room. Sunlight streamed in through the windows and there was a wooden rocking horse—white, with a red harness. He heard a child laughing, and with a jolt of shock he realised that the child was *him*. He couldn't have been at the orphanage, he realised, because he did not remember ever laughing there. He sensed that the room he could visualise was a nursery, and knew without knowing *how* he knew that he had felt safe there, and—his heart gave a lurch— *loved*. Was the vague figure in his mind whose face he could not quite see his *mother*?

'I saw Baines carrying your suitcase downstairs.'

Elin's voice jerked him back to the present, and to his bitter frustration the images in his head disappeared like smoke drifting up the chimney.

'Are you going back to the clinic in Austria?'

'No.' He felt a stab of guilt at his sister's concerned expression.

'How did you get on with Dr Maitland? She sounded nice when I spoke to her.' Elin gave him a close look. Is she pretty?' she asked mischievously.

He pictured Holly lying in front of the fire, with her silky brown hair spread around her shoulders and her naked body so unutterably beautiful that he had sunk to his knees and worshipped her.

'Pretty enough, I suppose,' he said dismissively. 'But I prefer fun-loving blondes to serious brunettes.'

Or that had been true in the past—before he had met his beautiful psychotherapist, he brooded.

'I'm going to Vostov,' he said abruptly, steering the conversation away from Holly.

'The principality has been in the news recently,' Cortez commented. 'Rumours abound that the ruling family of the House of Karadjvic may have been murdered during the conflict in the Balkans in the early nineteen-nineties. And there is another rumour that the royal children might have survived.'

'But those children would be adults now—surely they'd know if they were royalty,' Elin said.

Cortez shrugged. 'Perhaps they were too young at the time for them to remember.' He glanced at Jarek. 'Are you thinking of investing in Vostov? The low business taxes there have enabled the principality to establish a thriving economy.'

'I've arranged to meet someone to discuss various things,' Jarek said noncommittally.

If he told Elin of his crazy suspicion that their parents had been a prince and princess she would insist that he sought help from a psychiatrist. He could not tell anyone the real reason for his trip to Vostov was so that he could meet Asmir Sunjic.

Jarek was certain the old man's story was an elaborate hoax. But his nightmares were becoming more frequent and troubling, and he was determined to find out the truth about his past.

Twenty-four hours later Jarek rode the motorbike he had hired along a twisting mountain road in Vostov, on his way to a remote village. The landscape of tall pine trees and snow-capped mountains was similar to Alpine countries, which might explain why it seemed familiar. Harder to explain was the sense of belonging he'd felt the moment his private jet had landed at a small airfield. He had not wanted to draw attention to his visit by arriving at the principality's main airport.

He was sure he recognised the style of the traditional grey stone houses with steeply sloping tin roofs as he rode into the village. Some of the villagers came out to stare at him as he knocked on the door of a house. An elderly woman ushered him inside. She spoke in a language that sounded similar to Bosnian and Jarek guessed was Vostovian. He was startled to find that he understood some of the woman's words, but then his attention swung to the old man who slowly rose out of a chair next to the fire.

Time had left its mark on the man's features, but Jarek knew he had seen him before—a long time ago—and pain ripped through him as if he had been shot through his heart.

From the air, the tiny island of Paradis sur Terre looked like an emerald jewel set amid a cerulean sea. As the helicopter descended Holly saw that most of the island was covered in dense green forest and surrounded by pure white sandy beaches. Even the name which, translated from the French, meant Heaven on Earth, was a perfect description of the privately owned island in the Indian Ocean.

It was a pity there was a serpent in paradise.

Her stomach muscles tightened as the helicopter swooped low over the one building on the island— a charming colonial-style house with direct access onto the beach. A wooden jetty ran from the beach out over the crystal-clear sea, and at the far end of the jetty stood a blond-haired Viking.

Holly's heart gave a jolt when she caught sight of Jarek, and she almost asked the pilot to fly her back to the international airport in the Seychelles capital city of Victoria. She must have been mad to agree to his request to see him again, let alone fly halfway round the world to meet him, she thought for the hundredth time. Although Jarek had not so much requested as *demanded* that she be on the private jet he had sent to Austria to bring her to the Seychelles.

Her mind flew back forty-eight hours, to when she'd answered her phone without first glancing at the screen to check the name of the caller. The sound of Jarek's voice had nearly made her drop her phone which was still held together with tape after their last conversation three weeks ago had resulted in her hurling the handset at the wall.

'I've decided to take your advice and carry on with therapy,' Jarek had told her, ignoring any conventional greeting like *Hello, how are you?* Although even if he had asked she would have rather died than admit that she felt sick with misery and had lost her enthusiasm for life since he had left Austria.

'I think your decision is sensible.' She had been pleased that she sounded cool and calm when her heart had been pounding. 'All the clinical staff here at the Frieden Clinic are highly qualified to help you. I'll check with Professor Heppel to see which of them is available to give you counselling.'

'I don't want a different psychotherapist. I want you.'

Jarek's smoky voice had wreaked havoc with Holly's equilibrium. Just when she had been making progress in forgetting him, she'd thought, but had known she was fooling herself.

'I'm afraid that's not possible. My schedule is full and I will be working with other patients,' she'd told him crisply.

'Your other patients might change their mind and decide not to seek treatment from you if they hear about how you behaved so unprofessionally with me. Social media is *very* useful for spreading rumours,' he'd drawled. 'And when Professor Heppel reads my report concerning certain aspects of my experience as a patient at his clinic—which I will email to him if you refuse to see me—you may even find yourself out of a job.'

She'd felt sick 'You wouldn't do that.'

'I told you—I don't play fair, angel-face.'

'As a matter of fact, blackmail is illegal,' she'd said tersely.

'I admit I might have embellished a few details about the night we spent together in that mountain hut…'

Beneath his amused tone Holly had heard quiet determination and had felt her heart sink.

'Jarek…you must see that I can't be your psychotherapist,' she'd argued desperately. 'It wouldn't be right—'

'You are the only person I trust,' he had interrupted her harshly. And then, even more shockingly, 'I need you, Holly. I have to talk to you.'

Fool that she was, she had felt her heart melt at the rawness in his voice. The outrageous attempt to coerce her into agreeing to visit him on his remote island hideaway had struck her as strange behaviour from the feckless playboy he was portrayed as being in the tabloids. But Holly knew that behind his public image Jarek had integrity and compassion. He'd said he trusted her, and she could not allow her pride to prevent her from helping him deal with his demons.

The helicopter landed on a green lawn in front of the house, and Holly was greeted by a cheerful man in a white uniform who introduced himself as the butler, Rani.

'I'll take your case up to the house, Dr Maitland. Mr Dvorska is waiting for you on the beach,' Rani told her.

She soon discovered that walking on soft sand in kitten-heel shoes was no easy task. The late-afternoon sun was blazing in a cloudless azure sky, and by the time she stepped onto the jetty Holly felt hot and was tempted to take off her jacket. But she could not risk her body betraying her as she walked towards Jarek. Her grey wool suit and crisp white blouse were her armour against his potency.

He must have heard her heels tapping on the wooden boards because he turned around. Holly's footsteps faltered. She had thought about him constantly in the past weeks, but he was even more breathtaking than her memories of him.

He was wearing a pair of faded denim shorts that sat low on his hips. His chest was bare and his dark golden tan suggested that he had spent much of the past three weeks in the sun. Holly's eyes roamed over his flat stomach and the defined ridges of his impressive six-pack. Lifting her gaze higher to his face, she noted there was at least three days' growth of stubble on his jaw, and the too-long hair that he was pushing off his brow had been bleached even blonder by the sun.

His wide mouth crooked in a sexy smile, but his ice-blue eyes were as hard as diamonds and revealed nothing of his thoughts.

'Hello, Holly,' he murmured, in the gravelly voice that she had heard countless times in her dreams.

She felt a rush of heat to her breasts, and was conscious of the tendrils of sweat-damp hair that clung to her flushed cheeks. 'It's so hot!' she burst out, desperate to fill the awkward silence and disguise the thunderous beat of her heart. 'The temperature was minus two when I left Austria.'

'Is that why you are dressed for arctic conditions?' he said drily. 'The daytime temperature in the Seychelles at this time of year rarely drops below thirty degrees, and the dress code is informal. Wear as little as you like.' His wicked grin made her catch her breath. 'I hope you packed your gold swimsuit.'

'Stop right there,' Holly told him firmly. She held up her hand, as if she could ward off his charisma. 'I know that flirting is as natural to you as breathing, but you don't have to switch on your fake charm with me because you've already established that I'm nice but unmemorable.'

Something flashed in his eyes. 'I'm sorry I hurt you,' he said roughly.

He stepped closer to her and she immediately backed away from him.

'I'm old enough to cope with rejection gracefully, and I'm sure I'll survive having my ego dented.' She shrugged. 'I was simply under the misapprehension that you liked me.'

'Of course I bloody well *like* you.' He took another step towards her and caught hold of her arm. 'The night we spent together in that mountain hut was amazing. It was—'

'It was a mistake,' Holly insisted. She looked at him steadily. ' I'm prepared to try to help you, but I won't be fobbed off with excuses or chase you around the island like I chased you up that mountain. You say you want to talk to me—so talk.'

He stared at her, clearly surprised by her refusal to be a push-over, and there was reluctant admiration in his voice when he spoke. 'You've had a long journey to get here. Come up to the house and I'll show you to your room. I'm sure you want to change into something cooler,' he said, eyeing her thick skirt and jacket. 'I guessed you wouldn't have had a chance to buy beachwear in Austria, so I took the liberty of buying a few summer clothes for you.'

He started to walk back along the jetty and Holly had no choice but to follow him.

'I've asked the chef to prepare an early dinner,' he said over his shoulder. 'We'll talk then.'

Twenty minutes later Holly felt refreshed after taking a shower. Her bedroom was delightfully cool, thanks to the ceiling fan that was positioned over the huge bed. Sliding glass doors opened onto a balcony where pots of white jasmine grew in profusion, filling the room with their delicate fragrance. From the balcony she could see a turquoise infinity pool that looked tempting—although

she had definitely *not* packed the frivolous gold swimsuit
Jarek had referred to.

What would he think of her sensible blue costume? she
wondered, and then reminded herself that she didn't care
about his opinion of her.

She rifled through her clothes, which the maid had un-
packed and hung in the wardrobe, and realised she would
swelter if she wore any of the smart business suits she had
brought to the island with her.

Hanging on the rail next to her own clothes were the
summer outfits that Jarek had provided: pretty dresses in
lightweight fabrics that would be far more comfortable to
wear in the heat. She would insist on paying for the clothes,
Holly assured herself as she slipped on an elegant wraparound dress of aquamarine silk. Luckily she had packed
a pair of flat ballet pumps that looked fine with the dress.

She had just caught her hair up in a loose knot on top
of her head when the maid came to escort her to lunch.

Jarek was waiting for her beneath a gazebo next to the
pool, where the butler was laying out a buffet-style meal
on the table. Everything was so vivid, Holly thought, looking at the bowls of colourful salads and an array of fresh
fruits. Bright pink hibiscus flowers covered the wooden
frame of the gazebo, and the early-evening sunshine dap-
pled everything in a mellow golden light.

'This is an incredible place,' she said as she sat down
and picked up the glass of sparkling water that Rani had
served her. She was curious to see that Jarek had opted
for fruit juice rather than wine.

'I haven't drunk alcohol or smoked a cigarette for
weeks,' he told her. 'Sex is the only vice left,' he said, and
grinned when she blushed.

Holly silently cursed her fair skin. 'I don't suppose
you've given up *that* particular vice—even though there

has been a notable absence of scandalous stories about your love-life in the tabloids recently. Perhaps you have decided to conduct your affairs with more discretion,' she said sweetly.

His smile faded and he seemed suddenly tense. 'I've been here on the island—alone apart from the staff. I flew here straight after I'd visited my sister and my new niece. Paradis sur Terre belongs to a friend of mine, and only he and you know my whereabouts.'

'Why the secrecy?' Holly frowned.

Jarek handed her a letter.

'Read it,' he urged her grimly.

Jarek was tempted to add a shot of rum to his pineapple juice. He had kept away from vodka since he'd left Austria, because every time he'd thought about having a drink he'd had the crazy idea that Holly would be disappointed with him. As if he *cared* about her opinion of him, he brooded. Right now he wanted to drink enough alcohol to render him unconscious, but he sipped his fruit juice and waited for Holly to finish reading Asmir Sunjic's astonishing letter.

He watched the sunlight slanting through the blinds on the gazebo spill over her hair, so that it gleamed in myriad shades from dark chocolate through to russet. Oddly, he felt calmer than he'd done in days—weeks. Three weeks, to be exact. Since he had checked out of the Frieden Clinic believing he would never see Holly again.

Now she was here in front of him, looking even more beautiful than he remembered. How he was managing to hold himself back from walking around the table and snatching her into his arms so that he could claim her mouth with his, as he had done a thousand times in his dreams, was beyond him.

She put the letter down on the table and stared at him, shock and disbelief in her dark eyes.

'I'm guessing from the stilted wording that English isn't this man Asmir Sunjic's first language, but the letter is clear enough. Is it some sort of joke? There can't be any truth in what he says, can there?' She shook her head. 'His story seems so fantastical.'

'That's what I thought at first, but now I don't know. Maybe his crazy story *is* true.'

Jarek pushed away his uneaten dinner before standing up and walking to the side of the gazebo overlooking the beach. The sea was sapphire-blue and the silver sand stretched into the distance. He wanted to run along the water's edge and shut his mind to everything but the rhythmic sound of the waves crashing onto the shore.

He had been running for most of his life, he thought.

He heard Holly move as she came to stand beside him, and his stomach clenched when he caught the drift of her perfume. Lilies, he thought, pure and sweet and yet subtly sensual as Holly was herself.

'Why do you think Asmir might be telling the truth?' she asked quietly.

'Because I went to Vostov to meet him *and I recognised him*,' he said harshly. 'I remembered him from my childhood—before I went to live at the orphanage.'

'My God…' she said in a shaken voice. 'I need to read the letter again. I couldn't take it all in the first time.'

'I'll save you the trouble.' Every word of the letter was imprinted on Jarek's brain. 'You may know that Vostov is a small principality in the Balkans, closely allied to Bosnia Herzegovina. Twenty-five years ago the principality was affected by the Bosnian war when it was invaded by Serbian forces. The commonly held belief is that Prince Goran attempted to take his wife, Princess Isidora, and their children, Prince Jarrett and the infant Princess Eliana, to safety in neighbouring Croatia. But the car they were travelling in crashed on a remote mountain pass and it was believed that the family were all killed.'

Holly nodded.

'But according to Asmir—who says he was Prince Goran's personal assistant—he managed to escape from the car with the two children before the car burst into flames with the other adults still inside. Asmir states that the royal family had been ambushed by the military forces who had invaded Vostov.'

Holly's brow furrowed.

'If I understood the letter correctly, Asmir says he hid the royal children at an orphanage in Sarajevo, where his sister worked. He thought that even if the military leaders who by then were in control of Vostov realised the children were alive, no one would be able to find them. That was why he changed Jarrett and Eliana's names to…'

She trailed off into a stunned silence.

'Jarek and Elin.' Jarek finished her sentence. 'Asmir forged documents stating that the children's surname was Dvorska, which was his mother's maiden name.'

'Do you remember being told to call yourself Jarek instead of Jarrett?'

'I don't remember *any* of the events Asmir described.' Jarek's jaw clenched. 'At least I have no *conscious* memories—but my nightmares make more sense now. I often dream about being in a car that is travelling fast. I can't picture who else is in the car, but I sense they are scared. I hear loud noises—which might be gunfire. I hear screams, but I don't know who is screaming. I think it might be me.'

Jarek thought of the intense fear he felt whenever he climbed into a car, and frustration surged through him.

'I wish I could damn well remember.'

'We can work on recovering your lost memories,' Holly said. 'The fact that you remember Asmir is encouraging, and with intensive therapy I'm hopeful we will uncover your past.'

She put her hand on his arm, and the gentle expression in her eyes made him want to howl like the child he must have once been—before his emotions had been blunted by the struggle to survive the war in Sarajevo and protect his baby sister.

'The timing of the events Asmir mentions fits,' Jarek said heavily. 'The orphanage was bombed and Asmir's sister was killed. When he couldn't find the royal children he assumed they had also died. But by that time my sister and I had been adopted by the Saundersons and taken to live in England. All the records of children who had lived at the orphanage were destroyed when the building caught fire.'

'Why did Asmir send you the letter if he thought you were dead?'

'He explained that for years he had felt guilty that he'd failed to protect the royal children and had told no one his story. But a year ago he saw my photograph in a newspaper and recognised me as the young boy he had smuggled out of Vostov all those years ago.'

'It's incredible…' Holly's eyes were as round as buttons. 'If Asmir's story is true it means that you are…a *prince*.'

Jarek laughed bitterly. '"Incredible" is right. But even if the story is true, I'm no prince. Vostov's National Council asked me to have a DNA test to prove if I am a descendant of the House of Karadjvic.'

'So…did the test show that you *are*, in fact, Prince Jarrett?'

'I declined to have the DNA test.'

Jarek felt Holly's eyes search his face, but he could not bring himself to look at her.

'I don't understand,' she said slowly. 'You have always wanted to uncover your past and the DNA test would be a start. At the moment you don't even know *who* you are.'

He moved restlessly. 'Until Asmir saw my photograph in the newspaper he and everyone else believed that Vostov's royal family were all dead. What good will it do to dig up the past? Prince Jarrett doesn't exist, and Jarek Dvorska is no good. It's *true*,' he said roughly, when Holly shook her head. 'Ralph Saunderson was right when he called me destructive. I was responsible for my adoptive mother's death.'

His voice lowered to a raw growl.

'And maybe I did something else—something so terrible that my mind has blocked out the memories. Frankly, I don't want to know. If a DNA test revealed that I *am* the son of Prince Goran the press would look for skeletons in my past—and perhaps they would find some. The inescapable truth is that I am not good enough to rule Vostov.'

'Jarek...'

Holly's voice followed him as he strode down the beach, but he did not look back at her. His mind swirled with half-formed memories and dark shadows, and the compassion in her eyes filled him with a wildness that made him feel dangerously out of control.

He carried on running into the sea and dived beneath the waves, moving powerfully through the water as he swam across the bay, turned around and swam back in the opposite direction. He lost track of how many times he swam back and forth. The breath burned in his chest and his arms ached, but still he pushed himself, trying to exorcise his demons with hard physical exercise.

But even after he was exhausted his body still ached for Holly. She had followed him down the beach, and each time he'd swum across the bay he had seen her sitting on a rock, watching him. He had the strange feeling that she was guarding him, and the thought made him feel hollow inside.

The sun was low in the sky when he swam back to the shore and walked up the beach to the outside shower. He rinsed the sea water from his skin before heading towards Holly.

He hunkered down in front of her and stared into her big brown eyes. 'I don't need a guardian angel,' he said roughly.

'Listen to me,' she said fiercely. 'You are a good and honourable man. I truly believe that. I did some research about your charity work, and the huge amount of money you have raised for Lorna's Gift actually changes the lives of children who live in orphanages as you once did.'

Her belief in him scraped on emotions that had been buried deep inside Jarek since he was six years old and had walked into that forbidding institution for homeless children in Sarajevo. For the first few nights he had cried because he missed his parents, but he'd quickly learned that crying earned him a beating and he had never cried again—not even at Mama's funeral, even though he had felt as if his heart had been ripped from his chest.

He looked away from Holly, afraid that she would see too much—the part of himself that he'd kept hidden behind his carefully cultivated playboy image. 'I'm no hero,' he muttered.

'You protected your little sister in a war when you were just a child yourself. I think that's pretty heroic,' she said firmly. 'Jarek, you *have* to have the DNA test and accept your destiny. For what it's worth, I think you would be a great prince.'

'Come with me. I want to show you something.'

He stood up and held out his hand to pull her to her feet.

Her hand felt soft in his and he linked his fingers with hers as they walked along the beach.

'Where are we going?'

'You'll see.'

He led her around the headland and onto a small, secluded beach surrounded by palm trees. There was a double sun lounger on the sand and he sat down on it, patted the space beside him.

'Take a seat and watch the show,' he invited, pointing to the horizon, where the sun was a huge orange ball that appeared to be sinking slowly into the sea.

The sky was streaked in hues of pink and red that were reflected on the surface of the ocean. And as the fiery ball sank lower the entire beach was bathed in gold and the fronded leaves of the palm trees were silhouetted against the setting sun.

'How incredibly beautiful...' Holly murmured.

'Yes.'

But Jarek did not glance at the sunset. He only had eyes for her, and the heat inside him blazed like a wildfire—fierce and uncontrollable.

She turned to look at him and he heard her catch her breath when he removed the clasp that secured the knot on top of her head, so that her hair fell like a curtain of silk around her shoulders. She whispered his name and it was the sweetest sound he had ever heard. A siren's song that he could no longer resist.

He had spent three weeks on a paradise island feeling as miserable as sin. He'd missed her soft smile and her sharp wit. And if he did not make her his soon he thought he might die.

Her eyes widened when he leaned towards her, and he felt a quiver run through her as he brushed his lips over hers. She tasted divine, and what little restraint he had left cracked when she opened her mouth to him with a willingness that drove him over the edge.

With a low growl he hauled her into his arms and slid one hand to her nape, to angle her head so that he could kiss her deeply, hungrily. And somewhere in Jarek's mind was the thought that he had come home.

CHAPTER NINE

JUST ONE KISS, Holly promised herself. What harm could there be in one kiss?

The raw emotion in Jarek's voice when he had told her that he remembered Asmir from his early childhood had swept away her defences against him. Asmir's story that Jarek was in fact Prince Jarrett, heir to the throne of Vostov, was almost too astounding to be believable. But if a DNA test proved it to be true then Jarek would be desperate to regain his lost memories about his parents, and he would need her help in the form of therapy sessions.

Holly was aware that it was vital to set boundaries between a psychotherapist and her client. In fact, before she'd left Austria, she had explained to Professor Heppel that her relationship with Jarek had become personal, and she had taken unpaid leave from the Frieden Clinic in order to visit him in the Seychelles. Even so, she knew she should not be allowing Jarek to draw her into his arms and hold her so close that she could feel the hard thud of his heart beneath the hand that she had placed on his chest, intending to push him away.

But he filled her senses, and she could not resist sliding her hands to his shoulders, stroking her fingers over his satiny skin before moving them up to trace across his rough jaw. And all the while his mouth was fused to hers.

And he pushed his tongue between her lips as he deepened the kiss so that it became intensely erotic.

She kissed him back because she could not help herself. Because she had missed him the same way that she would miss drawing oxygen into her lungs after he had left the clinic in Austria. When he lay back on the sun lounger and pulled her down on top of him she pressed herself against his hard body and felt a quiver of feminine satisfaction at the feral sound he made.

He took his mouth from hers, and she should have seized that moment to end the madness and lift herself off him. But he trailed his lips down her throat and lower, to the valley between her breasts, and it was then that Holly discovered he had untied the wraparound dress. He pushed the edges of the dress aside, and when he smoothed his hand over her stomach she burned at his touch and every sensible thought flew from her head, leaving her mindless with desire.

In a fluid movement Jarek reversed their positions and flipped her over, so that she was lying beneath him. She ran her fingers through his silky hair and then cradled his face in her hands and kissed him with a hunger that she had never felt for any other man. He had fascinated her from the start, and she was helpless to deny her desire for him when he tightened his arms around her as if he never wanted to let her go.

The soft shadows of the gathering dusk stole around them, enclosing them in their private world, and Holly simply surrendered to the thunder of her heart and the increasing urgency of Jarek's passion. He pulled her bra cup aside and gave a husky laugh when he flicked his tongue across the hard peak of her nipple and heard her catch her breath.

A flame shot down from her breasts to the molten place between her legs and she forgot who she was—forgot that her body was flawed. Jarek used his hands and his mouth to caress her with such artistry, such reverence, that she forgot everything but the heavy pulse of her need that was centred *right there*, where his hand rested on the lacy panel of her knickers.

She lifted her hips towards him when he pressed his palm down hard, and gave a startled cry as the tight band of need inside her snapped and her body shuddered with the intense pleasure he had created simply with his touch.

'Holly…' Her name was a raw growl and his eyes glittered with a feral hunger that belatedly awoke her to the realisation of where this was leading.

'Jarek—' she began, but her voice was smothered when he captured her mouth once more and kissed her with a desperation that tugged on her heart.

She wanted him more than she had ever wanted anything in her life, and the stark look on his face warned her that he was barely holding on to his control.

He rose up onto his knees, and yanked down the zip on his shorts. 'I have to have you,' he said hoarsely. 'I can't wait, angel-face. You're driving me out of my mind.'

With one hand he began to tug her knickers down, and he used his other hand to free himself from his shorts.

Until that moment Holly had told herself that this time it would be all right. She was so turned on that surely her body would allow Jarek to penetrate her. But one look at the hard length of his erection brought her crashing back to reality. For her, having sex had to be a gradual process. If she rushed it would be bound to end in disappointment for Jarek and embarrassment for her.

He stood up to pull off his shorts and kick them away. Truly he was a work of art, his muscle-hard body as beautiful as any marble figure sculpted by Michelangelo. But Jarek wasn't made of stone. He was a hot-blooded male in his prime, and when he moved purposefully towards Holly it broke her heart to know she had to deny them both the satisfaction of the desire that burned like a white-hot flame between them.

'*No!*' she said frantically, holding out her hand to stop him lowering himself down onto her.

Taking advantage of his stunned expression, she rolled off the sun lounger and pulled her underwear back into place. Her hands shook as she refastened her dress.

'No?' There was disbelief in his voice. His eyes narrowed and she sensed he was struggling to control his angry frustration. 'What *is* this, Holly? An attempt to pay me back for rejecting you?'

She swallowed. 'I'm allowed to change my mind.'

'Of course.' His ice-blue eyes glimmered. 'But I'm curious to know *why*, exactly. You wanted me.' He swore, and then said with heavy self-derision, 'I've had enough experience of women to be able to tell if you were faking it.'

His casual reference to the fact that he had slept with countless women felt a knife in her heart. She was sure that none of his beautiful mistresses would have had an imperfect body like hers.

'We can't. I…I can't. I'm sorry,' she said in a choked voice, before she whirled away from him and tore across the beach.

Dusk fell quickly in the Seychelles, and the path up to the house was illuminated by fairy lights that glowed as bright as fireflies. Holly ran inside and up the stairs to her bedroom, and after locking the door she curled up on the bed and wept tears of frustration.

On the beach she simply hadn't felt confident that she would be able to make love with Jarek, or that he would want her when he discovered she had a medical condition which meant spontaneous sex was a problem for her.

'Holly, are you all right?'

Jarek's voice sounded through the door, and the doorknob rattled as he tried to turn it.

'Will you let me in? We need to talk.'

'There's nothing to say.' She sniffed. 'Stop harassing me.'

She heard him sigh. 'What happened, angel-face? You were with me all the way.'

She swallowed a hiccup. 'You think I led you on deliberately?'

'No, I don't. I said a stupid thing in the heat of the moment, but I know you're not a sexual tease.' His voice deepened. 'I *know* you, Holly. I guess you called a halt because maybe you're not on the pill, and you were right to be concerned that we were about to have unprotected sex. I promise you I have never been careless about contraception before,' he said gruffly.

She gulped. Jarek had no idea that she would never have to worry about an unplanned pregnancy. 'It wasn't that. You...you don't know me at all.'

'Are you *crying*?'

The doorknob rattled again and she heard him swear.

'Let me in.'

'Go away—*please*.' Her voice trembled. 'Just leave me alone.'

After a few minutes she heard his footsteps move away down the corridor. Holly didn't know how long she lay there, feeling sorry for herself, but after a while she decided she might as well go to bed and try to sleep, aware that in the morning she would have to face Jarek and somehow try to re-establish her role as his therapist.

She took off the badly creased silk dress and hung it up. Then realised the brushed cotton pyjamas she wore in Austria would be too hot here in the Seychelles, where the temperature at night only dropped a couple of degrees from the searing heat of the day.

Searching through a drawer for a T-shirt to wear in bed, she found the shirt Jarek had lent her when they had been stranded for the night in the mountain hut. She had packed the shirt so that she could return it to him, but it was the nearest she was going to get to sleeping in his arms, she thought as she slipped the shirt on and hugged it around her.

A noise from over by the sliding glass doors made her swing round, and her heart crashed against her ribs as she watched Jarek climb over the rail and drop down onto the balcony outside her bedroom.

'Are you *crazy*?' she demanded. 'It must be a ten-foot drop at least down to the ground. If you'd fallen you might have broken your neck.'

He ignored her protest and strode across the room, catching hold of her shoulders before she could back away from him. 'Why were you crying? Did I do something to hurt you or offend you?'

'No, of course not.'

'Then why did you run off like that?'

She looked away from his piercing blue eyes and shrugged. 'Is your ego so big that you find it hard to accept I didn't want to have sex with you?'

He spread his fingers wide on her shoulders and drew her closer to him. 'It has nothing to do with my ego. I *know* you are as hungry for me as I am for you.'

Oddly, considering his words, there was none of the old arrogance in his voice, and he spoke in a low, intense way—as if his emotions were on a knife-edge.

'If I demand that you give me back my shirt right here and now, I'm certain your body won't lie. Shall I put my theory to the test, Holly?' he said softly.

She swallowed when he unfastened a button on the shirt, and then another. The hard gleam in his eyes told her it was not by accident that his knuckles brushed over the upper slopes of her breasts. She felt her nipples become tight and hot and she was powerless to prevent her body from betraying her.

'Say it,' he muttered, and there was something strangely vulnerable in his rough voice. 'You are the most honest person I know. Tell me the truth, Holly.'

She put her hand over his to stop him unbuttoning the shirt any lower, and gave a defeated sigh. 'All right, yes. I wanted to make love with you on the beach. But I couldn't. I just *couldn't*—not easily. Can we leave it at that?' she whispered.

He moved his hands up from her shoulders and cradled her face in his palms. When he spoke, the unexpected tenderness in his voice brought more tears to her eyes.

'I have stripped my soul bare to you, angel-face. You know every one of my deepest, darkest secrets except for the ones I don't even know myself.' He rubbed his thumb-pad over the trembling of her mouth. 'I would never betray your trust in me, just as I know *here*—' he thumped his fist over his heart '—that you would die rather than reveal something told to you in confidence.'

Jarek's faith in her was humbling, and it made her want to cry even more.

Perhaps he could tell from the way her shoulders drooped that all the fight had gone out of her, because he scooped her up in his arms as easily as he had on the mountain after she had been injured in the avalanche and carried her over to the sofa. He sat down and settled her on his lap—as if she were a child in need of comfort instead of a highly qualified professional woman of thirty-one, Holly thought ruefully.

Before he had climbed up to her room he'd changed into jeans and a black T-shirt that clung to his muscular chest and felt soft against her cheek when she rested her head on his shoulder. She felt drained after her storm of emotions. Jarek stroked her hair, and her sense of being comforted and cared for by him was dangerously beguiling.

After a moment she began to speak. 'I have a rare syndrome which means that I was born with a gynaecological abnormality. As a teenager I had to have surgery which would enable me to have sex when I was an adult, and I was also advised by the doctor to use dilators regularly.'

Holly tensed as she waited for Jarek's reaction. In the past, when she had told a couple of boyfriends about her condition, they had reacted with varying degrees of shock. Their main concern had been that her imperfection might affect their enjoyment of sex with her. In each case she had decided not to take the relationship any further.

'That must have a tough experience to go through,' Jarek said, with no hint of shock or horror in his voice. 'Puberty can be a difficult time anyway.'

She nodded. 'I was fifteen when I was diagnosed, and I found it horribly embarrassing to have to discuss very personal details about my body with medical staff. I couldn't talk to my parents about my feelings, but inside I felt I was a freak and a failure as a woman.'

She was embarrassed, telling Jarek such intimate things about herself, but when she attempted to slide off his lap he tightened his arm around her.

'It was even worse when I started modelling,' she continued after a moment. 'Men desired me for the way I looked, but I knew I hid a shameful secret.'

'Why shameful?' he murmured. 'It's not your fault that you were born with a medical condition.' He continued to stroke her hair gently. 'Was the surgery you underwent to enable you to have sex successful?'

'Yes, but since my last relationship ended over a year ago I haven't had sex, I have used the dilators, but not as often as I should have done.'

'Did the relationship end because of your condition?'

'It was a factor,' Holly admitted.

In fact, when she'd first met Stuart she hadn't explained about her MRKH because she had used her dilators regularly. Sex with him had been uneventful—*and unexciting*, a little voice in her mind whispered. Stuart had finished with her after she had told him she was infertile, but there was no reason to explain that to Jarek.

'Were you in love with your ex?' Jarek frowned. 'I assume you must have been, as you've remained single and celibate for a year since your relationship finished.'

She hesitated. 'I believed that Stuart and I had a future together. I haven't dated anyone else because...' She halted, feeling utterly miserable.

It was all hopeless. She had no idea why she was telling Jarek so much about herself. How could he possibly understand? He probably regretted risking serious injury by climbing up to her balcony like a latter-day Romeo, only to discover that his Juliet was a dud.

His brows lifted. 'Because?'

'I can have sex, just the same as any other woman,' Holly burst out defensively. 'But it takes time for my body to be ready and most guys are too impatient.'

She stared at him—at the hard, beautiful face that made her heart twist. He was a golden, gorgeous playboy who could have any woman he wanted.

'Truthfully,' she whispered, 'what man would want to make love to me?'

'*This* man,' Jarek said softly.

He lifted his hand and brushed the tears from her cheeks. Holly turned her head away, afraid she would see pity in his eyes that would make her feel worse. But he slipped his fingers beneath her chin and steered her gaze back towards him, and the fierce gleam in his eyes set her foolish heart pounding.

'I told you the truth when I said you were driving me out of my mind, and nothing you have said has lessened my desire for you.'

He stared into her eyes with an intensity that made her tremble.

'I wanted you the minute I set eyes on you in Austria. You blew me away then and you blow me away now. The only difference now is that I know your beauty is not just skin-deep. You are brave and honest, compassionate and infuriatingly stubborn.' Jarek's mouth crooked. 'You are also the sexiest psychologist I've ever known.'

Despite everything, Holly melted at his smile. 'Have you known *many* psychologists, then?' she murmured.

'Only you, angel-face.' He still smiled, but his tone had become serious. 'I would like to make love with you—but this isn't about me…it's about what *you* want.'

'I want you,' she whispered. 'But I've told you…I have to take things slowly…you might get bored.'

Jarek stroked his fingers through her hair, but it no longer felt as if he was comforting her when he slid his hand to her nape and gave a gentle tug to angle her face towards his so that his mouth was a whisper away from hers.

'I promise you that neither of us will be bored,' he said softly. 'Forget those guys who were impatient, and your ex-boyfriend who is clearly a jerk. Your body is beautiful and unique to you, and if it takes a little time for you to become fully aroused and ready to make love what does it matter? We can take as long as we like. Anticipation adds another dimension to the overall pleasure,' he murmured, his voice very deep and very soft, like the caress of plush velvet across her skin.

Holly gave a low moan when Jarek finally claimed her mouth and kissed her with a bone-shaking sensuality that dispelled any doubts she might have had that he genuinely desired her. But she still couldn't relax, and he must have sensed her tension because he lifted his mouth from hers and cradled her cheek in his hand.

'I give you my word that I won't try to rush you before you feel ready.' He trailed his lips down her throat to the sensitive hollow at its base and murmured, 'The route to sexual pleasure has many pathways that we can explore.'

Holly felt like a teenager on a first date. She had been certain that Jarek would reject her, but he had promised to be patient. Her heart was thumping with a mixture of nerves and anticipation and she needed a few minutes to herself.

'I...I need to go to the bathroom.'

He lifted her off his lap and stood up, bending his head to drop a brief, hard kiss on her lips that left her wanting much more.

He grinned at her obvious disappointment when he took his mouth from hers. 'All in good time, angel-face,' he promised, in a husky growl that caused heat to unfurl in the pit of her stomach.

Five minutes later Holly was tempted to call through the bathroom door and tell Jarek she had changed her mind and did *not* want to make love with him. Except that she would be lying, she admitted to herself. Her lips were still tingling from his kiss and the heaviness in her breasts coiled all the way down to the hot, molten core of her.

She caught sight of herself in the mirror and grimaced

when she saw that her eyes were huge and dark, with enlarged pupils. There was a bloom of heat on her cheeks and the hard points of her nipples were clearly visible, jutting beneath the shirt she had borrowed from Jarek.

Was it love or lust that was responsible for her accelerated heart-rate and quickened breathing? She didn't know, and at that moment she did not care. Jarek had insisted that the medical condition she had been born with made no difference to his desire for her. She wanted to believe him, but she had spent the past five minutes in the bathroom to give him a chance to leave her bedroom. She wouldn't blame him if he decided that having sex with her sounded like too much trouble.

But when she opened the bathroom door and saw him sprawled on her bed, naked save for a pair of black briefs, she felt a flash of relief. Simultaneously her stomach tied itself into a knot.

He was diabolically handsome, she thought. Although thinking was difficult when she was fixated on his magnificent body—all that lean, golden hardness, and the sheer perfection of finely honed muscles. All that untamed blond hair that he flicked back from his face with a careless gesture, and those brilliant blue eyes that trapped her gaze from across the room and gleamed with a hunger that was too raw and intense for it not to be real.

'We can make love in the doorway if you like,' he murmured as she clung to the doorframe for support, 'but we will be more comfortable on the bed. Why don't you come over here?'

She licked her dry lips and fought the urge to lock herself back in the bathroom. Jarek was leaning against the pillows, watching her from beneath heavy lids. With a flare of misery Holly wondered how many times he had played out this very scene: him sprawled on a bed like an indolent sultan, waiting for his mistress—probably blonde and definitely beautiful—to join him on the silk sheets.

She gave herself a mental shake as she walked towards the bed. It wasn't as though she was a virgin, but she only had fairly limited sexual experience, and she was afraid that Jarek would find her disappointing.

'Do you trust me, Holly?'

'Yes,' she said, without hesitation. He had saved her life on the mountain and she knew that physically she was safe with him—although her heart was a different matter.

'Good,' he said softly. 'Before we begin you have to agree to two rules. Rule number one—and the most important—you must tell me if anything we do causes you discomfort and we will stop immediately. Secondly...' His smile was a wicked promise that made Holly's legs tremble beneath her. 'You have to agree to do whatever I tell you.' When she opened her mouth to argue he reminded her gently, 'You said you trust me.'

'I do,' she whispered.

'In that case I want you to return my shirt to me.'

'Now?'

Her heart missed a beat when he nodded.

She stared at him, lounging there against the pillows as if he was her lord and she was a serving wench bound to do her master's bidding. For the first time since she had fled from the beach in shame Holly's chin came up and she stopped feeling crushed. If Jarek wanted her to perform a striptease she would damn well give him a performance that would bring him to his knees!

Keeping her eyes focused on him, she lifted her hands and opened the top button of the shirt, and then slowly worked her way down, sliding the buttons out of their buttonholes. She pushed the heavy swathe of her hair back from her face and the action caused the half-open shirt to slip off one shoulder.

Jarek's eyes glittered and he no longer looked relaxed. The idea that *she* was the cause of his tension delighted Holly, and she unfastened the rest of the buttons without taking her gaze from his. She let the shirt slip from her shoulders—slowly, slowly, inch by tantalising inch—baring her breasts in all their proud, firm glory. Her nipples were flushed rose-red and they were hard...so hard they hurt.

Jarek made a thick sound in his throat. His skin was stretched tight over his sharp cheekbones and there was something predatory about his smile that made Holly think of a wolf—with very sharp teeth. She dropped the shirt and it fell to the floor, leaving her with just the fragile wisp of her lace panties to cover her femininity.

Jarek swallowed audibly. 'You are so beautiful,' he muttered, and she was startled to see dull colour flare on his face. 'See what you do to me, angel-face.'

She could not fail to notice the betraying bulge beneath his briefs, and the evidence of his arousal turned her insides to liquid. He made her feel beautiful and, still holding his gaze, she hooked her fingers in the top of her panties and pulled them down so that they fluttered to the floor.

Jarek growled something that might have been a prayer, and Holly gave a confident smile as she put her hands on her hips while he stared and stared at her naked body.

His breath hissed between his teeth. 'Witch. I *knew* you would be the death of me.'

He did not try to hide his desire for her, and the stark hunger in his eyes made her heart beat as hard as a drum when he held out his hand to her. It was anticipation, not trepidation, that shivered through Holly as she put her hand in Jarek's. He pulled her down onto the bed and stretched out beside her, tracing light circles with his fingertips around her navel before stroking his hand over her stomach.

Fire ignited in her belly and shot lower to between her legs when he ran his fingers over the neatly trimmed vee of dark hair that covered her womanhood. She could feel the molten heat of her arousal, but however much she desired Jarek she could not simply pull him down on top of her and take him inside her.

He must have felt her stiffen because he murmured, 'Holly…angel-face…what's wrong?'

'I *hate* my body. I wish I was normal.'

The words tumbled out of her mouth before she could stop them. The truth that she had denied to herself for years finally revealed. She tried to look away from Jarek, but he cupped her cheek in his hand and stared at her with an indefinable expression in his eyes that caused her heart to clatter.

'Then it is up to me to prove to you that your body is utterly perfect,' he said softly.

He laid his finger across her lips when she made an angry sound of denial.

'It's perfect because it's *you*, Holly, and I would not change a single thing about you. But instead of talking let me *show* you how lovely you truly are.'

He moved so that he was kneeling beside her on the bed, and took both her hands and lifted them behind her head so that her fingers brushed against the bars of the headboard.

'Hold on,' he ordered softly, with a sultry gleam in his eyes that caused butterflies to leap in her stomach. 'We're going to play a game. I'm allowed to touch you wherever I want to, but you're not allowed to touch me.'

'That's not fair—' She caught her breath when he

stroked his fingers across the soles of her feet before moving up to her ankles.

'That's the rules, angel-face.'

Jarek continued to skim his fingers up her legs with a light touch that nevertheless felt as if he was branding her skin. Holly tried not to tense when he stroked his fingers over the insides of her thighs, but to her surprise he did not touch her intimately, just moved up to her stomach and then higher so that his hands were just below her breasts. She swallowed and silently urged him to caress her breasts, and her nipples that were tight and hard.

But once again he avoided touching her where she longed to feel his hands and instead trailed his fingers lightly over her arms and shoulders, tracing the line of her collarbone and exploring the sensitive spot behind her ears. And all the while he watched her with his brilliant blue eyes, laughing huskily when he stroked the sides of her breasts but still didn't touch the rosy peaks of her nipples that jutted provocatively and ached for him to roll them between his fingers.

Holly felt as though every centimetre of her body was on fire, and she gave a moan when Jarek smoothed his hands over her thighs once again but made no attempt to touch her *there*, where she was so desperate for him to caress her.

'Please…' she whispered, lifting her hips towards his hands. She felt boneless, more turned on than she had ever felt before, and he had not even caressed her in any sexual way yet.

She realised that he was being true to his word and absolutely would not rush her. His patience as he aroused her body was allowing her to relax and put her trust in him utterly, and she couldn't restrain a gasp of pleasure when finally he bent his head and took her nipple into his mouth. The sensation of him sucking hard on the tender peak before he moved across to her other breast evoked a flood of molten heat at her feminine core.

If he didn't touch her *there* soon she thought she might die, but he ignored her soft plea and moved so that he was lying on his back and she was straddling his legs.

'Now it's your turn to touch me. Remember nowhere is off-limits,' he murmured. 'I'm all yours, angel-face.'

Her heart gave a sharp pang, because she knew he wasn't hers in the way she wanted him to be. But he was hers for this night, and he had given her free rein to explore his body. She would use her hands to imprint his male beauty onto her mind in the same way that a visually impaired person used braille, Holly decided as she ran her fingers over his face, along his sharp cheekbones and down to trace the contours of his sexy mouth.

She caught her breath when he drew her finger into his mouth and sucked. How could such an innocuous action be so erotic?

'It's my turn to touch…you're not allowed to touch *me*,' she complained.

He grinned. 'Ah, but I make up the rules.'

His gentle teasing gave her the confidence to be bold, and it was her turn to laugh when she skimmed her hand over his flat abdomen before tracing her fingers over the front of his briefs. He became instantly and impressively erect.

'I don't think I can be patient for much longer. I want to make love with you, Jarek,' she confessed, in a husky voice that did not sound like her own.

CHAPTER TEN

JAREK DID NOT understand what was happening to him. When Holly had admitted that she hated her body, the shimmer of tears in her eyes and the faint tremble of her mouth had ripped him apart. He'd been impressed by her courage when they had been caught in the avalanche in Austria, but her honesty tonight must have taken a hell of a nerve and he admired her more than ever.

But he was getting in too deep, a voice inside him warned. There were numerous reasons why he should not take his involvement with her any further, and none of them were to do with the rare syndrome she had been born with, and which he sensed affected her emotionally even more than physically.

When she had stripped for him, and teased him by taking her time to reveal her gorgeous body, he'd been so turned on that he'd had to restrain himself from ripping the shirt off her.

He tugged her down so that she was lying next to him and felt a hard kick of desire in his gut as he studied every beautiful inch of her body, from the delicate flush of rose on her cheeks and the darker pink of her nipples that contrasted with the pale cream of her breasts. He moved his gaze lower to the indentation of her waist and the sensual curve of her hips, before coming to rest at the tantalising junction between her soft thighs.

He wanted nothing more than to worship her with his hands and mouth, show her that she was Aphrodite, incomparable, the only woman who made him shake with need. But his needs were unimportant. All that mattered was Holly.

He was shocked by the surge of protectiveness that swept through him. The diagnosis of her medical condition when she was a teenager must have been devastating. It had let to a period of depression, but Holly had sought help from a counsellor and gone on to train as a psychologist and psychotherapist so that she could help other people overcome emotional trauma.

She was nothing short of amazing, Jarek brooded. He wanted to see the shadows in her eyes disappear, and he did not care to dwell on why making her happy was so important to him. He bent his head to her breast and captured her nipple in his mouth, smiling when he heard her soft gasp.

He forgot the tangled web of his life, the possibility that his name was not Jarek Dvorska and the intangible horror of his nightmares that he feared hid the truth about his parents' deaths. He forgot everything and dedicated himself to giving Holly more pleasure than he was sure she'd ever experienced with her crass ex-boyfriend.

The realisation that he hated thinking of her with other men should have set alarm bells ringing, but he shut his ears to everything but the thin cry she made when he sucked hard on her nipple before he moved across to her other breast and flicked his tongue over the taut peak at its centre.

He had assured her that they were in no rush, and he took his time to explore her body and encouraged her to explore his—although when she slipped her hand into his briefs and stretched her fingers around his burgeoning erection he had to stop her while he still had enough self-control.

'We want this to last, angel-face,' he growled, when she tugged his briefs down and ran her hands over his buttocks. 'Remember we're playing by *my* rules and you have to do as I tell you. Open your legs,' he ordered softly, and grinned as a scarlet stain spread across her face. 'If you're hot now, you'll be burning up by the time I've finished,' he promised.'

'You're *so* arrogant,' she choked, sounding appalled, although she allowed him to arrange her to his satisfaction, with a pillow beneath her bottom and her legs hooked over his shoulders.

'I'm so *good*,' he assured her, and proceeded to demonstrate that it was not an idle boast.

He tasted her feminine sweetness and used his tongue with devastating effect on her clitoris before he drew the tiny nub into his mouth and sucked. Holly plunged her fingers into his hair and held on as if she was anchoring herself while she threshed beneath his relentless onslaught. Suddenly she gave a guttural cry, and the sound of it made Jarek's gut twist.

While she was still shaking and trembling in the aftermath of her orgasm he gently ran his finger up and down her opening and slowly eased his smallest finger into her. At the same time he kissed her mouth, slow and deep, until he felt her relax. She released her breath slowly.

'Does that hurt?' he asked her.

'No, it feels good.'

She smiled, and Jarek felt something tug in his chest. His body was aching with the force of his desire, but he was determined to be patient and make sex a good experience for her.

He withdrew his finger and replaced it with his thicker middle finger while he rubbed his thumb pad lightly over her clitoris until Holly trembled.

'How about that? Does it still feel good?' he murmured.

'Yes, *so* good. *Oh...*' She moaned when he swirled his finger inside her. 'Jarek, I'm ready now,' she said, with an urgency in her voice that almost made him come there and then.

'Are you sure? I don't want to hurt you...'

He felt as if he was going to explode—especially when she slid her hand down and clasped his thickened shaft tightly in her hand.'

'You won't hurt me.'

She pushed her hair off her face. Her cheeks were flushed and her eyes were deep, dark pools.

'I want you,' she said fiercely, and Jarek knew then that he was never going to survive.

Holly made him feel things he hadn't believed he was capable of feeling, and she made him wish he was a different man from either of the men he thought he might be—a lost prince without a memory, or a feral boy scarred by his memories of a brutal war.

'I want you, Jarek,' she said again, softly this time, whispering her words against his lips as she cradled his face in her hands and urged him down onto her.

'I left a packet of condoms in my trouser pocket.' He remembered just in time, and kissed away her pout as he lifted himself off her.

There was something in her eyes—a flicker of hesitation...he didn't know what—before she murmured, 'It's okay. I won't fall pregnant. And it's safe. I haven't had a sexual relationship for over a year, and you said you have always been careful to use protection with other women.'

The fact that contraception hadn't entered his mind when he had been about to make love to Holly on the beach was a warning Jarek chose to ignore. He guessed since she had assured him it was safe that she was on the pill, or had protected herself against unwanted pregnancy some other way.

He ached to possess her—and it was not just his body, he realised, aware of a deeper ache in that empty vessel he had assumed was his heart.

He shoved the thought away. There would be a time of reckoning, when undoubtedly he would despise himself for his weakness for this woman with her sweet smile and her innocent belief that there was anything good about him. But for now he could fool himself that maybe she was right. And besides, he wanted her too badly to care about tomorrow.

His hunger for Holly bordered on the obsessional, Jarek acknowledged, but that did not make him forget that what she required from him was patience.

He stretched out on top of her and propped himself up on his forearms to take his weight. Her skin was satin-smooth, and she gave a little shiver when his rough chest hair scraped over her breasts. He laughed softly against her lips before he kissed her mouth, and as their breath mingled he pressed forward so that his hard length was there, at her opening.

'Stop me if it hurts,' he said roughly.

'If you stop I think I'll die,' she muttered. 'Please, Jarek, *now.*'

He eased further forward, entering her slowly to allow her internal muscles time to stretch around him. Her soft moan made him halt, but when he tried to withdraw she wrapped her legs around his back and urged him deeper inside her.

'It's fine…really,' she assured him. 'Actually, it's more than fine.'

She smiled, and that ache in his chest got a whole lot worse. He gathered her close and pushed deeper, taking her with exquisite care, making her his. He set a rhythm, slow at first, increasing in pace when she lifted her hips to meet him.

It couldn't last. He had wanted her for so long—a lifetime, it seemed—and the pressure inside him built with every smooth thrust he made into her. But his concern that it might be too much for her made him restrain his passion as he concentrated on giving Holly pleasure. With each steady stroke he took her higher, and he could tell from her quickened breathing that she was nearing the edge.

'Jarek…' She dug her fingernails into his buttocks and moved sensuously against him, urging him in a husky voice to go faster, deeper.

'I'm trying to be careful,' he muttered, struggling to hold back a surge of rampant need when she wriggled experimentally beneath him.

He felt her smile against his cheek. 'I know, and I love you for it. But I promise you're not hurting me.'

Her words jolted through Jarek. He wondered if she was aware of what she had said. What did *love* have to do with *him*? It was an emotion he viewed with deep mistrust. As for not hurting Holly… He cursed silently, because he knew with grim certainty that he *would* hurt her. It was in his nature. He should never have allowed things to get this far, but now it was too late.

'You can let go,' she whispered.

And then it really was too late for him to maintain any kind of control. The heat inside him became a furnace as he clamped his hands on her hips and his next thrust threw them both into the fire. She arched beneath him and gave a startled cry as her body shook and she convulsed around him. Jarek would have liked to take her high again, but for the first time in his life he was overwhelmed by the wildfire that ripped through him, and with a savage groan he came, hot and hard, and felt the burn of it right down to his soul.

After a few moments he lifted himself off her with a reluctance that worried him. He needed to regroup his thoughts and re-establish his boundaries. That word *love* had thrown him, and he couldn't understand why he was still in bed with her when his common sense told him to get the hell out of her room *and* her life.

But Holly seemed unaware of his inner turmoil and snuggled up to him. For a second Jarek froze. He did not *do* cuddling. So why did he draw her against his side and turn his head to breathe in the fragrance of her hair when she rested her head on his shoulder?

She sighed softly and he tensed, hoping she was not about to declare that she was in love with him, which would embarrass both of them. *Obviously* he hoped she wouldn't do that, he told himself.

'So that's what all the fuss is about,' she murmured. 'I never knew…'

He looked at her questioningly. 'Seriously? That was your first orgasm?' He'd suspected, but hearing her say it filled him with a possessiveness that was downright dangerous.

'First *two* orgasms, as it happens. It's nice to know that the press are right about some things.'

'Like what?'

'Well, you *are* often described in the tabloids as a stud.' She gave him an innocent smile while devilment danced in her eyes. 'Now I have proof that it's true.'

For a few seconds he stared at her, and the tight cords that had been lashed around his heart since the grim days of what should have been his childhood in Sarajevo loosened a fraction. Slowly a grin spread over Jarek's face, and for the first time that he could remember he laughed from deep in his gut—a genuine laugh rather than the sardonic humour he was renowned for on the social circuit of Mayfair, or Monte Carlo, or any of the other places where the rich and bored played.

He had never met a woman who made him laugh the way Holly did, with her dry wit and her refusal to be impressed by him. He was fascinated by the dimples that appeared at the corners of her mouth when she smiled, but he noted too the faint wariness in her dark eyes, and he realised that her teasing had been to disguise her uncertainty.

'Was it okay for you?' Colour flared on her cheeks. 'I mean...maybe sex is better with other women who don't have my...my problem.'

That was when Jarek knew he was in trouble. When that empty vessel in his chest that had never given even a slight twinge before contracted with pain. He closed his eyes briefly, trying to control emotions that were in free-fall. Her hair felt like silk when he slid his hand around her nape and tilted her face to him.

'It was the *best* with you, angel-face,' he assured her gently. 'So perfect, in fact, that when you are ready I think we will have to do it again.'

'I'm ready now,' she whispered against his mouth.

And Jarek couldn't help himself. He kissed her and the world went up in flames.

In paradise it was easy for Holly to pretend that the world did not exist. For a whole week she and Jarek had been cocooned from reality on Paradis sur Terre, and in that time they had barely been apart—or out of bed, she thought guiltily.

Making love with him had been a revelation, and under his patient tutelage she had learned that her body was capable of experiencing the most intense and indescribable pleasure. When she had explained that she did not need to use her dilators if she was having sex regularly he'd grinned, and assured her that they must heed medical advice and make love as often as possible.

'I'm following doctor's orders,' he said every time he reached for her in the big bed they shared, or tumbled her down onto the sand and made love to her with fierce passion coupled with exquisite tenderness while the waves running up the shore lapped around them.

And when they weren't consumed by their wild hunger for each other, which seemed to grow stronger every day, they talked.

At the beginning of the week Jarek had flown by helicopter to Mahe, the largest island in the Seychelles, and at a private clinic had met a representative of Vostov's National Council and given a DNA sample which might prove if he was the sole surviving male member of the House of Karadjvic.

'When will you have the result of the test?' Holly had asked when he had returned to the island, which she now realised really was a hideaway. No one—not even Vostov's Council, and certainly not the media—knew Jarek's exact location.

'It could take as long as two weeks. The standard paternity test which would show if Prince Goran was my father isn't possible because he is dead. A mouth swab is the usual method of collecting a sample. But it is possible to retrieve DNA from items used by a deceased person. Unfortunately the palace in Vostov was ransacked during the war, and most of the royal family's personal possessions were destroyed—which is why there are no photographs of the Prince and Princess and their children,' Jarek said heavily. 'However, a monogramed hairbrush which belonged to Prince Goran is being analysed, and it's hoped that enough DNA can be obtained to carry out a paternity test.'

'It sounds like something out of a spy novel,' Holly had murmured. 'So nothing exists that might trigger your memories of early childhood? That's a pity. Sometimes seeing an object—in your case perhaps a favourite toy— might be a reminder of the past.'

'In my dreams I often see a rocking horse,' Jarek had said slowly. 'But I don't know if it ever existed or if it's something I've imagined.' He'd hesitated. 'Sometimes in the same dream I sense the presence of a woman, although I can't see her. I think she might be my mother.'

Encouraged that Jarek had some vague memories, albeit in his dreams, Holly had planned various strategies which might help him to overcome his amnesia. But at the first session he had paced restlessly around the room and become increasingly frustrated when questions designed to prompt his memory had no effect.

'Why don't you start by telling me about the period of your childhood that you *do* remember, when you were at the orphanage in Sarajevo?' she suggested.

'You don't want to hear about the things I saw there,' he'd growled. 'Let's just say that war isn't pretty.'

'I've never thought it was, but you don't need to protect me,' she'd said gently. 'Not talking about the horrors you witnessed won't make the memories go away. You have to take the first step to unlocking the areas of your mind that you have been hiding from for years.'

He had stared at her for a long time, his jaw clenched,

and with a bleakness in his blue eyes that had made her want to wrap her arms around him and take away his pain. But neither of the two distinct sides of their relationship allowed her to comfort him, Holly reminded herself. They were lovers—for now—and she'd had sex with him. She was also here as his private psychotherapist and her role was to listen and try to help him, not to fall ever deeper in love with him.

'All right—you win. I'll bloody well talk,' he'd said harshly. 'But not here.' He'd grabbed her hand and pulled her to her feet. 'If you want to know what it was like in Sarajevo I'll tell you.'

And he had, while they'd walked on the beach. He'd told her how he had been scared and confused when he'd found himself in the orphanage, with no memories of his life before then. He'd told her about his nightmares and his illogical terror of travelling in cars. He had even admitted that 'Tarik' was not a boy he had known at the orphanage.

'I have no idea why in my nightmares I am shouting for Tarik, but I'm certain that the name is linked in some way to my amnesia.'

They had walked and walked on the soft white sand, with the crystal-clear sea sparkling and the sun blazing down from an azure sky. On an island called heaven Jarek had told Holly about hell.

His childhood memories of a war-ravaged city were the stuff of nightmares, and her heart ached for the scared, abandoned boy he had been in Sarajevo. It ached even more for the man she had fallen in love with, who was haunted by the faceless ghosts from his past.

Finally he had stopped talking, and on the secret beach where she had run from him on her first night on the island he had drawn her into his arms and they'd watched the sun turn into a giant ball of fire that sank slowly into the sea.

Beneath a bejewelled sky of pink and gold he had undressed her, then himself, before he'd lain her down on the sun lounger and worshipped her with his hands and lips, with his mouth on her breasts and at the slick core of her. The velvet dusk had closed around them and the cicadas' song had carried on the warm breeze.

'You can let go now,' Holly had whispered.

And with a groan torn from deep in his chest he had spilled into her and in the sweet aftermath of their passion held her close as if he would never let her go.

Which, of course, was an illusion brought about by her wishful thinking—as Holly kept reminding herself in the following days, when it had felt as though there was only her and Jarek and an island called paradise. One day soon the outside world would intrude on her fantasy that this time with him would last for ever...

The end began on a day towards the end of their second week.

'We'll take the boat out,' Jarek said when they were sitting on the veranda, finishing a very late breakfast after they had spent most of the morning in bed. 'We'll sail around the headland to a cove which is only accessible by boat. You mentioned that you wished you could see turtles, so I asked Rani if they nest on the island. He told me that turtles go to the cove to lay their eggs in the daytime, rather than at night, because the beach is so secluded and safe. With luck we might spot them.'

'That would be lovely.' Holly hesitated. 'I take it you haven't heard from the DNA testing clinic?'

'No.' Jarek frowned. 'But a story has been leaked to the media that "an unnamed male" is undergoing checks that might prove he is the heir to Vostov's throne, and several newspapers are speculating on who it might be.

Suggestions include a famous European football player and an American pop star,' he said drily. 'There has also been a poll in Vostov which shows that the majority of the Vostovian people are in favour of restoring a constitutional monarchy if it is proved that Prince Goran's son and heir is alive.'

'How do you feel about that?' she asked quietly.

He ran his hand through his hair and looked tense. 'I don't know what I feel about any of it. The idea that I could be Prince Jarrett is crazy, and yet—' He broke off and shook his head.

'And yet you see things in your dreams that make you think it could be true?'

'In that case why don't I remember my parents?' he said savagely. 'What horror is my mind trying so desperately to hide from me?'

He was still grim and uncommunicative when they boarded the small sailing dingy and he cast off from the jetty. Holly did not know the first thing about sailing, but Jarek was an expert—as he was at most things and especially sex, she thought as she recalled how wickedly inventive he had been when he had joined her in the shower earlier.

As they sailed around the headland and made for the cove Holly used the camera on her phone to take a few photos of the island. She became aware of a sound that grew louder, and glanced up to see a helicopter flying directly towards them.

Jarek swore. 'Lie down on the floor and hide your face,' he shouted to her. 'They're shooting.'

'*What?*' She stared at him.

Had the helicopter which was now right above them reminded Jarek of being in Sarajevo when the city had suffered air strikes? Holly wondered. She moved towards him to reassure him, but lost her balance. And as she lurched backwards on the boat she dropped her phone over the side. It immediately sank beneath the waves.

'Damn it. *Oh!*' She gave a cry as Jarek pushed her down to the floor of the boat.

'They are paparazzi in the helicopter—shooting pictures of us,' he told her grimly.

'Are you sure? No one knows that you are staying on the island, or indeed that you might be a prince. And the paparazzi are certainly not interested in *me*,' she said as she watched the helicopter fly away. 'Maybe they were wildlife photographers, come to film the turtles.'

Jarek made a disbelieving sound and continued to steer the yacht towards the cove.

Although his mood improved, and they spent a pleasant afternoon watching the turtles, the incident was another reminder that his life was about to get a lot more complicated if the result of the DNA test revealed that he *was* a prince, Holly brooded. Where, if anywhere, would she fit into his life once he knew the truth about his identity? she wondered.

When Jarek made love to her so beautifully she could not believe that he felt nothing for her other than desire, or that his hunger for her would fade. But maybe all those countless other women who had fallen for his lazy charm had believed the same thing, she thought bleakly.

Dinner that evening was a quiet affair. Jarek had reverted to being the brooding, unapproachable stranger who had gone to such great lengths to avoid her when they had been at Chalet Soline—a lifetime ago, it seemed. And Holly, who had questioned him endlessly about his past in an attempt to break his amnesia, was too afraid to ask him where their relationship was heading.

She pleaded tiredness and took herself off to bed early,

unable to deal with his palpable tension or hide her misery. But she still went to his room and climbed into his bed, which she had shared with him for the past two weeks. Surprisingly, she fell asleep almost instantly—only to be awoken in the dark of the night by Jarek reaching for her and pulling her close until that she felt his hard length press between her thighs.

She went to him with a silent sigh of relief that *this* hadn't changed. His fierce passion matched hers, and the underlying urgency she sensed in his caresses only made their coming together wilder, hotter, and so utterly magical that she pushed her doubts aside and showed him with her body the love that was in her heart.

CHAPTER ELEVEN

'*No!*' JAREK CLAWED his way out of the darkness of his nightmare and jerked his head off the pillows. His breath came in harsh pants, as if he had been running, and he remembered that in his dream he had been running through a forest, stumbling over tree roots, branches whipping across his face.

A man's voice was urging him to run faster. His father's assistant Asmir was ahead of him, holding the baby in his arms. Why wasn't his *mother* holding Eliana? Where were his *majka* and *tata*?

He turned his head to look for his parents and saw their car smashed up against a tree trunk. There was a loud bang and the bright orange glow of flames. Why didn't his parents come?

'Majka…' He started to run back to the burning car, but Asmir grabbed his arm and dragged him deeper into the forest…

Jarek swung his legs over the side of the bed and glanced at Holly as she stirred. But she did not wake up, and his heart twisted when she rolled into the space in the bed that he had just vacated. In the gossamer glow of dawn she looked like a sleeping angel, with her lovely face serene and her soft lips slightly parted. He would have liked to kiss her awake and tug the sheet from her body, to enjoy her one last time. But he dared not touch her now that he understood his nightmare. Now he knew what he had done.

'You destroy everything that is good,' his adoptive father had told him, and he knew now for certain that Ralph Saunderson had been right.

His phone was blinking, indicating that he had new messages. He pulled on a pair of jeans and walked out onto the balcony to read the email from the DNA testing clinic. Shock ripped through him, even though he had been half expecting to have confirmation that he *was* Prince Jarrett of Vostov.

There was a certain irony in the fact that he had received the result of the test on the same day that his amnesia had lifted, Jarek brooded. He was finally able to remember his parents, and he felt a deep sadness for what had happened to them and to him. He had spent most of his life unaware of his true identity, but now memories flooded his mind of his mother and father, and finally he was able to grieve for them.

His phone pinged constantly with new messages. Social media had gone mad, and he quickly discovered why when he read the news story that was making headlines around the world.

Vostov's Prince: Alive but Elusive! screamed one front page.

Where is Prince Jarrett hiding? asked another paper.

One of the tabloids had a photo of him and Holly on the boat, with the caption *Playboy Prince caught in Secret Tryst with Mystery Brunette.*

Who could have tipped off the press that he was Vostov's missing Prince? It had to be someone who worked at the DNA clinic, or even a member of Vostov's National Council, Jarek thought grimly. This was how his life would be from now on. The paparazzi were already fascinated by his playboy image, but their interest in him and those around him would be relentless now they knew that he was a prince.

He studied the images on his phone. At least Holly's face was obscured in the picture, and she was huddled on the floor of the sailing dingy. But it would only be a matter of time before she was identified, and then the paparazzi would stalk her and dig up every personal detail they could find about her.

He went cold at the thought that journalists might somehow get access to her medical records. Holly would be distraught if it was made public that she had been born with the rare syndrome. Despite his assurances that she was perfect, Jarek knew she struggled with body image issues.

The media machine was merciless, and he would have to move fast to protect her. The only way he'd be able to save her from unwanted press attention would be to make sure that Holly's identity remained a mystery.

He would *not* destroy her too, he vowed grimly as his adoptive father's accusation reverberated in his head. But that meant he must send her away from him and never see her again. He would accept his destiny, as Holly had once told him he must do, but he was aware that his life as a prince would be played out in the full glare of the public and the media spotlight.

A small sound from behind him made him turn his head, and he swallowed when he saw her standing there, wearing his shirt that she had never given back.

'I woke up and you were gone,' she said, her voice softly sleepy and so sexy that he was instantly painfully hard. Her dark eyes searched his face. 'Is everything all right?'

Nothing would ever be right again, but he did not tell her that. He shrugged. 'I've had the result of the DNA test and it proves beyond doubt that I *am* the only remaining male from the House of Karadjvic.'

'So you *are* Prince Jarrett. But in your heart you already knew that,' she murmured, 'because you'd remembered that Asmir worked for your father, Prince Goran.'

'I remember *everything*,' he bit out, and silently cursed himself—because he had not meant to say those words. He certainly did not intend to confide in Holly or confess his sins. Even an angel could not give him absolution.

'That's good,' she said gently. 'The secrets in your past have tormented you for too long.'

'Believe me, there is nothing *good* about my memories.'

She said nothing, and Jarek looked away from the deep pools of her eyes before he drowned in them.

'Tarik wasn't a person—he was a dog. My parents gave me a puppy when my sister was born.'

The words spilled out of him and he was unable to stop them. His grim little story had festered in his subconscious for so long, and in a strange way it was a relief to unburden himself to the one person he trusted absolutely.

'I was jealous of Eliana—Elin, as she is called now. Everyone made a fuss of the new baby, and I...'

He gripped the balcony rail as memories flooded his mind. He hadn't been a nice child, Jarek thought. He remembered feeling angry because his parents had loved the new baby more than him.

'I threw tantrums to gain attention. But then one day there was a puppy in the nursery—a cute little thing. Tarik was *my* dog, my father told me. But I would only be allowed to play with the puppy if I behaved like a young prince should.'

He closed his eyes and saw himself at six years old.

'One night my mother woke me up and told me that we were going on a trip in the car. We had to hurry, she said.

But I couldn't find Tarik, and I had a tantrum because I didn't want to leave without the puppy. My father was shouting at my mother to put me in the car.'

He let out a harsh breath.

'I'd never heard my father raise his voice before. My mother said I couldn't waste any more time searching for the dog. I had to be good and get into the car so that we could leave, or something bad would happen.'

He shook his head.

'I had no idea, of course, that Vostov had been invaded and my parents had been tipped off that the military dictatorship planned to ambush and kill the royal family.'

He swung round to face Holly.

'Don't you see?' he said savagely. 'It was *my* fault that my parents died. *My* bad behaviour caused my parents to delay escaping from the palace. Because of me something bad *did* happen—just as my mother had told me it would. My parents were trapped in the car when it exploded. My sister and I only lived because Asmir managed to get us out of the car in time, and then hid us at the orphanage in Sarajevo to protect us from being discovered by the military who ruled Vostov in place of my father.'

He stared at Holly and wondered why she hadn't recoiled from him in horror.

'Ralph Saunderson believed I was responsible for Lorna's death, but my ability to destroy began when I was a child,' he said rawly.

She shook her head. 'You said it yourself. You were a *child.*'

She walked across the balcony and stood in front of him, and the compassion in her eyes stunned Jarek because he knew he did not deserve it.

'Six-year-old boys have tantrums,' she said steadily. 'And an older child will often feel jealous of a new sibling.

These things happen in families everywhere, and just because you behaved like a normal six-year-old it does not make you responsible for the atrocity committed against your parents in a time of war.'

He almost believed her. But he heard his mother's voice telling him that something bad would happen if he wasn't good, and he saw the car with his parents inside burst into flames. He heard a shot fired from a gun and saw his adoptive mother fall to the floor, and he listened to Ralph Saunderson telling him he was reckless, destructive.

He tensed when Holly stepped closer to him and breathed in the sweet fragrance of her hair, which gleamed like raw silk in the pale gold light of early morning.

'I wish you could see the man I see,' she said softly. 'You don't destroy people. You saved your sister. You created a charity to help children living in orphanages have better lives.' She hesitated and lifted her eyes to his. 'You saved *me*.'

'It was my fault you were on the mountain when the avalanche struck,' he growled.

'I don't mean then. You didn't reject me when I told you about my medical condition. You were patient, and you helped me to accept my body instead of feeling ashamed that I need to use dilators so that I can have sex.' Soft colour came into her cheeks. 'And you made love to me with such wonderful passion that it's hardly surprising I…I fell in love with you.'

Jarek wanted to believe her. He wanted it so badly that he almost reached for her.

But he stopped himself because he knew the truth. He had been his adoptive father's heir but his parents had loved only his baby sister. Ralph Saunderson had barely tolerated him and his adoptive mother had pitied him. Elin had loved Lorna Saunderson, until he had ruined that for her, and now she loved Cortez.

No one had ever loved *him*, and he could see no reason why that would change—or why he should want it to, he reminded himself. Despite Holly's assurances he knew what he was, that he ruined lives. He was determined not to ruin hers.

'I warned you against falling in love with me,' he drawled, finding it harder that he'd expected to slip into the role he had carved out for himself years ago.

But somehow he needed to find the careless playboy who drank too much and laughed too hard. *God*, he would never laugh again—not the way Holly had made him laugh, with her wicked sense of humour and her warmth that felt like permanent sunshine.

He watched her expression change and become guarded, and the knowledge that she was guarding herself against him felt like a knife in his heart even as he told himself it was what he wanted. It was best for her.

'Could it be that you have ideas about being a princess?' His brows arched. 'You must admit that your timing is off. You tell me you love me ten minutes after learning that I am royal by birth?' he mocked.

She pressed her lips together and Jarek sensed that she would rather die than cry in front of him.

'You don't believe that,' she said, with a quiet certainty that rocked him. 'And, if you care to remember, I told you I love you the first time we slept together.'

He frowned. 'I assumed you said it in the heat of the moment and didn't mean it.'

'I never say things I don't mean. I've told you that I believe you are a good man and that you will be a great sovereign of Vostov. I understand why you are pushing me away, Jarek...'

Her gentle tone ripped him apart.

'But if you shut love out for ever I fear you will find life lonely at the top.'

It killed him to smile the lazy smile that had always come so easily to his lips at parties and meant nothing. But he had to protect her from the danger he knew he was.

'You obviously didn't read fairy tales when you were growing up,' he said, with a laugh that sounded fake to his own ears. '*Every* woman wants a prince, and I don't imagine I'll be lonely for long.'

He turned away from the hurt in her eyes and curled his hands around the balcony rail. The sun was rising over paradise, heralding a new day, but Jarek knew that from this day forward he would never watch the beauty of a sunrise without thinking of Holly.

'It will be better if we are not seen together, so we'll leave the island separately,' he told her. 'The helicopter will take you first and come back for me later today.'

'So this is goodbye?'

He did not hear her bare feet walking across the balcony, and he tensed when she was suddenly standing beside him. She put her hands on either side of his face and the ache inside him grew worse when she reached up and covered his mouth with hers. Somehow he held himself stiffly, and after a moment she ended the kiss and stepped back from him, her cheeks flushed and a betraying shimmer in her eyes.

'Be happy,' she whispered.

Jarek stared at the beach and did not turn to watch her walk away from him. He stood there, frozen, until he heard the helicopter take off, and when he looked up at the sky the sun was so bright that his vision was blurred.

It must be that, for it could not be tears that blinded him, Jarek assured himself. A man with an empty heart could not cry.

* * *

The window boxes outside the flat in Greenwich that Holly co-owned with her best friend Kate were ablaze with yellow daffodils. According to Kate, there had been snow in March, while Holly had been abroad, but April had arrived with pale sunshine, and the trees were sporting vibrant green leaves.

'A couple of items of mail arrived for you, but I couldn't forward them to you while you were staying at your secret location,' Kate told her. 'Are you allowed to reveal why you spent a month in Florida? Not that I'm jealous of your gorgeous tan!'

'I can't break a patient's confidentiality, but I can tell you I was giving counselling to a famous golfer who needed to work through some issues,' Holly explained. 'He chose not to check into the Frieden Clinic in Austria, so I stayed with him and his family at a secret location in Florida because he wanted to avoid the press finding out that he was seeing a psychologist.'

She found her unopened mail on the kitchen worktop, next to a pile of old newspapers ready to go into the recycling bin. Although Holly knew it was a form of masochism, she couldn't help herself from reading the numerous headlines about Vostov's return to a constitutional monarchy and its plans for the inauguration of Prince Jarrett. The Vostovian people were delighted to have their royal family back, and there had been many pictures of Princess Eliana, with her impossibly handsome husband Cortez and their two young children, when they had visited the Principality.

Elin was very beautiful, Holly thought as she studied a picture of Jarek's sister. It must have been a great shock to her when she had learned of her royal heritage.

There was much speculation in the press about Prince

Jarrett's need to find a bride to be his royal consort. The names of several minor royals and the daughters of aristocratic families across Europe were being mentioned. No doubt Jarek would marry a stunning bride with an impeccable pedigree and they would have beautiful children, Holly thought miserably.

While she had been in Florida she had focused on her job as a way of supressing her heartache, but as she stared at a photo of Jarek it all came hurtling back—his cold rejection and her stupid hope that if she kissed him she would reach the heart that she had glimpsed during those heavenly two weeks when they had been lovers in paradise. Holly went hot at the humiliating memory of how she had thrown herself at him.

She flicked through the pile of mainly junk mail addressed to her and opened a gold envelope, expecting it to contain advertising material.

An embossed card fell out, and she saw that it was an invitation to the Prince Jarrett's inaugural ball to be held at the royal palace in Vostov on the tenth of April.

The tenth was in two days' time, she realised.

Reading down, she discovered that she should have responded to the invitation a few days ago. At the bottom was a handwritten message, and her heart slammed into her ribs when she saw that it was from Jarek and said simply—*Please come. I need you.*

Twenty-four hours later Holly was following a footman along a corridor on her way to meet Jarek at his private apartment in the palace.

Everything had been a blur from the moment she had called the phone number on the invitation and given her name. A palace official had told her that a car would collect her from her London flat and take her to the airport, where Jarek's private jet would be waiting to bring her to Vostov.

She'd barely had time to pack, let alone question why she had agreed to see him when it was bound to end badly. But he had written on the invitation that he needed her, and like a fool she had rushed to him—again, she thought ruefully.

From the air, Vostov's royal residence had looked like a fairy tale palace, perched on a mountain, surrounded by higher snow-capped peaks and overlooking a gentian-blue lake. Inside, parts of the palace were still undergoing extensive restoration work, following the dark period of Vostovian history when a military dictatorship had imposed rule over the principality and the palace had been left to fall into ruin.

But now it was a new era, with the return of the monarchy, the footman told Holly. Prince Jarrett was already hugely popular, and he had published his plans to turn Vostov into a business hub and tourist venue which would bring wealth to the country.

The footman opened a door and stood aside for Holly to enter an elegant sitting room. Her stomach swooped when she saw Jarek standing in front of the fireplace. *He looked like a prince.* That was her first thought. His blond hair was shorter, although she noticed that he still pushed it off his brow, and for once he was clean-shaven. His face was leaner and even more handsome than the image of him that haunted her dreams.

The suit he wore was exquisitely tailored to show off his broad shoulders. But it was his eyes that held her attention: brilliant blue, and glittering with an expression she could not define but which made her heart-rate quicken when he crossed the room to stand in front of her.

'You look beautiful,' he rasped, almost as if it hurt his throat to speak.

She saw now he was closer that his skin was drawn tightly over his sharp cheekbones, making his resemblance to a wolf even more marked. She felt his gaze burn through the white silk jersey dress with its deep vee at the front. She had bought it in Florida and it had somehow seemed less revealing in the Sunshine State than it did in a palace. She was conscious of how the material clung to her curves and showed plainly that she wasn't wearing a bra. Jarek's eyes lingered on her breasts and she flushed as she felt her nipples harden.

'Where the bloody hell have you been for a month?' he demanded, making Holly flinch at the whiplash of his voice. 'Professor Heppel at the Frieden Clinic refused to reveal where you were, and your phone number was unavailable.'

'I had to get a new phone because I dropped mine over the side of the boat,' she reminded him.

She wished she could act cool, but she could feel the erratic thud of her pulse at the base of her throat, and with a flash of despair she realised that she would never escape from the spell he had cast over her—and she would never stop wanting him or loving him, a little voice in her head taunted her.

'How are you?' she whispered into the vast ache of tension that filled the room.

'Confused,' he said.

And now his voice did not feel like the sting of a whip. It was a low growl that made her skin prickle with sensual heat.

'You told me you love me, and yet ten minutes later you boarded a helicopter to take you off the island and effectively disappeared from the face of the earth. What kind of love is that?'

Her temper simmered. 'What did you expect me to do after you had made it so very clear that you didn't return my feelings?' she snapped. 'I had made enough of a fool of myself. There seemed no point in prolonging my embarrassment.'

His eyes narrowed on her scarlet face. 'Why did you come to Vostov? I'd given up hope that you would attend my ball when you ignored both the invitations that were sent to you. One went to Chalet Soline in Austria and the other to your London address,' Jarek said roughly.

'I didn't open it until I returned to London from Florida, where I'd been treating a patient. I came because you said you needed me. I assume you meant you needed to see a psychotherapist, and it isn't the first time I've flown across the globe at your command.'

Her eyes flashed at him.

'I definitely did *not* come to Vostov because I hope you will make me a princess,' she said sharply. 'From what I've read in the newspapers you won't have any problem finding a bride to be your consort. You're Europe's most eligible bachelor—I'm sure you haven't been lonely at all.'

Holly looked away from him, hoping he hadn't heard the scratch of jealousy in her voice.

'I've always been alone,' he said quietly. 'Until I met you. The vacancy for my bride is still open, as a matter of fact...' His casual tone was at odds with the intensity of his gaze. 'If you are interested.'

'Jarek—don't.' She couldn't keep it together, and knew the tremble in her voice betrayed her. 'If you asked me here so that you can carry out some kind of refined torture...'

He slipped his hand beneath her chin and tilted her face

up so that she was forced to look at him. And what she saw made her catch her breath.

'You told me to be happy,' he said, so grimly that she ached for him. 'And then you left. It felt like I'd been kicked in the gut. The truth was so clear but I had been so blind.'

His beautiful mouth shook and Holly's heart stood still.

'I had never been truly happy before I met you, and I knew as sure as hell that I would never be happy if I let you go.'

'Jarek…' Holly could not stop the tears that blurred her eyes from falling.

'I thought of all the things you had said,' he continued, in that rasp of a voice that was so raw it hurt her to hear it. 'You saw something good in me that nobody else saw and you made me think that I *could* be a better man, that I wasn't stuck for ever with the labels that Ralph Saunderson and others had put on me.'

He lifted his hand to her face and brushed away her tears.

'More importantly, you made me want to be a better man—a man you would be proud of.' He hesitated and stared at her, his expression unguarded and oddly desperate. 'A man you would love as deeply as I love you.'

She was afraid to believe him. 'You don't…'

'How could I *not* fall in love with you, angel-face?' he said softly. 'I thought I could protect you if I sent you away. But I was beyond miserable. And then I remembered you had told me you never say anything you don't mean, and I started thinking that if you *did* love me maybe you were as unhappy as I was.'

Holly's breath caught in her throat when Jarek dropped down onto one knee and reached into his jacket pocket. Through her tears she saw the sparkle of a diamond ring, and then he took her hand in his.

'Holly, my angel, will you marry me and be my wife, my Princess, and the love of my life?'

She shook her head, and her tears fell faster when the light in his eyes dulled and she saw the abandoned boy he had been in the face of the man she loved but had to let go.

'I can't marry you,' she choked. 'There's something you don't know about me.'

She pulled away from him and ran over to the door, but his voice stopped her.

'You mean the fact that you are unable to have children, don't you?'

'How do you know?' She turned slowly and watched him walk towards her.

'The syndrome you were born with is commonly known as MRKH, am I right?' At her nod, he continued gently, 'I did some research and I guessed you had been diagnosed with the syndrome when you hit puberty but your periods did not start because you were born without a womb.'

'I've come to terms with my infertility,' Holly said huskily. 'But you are a prince and you have to have an heir to continue the royal line.' She swallowed hard. 'I love you with all my heart...maybe I could be your mistress for a while, until you decide that you want to marry and have children.'

Jarek released his breath with obvious relief and his mouth curved into a grin. 'I hope you know that I will never let you forget that you propositioned me,' he murmured as he pulled her into his arms. 'I have already told Vostov's National Council that I intend to marry you, and I have explained that we won't have children. It has been agreed that the royal line will continue through my nephew. Elin's son Harry will be my heir, but if he chooses not to be the next Prince, Vostov will simply be ruled by the National Council after my death.'

'But you *must* want your own child?' she said painfully.

'I want *you*. You're all I'll ever want or need.'

The truth of his words was there for Holly to see in the fierce glitter in his eyes.

'I intend to combine my role as Prince with my work with Lorna's Gift, and I hope you will work with me. Your training as a psychologist will be invaluable to the many children in the world who need support.'

'I don't know what to say,' Holly whispered.

Moments ago the future had seemed hopeless and bleak, but now the look in Jarek's eyes—the *love*—filled her with a fragile hope.

'Just say yes to the following questions,' he told her, with a touch of his old arrogance that she adored because it was part of him. 'Do you love me?'

'Yes. More than life.'

'Will you marry me and be mine for ever?'

'Yes,' she said tremulously. 'If you will be mine.'

'I have always been yours, angel-face,' Jarek told her as he slipped an exquisite square-cut diamond ring onto her finger. 'I fell in love with you when you stood up in a hot tub, wearing the sexiest swimsuit I've ever seen.'

The heat in his gaze burned its way into Holly's soul so that when he kissed her she melted against him and kissed him back with love, with hope, and with a promise whispered against his lips that her heart was his for ever.

* * * * *

ROYALLY BEDDED, REGALLY WEDDED

JULIA JAMES

PROLOGUE

THE dark-haired figure seated at the antique desk and illuminated by an ornate, gold trimmed lamp slapped shut the leather folder, placed it on the growing pile to his right, and reached for yet another folder, opening it with an impatient flick. *Dio*, was there no end to these damned documents? How could so small a place as San Lucenzo generate so many of the things? Everything from officers' commissions to resolutions of the Great Council, all needing to be signed and sealed—by him.

Prince Rico gave a caustic twist of his well-shaped mouth. Perhaps he should be grateful the task seldom came his way. But with his older brother, the Crown Prince, in Scandinavia, representing the House of Ceraldi at a royal wedding, the temporarily indisposed Prince Regnant—their father—had for once been obliged to turn to his younger son to carry out those deputised duties he was generally excluded from.

Rico's eyes darkened for a moment with an old bitterness. Excluded from any involvement in the running of the principality—however tedious or trivial—yet his father still condemned him for the life he perforce led. The twist in his mouth deepened in cynicism. His father might deplore his younger son's well-earned reputation as the Playboy Prince, yet his exploits both in the world of expensive sports like powerboat racing, and on the glittering international social circuit—including the bedrooms of its most beautiful women—generated invaluable publicity for San Lucenzo. And, considering just how much of the principality's revenues derived from it being one of the world's most glamorous locales, his part in contributing to that glamour was not small. Not that either his father or older brother saw it that way. To them, his exploits brought the attention of the paparazzi and the constant risk of scandal— both of which were anathema to the strait-laced Ruling Prince of San Lucenzo and his upright heir.

Not, Rico grudgingly allowed, as he scanned through the document in his hand, that they were not sometimes justified in their concerns. Carina Collingham was an unfortunate instance in that respect—though how he could have been expected to know she was lying when she told him her divorce was through was beyond him.

Despite his instantly having dissociated himself from her the moment he'd discovered the unpalatable truth about the marital status of the film actress, the damage had been done, and now his father had yet another complaint to lay at his younger son's door.

His older brother, Luca, had taken him to task as well, berating him for not having had Carina security-checked adequately before bedding her. Better to exercise some self-restraint when it came to picking women out of the box like so much candy.

'There's safety in numbers,' Rico had replied acerbically. 'While I play the field, no woman thinks she has the ticket on me. Unlike you.' He'd cast a mordant look at his brother, along whose high Ceraldi cheekbones a line had been etched. 'You watch yourself, Luca,' he'd told him. 'Christabel Pasoni has plans for you.'

'Christa's perfectly content with the way things are,' Luca had responded repressively. 'And she does *not* cause a scandal in the press.'

'That's because her fond papa owns so much of it! *Dio*, Luca, can't you damn well ask her to tell *Papa* to instruct his editors to lay off me?'

But Luca had been unsympathetic.

'They wouldn't write about you if they had nothing to write. Don't you think it's time to grow up, Rico, and face your responsibilities?'

Rico's expression had hardened.

'If I had any, I might just do that,' he'd shot back, and walked away.

Well, he'd wanted responsibilities and now he'd got some—signing documents because there was no one else available to do so, and atoning for having had a misplaced affair with a still-technically-married woman.

Maybe if I sign every damn document in my best handwriting before Luca gets back I'll have earned a royal pardon...

But his caustic musing was without humour, and impatiently he scanned the document now in front of him. Something to do with a petition from a convent to be rescinded of the obligation to pay property tax on land on which a hospital had been built in the seventeenth century—a petition which, so the helpful handwritten note appended by his father's equerry reminded him, was nothing more than a *pro forma* request, made annually and granted annually since 1647, requiring nothing more than the customary royal assent. Dutifully, Rico scrawled the royal signature, put down the quill, and reached for the sealing wax, melting the required dark scarlet blob below his name, and then waiting a few moments for it to cool before impressing on it the royal seal. He was just replacing the seal when his phone went.

Not the phone on the desk, but his own mobile—to which very, very few people had the number. Frowning slightly, he slid a long fingered hand inside his jacket pocket and flicked open the handset.

'Rico?'

He recognised the voice at once, and his frown deepened. Whenever Jean-Paul phoned it was seldom good news—certainly not at this late hour of the night. The hour when, Rico knew from experience, the press went to bed. And what a certain section of the press across Europe all too often went to bed with was a story of just who *he* had gone to bed with.

Damn—had the vultures stirred yet more trouble for him over Carina Collingham? Had she been milking the situation for yet more publicity for her career?

'OK, Jean-Paul, tell me the worst,' he said, when foreboding.

The gossip-columnist, who was also the impoverished grandson of a French count, as well as a rare genuine friend in the press, started to speak. But the story that he'd heard was about to break had nothing to do with Carina Collingham. Nothing to do with any of Rico's *affaires*.

'Rico,' said Jean-Paul, and his voice was unusually grave, 'it's about Paolo.'

Rico stilled. Slowly he released his hand from the back of his neck and slipped it down on to the leather surface of the desk. It tensed, unconsciously, into a fist.

'If *anyone*—' his voice was a soft, deadly snarl '—thinks they are going to dig any dirt on him, they are—'

He could hear the wariness in the other man's voice as he interrupted.

'I wouldn't call it dirt, Rico. But I would…' he paused minutely '…call it trouble. Seriously big trouble.'

Emotion splintered through Rico.

'*Dio*, Paolo is *dead*. His broken body got pulled from the wreckage of a car over four years ago.'

Pain stabbed him. Even now he could not bear to think about, to remember, how Paolo—the golden prince, the only one of his father's three sons who had ever won his parents' indulgence—had been snuffed out before he was even twenty-two. Like a bright flame extinguished by the dark.

The news had devastated the family. Even Luca had wept openly at the funeral, where the two of them had been the chief pallbearers who had carried their young brother's black-swathed coffin into the cathedral on that unbearable day.

And now, years later, some slimeball hack *dared* to write some kind of sleaze about Paolo.

'What kind of trouble?' he demanded icily. On the desk, his hand fisted more tightly.

There was a distinct pause, as if Jean-Paul were mentally gathering courage. Then he spoke.

'It's about the girl who was in the car crash with him…'

Rico froze.

'What girl?' he asked slowly, as every drop of blood in his veins turned to ice.

Haltingly, Jean-Paul told him.

CHAPTER ONE

*'Oh my darling, oh my darling, oh my darling Benjy-mine—
You are mucky, oh, so mucky, so it's Benjy's bathy-time.'*

Lizzy chirruped away, pushing the laden buggy along the narrow country lane as dusk gathered in the hedgerows. Crows were cawing overhead in the trees near the top of the hill, and the last light of day dwindled in the west, towards the sea, half a mile back down the coombe. It was still only late spring, and primroses gleamed palely in the verges and clustered in the long grass of the lower part of the hedge. The upper part was made of stunted beech, its branches slanted by the prevailing west wind off the Atlantic, which, even now, was combing along the lane and whipping her hair into yet more of a frizz—though she'd fastened it back as tightly as she could. But what did she care about her awful hair, charity shop clothes and total lack of looks? Ben didn't, and he was all she cared about in the world.

'Not *mucky*, Mummy. *Sandy*,' Ben corrected her, craning his head round reprovingly in the buggy.

'Mucky with sand,' compromised Lizzy.

'Keep singing,' instructed Ben.

She obeyed. At least Ben was an uncritical audience. She had no singing voice at all, she knew, but for her four-year-old son that was not a problem. Nor was it a problem that everything he wore, and all his toys—such as they were—came from jumble sales or from charity shops in the local Cornish seaside town.

Nor was it a problem that he had no daddy, like most other children seemed to have.

He's got *me*, and that's all he needs, Lizzy thought fiercely, her hands gripping the buggy handles as she pushed it along up the steepening road, hastening her pace slightly. It was growing late, and therefore dark, but Ben had been enjoying himself so much on the beach, even though it was far too cold yet to swim, that she had stayed later than she had intended.

But its proximity to the beach had been the chief reason that Lizzy had bought the tiny cottage, despite its run-down condition, eleven months ago, after selling her flat in the London suburbs. It was much better to bring a child up in the country.

Her face softened.

Ben. Benedict.

Blessed.

That was what his name meant, and it was true—oh, so true! He had been blessed with life against all the odds, and *she* had been blessed with him. No mother, she knew, could love her child more than she did.

Not even a birth mother.

Grief stabbed at her with a familiar pain. Maria had been so *young*. Far too young to leave home, far too young to be a model, far too young to get pregnant and far too young to die. To be smashed to pieces in a hideous pile-up on a French motorway before she was twenty.

Lizzy's eyes were pierced with sorrow. Maria—so lovely, so pretty. The original golden girl. Her long blonde hair, her wide-set blue eyes and angelic smile. Her slender beauty had been the kind of beauty that turned heads.

And sold clothes.

Their parents had been aghast when Maria had bounded in from school, still in her uniform, and told them that she'd been spotted by a scout for a modelling agency. Lizzy had been despatched to chaperon the eighteen-year-old Maria when she went up to the West End for her try-out shoot. The two girls had reacted very differently to the experience, Lizzy recalled. Maria had been ecstatic, instantly looking completely at home in the fashionable milieu, while Lizzy couldn't have felt more out of place or more awkward—as if she were contaminated by some dreadful disease.

Lizzy knew what that disease was. She'd known it ever since her blue-eyed, golden-haired sister had been born, two years after her, when, overnight, she had become supremely unimportant to her parents. Her sole function had been to look out for Maria. And that was what she'd done. Walked Maria to school, stayed late at clubs Maria had belonged to, helped her with her homework and then, later, with exam revision. Although Maria, being naturally clever, had not, so her parents had often reminded her, needed much help from her—especially as Lizzy's own exam results had hardly been dazzling. But then, who had *expected* them to be dazzling? No one. Just as no one had expected her to make any kind of mark in the world at all. And because of that, and because going to college cost money, Lizzy had not gone to college. The pennies had been put by to see Maria through university.

But all their hopes had been ruined—Maria had been offered a modelling contract. She'd been over the moon, telling her parents that she could always go to university later, and pay for it herself out of her earnings. Her parents had not been pleased, they had looked forward to spending their money on Maria.

'Well, now you can pay for Lizzy to go to college instead,' Maria had said. 'You know she always wanted to go.'

But it had been ridiculous to think of that. At twenty, Lizzy had been too old to be a student, and not nearly bright enough. Besides, they'd needed Lizzy to work in the corner shop that her father owned, in one of London's outer suburbs.

'Lizzy, leave home,' Maria had urged, the first time she'd come back after starting her new career. 'They treat you like a drudge like some kind of lesser mortal. Come up to London and flat with me. It's a hoot, honestly. Loads of fun and parties. I'll get you glammed up, and we can—'

'No.' Lizzy's voice had been sharp.

Maria had meant it kindly. For all her parents' attention to her she had never been spoilt, and her warm, sunny nature had been as genuine as her golden looks. But what she'd suggested would have been unbearable. The thought of being the plain, lumpy older sister dumped in a flat full of teenage models who all looked as beautiful as Maria had been hideous.

But she should have gone, she knew. Had known as soon as that terrible, terrible call had come, summoning her to the hospital in France where Maria had been taken.

If she'd been living with Maria surely she'd have found out about the affair she'd started? Perhaps even been able to stop it? Guilt stabbed her. At least she'd have known who Maria was having an affair *with*.

Which would have meant—she glanced down at Ben's fair head—she would have known who had got her pregnant.

But she did not know and now she would never know.

She paused in her tuneless singing. Further back down the lane she could hear the sound of a car engine. Instinctively she tucked the buggy closer to the verge. There was a passing place further along, but she doubted she could reach it before the approaching vehicle did. Wishing it weren't quite so dusky, she paused, half lifting one set of buggy wheels on to the verge, and warning Ben that a car was coming along.

Headlights cut through the gathering gloom and swept up the lane, followed by a powerful vehicle. It slowed as the lights picked her out, and for a moment Lizzy thought it was going to stop. Then it was past them, and accelerating forward. As it did so, she frowned slightly. The lane she was walking along led inland, whereas the road back to the seaside town ran parallel to the coast. Little traffic came along this lane. Well, maybe the occupants were staying at a farm or a holiday cottage inland. Or maybe they were just lost. She went on pushing the buggy up the final part of the slope, and then around the bend to where her cottage was.

As she finally rounded the curve she saw, to her surprise, that the big four-by-four had parked outside her cottage.

A shiver of apprehension flickered through her. This was a very safe part of the world, compared to the city, but crime wasn't unknown. She slid her hand inside her jacket and flicked her mobile phone on, ready to dial 999 if she had to. As she approached her garden gate she saw two tall figures get out of the car and come towards her. She paused, right by her gate, one hand in her pocket, her finger hovering over the emergency number.

'Are you lost?' she asked politely.

They didn't answer, just closed in on her. Every nerve in her body started to fire. Then, abruptly, one of them spoke.

'Miss Mitchell?'

His voice was deep, and accented. She didn't know what accent. Something foreign, that was all. She looked at him, still with every nerve firing. His face was shadowed in the deepening dusk; she just got an impression of height, of dark eyes—and something else. Something she couldn't put a name to.

Except that it made her say slowly, 'Yes. Why do you want to know?'

Instinctively she moved closer to the buggy, putting herself between it and the strangers.

'Who are those men?' Ben piped up. His little head craned around as he tried to see, because she'd pointed the buggy straight at the gate to the garden.

She heard the man give a rasp in his throat. Then he was speaking again. 'We need to speak to you, Miss Mitchell. About the boy.' There was a frown across his brow, a deep frown, as he looked at her.

'Who are you?' Lizzy's voice was shrill suddenly, infected with fear.

Then the other man, more slightly built, and older, spoke.

'There is no cause for alarm, Miss Mitchell. I am a police officer, and you are perfectly safe. Be assured.'

A police officer? Lizzy stared at him. His voice had the

same accent as the taller, younger man, whose gaze had gone back fixedly to Ben.

'You're not English.'

The first man's eyebrows rose as he turned back to her. 'Of course not,' he said, as if that were a ridiculous observation. Then, with a note of impatience in his voice, he went on, 'Miss Mitchell, we have a great deal to discuss. Please be so good as to go inside. You have my word that you are perfectly safe.'

The other man was reaching forward, pushing open the gate and ushering her along the short path to her front door. Numbly she did as she was bade. Tension and a deep unease were still ripping through her. As she gained the tiny entrance hall of the cottage she paused to unlatch Ben from his safety harness. He struggled out immediately, and turned to survey the two tall men waiting in the doorway to gain entrance.

Lizzy straightened, and flicked on the hall light, surveying the two men herself. As her gaze rested on the younger of the two, she saw he was staring, riveted, at Ben.

There were two other things she registered about him that sent conflicting emotions shooting through her.

The first was, quite simply, that in the stark light of the electric bulb the man staring down at Ben was the most devastatingly good-looking male she'd ever seen.

The second was that he looked terrifyingly like her sister's son.

In shocked slow motion Lizzy helped Ben out of his jacket and boots, then her own, then folded up the buggy and leant it against the wall. Her stomach was tying itself into knots. Oh, God, what was happening? Fear shot through her, and convulsed in her throat.

'This is the way to the kitchen,' announced Ben, and led the way, looking with great interest at these unexpected visitors.

The warmth of the kitchen from the wood-burning range made Lizzy feel breathless, and the room seemed tiny with the two men standing in it. Instinctively she stood behind Ben as he climbed on to a chair to be higher. Both men were still regarding him intently. Fear jerked through her again.

'Look, what *is* this?' she demanded sharply. Her arm came around Ben's shoulder in a protective gesture. The man who looked like Ben turned briefly to the other man, and said something low and rapid in a foreign language.

Italian, she registered. But the recognition did nothing to help her. She didn't understand Italian, and what the man had just said to the other one she'd no idea. But she understood what he said next.

'*Prego,*' he murmured. 'Captain Falieri will look after the boy in another room while we…' he paused heavily '…talk.'

'No.' Her response was automatic. Panicked.

'The boy will be as safe,' said the man heavily, 'as if he had his own personal bodyguard.' He looked down at Ben. 'Have you got any toys? Captain Falieri would like to see them. Will you show them to him? Can you do that?'

'Yes,' said Ben importantly. He scrambled down. Then he glanced at Lizzy. 'May I, please?'

She nodded. Her heart was still pounding as she watched the older man accompany Ben out of the kitchen. Supposing the other man just walked out of the house with Ben. Supposing he drove off with him. Supposing…

'The boy is quite safe. I merely require to talk to you without him hearing at this stage. That much is obvious, I would have thought.'

There was reproof in the voice. As though she were making trouble. Making a nuisance of herself.

She dragged her eyes to him, away from Ben leading the other man into the chilly living room.

He was looking at her from across the table. Again, like a blow to her chest, his resemblance to Ben impacted through her. Ben was fair, and this man was dark, but the features were so similar.

Fear and shock buckled her again.

What if this was Ben's father?

Her stomach churned, his heartbeat racing. Desperately she tried to calm herself.

Even if he's Ben's father he can't take him from me—he can't!

Faintness drummed through her. Her hand clung on to the back of the kitchen chair for strength.

'You are shocked.' The deep, accented voice did not hold reproof any more, but the dark eyes were looking at her assessingly. As if he were deciding whether she really was shocked.

She threw her head back.

'What else did you expect?' she countered.

His eyes pulled away from her and swept the room. Seeing the old-fashioned range, the almost as old-fashioned electric cooker, ancient sink, worn work surfaces and the scrubbed kitchen table standing on old flagstones.

'Not this,' he murmured. Now there was disparagement clear in his voice. His face.

The face that looked so terrifyingly like Ben's.

'Why are you here?' The words burst from her.

The dark eyebrows snapped together. So dark, he was, and yet Ben so fair. And yet despite the difference in colouring, the bones were the same, the features terrifyingly similar.

'Because of the boy, obviously. He cannot remain here.'

She felt the blood drain from her.

'You can't take him. You can't swan in here five years after conceiving him and—'

'*What?*' The single word was so explosive that it stopped Lizzy dead in her tracks.

For one long, shattering moment he just stared at her with a look of total and utter stupefaction on his face. As if the world completely and absolutely did not make sense. Lizzy stared back. Why was he looking at her like that? As if she were insane. Deranged.

'*I* am not Ben's father.'

The words bit from him. Relief washed through her, knocking the wind out of her. The terror that had been dissolving her stomach—the terror that, for all her defiance, this man invading her home had the power to take Ben from her, or at the very least to demand a presence in her son's life—the fear that had gripped her since she had seen the startling resemblance in their faces, began to subside.

'I am Ben's uncle.' The words were flat. Irrefutable. 'It was my brother, Paolo, who was Ben's father. And, as you must know, Paolo—like your sister Maria, Ben's mother—is dead.' Now his voice was bleak, stark.

Lizzy waited for the flush of relief to go through her again. The man who had got her sister pregnant was dead. He could never threaten her. Could never threaten Ben. She should feel relief at that.

But no such emotion came. Instead, only a terrible empty grief filled her.

Dead. Both dead. Both parents. And suddenly it seemed just so incredibly, blindingly sad. So cruel that Ben had had ripped from him both the people who had created him.

'I'm…I'm sorry,' she heard herself saying, her throat tight suddenly.

For just a moment the expression in his eyes changed, as if just for the briefest second they were both feeling the same emotion, the same grief at such loss. Then, like a door shutting, it was gone.

'I've…I've never known who Ben's father was.' Lizzy's voice was bleak. 'My sister never regained consciousness. She stayed in a coma until Ben was full-term, and then—' She broke off. Something struck her. She looked at the man who looked so much like Ben, who was his uncle. 'Did…did you know about Ben?'

The brows snapped together. 'Of course not. His existence was entirely unknown. That might seem impossible, given the circumstances of his parents' death, which seem to have concealed even from you the identity of his father. However, thanks to the mercenary investigations of a muck-raking journalist, about which thankfully I have been recently informed, his existence is unknown no longer. Which is why—' his voice sharpened, the initial impatience and imperiousness returning '—he must immediately be removed from here.' His mouth pressed tightly a moment. 'We may have located you ahead of the press, but if we can find you, so can they. Which means that both you and the boy must leave with us immediately. A safe house has been organised.'

'What journalist? What do you mean, the press?'

A frown darkened his brow.

'Do not be obtuse. The moment the boy's location is discovered, the press will arrive like a pack of jackals. We must leave immediately.'

Lizzy stared uncomprehendingly. This was insane. What was going on?

'I don't understand. I don't understand any of this. Why would the press come here?'

'To find my nephew. What do you imagine?' Impatience and exasperation were snapping through him.

'But why? What possible interest can the press have in Ben?'

He was staring at her. Staring at her as if she were completely insane.

Across the hall, Ben's piping voice came from the living room, talking about his trainset.

'This is the level crossing, and that's the turntable.'

His voice faded again.

The man who was Ben's uncle was still staring at her. Lizzy started to feel cold seep through her.

'We haven't done anything.' Her voice was thin. 'Why would any journalist be interested in Ben? He's a four-year-old child.'

That look was still in his eye. He stood, quite motionless.

'He was born. That is quite enough. His parentage ensures that.' Exasperated anger suddenly bit through his voice. 'Surely to God you have intelligence enough to understand that?'

Slowly, Lizzy took another careful step backwards. She did

not like being so physically close to this man. It was overpowering, disturbing. Her heart was hammering in her chest.

What did he mean, Ben's parentage? She stared at him. Apart from his being so extraordinarily, devastatingly good-looking, she did not recognise him. He looked like Ben, that was all. A dark version. Very Italian. He must be quite well-off, she registered. The four-by-four was a gleaming brand-new model. And he was wearing expensive clothes; she could see that. He had the sleek, impeccably groomed appearance of someone who wore clothes which, however deceptively casual, had cost a lot of money. And he had that air about him of someone who was used to others jumping to do his bidding. So he could easily be rich.

But why would that bring the press down in droves? Rich Italians were not so unique that the press wrote stories about them.

A frown crossed her face. But what about his brother, Paolo? His dead brother who was Ben's father. Had he been someone the press would be interested in?

He'd said that surely she must know that Paolo was dead. But how should she? She knew nothing about him.

Carefully, very carefully, she spoke.

'My sister was not a supermodel, she was just starting out on her career—just making a name for herself. No journalist would be interested in her. But your brother—the man she…she had a child by. Was he—I don't know—someone well known in Italy? Was he a film star there, or on the television? Or a footballer, a racing driver? Something like that? Some kind of celebrity? Is that what you mean by Ben's parentage?'

She stared at him, a questioning look on her face. Slowly, it changed to one of bewilderment.

He was looking at her as if she were an alien. Fear stabbed her again.

'What—what is it?'

His eyes were boring into her face. As if he were trying to penetrate into her brain.

'This cannot be,' he said flatly. 'It is not possible.'

Lizzy stared. *What* was not possible?

He was holding himself in; she could see it.

'It is not possible that you have just said what you said.' His expression changed, and now he was not talking to her as if she were retarded, but as if she were—unreal. As if this entire exchange were unreal.

'My brother—' he spoke, each word falling as heavy as lead into the space between them '—was Paolo Ceraldi.'

Nothing changed in her expression. She swallowed. 'I'm sorry—the name does not mean anything to me. Perhaps in Italy it might, but—'

A muscle worked in his cheek. His eyes were like black holes.

'Do not, Miss Mitchell, play games with me. That name is *not* unknown to you. It *cannot* be. Nor can the name of San Lucenzo.'

Her face frowned slightly. San Lucenzo? Perhaps that was where Ben's father had come from. But, even if he had, why the big deal?

'That's…that's that place near Italy that's like Monaco. One of those places left over from the Middle Ages.' She spoke cautiously. 'On the Riviera or somewhere. Lots of rich people live there. But…but I'm sorry. The name Paolo Ceraldi still doesn't mean anything to me, so if he was famous there, I'm afraid I just don't—'

The flash in his eyes had come again. With cold, chilling courtesy he spoke, but it was not civil.

'The House of Ceraldi, Miss Mitchell, has ruled San Lucenzo for eight hundred years,' he said sibilantly.

There was silence. Complete silence. Some incredibly complicated arcane equation was trying to work itself out in her brain, but she couldn't do it.

Then the deep, chilling voice came again, icy with a courtesy that was not courteous at all.

'Paolo's father is the Ruling Prince.' He paused, brief and deadly, while his eyes speared hers. 'He is your nephew's grandfather.'

CHAPTER TWO

MIST was rolling in, like thick cotton wool. She felt the room start to swirl around her. Instinctively, she grabbed out with her hand and caught the edge of the kitchen table. She clung on to it.

Not true.

Not true. Not true. Not true.

If she just kept saying it, it would be true. True that it was *not* true. Not true what this man had just said. Because of course it wasn't true. It couldn't be true. It was absurd. Stupid. Impossible. A lie. Some stupid, absurd, impossible lie—or joke. Maybe it was a joke. That must be it. Just a joke. She threw her head back to suck in deep draughts of air. Then she steadied herself, forcibly, and made herself look across at the man who had just said such a stupid, absurd, impossible thing.

'This isn't true.'

Her voice was flat. As flat, she realised, with a hideous, gaping recognition in her guts, as his had been when she'd said she had no idea who…

Ben's father. Ben's father was.

'No.' She'd spoken out loud. Her legs were starting to shake. 'No. This is a joke. It's impossible. It has to be. It's just not possible. I haven't understood it properly.'

'You had better sit down.' The voice was still chill, but less so. Lizzy gazed at him with wide, shock-splintered eyes. Her eyebrows shot together in a frown.

That complicated, arcane equation was still running in her head.

He had just said that Ben's father had been the son of…she forced her mind to say it … the son of the Prince of San Lucenzo. But he had said he was Ben's uncle. His dead father's brother. Which meant that *his* father was also…

She stared. It wasn't possible. It just wasn't possible.

He let her stare. She could see it. Could see he was just standing there while she clung to the edge of the table in the kitchen in her tiny little Cornish cottage where, a few feet away, from her stood.

'I am Enrico Ceraldi,' he enlightened her.

She sat down. Collapsing on the kitchen chair with a heavy thud.

He cast a look at her.

'Did you really not know who I was?' There was almost curiosity in his voice. And something flickered in his eyes.

'Of course I bloody didn't.' The return burst from her lips without her thinking. Then, as if she'd just realised what she'd done, her face stiffened.

'I'm sorry,' she spoke abruptly. 'I didn't mean to be—' She broke off. Something changed in her face again. She lifted her chin, looking directly into his eyes. 'I didn't mean to speak rudely. But, no,' she said heavily, yet still with her chin lifted, 'I did not recognise you. I've heard of you—it would be hard not to have.' Her voice tightened with disapproval. 'But not with the surname, of course. Just your first name and…' she paused, then said it '…your title.'

She got to her feet. The room swayed, but she ignored it. A bomb had exploded in her head, ripping everything to shreds. But she had to cope with it. She straightened her spine.

'I find this very hard to deal with. I'm sure you understand. And I am also sure you understand that I have a great many questions I need to ask. But also—' she held his eyes and spoke resolutely '—I need time to come to terms with this. It is, after all, quite unbelievable.'

She looked at him directly. Refusing to look away.

Long, sooted lashes swept down over his dark eyes. Eyes, she realised, with the now familiar hollowing still going on inside her stomach, that were more used to looking out of photographs in celebrity magazines and the gossip pages of newspapers.

I didn't recognise him. I simply didn't recognise him. He's all over the press and I never recognised him.

But why should I? And why should I think that someone like him could turn up here and tell me that...that Ben is...

Shock kicked through her again.

She bowed her head. It was too much. It was all too much.

'I can't take any more.'

She must have spoken aloud, defeat in her voice.

For one long, hopeless minute she just stared blankly into the eyes of the man standing opposite her. The brother of Ben's father. Who was dead. Who had been the son of the Reigning Prince of San Lucenzo. Who was also the father of the man standing opposite her.

Who was therefore a prince.

Standing in her living room.

'I can't take any more,' she said again.

Rico shifted his head slightly, and glanced behind him as the occasional dazzle of other traffic on the motorway illuminated the interior of the vehicle.

She was asleep. So was the boy. She was holding his hand, reaching out to him in the child seat he was fastened into.

His mouth pressed together and he looked away again, back out over the glowing stream of red tail-lights ahead of him. Beside him, Falieri drove steadily and fast, the big four-by-four eating up the miles.

Rico stared out over the motorway.

Paolo's son. Paolo's son was sitting in the car. A son that none of his family had known about.

How could it have happened?

The question seared through him, as it had done so often since Jean-Paul had told him the story that was set to break in the press. It seemed impossible that Paolo's son should have disappeared, without anyone even knowing of his existence. And yet, in the nightmare of that motorway pile-up in France all those years ago, with smashed cars and smashed bodies, he could see how rescue workers, finding the female occupant of Paolo's car still alive and clearly pregnant, had cut her free first and rushed her to hospital. A different hospital from the one where Paolo's mangled body had been taken hours later, when all those still living had been dealt with.

Cold horror chilled through him. In the carnage no one had made the connection between the two—the dead Prince Paolo Ceraldi and the unknown young woman, comatose and pregnant.

Never to regain consciousness.

Never to tell who had fathered her child.

And so no one had known. No one until some get-lucky hack had decided to see if there was any mileage in a rehash of the tragedy of Paolo's death, and his investigations had turned up, against all the odds, a French fireman who'd mentioned he had freed a woman from the wreckage of the very type of sports car that the journalist knew Paolo Ceraldi had been driving. From that single item the hack had burrowed and burrowed, until he had pieced together the extraordinary, unbelievable story.

How Prince Paolo Ceraldi, dead at twenty-one, had left an orphaned son behind.

The story would blaze across the tabloids.

'*Get the boy.*'

Luca's urgent command echoed in Rico's head. He'd phoned Luca the moment he'd hung up on Jean-Paul.

'We have to get the boy before the press does,' Luca had said. 'Get Falieri on to it tonight. But, Rico, it's essential we look as if we don't know about the story. If they think we are trying to stop it, they'll run with it immediately. In the meantime—' his voice had hardened '—I will contact Christa. Maybe for once

I will, after all, exact a favour from her father…it won't stifle the story, but it may just delay it. Buy us some time. Enough for Falieri to get the child safely out of their reach.' He'd paused, then gone on, his voice dry. 'It seems, just for once, Rico, that your close proximity to the press has come in handy.'

'Glad to be of use,' Rico had replied, his voice even drier. 'For once.'

'Well, you can really be of use now,' Luca had cut back. 'I can't leave this wedding, if I did it would simply arouse suspicion, so I'm stuck here for the duration. I'm counting on you to hold the fort. But Rico?' His voice had held a warning note in it. 'Leave it to me to tell our father about this debacle, OK? He'll take it a lot better from me.'

Rico hadn't stuck around to find out how his father had taken the news that the Ceraldis were about to face their biggest trial by tabloid yet. He'd had only one imperative. To find Paolo's son.

Emotion buckled him. He'd been holding it back as much as he could, because there had been no time for it. No time to do anything other than get hold of Falieri and track down the child his brother had fathered.

He felt his heart squeeze tightly. It was incredible that here, now, just in the seat behind him, his brother's son was sleeping. It was almost like having Paolo back again.

Debacle, Luca had called it. And Rico knew he was right. He loathed the thought of all the tabloid coverage that was inevitably going to erupt, even with the boy safely with him now, but far more powerful was the sense of wonder and gratitude coursing through him.

He turned in his seat, his eyes resting on the sleeping form of the small boy.

His heart squeezed again. Even in the poor light he could see Paolo's features, see the resemblance. To think that his brother's blood pulsed in those delicate veins, that that small child was his own nephew.

Paolo's son. His brother's child. The brother who had been killed so senselessly, so tragically.

And yet—

He had had a son.

All these years, growing up here, in this foreign country, raised by a woman who was not even his own mother, not knowing who he was.

We didn't know. How could we not have known?

A cold, icy chill went through him.

For a long moment his eyes watched over the sleeping boy, seeing his little chest rise and fall, the long lashes folded down on his fair skin.

Then, slowly, they moved to the figure beside the child seat.

His expression changed, mouth tightening.

This was a complication they could do without.

His gaze rested on her. A frown gathered between his brows. Had she really not realised who he was? It seemed incredible, and yet her shock had been genuine. His frown deepened. He had never before encountered anyone who did not know who he was.

He dragged his mind away. It was irrelevant that his reaction to her evident complete ignorance of his identity had…had what? Irritated him? Piqued him? No, none of those, he asserted to himself. He was merely totally unaccustomed to not being recognised. He had been recognised wherever he went, all his life. Everyone always knew who he was.

So being stared at as if he were the man in the moon had simply been a new experience for him. That was all.

Dio, he dismissed impatiently. What did he care if the girl hadn't realised who he was? It was, as he had said, irrelevant. She knew now. That was all that mattered. And once she'd accepted it—not that the look of glazed shock had left her face until she'd fallen asleep in the vehicle—it had at least had the thankful effect of making her co-operate finally. Silently, numbly, but docilely.

She'd made sandwiches and drinks for herself and Ben,

telling him while he ate that they were going on an adventure, and then heading upstairs to pack. Ben had shown no anxiety, only curiosity and excitement. Rico had done his best to give him an explanation he could understand.

'I...' He had hesitated, then said it, a shaft of emotion going through him as he did so. 'I am your uncle, Ben, and I have only just found out that you live here. So I am taking you on a little holiday. We'll need to leave now, though, and drive in the night.'

It had seemed to suffice.

He had fallen asleep almost instantly, the car having only gone a few miles, and it had not taken a great deal longer for the aunt to fall asleep as well. Rico was glad. A car was not the place for the next conversation they must have.

He glanced at her now, his face tightening in automatic male distaste at the plain-faced female, with her unflattering frizzy hair and even more unflattering nondescript clothes.

She couldn't be more different from Maria Mitchell. She possessed not a scrap of her sister's looks. Maria had been one of those naturally eye-catching blondes, tall and slender, with wide-set blue eyes and a heart-shaped face. No wonder she'd become a model. The photos Falieri had dug up of her had shown exactly how she must have attracted Paolo.

They would have made a golden couple.

Pain bit at him, again. *Dio*, both of them wiped out, their young lives cut short in a crush of metal. But leaving behind a secret legacy.

Rico's eyes went back to his nephew, softening.

We'll take care of you now—don't worry. You're safe with us.

Oblivious, Ben slept on.

Lizzy stirred. Even as the first threads of consciousness returned, she reached automatically across the wide bed.

It was all right. Ben was there. For a moment she let her hand rest on the warm, pyjama-covered back of her son, still fast asleep on the far side of the huge double bed. They were in some kind of private house, at which they'd arrived in the middle of the night—specially rented, and staffed by San Lucenzans flown in from the royal palace, or so she had been told by Captain Falieri. A safe house. Safe from prying journalists.

Disbelief washed through her, as it had done over and over again since that moment when she'd stared at the man who had invaded her cottage and realised who he was.

She was still in shock, she knew. She had to be. Because why else was she so calm? Partly it was for Ben's sake. Above all he must not be upset, or distressed. For his sake she must treat this as normal.

Impossible as that was.

What's going to happen?

The question arrowed through her, bringing a churning anxiety to her stomach.

Was the Prince still here? Or had he left her with Captain Falieri. She hoped he was gone. She was not comfortable with him.

She shifted in her bed. Even had he not been royal, let alone infamous in the press—what did they call him? The Playboy Prince? Was that it?—she could never have been comfortable in his company. No man that good-looking could make her feel anything other than awkward and embarrassed.

Just as, she knew with her usual searing honesty, a man like that could never be comfortable with *her* around. Men like that wanted to be surrounded by beautiful women—women like Maria. Females who were plain and unattractive, as she was, simply didn't exist for them. Hadn't she learnt that lesson early, knowing that for men she was simply invisible? How many times had male eyes slid automatically past her to seek out Maria?

She jerked her mind away from such irrelevancies, back to what she did not want to think about. The paternity of her son.

And his uncle. Prince Enrico Ceraldi.

He won't be here still, she guessed. He'll have left—returned to his palace and his socialite chums. Why would he hang around? He probably only came to the cottage in person because he wanted to check out that Ben really did look like his brother.

She opened her eyes, looking around her. The bedroom was large, and from what she could tell the house was some kind of small, Regency period country house. Presumably sufficiently remote for the press not to find Ben. How long would they need to stay here? she wondered anxiously. The sooner the story broke, the better—because then the fuss would die down and she and Ben could go home.

She frowned. Would Ben be upset that this mysteriously arrived uncle had simply disappeared again? She would far rather he had not known who he was. Her frown etched deeper. Why had he told Ben? It seemed a pointless thing to do. The news story would just be a nine-day wonder, and, although she could understand why the Ceraldi family would want to tuck Ben out of sight while it was going on, there was no need to have told Ben anything.

She'd have to tell Ben that even though Prince Enrico was his uncle, he lived abroad, and that was why he wouldn't see him again.

Even so, it seemed cruel to have told him in the first place. Ben had asked about his father sometimes, and all Lizzy had been able to do was say that it had been someone who had loved the mummy in whose tummy he had grown, but that that mummy had been too ill to say who his daddy was.

For the hundredth time since the bombshell about Maria's lover had fallen, Lizzy felt disbelief wash through her. And a terrible chill. With all the horror of having to rush out to France, to the hospital her mortally injured sister had been taken to, the news that the pile-up had claimed the life of the youngest prince of San Lucenzo had simply passed her by. She had made no connection—how could she have?

And yet he had been Ben's father. Maria had had an affair with Prince Paolo of San Lucenzo. And nobody had known. No one at all.

It was extraordinary, unbelievable. But it was true.

I have to accept it. I have to come to terms with it.

She stared bleakly out over the room. Deliberately, she forced herself to think instead of feel.

It makes no difference. Once all the fuss in the news has died down, we can just go back home. Everything will be the same again. I just have to wait it out, that's all.

Beneath her hand, she could feel Ben start to stir and wake. A rush of emotion went through her.

Nothing would hurt Ben. Nothing. She would keep him safe always. Nothing on this earth would *ever* come between her and the son she adored with all her heart. Ever.

CHAPTER THREE

'GOOD morning.'

Rico walked into the drawing room. Ben was sitting on the floor in the middle of the room, occupied with a pile of brightly coloured building blocks. His aunt was beside him. He nodded brief acknowledgement of her, then turned his attention to Ben.

'What are you making?' he asked his nephew.

'The tallest tower in the world.' Ben announced. 'Come and see.'

Rico did not need an invitation. As his eyes had lit on his nephew, his heart had squeezed. Memories flooded back in. He could remember Paolo being that age.

A shadow fleetingly crossed his eyes. Paolo had been different from Luca and himself. As his adult self, he knew why. Luca had been born the heir. The firstborn Prince, the Crown Prince, the heir apparent, destined to rule San Lucenzo just as their father, Prince Eduardo, had been destined to inherit the throne from his own father a generation earlier. For eight hundred years the Ceraldis had ruled the tiny principality, which had escaped conquest by any of the other Italian states, or even the invading foreign powers that had plagued the Italian peninsula throughout history. Generation after generation of reigning princes had kept San Lucenzo independent—even in this age of European union the principality was still a sovereign state. Some saw it as a time-warped historical anomaly, others merely as a tax haven and a luxury playground for the very rich. But to his father and his older brother it was their inheritance, their destiny.

And it was an inheritance that would always need protection. Not, these days, against foreign powers, or any territorial interests of the Italian state—relations with Italy were excellent. What made San Lucenzo safe was continuity. The continuity of its ruling family. In many ways the principality was the personal fiefdom of the Ceraldis, and yet it was because of that that it retained its independence. Rico accepted that. Without the Ceraldis it would surely have been merged into Italy, just as all the earlier duchies and city states and papal territories had been during the great Risorgimento of the nineteenth century, that had freed Italy from foreign oppression, and united it as a nation.

The Ceraldis were essential to San Lucenzo, and for that reason, it was essential that every reigning prince had an assured heir apparent.

And—Rico's mouth tightened—that the heir apparent had a back up in case of emergency.

The traditional 'heir and a spare'—with himself as the spare.

It was what he had been all his life, growing up knowing that he was simply there in case of disaster. To assure continuity of the Ceraldi line.

But Paolo—ah, Paolo had been different. He had been special to his parents because he'd been an unexpected addition, coming several years after their two older sons. Paolo had had no dynastic function, and so he had been allowed merely to be a boy. A son. A golden boy whose sunny temper had won round even his strait-laced father and his emotionally distant mother.

Which was why his premature death had been all the more tragic, all the more bitter.

Rico hunkered down beside his nephew, taking scant notice of the way his aunt immediately shrank away. Yes, Paolo's son. No doubt about it. No DNA tests would be required; his paternity was undeniable, blazing from every feature. Perhaps there might be a little of his birth mother about him, but one look at him told the world that he was a Ceraldi.

Benedict. That was what he'd been called. And it was a true name for him.

Blessed.

His heart gave that familiar catch again. Yes, he was blessed, all right. He didn't know it yet, but he would. And he was more than blessed—he was a blessing himself.

Because, beyond all the publicity and press coverage and gossip that was going to explode at any moment now, the boy was going to be seen as the blessing he was.

The final consolation to his parents for the son they had lost so tragically.

Lizzy moved backwards across the carpet and lifted herself into a nearby armchair. She had hoped, at the fact that she and Ben had had the breakfast room to themselves, that it meant Prince Enrico had gone.

She wished he had.

She felt excruciatingly awkward with him there. She tried not to look at him, but it was hard not to feel intensely aware of his presence in the room. Even without a drop of royal blood in him he would have been impossible to ignore.

By day he seemed even taller, outlined against the light from the window behind him, and his startling good looks automatically drew her eyes. He was wearing designer jeans, immaculately cut, and an open-necked shirt, clearly handmade. Immediately she felt the full force of just how shabbily she was dressed in comparison. Her cheap chainstore skirt and top had probably cost less than his monogrammed handkerchief.

At least, apart from that brief initial nod in her direction, he wasn't paying any attention to her. It was all on Ben, or helping him build his tower.

Resentment and embarrassment warred within her.

Ben was chattering away confidently, without a trace of

shyness, his smiles sunny. He was like Maria in that, Lizzy knew. Hindsight over the years since her terrible death had made things clearer to her. It had been a miracle that Maria's sunny-tempered nature had not been warped by her upbringing. Despite the way her parents had doted on her, obsessed over her, she really had seemed to escape being spoilt. And yet, for all her sunny nature, she had known what she wanted, and what she'd wanted was to be a model, to live an exciting, glamorous life. And that was what she'd done, smiling happily, ignoring her parents' dismay, and waltzing off to the life she'd wanted.

And the man she'd wanted.

Disbelief was etched through Lizzy for the thousandth time. That Maria had actually had an affair with Prince Paolo of San Lucenzo and none of them had known. Not even his family, let alone hers.

How had they managed it? He must have been very different from his brother. Even though she hadn't recognised Enrico, she'd still heard of him—and of his reputation. The Playboy Prince. Her covert gaze rested on him a second. He certainly had the looks for it, all right. Tall, broad-shouldered, sable-haired, with strong, well-cut, aristocratic features.

And those eyes.

Dark, long-lashed, with flecks of gold in them if you looked deeply. Not that she could—or would.

She looked away. It was completely irrelevant what he looked like. It was nothing to do with her. All she had to be concerned about was how long she and Ben would have to hide here before they could go back home.

Ben had paused in his tower-building. He was looking curiously at his helper.

'Are you really my uncle?'

Immediately Lizzy stiffened.

'Yes,' he answered. He spoke in a very matter of fact way. 'You can call me Tio Rico. That means Uncle Rico. My brother was your father. But he died. It was in the car crash with your mother.'

Ben nodded. 'I was still growing in her tummy. Then I came out, and she died.'

The Prince's eyes were carefully watching his nephew. Lizzy could see as she held her breath.

Please, *please* don't say anything about the royalty stuff. Please.

There was no point Ben knowing. None at all. It wouldn't make sense to him, wouldn't mean anything. One day, when he was much older, she would have to tell him, but till then it was an irrelevance.

Then, to her relief, Ben himself changed the subject.

'We've finished the tower,' he announced. 'What shall we make next?'

He seemed to take it for granted his helper would stick around. But the Prince got to his feet.

'I'm sorry, Ben. I don't have time. I have to leave very soon, and first I must talk with your aunt.'

He flicked his gaze across to the figure sitting tensely in the armchair. She got to her feet jerkily. Rico found himself regarding her without pleasure.

How could any female look so dire? No figure, no face, and hair like a bush. His eyes flicked away again, and he did not see her face mottle with colour.

'Please come this way,' he said, as he headed towards the door.

He went through into a room that was evidently a library, courteously holding the door open for the aunt, who walked hurriedly past him. He took up a position in front of the fireplace. She stood awkwardly in the middle of the room.

'You had better sit down.'

His voice was cool and remote. Very formal.

Lizzy tensed even more. The ease of manner he'd displayed towards Ben had disappeared completely.

What did he want to talk to her about? Hopefully it would be to tell her how long she and Ben had to stay here. She hoped it would not be long. This was so unsettling for Ben. She wanted to get him home again. Back to normal. Back to the cottage, where she could try to forget all about who Ben's father had been.

She took a seat on the long leather sofa facing the fire about ten feet away. The Prince went on standing. He seemed very tall. Lizzy wished she had remained standing too.

He started to speak.

'I hope you have begun to come to terms with what has transpired. This has been a considerable shock; I acknowledge that.'

'I still can't really believe it,' Lizzy heard herself say, giving voice to her thoughts. 'It just seems so impossible. How on earth did Maria get to meet a prince?'

Prince Enrico arched an eyebrow. 'Not as impossible as you might think. Your sister's career as a model would have taken her into the social circles frequented by my brother.'

She could read his expression quite clearly. Maria's life had been a world away from her own.

'However, now that you are aware of the situation, clearly you will appreciate that the first priority must be Ben's wellbeing.'

Lizzy's expression tightened. Did he think she didn't know that?

'How long are we going to have stay here?'

The question blurted from her.

There was a pause before the Prince answered her. Lizzy didn't care if she'd offended him, or annoyed him by asking a question of him like that. Simply being in the same room with him was just too embarrassing for her to want anything but to minimise the time she had to endure it. Besides, she didn't want to leave Ben on his own any longer than she had to.

'It is expected that the news story will break any day,' Prince Enrico informed her tersely. 'I doubt that it can be put off any longer. As for how long the story will run—' He took a sharp intake of breath. 'That depends on how much the press are fed.'

Lizzy's eyes sparked. Was that some kind of sly remark

about whether *she* would talk to any journalists when she got back home again?

But the Prince was speaking still.

'The press feed off each other, each trying to outdo the other, rehashing each other's stories, then seeking to add their own exclusive "revelation" to milk the story as much as they can, for as long as they can. It's cheap copy.'

There was a bitter note in his voice she would have had to be deaf not to hear. It was obvious he was speaking from experience. For a moment she felt a tinge of sympathy for him, then she pushed it aside. Prince Rico of San Lucenzo had not had his playboy lifestyle forced upon him, and if he didn't like being hounded by the press he shouldn't live the way he did. But Ben was innocent, a small child.

She could feel her fiercely protective maternal instincts take over. Ben was not responsible for his parentage. So Prince Paolo of San Lucenzo had taken a shine to Maria, had an affair with her, and got her pregnant—well, that was not Ben's fault.

'How long will we have to stay here?' she urged again.

'As long as is necessary. I can say no more than that.' His expression changed. 'I am returning to San Lucenzo this morning. I must report on the situation to my father. You and my nephew will stay here. You will be well looked after, naturally, but you will not be allowed to leave the house and gardens.'

Lizzy frowned. 'You don't imagine I *want* to run into any journalists, do you?'

'Nevertheless.' There was a note of implacability in the Prince's voice.

Lizzy looked at him. Did the Ceraldis think that she *wanted* this nightmare to be true? Did they really think she would do anything to make what was already a horrible situation worse by talking to the press?

Well, it didn't matter what Prince Rico or any of the Ceraldi family thought about her intentions. Right now she was in no position to do anything other than accept that she and Ben could not be at home, and she might as well be relieved—if not actually grateful—that the Ceraldis had moved so swiftly to get her and Ben away.

'However—' The Prince had started speaking again, addressing her in that same terse, impersonal tone, but he broke off abruptly. '*Si?*'

His head swivelled to the door, which had opened silently. A man stood there, quite young, but tough and muscular-looking, despite his sober dark suit. He looked like a body-guard, Lizzy realised. He said something in low, rapid Italian, and the Prince nodded curtly. Then he turned back to Lizzy.

'I am informed my plane is on standby and has air traffic clearance. Excuse me. I must leave.'

Lizzy watched him go. It was frustrating not to know how long she would have to stay here, but presumably not even the San Lucenzan royal family could know exactly what the press would do, or how long it would take for the story to die away.

Her mouth tightened. Had Prince Enrico really implied that she might try and talk to the press herself? It was the very last thing on earth she'd do.

She gave a mental shrug. There was no point her getting angry over it. Royals lived in a goldfish bowl; their wariness was understandable.

She went back to Ben, next door. He seemed to be taking all this in his stride, and she was grateful. Nor did he seem bothered by their enforced incarceration.

He seemed to take the following days in his stride too. They were left very much to themselves. Captain Falieri and the man who was probably Prince Enrico's bodyguard had disappeared as well, and she saw no sign of anyone else in the house except for the efficient Italian-speaking staff.

She was glad of the time to herself. Her mind seemed completely split in two. On the one hand she was as normal as she could be with Ben—playing with him, reading to him, taking him swimming, to his huge excitement, in the covered swimming pool built into a conservatory-style annexe off the main house— but inside her head her thoughts teemed with emotion.

She was still reeling from it all, but she did her best to hide it from Ben. He was, thank heavens, far too young to understand. He took what had happened at face value, absorbing it into his life as naturally as he had anything else, just as when they'd moved to Cornwall. The centre of his life was her, not his surroundings, and providing she was there, everything, for him, was as it should be.

It was inevitable, however, Lizzy acknowledged, that Ben would ask questions about the man who had so unnecessarily told him that he was his uncle.

'Where has he gone?' Ben asked.

'To Italy.' Lizzy told him. 'That's where he lives.'

'Will he come back?'

'I don't think so, Ben.'

Inwardly she cursed the man. Why had he gone and told Ben he was his uncle? Obviously a child would be interested—especially one who had no other relations. But what possible concern was Ben to Prince Enrico, other than being the unfortunate target of a salacious news story which threatened scandal to the San Lucenzan royal family?

Ben frowned. 'Well, what about Captain Fally-eery? Will he come back? He played trains with me.'

Lizzy shook her head. 'I don't think he'll come back either, Ben. He lives in Italy too.' Deliberately, she changed the subject. 'Now, shall we go and have our tea?'

Ben looked at her. 'Is this a hotel, Mummy, where they cook for you?'

She nodded. 'Sort of.' It seemed the easiest explanation to give.

'I like it here,' said Ben decidedly, looking around him approvingly. 'I like the swimming pool. Can we swim again after tea?'

'We'll see,' said Lizzy.

* * *

Rico stood at one of the windows of his apartments in the palace. It gave a dazzling view over the marina, with its brightly lit-up yachts, and the elegant promenade beyond. Paolo's apartments had been nearby, and had enjoyed similar views. His eyes shadowed.

To think that Paolo's young son was alive in England. That he had been there all along, brought up by a woman who did not even know who he was. It seemed incredible.

His thoughts went back to that ramshackle cottage he'd extracted his nephew from. His eyes darkened. It had shocked him to find Paolo's son living in such conditions.

Paolo's son.

He had known it the instant he had set eyes on him. And so he had told Luca.

'There won't be any need for DNA tests,' he'd told him.

'Well, they'll be done anyway. It's necessary.'

Rico had shrugged. He could understand it, but he also knew that when his family saw Ben in the flesh they would know instantly he was Paolo's child.

'And this aunt? What about her?' Luca had gone on.

'Shocked. That's understandable. She really seemed to have no idea at all.' He'd decided not to tell his brother that she'd failed to recognise him. Luca would find that darkly humorous.

'Can't believe her luck, more likely. She's got it made now.' There had been a cynical note in Luca's voice, and Rico frowned in recollection. Ben's aunt had given no indication of any emotion other than disbelief, and dread of the impending news story.

Then Luca had picked up one of the modelling shots of Maria Mitchell that was in the dossier Falieri had compiled, and glanced at it.

'Blonde bimbo like the sister?' he'd asked casually.

Rico had snorted. 'You're joking. Utterly plain.'

His brother had laughed sardonically. 'Well, at least that

should stop the press being interested in her, and that's all to the good. She won't make good copy if she's nothing to look at.'

Rico, his attention half taken by the latest version of a particular super-car that he liked to drive, which was wending its way along the edge of the marina, found himself frowning again at Luca's comment. It was a cruel way to speak about the girl, even if it was true.

He shifted his mind away from her. Ben's aunt was a complication that would be sorted out very soon now.

His father, during a brief interview with him, had made his wishes clear. And his instructions.

'I leave you to handle the matter,' his father had said.

Rico's mouth twisted. He need not take it as a compliment. As Luca had pointed out, 'It has to be you, Rico. You're the only one of us that can come and go freely. And besides—' the sardonic glint had been clear in his brother's eye '—if there's a female in the equation you're the expert—just as well she's plain, mind you. You'll be immune to her.'

He stepped away from the window. The woman who was his nephew's aunt was of no concern to him.

Only his nephew.

The news story on Paolo Ceraldi's unknown son broke the following morning. The lurid exclusive in a French tabloid was instantly picked up, and exactly the kind of media feeding frenzy ensued that his father so deplored. As Rico knew too well from personal experience, when he had been the subject of press attention.

There was nothing to be done about it except ignore it. His father ordered a policy of silence, and to carry on as if nothing had happened. The royal family's public life was not altered in any way. Rico's mother attended her usual opera, ballet and philharmonia performances, his father carried out his customary duties and Luca his. As for himself, he flew down to southern Africa to participate in a gruelling long-distance rally, as he always did at this time of year.

'No comment,' became his only words in half a dozen languages during the checkpoints, and he couldn't wait to get back into the driving seat and head out across the savannah again.

But there was something else he couldn't wait to do either. Get back to his nephew again. He was counting the days.

CHAPTER FOUR

LIZZY walked into the breakfast room and stopped dead. Prince Enrico was sitting at the table.

She'd had absolutely no idea that he was here.

At her side, Ben showed only pleasure.

'Tio Rico! You came back.'

Lizzy watched the Prince lever his long frame upright.

'Of course. Especially to see you.'

Ben's expression perked expectantly.

'Will you play with me?'

'After breakfast. Would you like to go swimming later?'

'Yes, please.'

'Good. Well, let's have breakfast first, shall we?'

He waited pointedly while Lizzy took her place, Ben beside her, before resuming his.

Lizzy watched as Ben chatted to his uncle. Tension laced through her instantly. He must have arrived back late last night. She had heard nothing.

But then she did not stay up late. In the strange, dislocated days she had spent here she had always retired with Ben, after supper, and once he was bathed and asleep she would spend the time in their room reading. The house came with a well-stocked library, and she was grateful for it. She had made a point of not watching television, quite deliberately. She had not wanted to catch anything of whatever the press might be saying by now about her sister and Ben. She didn't want to think about it.

But now, with Prince Enrico sitting at the head of the breakfast table, it all suddenly seemed horribly real again.

Her eyes had gone to him immediately as she'd entered the room—but then it would have been difficult for them to do otherwise, prince or no prince. He was the kind of man that drew all eyes instantly. She felt again that squirming awkwardness go through her, and wished that she and Ben had got up earlier, and so missed this ordeal.

Not that Ben thought it was an ordeal, evidently. He was chatting away with his uncle, and Lizzy felt her mouth tighten with disapproval.

'There is a problem?'

The accented voice was cool. Lizzy realised that Prince Enrico was looking at her.

'Why are you here? Has something happened? Something worse?'

Her voice was staccato, and probably sounded abrupt. She didn't care.

A frowning expression formed on his face.

'Is there more bad news?' Lizzy persisted.

'Other than what was expected? No. Did you not see any of the coverage?'

'No. It was the last thing I wanted to do. But in which case, if nothing worse has happened, why are you here?'

He looked at her. He had that closed expression on his face. Obviously he wasn't used to being spoken to like that, thought Lizzy. But she didn't care. Tension bit in her.

'I am here at the behest of my father. For reasons that must be obvious even to yourself, Miss Mitchell.'

His words were terse.

She looked blank. 'I don't understand.'

His mouth pressed together tightly, and he looked impatiently at her.

'We will discuss this matter later.' He turned his attention back to Ben. Shutting her out.

Dismissing her.

Anxiety and tension warred within her.

How she got through breakfast she did not know. She could not relax, and, although she deplored it, she knew she was grateful that Ben was chattering away to the Prince, making it possible for her to swallow a few morsels of food through a tight throat.

The moment Ben had finished, she got to her feet.

'Come along, Ben,' she said.

'Tio Rico said we'd go swimming,' Ben protested.

'Not straight after eating,' she said quietly. 'You'll get a sore tummy. And anyway, you need to brush your teeth,' she added, steering him out of the room.

As she gained the large hallway, she felt her stomach sink. Oh, God, now what? Why had he come back here? And why should it be *obvious* to her? Nothing was obvious to her. Nothing. Only that she was desperate for all this to be over, and for her to be able to go home with Ben.

But it seemed that she would have to get through another morning here.

After Ben had brushed his teeth they went back down to the drawing room, where Ben's toys were.

Prince Enrico was there before them. Lizzy tensed immediately.

'This is a good train track, Ben,' he said.

Ben trotted forward eagerly. 'My one at home is bigger, because we didn't bring all the pieces. And some of the engines are at home. But I will tell you who these are that I've got here.' He settled himself down by the track and started to regale the Prince, who had hunkered down.

Abruptly, Lizzy snapped her eyes away from the way the material of his immaculately cut trousers strained over powerful thighs.

Oh, God—isn't it bad enough that he's a prince?

She sat herself down on the sofa. Would the man never clear off?

It seemed not. To Lizzy's dismay, he seemed to be settling himself in. She picked up her book. Ben was happily chattering away, talking about his beloved trainset. She tried to concentrate on her book, and failed completely.

After what seemed like for ever, Ben suddenly stood up.

'Is it time to go swimming yet?'

She got to her feet, relieved. 'Good idea. Let's get your things.' She gave an awkward nod to the Prince, who had stood when she did.

She scurried off with Ben. But to her dismay, when they came back downstairs with the swimming kit and went into the pool room, there was already someone in the water.

The Prince's long, lean body cut through the water in a swift crawl, but when he reached the end of the pool he stopped.

'Ah, Ben, there you are,' he said. 'In you come.'

Lizzy stared in horrified fascination. The Prince had half levered himself out of the water, his arms folded down over the edge. She could see the water draining off his torso.

It was smooth, and perfectly muscled, honed like a sportsman.

She tore her eyes away. Ben was scrambling out of his clothes as fast as he could. With gritted teeth she inflated his armbands and slid them over his arms.

'Hurry, hurry,' said Ben, jiggling around. The moment he was fitted, he ran and jumped into the water.

Jerkily, Lizzy picked up his clothes, and went to sit on one of the padded seats that were dotted by the glass wall.

Thank God I wasn't in the water already.

That would have been the ultimate horror. She sat, feeling far too hot in what she was wearing in this sun-heated area, but there was nothing she could do about it. She felt her cheeks grow flushed as she watched Ben playing in the water.

The Prince seemed ludicrously enthusiastic about entertaining a four-year-old child. He ducked and dived and raced, and pounced on Ben like a shark, eliciting squeals of glee.

She felt resentment and anger mounting in her. What was the point? What was the *point* of Prince Enrico doing this? It would just unsettle Ben, that was all. Make him want something that he wasn't going to have.

He hasn't got a father. He hasn't got an uncle. He hasn't got anyone—he's just got me.

And it wasn't fair on him to let him get a taste of what it might be like if he had a father. A father to play with him, to pay attention to him.

Make him laugh the way he was laughing now.

I want to go home. I just want to go home. I want this over. Done with. Forgotten.

Rico helped Ben out of the pool for the last time, and glanced across at where his aunt was sitting. Her face had gone red in the heat, and she looked worse than ever. She also had a face like sour milk.

His brother's words came back to him, half-taunting, half-mocking—which was Luca's usual attitude towards him on this subject.

'If there's a female in the equation you're the expert—just as well she's plain, mind you. You'll be immune to her.'

Well, the latter was true. No doubt about that. With a dispassionate mind he could only feel sorry for any female as unattractive as this one. But as someone he actually had to deal with, however briefly, he could do without it. As for the former—well, females of this variety were definitely ones he was not expert in.

He launched himself out of the pool, effortlessly lifting himself on his arms. The boy's aunt had already busied herself wrapping Ben in a towel and getting him dry. He strolled off to get changed himself, in the cabanas provided for the purpose.

His mouth set. The sooner he'd settled the business here and was back in San Lucenzo the better.

But it had been good to start getting to know Ben.
Paolo's son.
His expression softened
I'll make sure he's OK, Paolo—I promise you.

Lunch had been just as much an ordeal as breakfast. Once again, the source of both her concern and her relief had been that Ben had dominated the proceedings, talking nineteen to the dozen to Prince Enrico. All she'd been required to do was sit there and try to eat through a throat that was getting tighter every moment.

What had happened? Why was Prince Enrico back here? He'd said he'd talk to her later—but when was later?

It was after lunch, it transpired. As they left the dining room he turned to her.

'Settle Ben with some toys, if you please. I shall await you in the library.'

'He has a nap after lunch. I'll come down when he's asleep.'

He gave a curt nod, and she took Ben upstairs, nerves jumping.

Typically, Ben took for ever to go to sleep, and her nerves were stretched thin by the time she could finally leave him, curtains closed, door ajar, and head downstairs.

He was, as he had said, in the library. A raft of daily papers, in both English and Italian, were on the low table, and he was sitting in a leather chair perusing *The Times*.

Surely such a respectable newspaper had not carried such a scurrilous story? she wondered.

But the page he was reading seemed to be about international politics. He cast the paper aside and stood up, indicating the chair opposite him, across the hearth of the unlit fire.

'Please sit down.' His voice was cool..

She sat nervously, stomach knoting.

'We must resolve, as a matter of urgency, as I am sure you will appreciate, the matter of my nephew's future.'

Lizzy stared.

'What do you mean?' she said.

A flicker of irritation showed briefly in the dark eyes, then it was suppressed.

'I appreciate,' he said carefully to her—as if, Lizzy thought, she was stupid, 'that the news of Ben's parentage has come as a profound shock to you. Nevertheless, I must ask you to focus on the implications of that discovery. Like yourself, his father's family were, unfortunately, but in the tragic circumstances understandably, equally unaware that Paolo had a son. Now that this is no longer the case, obviously steps will be taken as soon as possible to rectify the situation.'

She was still staring blankly.

'Rectify?' she echoed.

She saw him take a breath. 'Of course. Ben will now make his life in San Lucenzo.'

Cold went down Lizzy's back. She could feel it—as if her spine was turning to ice.

'No.'

The word was instinctive. Automatic.

She saw the Prince's face first tighten, then take on the same expression that it had had when she had failed to recognise him. Disbelieving.

She didn't care. Didn't care about anything. Except to refute, absolutely, what she had just heard him say.

His expression changed, as if he were making a visible effort. Again he addressed her as if she were stupid.

'Miss Mitchell, do you really not understand that your nephew's circumstances have changed now?' His tone, quite blatantly, was patronising, and Lizzy felt her hackles rise through the ice in her spine. 'It is inconceivable that my brother's orphaned son should live anywhere but in his own country.'

She stared at him.

'I can't believe you're saying that,' she cut across him. 'We're going home—back to Cornwall the moment we can. The sooner the better.'

She saw his face tighten.

'That is no longer possible.' His voice was flat. Implacable.

'What do you mean "no longer possible"?' she demanded. Her voice was rising, she could tell, and she could feel the adrenaline churning in her system. 'Ben and I are going home. That's all there is to it.'

'Ben's home will now have to be in San Lucenzo.'

The voice was still flat, still implacable.

'There's no "have to" about it. No *question* of it!'

Dark, long-lashed eyes stared at her.

'Miss Mitchell—are you being deliberately obtuse?' The question was rhetorical, for he plunged straight on. 'There is no going back. Do you not understand that? Your nephew cannot return to the life you gave him. He must come to his own country to live.'

She leant forward, tension in every line of her body.

'This is ridiculous. Absurd,' she responded vehemently. Emotion was surging through her. 'Completely out of the question. I can understand your reaction to the nightmare of this news story, and I have my sympathies for you and your family. If there is one thing I do feel sorry about for royalty, it's that their private lives are raked over by the press—even when they do not conspicuously court such publicity,' she threw in, with a glancing look in her eyes at him that drew an answering flash and a compression of his mouth. But she allowed him no time to interrupt her. 'If anything, Ben's presence in San Lucenzo could only be an further embarrassment to you. Why on earth would your family want to be landed with your late brother's illegitimate child—"love child", as I suppose the tabloids will coyly call him—as an ever-present reminder of his affair with my sister? Look,' she went on, trying to be reasonable, even with the adrenaline running in her like a river in flood, 'if you are worried that I might, God help me, be insane enough to speak to the press at any point in the future, then I'll sign any gagging papers you want. The *only* thing I want for Ben is a happy, unspoilt childhood. He can't help his parentage, and I won't let it affect him adversely.'

He was staring at her again. She wished he wouldn't do that. Not just because his eyes were the most extraordinary she'd ever seen, but because he was looking at her as if she were from another planet.

His mouth tightened. Italian broke from him, angry and incomprehensible.

Then, as if he were making a monumental effort to control his reaction, he spoke again, and she stared wildly at him, stomach churning.

'You do not seem to understand. My brother did *not* have an affair with your sister.'

'But you've just said—' she launched.

His hand shot up, silencing her.

His dark eyes were completely opaque again.

'He married her.'

Lizzy felt her mouth fall open. Her jaw drop like a stone. With numb, unconscious effort she closed it again, then spoke.

'My sister *married* your brother?' Her voice was dazed.

'Yes. The day before their fatal car crash. I have seen the marriage certificate. It is...' he paused '...quite legal. Apparently—' his voice was as dry as sand '—the name Ceraldi was also unknown to the celebrant.'

She got to her feet, staring at him blindly.

'I don't believe it.'

It was denial again. Just the same as when the man standing in front of her had told her he was a royal prince—and so had his brother been.

And if Maria had married him that meant Ben was—

No—no, it could not be. It was impossible. Ben was just... Ben, that was all.

But if her sister had been married to his father, and his father was a prince of San Lucenzo, then Ben...

She sat down. Her legs felt weightless somehow.

'It's not true.' Her voice was faint. Her eyes wide. She stared across at him. 'Please—please say it isn't true. Please.'

Rico looked at her. She could not have meant what she'd just said. No one could. Certainly no woman in her situation could mean it. She had just been told that her nephew was a royal prince. And yet she was begging him to tell her it was not true.

He inhaled sharply.

'It is hardly a subject for jest. And now that you know, you must realise why there is no question but that Ben be brought up in his own country, with his own family.'

Her eyes blazed with sudden fierce light.

'I don't care if you tell me that Ben is the King of Siam. I'm not uprooting him from his own life, from everything he knows. So *what* if he *is* legitimate? Your brother Paolo was the youngest brother, so Ben isn't going to inherit the throne or anything, is he?'

The strident voice grated on Rico's already stretched nerves. The girl's reaction was incomprehensible. Was she particularly unintelligent? It seemed he would have to spell everything out to her.

'A royal prince of the house of Ceraldi cannot be brought up as a private citizen in a foreign country.' He spoke heavily, hoping to God the damn woman would finally get through her skull what the reality of the situation was. 'He must be raised by his family—'

'*I* am his family.'

Rico's face closed.

'You are his aunt. Nothing more than that. I appreciate that you have worked very hard to raise my brother's son, and—'

Her strident voice interrupted him again. Rico felt his impatience mounting. It was not just her unbelievable pig-headedness and her exasperating lack of intelligence that got to him, but her appalling habit of cutting across him.

Her eyes were stabbing at him, and she was getting ludicrously worked up.

'I am Ben's legal guardian. He is solely my responsibility.'

Rico fought for self-control. 'Then, as his legal guardian, you will want the best for him, no? And clearly—' he tried hard to keep the withering sarcasm out of his voice '—Ben's interests will be served by his being raised by his father's family.' And now the sarcasm did creep in. He couldn't stop it, such were the emotions biting through him at the woman's incomprehensible objections. 'Or did you imagine it would be suitable for my brother's son to be raised in a semi-derelict peasant cottage?'

A line of colour leached out across her cheeks, and Rico, despite his mounting temper, felt a stab of regret. She could not help being poor, and she had, after all, done the best she could for Paolo's son, within her means.

But that was irrelevant now. Whether she liked it or not, she had to accept the truth of the matter—the Ceraldis had a new prince, and his place was with them. Swiftly, he moved on. His father had given him full authority to do whatever was necessary to ensure Ben returned to San Lucenzo as soon as possible.

He held up a hand, forestalling any further comeback from her.

'Miss Mitchell—the matter is not open for debate. I make allowances for your sense of shock, but you must face up to the necessity of the situation. My nephew must go to San Lucenzo with the minimum of delay to start his new life. You must see that.'

She shook her head wildly.

'No, I don't. I don't see anything of the sort. You can't possibly think his life should be turned upside down like that.'

Rico pressed his mouth together, willing himself to stay calm.

'And you, Miss Mitchell, cannot possibly think that Ben's life will not be immeasurably better when he is surrounded by his family. What possible justification can you have for your objection? How can you possibly not welcome this? You live in poverty—all that has changed. Changed completely. Have you not realised that?'

His eyes narrowed infinitesimally as he watched for her reaction. But her face just seemed totally blank. Obviously he would need to be blunter, distasteful though it was.

'You will not suffer by the change in Ben's life, Miss Mitchell. You will always be his aunt, and, although Ben's new life will inevitably be vastly different from what he has been used to so far, you will benefit too. It would not be appropriate for my nephew's aunt to live in poverty,' he said carefully, his eyes watching her. 'Therefore generous financial arrangements will be made in your favour, in appreciation for what you have done for my nephew. You have given up four years of your life to look after him—it is only right that your invaluable contribution should be recognised. But now you will be able to resume the life of a young woman, independent of the responsibilities you have had to assume up till now.'

His eyes rested on her as he waited for the penny to drop. But her face was still quite expressionless.

It irritated Rico. Did he have to spell *everything* out in excruciatingly vulgar detail? Evidently so. His mouth tightened. He took a controlled breath, and prepared to speak again.

But before he could say anything she got to her feet.

It was a jerky movement, like an automaton. Her eyes were pinned on his. There was something in them that took him aback. Then she spoke. Her voice was strange.

'You do not seriously think I am going to let you part me from Ben, do you?'

She was trembling like a wire strung out to breaking point. Emotion poured through her, terror and fury storming together. They spilled over into a torrent of words.

'Do you really think I would ever, *ever* allow Ben to be taken from me? Do you? How can you even imagine that for a moment? I'm his *mother*—the only mother he's ever known.'

A burning, punishing breath seared through her lungs. 'Listen to me and listen well. Because I will say this over and over again until I get you to understand it. I am Ben's mother—his guardian. And that means I guard him—I guard him from anything and everything that threatens him, threatens his happiness, his emotional and physical well-being, his long-term stability…*everything*. I love him more than my own life—I could not love him more if he were my birth child. He is all I have left of my sister, and I made a vow to her that I would keep her child safe, that I would be the mother to him that she was not allowed to be. He is my son and I am his mother. It would *devastate* him to be taken from me—how could you even *think* of doing so? Nothing will come between us. I will never let him be taken from me. *Never.*'

Her face was contorted, but she could not stop. She had to make him listen—had to make him hear.

'You must be completely insane to think of taking him from me. How do you even *begin* to think I would consent to it? Consent to Ben losing the only mother he's known. Are you mad, or just evil, even to *think* of separating us? No one takes a child from its mother. *No one.*' She shut her eyes. Her throat was burning, her breath choking. 'Oh, God, how could this nightmare ever have happened. How?'

Her anguished question rang into silence, complete silence. She stood there, shaking like a leaf.

Then, slowly, a voice spoke. Deep and resonant.

'No one will take Ben from you. You have my word.'

Rico was in his bedroom. The phone was against his ear. He stood with one arm extended, resting his hand on the folded wooden shutters that framed the sash windows. From where he stood he could see the gardens. Ben and his aunt were on the lawn, in the last of the early-evening sunshine, playing football. Two goals were roughly marked out with sticks. Ben kicked, and scored, and ran around gleefully in imitation of professional footballers. His aunt threw up her hands in exaggerated defeat, and took a goal kick. It was a very bad one, and Ben returned it instantly, scoring yet another goal. He crowed with triumph.

At the other end of the phone line, Rico's brother was speaking.

'What do you mean, she won't give him up? She's nothing more than his aunt—what claim can she have?'

'A watertight legal one,' replied Rico dryly.

There was a pause. Then Luca spoke.

'She wants more money, I take it?' His voice was sharp.

'She wants her son.' Rico realised his voice was equally sharp.

'The boy is only her *nephew*,' riposted his brother.

'She's raised him as her son, and he regards her as his mother. Which, legally, she is. She adopted him at birth. So, if she does not want to part with him, we have to accept that.'

There was a pause again.

'How much did you offer her?' Luca asked.

'Luca—this is not *about* money. She's not prepared to consider it, OK?' He paused, then spoke again. 'And neither am I any longer. The attachment between them is definitely that of mother and child. I've been with them all day—so far as Paolo's son is concerned, the woman is his mother. There's nothing we can do about that. We may not like it, but that's the way it is. Our only way forward is for her to live in San Lucenzo with the boy. I have to persuade her of that, and I will do my best to do so. But—' he took a sharp breath '—I gave her my word we would not try and take the child from her.'

There was another pause. Outside in the garden Ben was still playing football. Rico felt a sudden urge to go and join in.

Luca was speaking again. 'Rico, do and say nothing for the moment. I'll report this back to our father. He won't like it but…' Rico could almost hear Luca shrug. 'Look, I'll phone you back.'

The line went dead. Rico's gaze dropped again to the figure playing on the lawn below with Ben. She was wearing some kind of grey tracksuit, baggy and shapeless, and her frizzy hair was tied back in an unflattering bunch. She looked overweight and lumpy. She really was extraordinarily unappealing. Yet what did her appearance matter to Ben? Even as he watched, he saw Ben trip as he ran to intercept the ball, and fall sprawlingly on the grass. She was there in an instant, hugging him, inspecting his grass-stained knee, then dropping a kiss on it before resuming play again. An ordinary maternal gesture.

Memory shafted through him. Or rather, lack of it. Who had picked him up when he'd gone sprawling like that? A nanny? Whichever of the nursery floor staff was looking after him at the time? Not his mother. He'd only ever seen his mother at five in the afternoon, when she had taken tea and interviewed both himself and Luca as to their progress in lessons that day.

A frown creased his brow. Paolo had been the only one of them ever to sit beside his mother on the exquisite silk-upholstered sofa in her sitting room. The only one of them he could remember her embracing.

He felt his heart squeeze again. He would bring her Paolo's son.

He glanced at his watch. He doubted Luca would phone back within the hour. Time enough for Rico to teach his nephew some football moves. He headed downstairs.

'It's no good, Ben, it's definitely bedtime.'

'Mummy—one more goal. Just one.'

'Golden goal,' said Rico.

'All right, then,' conceded Lizzy.

She had just passed the strangest half-hour. Out of nowhere, the Prince had emerged on to the lawn and joined in their game of football. Or rather taken it over.

Ben was ecstatic.

'You can ref, Mummy,' he instructed her.

She sat in a heap at the side of the pitch area, and watched. Her emotions were still in turmoil, but at least she was calmer than she had been.

You have my word, he had said.

Did he mean it?

He had seemed different when he'd said that to her. She didn't know why, or how, but he had.

And he'd looked at her. Looked at her into her eyes.

As if she were a real person suddenly.

And something had happened in that look. Something that for the first time had made the hard, fearful knot inside her ease.

Just by a fraction.

Something had changed.

Something had changed as she'd poured out her horror and terror in front of him. Telling him—screaming at him—that she would never let Ben be taken from her, that she was his mother by everything but physical birth. That she would never, ever, let such harm come to him as to be wrested from the only person he knew to be his mother.

Who had been the only person in the world to him.

Until now.

She felt emotion move and shift within her.

A pang went through her. Yes, she was Ben's mother—she would be all her life. Nothing could ever change that.

But now he's got an uncle. Two uncles. And grandparents too.

A family.

A family to whom Ben was not just the embarrassing result of an affair—someone they would wash their hands of, hide away out of sight.

They wanted him. They wanted him because he was the son of their dead son, their dead brother.

Emotion twisted within her.

If they were anything other than what they are, I'd be over-joyed at their discovering Ben's existence.

But that was the trouble. They *were* who they were. It was unbelievable, unreal—and the truth.

Depression rolled over her. Whichever way you looked at it, the whole situation was impossible.

Anguish filled her. There could be no resolution to this. How could there be? Two worlds had collided—the normal world, and the world the Ceraldis lived in. A world that was totally unreal to everyone except themselves.

And Ben was caught in the middle. Crushed between them.

And so was she.

CHAPTER FIVE

RICO stared at his brother. He had been summoned back to San Lucenzo the following morning, and now that he was here Luca had dropped a bombshell on him.

'This is a joke, right? And, as such, it isn't funny.'

The Crown Prince of San Lucenzo looked back at him with dispassionate eyes. He was good at dispassion, thought Rico viciously. Great at dispensing insane ideas as if they were commonplace, obvious no-brainers.

'It would solve the problem we are facing.'

'Are you mad? It's not a question of solving problems—this is about my *life*. And I am *not* about to sacrifice it for the reasons you think I should.'

'It's hardly a permanent sacrifice. Besides, I thought you said you had really taken to the boy.'

Rico's eyes flashed angrily.

'That doesn't mean I have to—'

His brother held up his hand. 'Yes, I understand. But listen, Rico—what other option is there? She's the legal guardian of Paolo's son. She won't relinquish the boy. You're saying that the only way for us to have Paolo's son is to have her as well. But how? We *cannot* have an English unmarried mother, a commoner, whose father kept a shop, living here with legal responsibility for a child who just happens to be our nephew and therefore a royal prince.' His face tightened. 'It will cause serious problems of protocol and security. What I've suggested cuts those problems right out.' Both the tone of his voice and his expression changed. 'I don't have to tell you that your co-operation in this matter would be appreciated by our father.'

He pressed on.

'We're talking a year—eighteen months at the most. That's all, Rico. Enough to serve the proprieties. Make everything watertight.'

His eyes rested on his younger brother.

'You're always talking about having a more active role in affairs. Wanting to take on responsibilities. All your life you've chafed at being the "spare". Well, now you can do something about that. No one else can do this, Rico—only you. You know that. Only you.'

There was an intensity in Luca's gaze that bored into Rico. For a long, endless moment Rico met his brother's eyes. Then, with a curse, he broke away.

'Damn you for this, Luca.'

Luca raised sardonic eyebrows. 'Damn me all you like—but do this for us all,' he retorted coolly.

His brother's voice, when he replied, was even cooler. 'I'll do it for Paolo,' he said.

The sleek, powerful car ate up the miles between the airfield and the rented house. But for Rico it was still too slow. He wanted to drive faster—much faster.

And in the opposite direction.

Instead, he was heading into a cage. He was going to have to put his head into a noose and let it be pulled tight.

His mood was grim. At his side, in the passenger seat, Falieri kept silent. Rico appreciated it. Falieri had been fully briefed, he knew, either by Luca or their father, and he knew exactly what Rico was about to do.

'Tell me I'm insane,' Rico demanded.

'It makes sense, what you are going to do,' Falieri said quietly.

'Does it?' Rico retorted bitterly. 'Keep reminding me of that, will you?'

'You are doing it for the boy,' said Falieri. 'And for your late brother.'

'Keep reminding me of that too—' said Rico.

He slammed on the brakes and changed gear viciously, ready to turn off the road.

Heading into that noose.

Ben greeted him excitedly, rushing to him with a cry of pleasure. Rico scooped him up. The boy's little arms wound around his neck, his sturdy body strong against Rico's chest. The hard, tight band around his lungs seemed to lighten fractionally.

I can do this. I can do it for Paolo. I can do it for Ben.

Gently, he lowered his nephew to the ground again. His eyes slid past him to the figure standing there, looking as out of place as she always did.

Dio, she looked worse than ever. Her skin had gone mottled, and her hair seemed frizzier than ever. She was wearing faded cotton trousers and an ill fitting top.

Revulsion raced through him.

He crushed the instinctive rejection. He'd committed to this course of action and there was no way out now. It might be insane—but he'd said he'd do it.

And there was no point putting it off. He had to do it now, before his feet hardened into ice. So, as he lowered Ben to the floor, he made himself look at her again.

'How have you been?' he asked.

She gave a half-shrug and didn't quite meet his eyes. She never did, he realised. Except that time when she had laid into him about being Ben's legal guardian and never parting from him.

His expression sobered. The intensity of her reaction had shocked him. More than shocked him. It had made him realise, for the first time since discovering about Paolo's son, that it didn't matter that the girl was only Ben's biological aunt—in emotional reality she was much, much more.

And she was right. Completely and indisputably right. To take Ben from her would be an unspeakable cruelty to the child. And to her—and she did not deserve that.

It must have been hard, taking on an orphaned child all on her own, in her circumstances.

'How did your father take it?' She swallowed. 'The fact that I won't let Ben be parted from me?'

He could hear the tension in her voice, like wires around her throat.

He looked at her.

'Another way of resolving the situation has been arrived at.'

Her eyes flashed.

'Anything involving taking Ben from me is—'

He held up a hand, silencing her.

'That will not happen. However,' he spoke heavily, steeling himself to do so, 'this is not the place to discuss this matter.' He cast a speaking look at Ben, who had gone back to his trainset, to rearrange some points. 'Have you dined?'

She pressed her lips together. 'I eat with Ben,' she said. 'It saves the staff doing two meals.'

'Very considerate,' said Rico dryly. 'Well, I have not. So I suggest that I do so while Ben is in his bath and then, when he is asleep, you will appreciate that we cannot postpone any longer a discussion about his future.' He cast a look at her. 'This must be done—none of us has any choice in that.'

Her expression had become strained, and she looked away. Ben piped up, and Rico was grateful.

'I've finished the track now—come and play,' he invited him. 'Let's race engines.'

Rico grinned, his face lightening.

'A race? Then prepare to be beaten, young man.'

For his pains he got a withering look. 'Silly you. I've got the express train,' he told Rico pityingly.

Out of the corner of his eye, Rico saw Ben's aunt slip away. He settled down to play with his nephew. It was a lot easier when she wasn't around.

Then he remembered what he had committed to do, and he felt his heart sink like lead. Even for Paolo's sake, this was going to be excruciating.

Ben was asleep, drifting off even as she finished reading his bedtime story to him. Usually Lizzy just had a bath herself, then read until she fell asleep. Ben woke early, and there was no question of a lie-in. So she never minded early nights.

But tonight she had to go downstairs again.

And face the Prince.

Her stomach knotted itself. She couldn't see what his solution might be—how this nightmare could be resolved.

Round and round her tired head went the drearily familiar litany. Two worlds colliding—no way out. No way out.

She knew only one thing—whatever the Ceraldis wanted, they were not going to part Ben from her. Not while she had breath in her body.

Grimly, she left the door to the bedroom ajar, letting in light from the landing, and then headed downstairs.

She was shown into the drawing room, and the Prince was already there, standing staring out over the near-dark gardens, the curtains undrawn. He had a glass of brandy in his hand, Lizzy registered.

She also registered something else. Something she instantly did her best to suppress. And yet it was impossible.

Impossible for her and every other woman in the world. Impossible to ignore that he was the most drop-dead gorgeous male she'd ever seen.

Embarrassment flushed through her. It seemed wrong to be so aware of his ridiculous good-looks. She had no business being aware of them.

Yet with that brooding expression on his face he just looked even more compelling.

He turned as she advanced into the room, and his eyes rested on her.

Immediately she felt her face mottling, as it always did whenever she came into his eyeline. Making her horribly conscious of her grim appearance.

Yes, I know—I look awful. There's nothing I can do about it. So, please, just don't look at me.

'Won't you sit down?'

Awkwardly, Lizzy lowered herself on to the sofa. She watched the Prince walk across and take a seat opposite her, separated by a large square coffee table. He swirled the brandy slowly in his glass for a moment, staring down into it. Then his head lifted.

He started to speak.

'I know you have found it very hard to accept what has happened,' he began, his voice slow and careful, 'but I hope that the reality of the situation has now finally sunk in. And that you have begun to appreciate that Ben's life cannot continue as it was.'

She opened her mouth to speak, but he hadn't finished.

'Hear me out. Before you say anything, hear me out.' He took a breath. It rasped in his lungs. 'As I said, I understand that it's difficult to accept, but you must—you have no choice. Ben is no longer the boy you thought he was. Whether you like it or not, you cannot deny his heritage. He is my brother's son— the offspring of his marriage to your sister. The circumstances of their deaths are tragic beyond belief, but we must deal with the outcome. And the outcome is Ben—our mutual nephew and your adopted son. This is the reality. And the reality of his paternity is, therefore, that he is a prince. Nothing can change that. Not all the wishing in the world.'

His expression changed. Emotion flared in his eyes suddenly. 'And I do not wish it. I would not wish it for a fraction of a second. Ben is a blessing—a gift from God. My dead brother's son restored to us. No. Do not blanch.' His voice had changed again, become measured and formal. 'Just because he is a gift to us, to my family, it does *not* imply that he is not precious beyond price to you. Or...' He paused, then said deliberately, 'Or you to him. That is not the issue. I gave you my word I would not pursue any avenue of resolution to this situation that was premised upon Ben leaving your care. But...' He paused again, then resumed, with absolute emphasis on each word. 'You *must* accept that his old life has gone. It cannot continue. Ben is a royal prince of the House of Ceraldi. Nothing can change that. His future must be based upon that fact.' He took another sharp intake of breath. 'And that means that he cannot live an ordinary life any more. He must come to San Lucenzo. With you.'

She had gone white, he could see. Her hands were clenched in her lap, and her breathing was uneven. But at least she was not interrupting him. He took another swift mouthful of brandy, feeling the fiery liquid burning in his throat.

He started speaking again.

'There is no easy way out of this situation. But a way does exist. And that is what I am going to propose to you. We have a situation which urgently requires resolution. And there is a way to do so. A drastic way, but nevertheless, in the circumstances, the only way forward.'

He could feel cold pooling in his legs, slowly turning his feet to ice. He had to say this—he had to say this now. Before he cut and ran. Ran as if all the devils in hell were after him.

He stared blankly into the face of the woman sitting opposite him. A woman who was a complete stranger. But to whom he *had* to say the following words.

'We get married,' said Rico.

She didn't move. That was the most unnerving thing of all. She just went on sitting there, hands clenched in her lap, face white. Rico felt his guts tighten. Had he really just said what he had? Had he been *that* insane?

And yet he knew it was not insanity that had made him say the words, but something much worse.

Necessity. Because, loathe Luca as he might for what he had suggested, Rico could see the unavoidable sense of it. The *impasse* they were in was immovable. Ben and his adoptive mother came as a package—that was all there was to it. A package that had to be incorporated somehow—by whatever means, however drastic—into the fabric of the San Lucenzo royal family. Ben alone would have been no problem—but Ben with the woman who had raised him, whom he thought of as his mother and who was in the eyes of the law indeed that person, that was a whole lot more impossible to swallow.

And yet she had to be swallowed. No alternative. No choice.

And he was the one who was going to have to do it. Luca had been right, and Rico hated him for it. But it didn't stop him being right. It would solve everything.

A marriage of convenience—for everyone except himself!

He felt his jaw set even tighter, and unconsciously his hands pressed against the rounded brandy glass. He wanted to take another mouthful, but knew he should not. He'd already drunk wine with dinner, to fortify himself, and although he wanted to drink himself into oblivion he knew it was impossible.

Why wasn't she responding? She hadn't moved—not a muscle. A spurt of anger went through him. Did she imagine this was easy for him? Abruptly he found himself raising the brandy glass anyway, and taking a large mouthful.

Something moved in her eyes minutely.

Then, as if a lever had suddenly been pulled, she jerked to her feet.

'You are,' she said, and there was something wrong with her voice, 'completely mad.'

Rico's eyes darkened. He might have expected this.

'Not mad,' he said repressively, 'just facing facts. Sit down again, if you please.'

She sat. Rico got the feeling it was not to obey him, but

because her legs wouldn't hold her upright. The bones of her face were standing out, and the blood had drained from her skin, which now looked like whey.

'If you marry me,' he began, 'a great many problems simply disappear. We have already established that your old life has gone—there can be no doubt about that. Ben is a royal prince of the House of Ceraldi, and he must be raised as such, in the land of his patrimony. He cannot be raised in this country, and he cannot be raised by you alone. But…' He took an inhalation of breath. 'Were you to marry me, this problem would immediately disappear. You and Ben would be absorbed into the royal family as a unit, and Ben would make the easiest transition possible to his new life. You must see that.'

Her mouth opened, then closed, then opened again.

'No, I don't.'

Rico's mouth pressed tightly.

'I appreciate,' he began, in that same deliberate fashion, 'that you may find this hard to comprehend, let alone accept, but—'

'It's the most insane, tasteless thing I've ever heard.' The words burst from her. 'How can you say it? How can you even *say* it? You can't sit there and say something like that—you *can't*.'

Agitation shook her visibly.

Abruptly he held up a hand.

'It is a matter of expediency, that is all.'

She was staring at him as if he were speaking Chinese. He ploughed on.

'The marriage would take place for no other purpose than to regularise my nephew's existence. As my wife you will become a Ceraldi, with a due place in the royal family, a rank appropriate to the adoptive mother of the Reigning Prince's grandson. You will have a suitable place in all the events of his life. The marriage itself will be a formality, nothing more. Be assured of that.'

There was an edge in his voice, and he continued before she could interrupt him again.

'You may also be assured that the marriage will only be temporary. Once Ben is settled into his new life, and once you are settled into yours, and can move within it in an appropriate manner, then the marriage will be annulled. We will need to observe the proprieties, but my father has agreed that he will sanction a short duration—little more than a year—after which the marriage will have served its purpose and can be dissolved.'

She was still sitting there, looking as if he'd just hit her over the head with a sledgehammer. Well, that was what he *had* done, of course. He, at least, had the last forty-eight hours to accustom himself to what had been proposed as the way through the *impasse*.

'I don't believe that you are saying what I hear you to be saying,' she said very slowly, her voice hollow. 'You cannot be. It's impossible.'

Rico felt anger welling in him, and fought to subdue it.

'I appreciate,' he began again, 'that this is difficult for you to fully take on board, but—'

'Stop saying that. Stop saying I don't understand.' She jerked to her feet again. Her eyes were flaring with emotion. 'What I'm saying is that it's insane. It's *grotesque*.'

Rico's expression froze.

'Grotesque?' The word echoed from him, as though it were in a foreign language. Hauteur filled his face. 'In what way?' he bit out. He got to his feet without realising it, discarding his brandy glass on a side-table as he did so.

She was staring at him wild-eyed, her face working.

'What do you mean, "In what way?"?' she demanded. 'In *every* way. It's grotesque—absolutely grotesque—to think of me marrying you.'

Cold anger filled Rico. To use such a word about such a matter—

He had taken a great deal from this woman, made allowance after allowance for her circumstances, but for her to stand there and tell him that his offer was *grotesque*—

'Would you do me the courtesy of explaining why?' His voice was like ice.

She stared at him. For one long moment she met his gaze, and then, as if in slow motion, he saw her face seem to fracture.

'What else can it be?' she said, in a low, vehement voice.

His voice was stiff with tightly leashed anger. 'I do not see why—'

She cut across him.

'*Look at me.*'

She stood dead in front of him.

'How can you even think of it? *Look at me.*' Her voice was taut. 'It's *grotesque* to think of me...of me...marrying... marrying...you—'

She broke off. Her head dropped.

Rico stood looking at her. His anger had gone. Vanished. In its place...an emotion he was unused to feeling.

Embarrassment.

And pity.

Then, quietly, he said, 'We'll find another way to sort this out.'

Lizzy lay in bed, but she was not asleep. Beside her, on the far side of the bed, Ben's breathing rose and fell steadily, soundlessly. Lizzy stared into the darkness. Even now, if she did not steel herself, she could feel the hot tide of all-consuming mortification flooding through her. It had been one of those excruciating moments—like a dream in which she found herself walking down the street naked—that she would remember all her life.

How could he have done it? How could he have actually sat there and said that to her face? How could *anyone* in his insane family have thought of it?

She felt a cold sweat break out on her.

Grotesque, she had called it, and that was the only word for it. The very *idea* of someone who looked like her marrying someone who looked like him—for whatever reason.

As if someone were running a sadism course in her mind, she made herself think about it. Made herself see it as if it were real.

Made herself see the headlines. Forced herself to.

The Playboy Prince and the Poison Pill.

Prince Rico and his Bride of Frankenstein.

They'd have a field-day.

She gazed out, wide-eyed and unseeing. Unseeing of anything except the cruel, unforgiving reflection that greeted her every day of her life.

Then, juxtaposed beside it, the image of Prince Rico Ceraldi.

The contrast was…grotesque.

She shut her eyes, as if to banish the image in her head.

All her life she'd known that she was not just unattractive, but actively repellent. It was a harsh word, but it was true. She had proof of it, day after day. She'd learnt to see it in men's eyes—that instant dismissal and rejection.

It was the exact opposite of the reaction Maria had got. Maria, with her tall, slim figure and her lovely face, her long golden hair.

Lizzy hadn't been jealous. What would have been the point? Maria had been the beautiful sister, she the plain one. It was the way it had always been.

Maria, in her kindness, had offered to try and do something to improve her appearance, but Lizzy had never let her. It would have been too embarrassing. Even worse than looking so repellent naturally would have been trying not to, trying to do something about it—and failing.

Because of course she would have failed.

'You can't make a silk purse out of a sow's ear,' her mother would say to her, her mouth pressing tightly in displeasure as she looked over her older daughter.

So she had never tried. She had accepted herself for what she was.

Totally without the slightest attraction to the male sex.

And with Ben it just didn't matter. What did a child care if its mother was ugly? For Ben, it was her love for him that counted, her devotion to him. All he needed from her was her care and her hugs. That was all.

Ben.

Instinctively she reached out her hand and touched his folded little body, lightly brushing his hair before taking her hand away again.

Anguish filled her.

I want to go home. I want to go back home, to Cornwall—I want this nightmare never to have happened. Please, please let it not have happened. Please.

But her prayers were hopeless. The nightmare *had* happened, and she was caught in it. She would never be free of it.

Heaviness crushed her.

'We'll find another way to sort this out,' the Prince had said.

But what other way? The Ceraldis must have been desperate to even entertain what he had come up with—a temporary marriage of convenience to turn her into a princess and therefore a suitable mother for Prince Eduardo's grandson.

The weight on her chest intensified.

I'm nothing but a nuisance to them...

Then she rallied. Tough. Tough that she was nothing but a nuisance to the San Lucenzan royal family. Tough that she was a problem that had to be solved. Tough that their precious grandson just happened to come encumbered by a stand-in mother.

I don't care—I don't care about them, or what an inconvenience I am! I don't care about anything except Ben and his happiness. Ben needs me...and that's all that matters. And for him I'll do anything—anything at all.

Except marry his uncle.

Rico stood under the shower and let the stinging needles of water pound down over his head.

He should be feeling relieved. He should be feeling like a

condemned man reprieved. But he wasn't. An uncomfortable, writhing emotion twisted within him.

He kept hearing that word in his mind.

Grotesque.

How could any woman say that about herself? Feel that about herself?

OK, she was plain. But that was not her fault. So why did she seem to flay herself so for it?

A cynical voice spoke in his head.

She's just facing up to the truth, that's all. No man will ever want her, and she knows that. She knows just what an unlikely couple the two of you would make—the talking behind her back, the whispering, the scornful looks, the offers to comfort you for your affliction in having had to marry such a female.

He silenced the voice. Ruthlessly.

Instead, deliberately, he called another image to mind. The way she was with Ben. Endlessly patient, always loving and affectionate, supportive and encouraging.

She'd brought him up well.

More than well.

He frowned. It must have been hard for her.

She could have so much easier a life now. If he could just get her to see that.

He cut the water off and stepped out of the shower.

OK, so maybe it wasn't ideal having Ben's mother floating around San Lucenzo like a loose cannon. But even if she was a commoner, and an Englishwoman, so what? Something could be sorted, surely? Yes, it would make life awkward—but too bad. Wasn't Paolo's son worth some degree of inconvenience, some rearrangement of protocol and expectation?

He whipped a towel around his lean, honed body, then grabbed a hand towel to roughly pat his hair dry.

Once she and Ben were in San Lucenzo she would start to see for herself how a new life there would be possible. And he would have to make Luca and his father realise that somehow they had to set up a situation where Ben and his mother could live there.

His mind raced on. They didn't have to live in the palace, or the capital itself. The Ceraldis owned enough property in the principality—one of their numerous residences would prove suitable.

A villa by the sea—they'd like that.

He could see Ben in his mind's eye, playing on the beach—a warmer, less windy beach than the one in Cornwall.

I could visit him a lot then. Get to know him. Spend time with him.

Another thought came to him as he shrugged on a bathrobe and discarded the towels.

I'll get something done about her—for her. With good clothes, a decent haircut, make-up—surely she'd look better?

It would be a kindness to her.

He headed for bed, feeling virtuous.

And finally relieved.

CHAPTER SIX

THE jet was starting its descent. Rico could feel the alteration in pitch.

'We're starting to go down, Ben,' he announced.

Ben, captivated, stared out of the porthole, at the tiny patchwork of fields and valleys and rivers spread below. He had taken the journey in his stride so far—and so, to Rico's relief, had his mother.

'Will you at least agree to a visit?' he had asked her the next day. 'Nothing more than that. To allow my parents and brother to meet Ben.' His voice had changed. 'I do not have to tell you how much they long to meet him at last. Please do not deny them that,' he'd finished quietly. 'It will be a very emotional moment for them.'

She had nodded. Something seemed to have changed between them. He didn't know what, but somehow it was easier to talk to her. She, too, and he was sure it was not just his imagination, seemed less tense, less awkward in his presence.

Maybe, he thought sombrely, the scene that night had brought everything to a head.

Whatever it was, he was grateful. Grateful that she had agreed to move forward, even in this circumspect way, that she finally seemed to have moved beyond the stonewalling denial that had made her so difficult to deal with.

He had spoken to Luca that morning, telling him they were

going to fly out the following day. What he hadn't told him was that it was only for a visit, not permanently. He would tell Luca privately that there could be no question of a marriage of convenience. That the situation would have to be resolved differently, in a way that Ben's adopted mother was comfortable with.

Luca had not been communicative, had merely wanted to know that Ben was finally on his way and when they would be landing. He'd seemed tense, preoccupied.

Well, it had been a stressful time, Rico acknowledged. Their father was not an easy man, and Rico had sympathy for Luca being the one to bear the brunt of it. However much of a miracle Ben's existence was, it had come with a price tag—one that his father hated to pay. The focus of the world's tabloid press on his family's private affairs.

The stewardess came forward into the cabin to request they put their seat belts on. Rico smiled reassuringly across at Ben's mother. She seemed outwardly calm, but he wondered how real it was.

Ben simply seemed excited.

Ironically, thought Rico, Ben seemed a lot more excited about flying in a plane than he did about the news, broken to him tactfully and carefully the previous afternoon by his uncle and his aunt, that he was, in fact, a royal prince.

'Will I have a crown?' had been his only question, and, when a negative answer had been returned to him, had lost interest in the matter.

His interest in royalty was revived momentarily when they transferred to the car waiting for them at the airfield. The car was flying a colourful standard from its bonnet, and Ben wanted to know why.

'It's your grandfather's flag,' Rico answered. 'Because he's the Ruler of San Lucenzo. We are going to meet him. And your grandmother and your other uncle. The one I told you about yesterday.'

The car glided off. Ben chattered away to Rico, asking him

question after question. Beside him, Lizzy sat, willing herself to stay calm.

But it was hard.

In England, cocooned in the safe house, it had been hard to appreciate the reality of Ben's patrimony. Now that they were here, in San Lucenzo itself, it was suddenly all too real. Fear and apprehension gouged at her, and she could feel her muscles tensing.

She was so completely out of place here. It had been bad enough in England, in that country house, but boarding a private San Lucenzan-registered jet, flying in luxury, with the stewardess saying 'Highness' to Ben's uncle every time she opened her mouth, and a uniformed airfield commander greeting them as they deplaned, and now a bodyguard, Gianni, sitting next to a peak-capped chauffeur driving them in the sleek, official-looking limo with the royal standard on it… It was all telling her that this was a world to which she did not belong.

A world as alien to her as if she'd landed on another planet.

Anxiety and nerves bit through her with merciless pincers.

'It will be all right. Trust me.'

Prince Rico had spoken in a low voice, but there was a note of consideration…kindness, even…that she was not used to. Perhaps it was simply because she was finally doing what the Ceraldis wanted her to do—bringing Ben out to San Lucenzo to meet his royal relatives.

But it seemed more than that.

And Lizzy knew why.

He's sorry for me. He's sorry for me because he knows that I know that the insane idea of a marriage of convenience was just grotesque.

His kindness should have made her feel more embarrassed than ever. And yet, strangely, it seemed to achieve the opposite.

She looked across at him, to where he was patiently answering Ben's questions. Ben was completely at ease with him now—and Rico with Ben, Lizzy could see. He was warm and affectionate, open and demonstrative with his nephew.

It brought a reassurance to her that she badly needed.

If he's like that with Ben, it means his parents and his brother will be too. OK, so they happen to be royalty—but what does that matter in the end? They want Ben to love, because they loved his father, and that's all that matters.

It would be all right—she had to believe that. It would be all right.

And if it wasn't—well. She took a heavy inhalation of breath as she reminded herself she had committed to nothing in coming out here. Ben, like her, was a British citizen, and she was his legal guardian. Nothing happened to him without her consent.

Her eyes went to Ben's uncle again.

Besides, he had given her his word.

He, a royal prince, wouldn't give that lightly or trivially. When he gave it, he would mean it.

Her reassurance deepened.

The windows of the car were tinted, so that although the occupants could see out, no one could see in.

'They are used to the cars of the royal family on the roads,' Rico remarked, as the car wound its slow way through the narrow streets of the city towards the royal palace.

'Does anyone else know we are coming here?' asked Lizzy.

Rico shook his head.

'The pavements would be mobbed with paparazzi if they knew,' he said. 'So far as the press is concerned, you and Ben are still in England. Eventually there will be an official statement from the palace, confirming both Ben's existence and yours, and also officially recognising him as Prince Paolo's son and a member of the royal family. But my father will not be hustled into making any announcements in reaction to the recent stories.'

'So no one knows we're here?' said Lizzy.

'No, you are quite safe. It will be a completely private visit.'

Her tension eased a fraction.

But not by much. The car was already approaching the wide gates of a palace, driving across its wide-paved concourse. The sugar-white, *faux*-castellated royal palace looked as if it was made out of children's candy, Lizzy thought. And the flanking guards were in picturesque antique costume and helmets as they swept past them and into the inner courtyard.

The car drew to a halt in front of a huge double door at the rear of the cobbled courtyard. As it stopped the doors were thrown open and two footmen emerged. One came to open the car door.

Prince Rico got out first, then turned to help lift Ben out and offer his hand to Lizzy. She managed to get out of the car without taking it.

As she straightened, she felt the warmth of the Mediterranean air in her lungs after the air-conditioned car.

Then they were heading indoors, and the cool of marble floors enveloped her as she walked beside Ben, his uncle on his other side, across the wide expanse of an entrance hall.

I'm in a palace, thought Lizzy, and the thought seemed bizarre and unreal.

One of the footmen was processing in front of them, the other bringing up the rear. Ben was still asking Rico questions. Lizzy glanced covertly either side of her, at the ornate walls, with alcoves inset with statuary.

Ahead was a huge flight of stairs, carpeted in royal blue. Prince Rico ascended lithely.

This is his home—he must do this every day of his life.

Her sense of unreality deepened.

So did the sense of oppression that had started to weigh her down.

How could she ever move in this world, even if only on the edges, as the legal mother of the Ruling Prince's grandson? It was impossible.

Grotesque…

The cruel word pincered at her.

They gained the top of the stairs, and a wide landing that

seemed to stretch endlessly in either direction. Off its length sets of double doors marched away.

Everywhere was marble and gilt, and there was the kind of hush that went with a deserted museum.

A man stepped forward, out of a doorway she hadn't even noticed.

The procession halted, and the man bowed briefly to Prince Rico, dismissing the footmen. The man was wearing a suit, and was clearly not a servant but one of the royal staff.

What were they called? Lizzy found herself wondering. Equerries? Was that it?

The man, who was quite young, and wearing pale spectacles which obscured his eyes, was addressing Prince Rico. His glance had gone briefly to Ben, but not to herself.

What am I? Invisible?

The caustic thought merely made her unease deepen.

Prince Rico was frowning, saying something in a sharp voice in Italian to the man. The man's expression did not change, remaining impassive. Unreadable.

Prince Rico turned towards Lizzy, shutting out the other man.

'My father and mother would like to meet Ben on his own for the first time,' he said to her. 'Please do not take offence at this. Were you to be there, they would be constrained to be formal, to behave as the protocols dictate. I hope you will understand?'

Fear flared in her eyes. Then, to her astonishment, her hand was taken.

'It will be all right. You have my word.'

His hands were warm across hers. His eyes, as he looked into hers, were rich with sympathy.

'Trust me,' he said in a low voice. 'Do not be afraid.'

Slowly, very slowly, she nodded. There seemed to be a lump in her throat.

He let go of her hand.

'You will be shown to your apartments, where you can

refresh yourself. I will bring Ben to you. In the meantime, rest and relax. Then, when I've brought Ben back, I will show you around.'

He glanced down at Ben.

'We're going to meet your grandparents now, Ben, and your other uncle. Your mother is going to have a little rest, and then we'll go exploring. There's a lot to see in this palace.' He bent forward conspiratorially. 'Even a secret passage.'

Ben's eyes widened. He slipped his hand into his uncle's, and Prince Rico started to walk off with him, still talking to him.

Lizzy watched them go.

'*Signorina?*'

It was the equerry, or whoever he was.

'I will show you to your new quarters,' said the man.

Numbly, Lizzy followed after him.

Tension netted her like a web.

Rico looked about him and frowned. His parents' private sitting room, which he'd just been ushered into with Ben, was deserted. Yet he'd been told to present Ben immediately. So where was everyone?

'Rico—finally.'

He turned abruptly. Luca had walked in from one of the antechambers. His brother's eyes went swiftly from himself to the small figure holding Rico's hand. For a moment he said nothing, just looked. Then he spoke.

'Yes—difficult to deny his paternity. Far too much Paolo in him.' His eyes flicked back to Rico. 'We were beginning to think you'd never get him here,' he said. 'You must be slipping.' A jibing note entered his voice. 'For a man who can charm any woman he wants into bed in the blink of an eye, it should have been a piece of cake for you to get the boy's aunt eating out of your hand.'

'Cut the sniping, Luca,' said Rico. His voice was sharper than usual. 'Where are the parents?'

His brother's eyebrows rose with a sardonic curve.

'It's Grand Council today—you know our father's never late for those sessions. And as for our fond mama, she always goes back to Andovaria for her fortnight's spa this time of year—had you forgotten?'

Rico stared. '*What?* Di Finori told me Ben had been summoned immediately.'

'Well, of course,' Luca responded impatiently. 'We've had to wait long enough to get him. But—' his mouth pressed '—at least we've got him now.' His voice changed again. 'So we can all relax finally. Especially you.' The jibing note was back in his voice. 'Poor Rico—actually reduced to offering to make the ultimate sacrifice—marriage. And to *such* a bride. I've just checked her out on the security cameras. *Dio*, if I'd known she was that bad even *I* might have thought twice before I did that number on you. Still, it did the business—as I knew it would. She must have snapped your hand off the minute you trotted out the marriage-of-convenience fairytale.'

'You never intended me to go through with it?' Rico's voice was edged like a knife.

Luca gave a laugh, abruptly cut off. 'Thump me one if you want, Rico, but you gave us no choice. I had to be convincing. I had to make sure you believed you were going to have to go through with it.' His mouth thinned. 'Why the hell you gave this Lizzy Mitchell your word that you wouldn't try and take the boy from her is beyond me. That's not something to lie about. That's why I didn't want to put you in a position where you knew you were lying about a marriage of convenience.'

The expression in Rico's eyes flickered minutely. 'I gave her my word to get her to trust me,' he said.

'Bad move.' Luca shook his head. 'You'll be glad to know I didn't mention it to our father—it wouldn't have gone down well. Still, like I said, everything's worked out finally. And now we can finally get this damn mess sorted.'

His eyes went to Ben, who had a blank, confused look on his face at all the incomprehensible Italian being spoken over his head, then to his brother again. For a moment Rico thought he saw something in Luca's eyes. Then it was gone. His voice, when he spoke next, was brisk and businesslike.

'The boy's personal household has been selected, and they're waiting to take him now. He'll have apartments here in the palace to begin with, where security is tighter. Later he'll be moved out to somewhere more remote—up in the hills, probably, to keep him out of circulation. Boarding school's a possibility when he's older, but that's a few years ahead yet. For the moment it's just a question of nannies and tutors. And keeping his profile as low as possible, of course. Everything necessary will be done to mitigate the situation and minimise his presence.' His expression changed again, and he gave a short, angry rasp. '*Dio*, what an ungodly mess! It's been hell dealing with it here, I can tell you!'

'I had the feeling,' Rico said, his eyes narrowing, 'that the idea of a grandson was welcome.'

Luca laughed shortly without humour.

'You've been reading too much of that trash in the press. Yes, of course that's the line the hacks took—they would, wouldn't they? All cloying sentimentality. You don't seriously imagine that our parents would *ever* welcome the news that Paolo had disgraced himself—and us all—by going and impregnating some two-cent bimbo and then *marrying* her?'

Rico gave a shrug. 'Could be worse—the bimbo could still be alive. As it is, it's just the frump of an aunt. What happens to *her* now, by the way?' His voice was offhand.

'Secure apartment here, in the south tower—she's being taken there now—then she'll be deported as *persona non grata* to the principality. Once outside the borders she can do what she wants. She won't get the boy back. Even if the press bankroll any counter-custody claim by her for the publicity, it will take years. While she had the boy and they were still in the

UK we were hamstrung—the law was weighted in her favour. But now it's a different story. We have possession, and that's what counts. She's finished. And you, my dear brother—' Luca clapped him on the back, his slate eyes sparking with his familiar sardonic expression '—are finally off-duty. You're free to celebrate a job well done. Mission accomplished.'

'Not quite,' said Rico.

His right hand slipped from Ben's, fisted, and landed on his brother's left temple with the full weight of his body behind the blow. Luca crumpled, unconscious, to the floor.

Ben had given a gasp, but Rico just took his hand again and started to hurry towards the door.

'Change of plan, Ben,' said Rico.

His voice was tight with fury.

The corridors seemed endless. Like a twisting maze. Numbly, Lizzy followed behind the bespectacled equerry. He said nothing to her, and walked at a pace that was slightly too fast for her. They went up stairs, and along more corridors, and then more stairs, leading upwards.

The décor was getting less palatial with every corridor. Finally he took her through a set of doors and into one more corridor. Lizzy looked about her. This wasn't just less palatial—this was…unused. It was the only word for it. A faint sheen of dust was on the floor, the skirting boards, and the air had a musty smell to it.

'*Signorina?*'

The equerry, or whoever he was, had opened a door and was waiting for her to go in. She hesitated a moment, then, not knowing what else to do, went in. It was more like a room in a budget hotel than a palace, with a plain bed and furniture, and a small and not very clean window that, Lizzy could see, over-looked some kind of delivery area.

Her suitcase was standing on a slightly frayed rug beside the bed.

It was a single bed, she noticed, frowning slightly, and she glanced around towards the door into what she presumed must be Ben's bedroom. But when she opened it it was only a small, windowless shower room, with no further door leading out of it. She turned.

'Where is my son's bedroom?' she asked. There was sharpness in her voice.

But it was wasted.

The door to the corridor was closing, and as it did she heard a distinct click.

A spurt of alarm went through her, and she hurried to the door, twisting the handle urgently.

It was locked.

The corridor was dingy, clearly disused. Emotion stabbed at Rico, and he suppressed it. There was no time for emotion now. None at all. Methodically he walked along the length of the corridor, testing each handle. Each one yielded to an empty room. They must have been servants' quarters at some point.

The fifth door refused to yield. He paused a moment, listening. There was no sound. Had she tried to scream? Or would she have realised it was bound to be pointless? No one would hear her here.

Emotion stabbed again, like a hornet stinging him. He suppressed it once more. He felt the strength of the lock with his hand, twisting the handle, then stepped back.

It hurt. In films it never looked as if it did. But the jarring pain in his shoulder as the door cracked was irrelevant.

What was not was the huddled figure on the bed. She had just launched up into a sitting position, he could tell.

Even from the shattered doorway he could see the look of terror on her face.

And the streaks of tears.

Her face contorted. Contorted into rage. Fury. Incandescent despair.

'I've got Ben—let's go.' He spoke urgently. 'We have no time—come now. *Now.*' His eyes bored at her. *'Trust me.'*

He could see the emotion in her face. An emotion that he never, ever wanted to see again on a woman's face. Then, abruptly, she hurled herself forward.

'Where is he?'

'At the end of the corridor, keeping watch. He thinks it's a game. He's not upset—he didn't realise what was happening. Don't ask questions—we've got *one* chance to get out of here, and that's all.'

How long would Luca stay out cold? He had no idea. He only knew that precious minutes were ticking by. He seemed to be divided into two people. One of them was raging with fury—the other was deadly calm. It was the latter he kept uppermost.

'Ben—' Her cry was almost a scream, but stifled in her throat.

Rico saw the child turn from his position at the end of the corridor.

'Mummy—come on.' He beckoned her furiously, his little face alight with excitement.

The palace was labyrinthine, but Rico knew it like the back of his hand. Knew exactly which levels were most likely to be deserted. He walked rapidly, blood pounding, her suitcase in one hand and Ben's hand in the other. Ben trotted beside him, his mother behind him, both instructed not to talk, not to ask questions. He mustn't think, mustn't feel. Just keep moving. Fast, urgent. Undetected. Every corner was a risk—someone, anyone, could be there.

But there was no one. No one right up to the service door to his own apartments. Ungently, he shoved Ben and his mother inside even as he yanked out his mobile phone and punched a number.

Thank God Gianni was there, in position. He'd phoned him the moment he'd left his brother out cold on the floor, to give him instructions. He snapped the phone shut and turned to Ben.

'Time for the secret passage,' he said.

Ben's mouth opened wide in wonder.

'Here it is,' said Rico. He'd crossed to the wall into which a fireplace had been set, and felt for the concealed button that operated the door mechanism. He hadn't used it in a while, but it still worked, if creakingly, revealing a narrow entrance to an even narrower staircase.

He gave a sudden grin, his mood lightening for a nanosecond.

'It's the reason I chose these apartments as a teenager. It was a great way to evade curfew. Come on.'

Ben needed no second invitation. He surged forward, his expression blissful, and Rico had to hold him while he flicked on the interior light, got them all inside, and then shut the door.

The concealed staircase opened into a side street in the palace precincts. The car was waiting, its tinted windows closed. Even so, he made his nephew and his mother lie on the floor of the back seat.

'Drive,' he instructed Gianni.

Only as he sat back in his seat, Ben excitedly clutching at his leg and asking him if it were another adventure, did the emotions start to come through.

The violence of them shook him to the core.

They made it to the border in under twenty minutes. He'd debated between speed via the coastal *autostrada* versus heading for the hills, and had gone for the former. He had to take a gamble, and it was absolutely vital they get on to Italian soil.

As they passed through the unmanned border he spoke.

'We're out,' he said. He leant down to haul up Ben, followed by his mother. She busied herself with seat-belts.

'What now?' she asked. Her voice was expressionless, but Rico heard the tremor in it. Heard the tightness of her throat. Heard the fear. The terror.

He looked at her. The chalky complexion, the bones stark

in her face. Emotion surged in him, and he clamped it down yet again.

'We get to a priest,' he said.

CHAPTER SEVEN

THE savage irony of it was that she still balked at marrying him. In the end he had to be brutal.

'It is the only way I can protect you. Protect Ben.'

She stared at him, her face a web of fear.

'It's another trick. A trap.' Her voice was hollow.

'*No*, I swear it. I swear I did not know what they were planning—I swear. If I could, I would get you back to England—but I can't. I've got you into Italy, and now you are safer, because my father will have to work through the Italian authorities and that will slow him down. But if you try and return to England you'll be taken into custody. I can't even get you into Switzerland. All the Italian borders will be watched. And don't think my father won't be able to do it—he'll have some charge against you trumped up. It doesn't matter what—it matters only to prevent you taking Ben back to the UK. You'll be separated, and there'll be some kind of court order taking him into care—something. Anything. Whatever it takes to separate you. And he'll find a way to keep you separated.'

He took a searing breath. 'The only way I can keep you safe is by doing what I've just said. Once we're married they can't touch you, and they can't touch Ben. Neither legally nor because of the publicity. They will have to accept a *fait accompli*. I know my father—he won't risk an open break with me. He won't cause that kind of scandal.'

He looked at her as she sat, her arm tight around Ben, who had lolled off to sleep with the motion of the car, steadily being driven further north towards the alpine foothills. 'I'm the only person who can protect you—keep you and Ben together.'

She stared at him.

'Why?' The question was a breath, almost inaudible. 'Why do you want to do that?'

It echoed through him, reverberating through his being.

Why? She had asked why.

'I gave you my word,' he said. 'Not to let Ben be parted from you. That's why.'

In his head he heard again Luca's voice, describing the nightmare childhood that had been planned for Ben.

Anger blinded him.

Anger at his father, his mother, his brother…the whole damn, twisted, duplicitous, hard-hearted, *callous* lot of them.

How could they do it? How could they even think it?

But he knew how. To them, the only important thing was duty and reputation, avoiding scandal, awkwardness, embarrassment.

And to achieve that they were prepared to take a four-year-old child and wrench it from its mother—trick the mother into coming here in good faith and then throw her out like a piece of rubbish.

His eyes went to her, went to her arm so tight around Ben, and to Ben, his head resting on her side, his hand lying in her lap. Mother and child.

Genetically she might only be his aunt, but to Ben she was everything—the whole world. So what if she were some ordinary member of the masses, utterly unfit to be a royal princess, the mother of a royal prince?

His lips pressed together. And so what that she was utterly unlike any woman he would have chosen for his wife? A woman who knew that brutal, cruel truth…

Grotesque.

That was what she thought a marriage between them would be.

Grotesque. The word tolled through him again.

Shaming him.

Shaming him with its pitiless honesty.

Well, now it didn't matter. Didn't matter what either of them thought about such a marriage. Because neither of them was important now—only Ben.

And this was the only way to keep him safe.

Savage humour filled him. So Luca had set him up like a patsy, had he? Despatching him to mount a charm offensive on Ben's aunt that would steal her child from her, duping him into offering to marry her simply to lull her into a false sense of security. His mouth tightened.

Thanks for the idea, Luca—it's a really good one.

And it would beat his family on all points.

And keep Ben safe with his mother.

His eyes went to the boy. He was still asleep, lolling against his mother.

He met her eyes. They were huge, strained.

'Thank you,' she said, her voice low and tight.

She felt as if she was falling. Falling very far, into a deep, bottomless pit. All she had to cling to was Ben. And it was imperative she did. Imperative she keep hold of him, never, ever to loosen her hold on him—because otherwise he would fall away from her and be lost for ever.

Fear shot through her like a grid of hot wires in her veins. Over and over again the horror of what had happened in the palace, when she had realised she had been locked in that room, when she had realised that it could mean only one thing, still drenched through her.

Her eyes went to the man standing beside her in the chill, stone-built church, his expression drawn and shuttered.

Trust me, he had said.

I give you my word, he had said.

Could she trust him? Was he really rescuing her? Or simply tricking her again?

But how could he be tricking her? He was prepared to do something that would change his life for ever. Something so drastic that it made her feel faint with the enormity of it. He had disobeyed his father, knocked his own brother out cold so he could rescue her, so he could get Ben and her away to freedom…safety.

Safety with him.

He's doing it for Ben. Because he knows it would be unspeakably cruel for him to lose me. And that was why she'd do it too. For Ben.

Nothing else mattered.

The priest was starting to speak. The dimly lit, tiny whitewashed church, scarcely more than a chapel, was in a small village somewhere in the hills. She had no idea where. There had been a low-voiced, urgent conversation in the car between the Prince and his bodyguard, who was, so it seemed, not merely loyal enough to his employer to have stood by him, but also possessed of a great-uncle who was a priest.

A frail, elderly man, he stood before them now, clasping their hands together with his and intoning words she did not understand, but which, she knew, were binding her in holy matrimony to the man at her side.

She went on falling.

It was done. Ben and his mother were safe. Relief sluiced through Rico. As he thanked the priest, mentally vowing that he would take every measure to avoid the man getting into the slightest trouble over what he had done, and thanked the housekeeper who had been the witness to the ceremony along with Gianni, Rico knew that there was one more thing to be done.

He ushered Ben and his mother back into the car. Gianni slid into the driver's seat. He knew where to go, what to do.

'I'm hungry,' announced Ben. He had woken up, stood beside Gianni during the brief, hurried ceremony, passively accepting, as children did, without comprehension, what was happening to the grown-ups around him.

'We'll have some food soon—very soon, I promise,' Rico said, ruffling his hair. It was still not quite dark, but they had a way to drive. He would have preferred to fly, but that was out. There was no way he could take a helicopter up without air traffic control knowing about it. But they would head cross country, by obscure routes if they could.

This car was different anyway—a lot less conspicuous. Gianni had fixed the swap—the guy was heading for an all-time bonus. Now he came up trumps yet again.

'You like pizza?' he asked, and passed back a large, double wrapped plastic bag. 'Cold, but good. From my great-uncle's housekeeper, for the *bambino*.'

Ben's face lit.

'Yes, please,' he said.

Rico watched as his mother unwrapped the food and handed it with some paper towels to his nephew, who tucked in hungrily. As they ate, he slid his hand into his pocket and took out his phone. It took a while to be answered, but when it was, he wasted no time.

'Jean-Paul, I've got a story for you…'

The conversation was lengthy, in rapid French, and when he disconnected Rico felt another wave of relief go through him. He also felt anxious eyes on him. He turned his head.

'That was a friend of mine. The one who alerted me that there was a story building about Paolo's long-lost son. He's a good friend, and I trust him absolutely. I've told him we've just got married. That we're making a family for Ben. He'll sit on the story until I give him the word to run with it. That's the weapon I can hold over my father. I'll give him some time to come round, to accept what's happened, but if he stonewalls then Jean-Paul can run the story the way I've given it to him— without any co-operation from the palace. That's the only choice my father gets.'

His voice was grim as he finished.

He slid the phone into his jacket pocket again.

'I still cannot believe that my father did what he did. I knew he was not sentimental about Luca and myself, but Paolo— Paolo was different.' His eyes slid away into the past as he spoke, his voice low. 'Paolo was the one son my parents could treat not as a prince, but as…as a child. As someone in his own right. Someone without a royal function. Who could just be himself. That's why—' His voice halted a moment, then he went on. 'That's why I thought they really wanted Ben. Because he's Paolo's son. I thought they would…' He swallowed. 'I thought they would love him. Love him enough to know that what was important for Ben was what should be done. Love him enough to know that *you* were important to him.'

His eyes looked troubled. 'I am ashamed of them. Ashamed of what they did to you.'

Suddenly, out of nowhere, he touched her arm. Lightly. Just for a moment.

'And I am ashamed of myself as well.'

Lizzy's expression was troubled.

'You're taking the fall for this,' she said, and her voice was low and strained. 'I'm sorry—I'm really, really sorry that you had to…had to do what you've just done. I'll try…I'll try not to be—' She swallowed, then fell silent.

What could she say? *I'll try not to be too grotesque a wife to you?* She felt her throat tightening.

He was silent a moment. Then he spoke.

'It will work out. For all the reasons I told you in England, when I believed that this marriage was what my father wanted. All those reasons are still true.'

She could not reply. What could she say?

That the reason for her refusing him in England was still the same as well?

Well, it was too late for that.

The car drove on into the night. At her side, Ben finished

his pizza. She cleared away the remains, then let him cuddle against her and fall asleep. His little body was warm and sturdy, and her love for him flooded through her.

I've done the right thing. I've done the only thing. The only thing possible to keep him safe.

Her eyes met his uncle's, on the other side of Ben.

A strange emotion pricked through him.

He had done what he had had to do. No other course of action had been possible—anything else had been unthinkable.

I did what I had to do. That is all.

It was my duty.

Duty. But of a different type.

Carrying, strangely, no burden of resentment. Only relief.

Relief that he had done, if nothing else, the right thing. By Paolo, by his son, and by the girl whom he now protected. Who had no one but him to do so. The strange emotion quickened. Quite different from all the emotions that had stormed through him since Jean-Paul's first phone call to him, which seemed now to have been a long, long time ago. He tried to think what the emotion was, to identify it. Then it came to him.

It was a sense of purpose. Doing something that mattered.

A new emotion for him.

'Where are we?' Lizzy's voice sounded bleary, even to her own ears. She had been roused from heavy, uneasy sleep as the car had come to a stop. She straightened up, feeling stiff. Ben was still slouched heavily against her, fast asleep.

'Capo d'Angeli. Jean-Paul has hired a villa here for us. We can stay here as long as we want. No one will disturb us.'

She let him undo the safety catch and she scooped the sleeping Ben into her arms, while Gianni helped her out of the car. A cool breeze came in the night, and all she could make out was a house with a gravelled drive immediately beneath her feet, and a front door opening. She heard Italian spoken, and then she and Ben were being ushered inside. There were people, more Italian, but she was too tired to do anything other than carry Ben upstairs, following the tall, besuited figure ascending in front of her, blocking out of her head everything except the overriding need to get to bed. Get back to sleep.

Like a zombie, she followed him into a room—a large bedroom with a larger bed. A maid was turning it down on either side. She hurried forward to help Lizzy, and within a few minutes—blessedly so—Lizzy was laying her head down on the pillow beside her sleeping son, her eyelids closing.

She wanted to sleep for ever and never wake up. Never face up to what she had just done.

Married Prince Enrico of San Lucenzo.

Downstairs, Rico took out his mobile once more, and pressed the number he knew he had to call.

Luca answered immediately. His voice was taut with fury. Incomprehension. Rico cut him off in mid-denunciation. He called his brother a word he had never used to him before. It silenced Luca long enough for Rico to tell him the new situation. Then, slowly, in a different voice, his older brother spoke again.

'Rico—it's not too late. We'll send a helicopter, and you and the boy can be back here by morning. We'll fix an instant annulment. The girl can be taken care of—we can get her deported from Italy. We can—'

'Wrong again.' Rico's voice was a tight, vicious drawl. 'All you and our father can do is—' He gave instructions that were crude—and anatomically impossible. 'And now, if you please, you can inform my revered father that I am going to start my honeymoon, with my bride and my new son. And there is *nothing* you can do about it. Do you understand me? Nothing. They are in my care now. Mine. And if you had a shred of honour in you, you would never speak to our father again.'

He hung up.

* * *

Lizzy was dreaming. She was back in that hospital, with her sister. But her sister was not in a coma. Instead she was sitting up, cradling a baby, her golden hair like a veil. There was someone else sitting on the bed—a young man with blond hair. They were both fixated on the baby in Maria's arms. They didn't see Lizzy. Didn't even look up.

Then her parents were coming into the ward. They walked past Lizzy, their arms full of presents wrapped up in baby blue. She tried to walk forward, but she couldn't. She had a present for the baby, but there was only room to put the present on the end of the bed. It slid onto the floor. Her mother looked round sharply.

'What are you doing here?' she demanded. 'Maria doesn't need you. No one needs you. And no one wants you either.'

She reached for the curtain and drew it around Maria's bed. Shutting Lizzy out.

Lizzy woke up.

Guilt drenched through her.

She had taken something that was not hers to take. Something she'd had no right to. She turned her head. Ben was asleep on the far side of the huge double bed, his little figure swathed in the light coverlet. Ben—her sister's son. Not hers. Not hers at all.

Anguish filled her. Her hand reached to him, touching his hair. Soft and golden. Like his mother's. His father's.

Not like hers at all.

Not mine. Not mine. Not mine.

The litany rang through her head.

And now she had taken something else she'd had no right to take. Something else she didn't deserve.

And yet she knew bitterly that the theft had come with its own punishment. Heat flushed through her—the heat of mortification. *Grotesque*, she had called the very idea of a marriage between them, the two most opposite people in the world. And yet she had gone ahead with it. She had inflicted herself on him because there was no other way to keep safe the child she had taken from her sister. The child she had no right to. No right to love the way she did.

She felt Ben stir and wake. His eyes opened. Trusting. Instantly content to see her. Knowing that if she was there, then all was well.

Cold iced along her veins. It had so very nearly been different.

I could have been on my way back to England—deported. Ben imprisoned in that palace, never to see me again.

The horror of what had so nearly been consumed her.

Prince Rico had saved them.

Guilt stabbed at her again. He had saved them—and she had repaid him by chaining him to her.

'Mummy?'

Ben was sitting up.

'Is it getting-up time?' he asked brightly. 'Is Tio Rico here?' He looked around expectantly, then, in a puzzled voice, 'Where are we, Mummy? Have we gone back to the palace again?'

She shook her head. A steely hardness filled her.

'No, darling. We're not going back there.' She threw back the bedclothes. 'Come on, let's find out where breakfast is. I'm starving.'

She looked around her. The room was large and airy, and filled with sunlight diffused through bleached wood Venetian blinds. The furniture was simple, but elegant, the walls white, the floor tiled. She found her spirits lifting.

Capo d'Angeli. She had heard of it vaguely, but nothing more. A place where rich people went, but not flash or sophisticated. Discreet and classy. An exclusive, luxury resort on the Italian coast where there were no hotels, only villas, with large private grounds, each nestled into its own place on the rocky promontory overlooking the sea.

Someone had brought up her suitcase. There was not a great deal in it—even less than she'd taken from Cornwall—but there was enough to serve. Ben fell with a cry of pleasure upon his teddy bear, as well as a clutch of his favourite engines.

It did not take long to dress, and when they were both ready

Lizzy drew up the Venetian blinds. French windows were behind them, and a wide terrace, and beyond the terrace—

'Mummy—the sea! It's bluer than my paintbox. Much bluer than home.'

Lizzy opened the French windows and warm air flooded in like an embrace. Ben rushed out, clutching the stone balustrade and staring eagerly out over the tops of the pine trees set below, out to the cerulean sea beyond, sparkling in the morning light.

'Do you think there's a beach?' he asked, his voice pitched with excitement.

'Definitely a beach, Ben.'

The voice that answered him was not hers. It came from further down the terrace, where an ironwork table was set out under a large blue-striped parasol. The table was set with breakfast things, but Lizzy had no eyes for them. All she had eyes for was the man sitting in the pool of shade.

She felt her stomach clench. Oh, God, he just looked so fantastic. He was wearing a bathrobe, and its whiteness contrasted dramatically with the warm tan of his skin tones, the deep vee of the crossover revealing a smooth, hard surface that she flicked her eyes away from jerkily. Not that it did any good to look at any other part of him. His forearms were bare, too, the sleeves of the robe rolled up, and his damp hair was feathering in the warmth. As for his face—

She felt her stomach clench again. He was a ludicrously attractive male, and up to now she'd only seen him in formal attire. Seeing him like this, fresh from his shower, was…

Different.

Completely, utterly different.

And he seemed different too. The tension that had been in him throughout their time together at the safe house, culminating in the extreme emotion of their flight from the palace had gone. Disappeared.

Now he seemed…relaxed.

Carefree.

Ben was running forward. 'Tio Rico, can we go down to the beach?' he asked eagerly.

His uncle laughed. Lizzy's stomach churned yet again. The laughter lit his face, indenting lines around his mouth, lifting his eyes, showing the white of his teeth. Making him look a hundred times more gorgeous. A hundred times sexier—

Oh, God, how am I going to cope with this?

Misery filled her, and with horrible self-conscious awkwardness she walked forward. As she approached, he got to his feet.

'Buon giorno,' he said. There was still a smile in his eyes. Left over from Ben, obviously.

Lizzy swallowed, and gave a sort of half nod. She couldn't look at him—not look him in the eye and know that last night, in some unreal, disorientating, panicked ceremony, she had become this man's wife.

She pulled out a chair and sat down.

'Did you sleep well?' There seemed to be genuine enquiry in his voice.

She swallowed, and nodded again. Jerkily she reached for a jug of orange juice and began to pour herself a glass. Ben was chattering away to his uncle.

His stepfather? A stepfather who could take him away from her—

The breath tightened in Lizzy's throat as the realisation hit her. It was followed by panic. Blind, gut-wrenching panic. Was this another trick? A trap like the one that had brought her to San Lucenzo, with one object only, to take Ben from her?

'Don't look like that.' His voice was low, but it penetrated her panic. Her eyes snapped up. Locked with his. 'It will be all right. *It will be all right.* There is no need for you to fear anything now.'

She felt her throat tighten unbearably.

'Trust me,' he said.

His dark eyes were looking into hers. 'I promised you,' he said slowly, clearly, as if to a frightened child, 'that I will keep you and Ben safe, together, for as long as is necessary. I will *never* allow you to be separated from him. You have my word.'

And slowly, very slowly, Lizzy felt the panic still, the fear drain from her. He held her eyes for one moment longer, and then, with a slight, humorously resigned twist to his lips, he turned to Ben, who was tugging at his sleeve to get his attention back and find out whether he could get down to the beach right away.

'Breakfast first, young man,' he said. 'Then we'll go exploring. When I've got some clothes.' He looked across at Lizzy, who was sipping her orange juice. 'I am having some new clothes sent up to the villa. They should be here soon. The palace may send my own on; they may not. In the meantime, the on-site boutiques by the marina here can supply whatever we want.' His eyes flicked to her and Ben. 'They'll get you two sorted out as well.'

'Oh, no—please. I'm sure I can cope with what I've brought,' Lizzy said hurriedly.

'That will not be necessary.' His expression stilled a moment. 'I know this is hard for you, but everything is different. However...' his voice changed again '...today we shall spend very quietly, giving us time to get used to what has happened. I think we deserve some calm after the storm, no? So, tell me, what do you think of the villa?'

'It's unbelievably beautiful,' Lizzy said.

Rico nodded. 'I agree. Jean-Paul chose well. It's also one of the most remote villas on the Capo D'Angeli estate. Not that we need to worry. Security on the whole estate is draconian. Everyone who stays here wants privacy above all—even from each other. And by the same token,' he said reassuringly, 'you do not need to worry about the staff. They are used to all guests wanting absolute discretion. We can relax completely here—I have even sent Gianni off to take a well-deserved holiday.'

He smiled encouragingly.

On cue a manservant appeared, bearing a tray of fresh coffee and breakfast rolls. Ben needed no encouragement, and was swiftly tucking in.

'He seems to have taken it all in his stride,' said Rico contemplatively. 'I think he will like it here.' He glanced across at Lizzy. 'I think we will like it here.'

She met his eyes. It was getting easier. Not easy, but easier.

'Thank you,' she said, in a low, intense voice. 'Thank you for what you have done.'

'We did what we had to do. There was no other way. No other choice. And now—' his expression changed '—I want to hear no more on it. We have been through a great deal—we deserve a holiday. And this is a good place for one.'

He grinned suddenly, and yet again Lizzy felt that hopelessly inappropriate reaction. She crushed it as much as she could, but dread went through her. How was she going to cope? It was impossible—just impossible.

She steeled herself. Prince Rico was going to have to cope, and so was she. If he could use his upbringing to handle any situation, then she would too. She would force herself.

'What…what will happen today?' she ventured.

'Today? Today we take things easy. Ben must go down to the beach—we'll have a revolution on our hands if we don't take him. The cove at the base of the villa gardens is private to us, so we will not be disturbed. There is a swimming pool here too, of course, on the level below this one. As for toys—well, the villa comes with a fully stocked children's playroom, and for anything else the internet is a great provider. So, you see, we shall have everything we need for the perfect holiday.'

He smiled at her again, then turned his attention to Ben.

'How are you at building sandcastles?' he asked him.

'Really good,' said Ben enthusiastically. 'At home we build them when the tide comes in, and then we make big walls to stop the waves. But the waves always win in the end.'

Rico made a face. 'Alas, there is no tide here—the Mediterranean sea is too small for tides. And the waves are very small too. But the water is lovely and warm. You won't get cold. We can go on a boat, too.'

'Today?' demanded Ben.

'Not today. Perhaps tomorrow. We'll see.'

Ben's expression darkened. '"We'll see" means no,' he said gloomily.

'It means I don't know yet. This is a holiday, Ben. We're going to take it one day at a time. Isn't that right?'

Rico's eyes suddenly flicked to hers.

'One day at a time,' he repeated. 'For us too.'

For a long moment he held her eyes, then Ben reclaimed his attention with yet another question.

She needed time, Rico knew. So much had happened to her since he'd showed up at her ramshackle cottage in Cornwall. And for her, he had to appreciate, it had all been bad. The life she'd known had been ripped away from her. For her, there was no going back.

A surge of determination went through him.

I'll make that life better now. All the fear and trauma is over now.

His eyes flickered over her fleetingly, without her knowledge, as she poured herself more coffee.

I don't believe she has to look this bad. I just don't.

Covertly he studied her. It was hard to see much of her figure, as even in this warmth she was wearing a long-sleeved baggy top that seemed to flow shapelessly into long baggy cotton trousers. Both garments were cheap and worn. She dressed for comfort, not style, that much had always been apparent, but the perpetual bagginess of her clothing made it hard to judge just what her figure really was. She was no stick-thin model, that was for sure, but how overweight was she *really*? And even so, well-cut clothes could conceal a multitude of evils, surely…?

He moved on to try and evaluate her features. That was hard to do too. The unsightly frizz of her hair which, even when tied back as it was now, still seemed to straggle round her face, drew all the attention. He tried to imagine her face without it. It was difficult, he realised, to judge it accurately. The heavy eyebrows didn't help, of course, and nor did the pallid skin. But there wasn't anything actively disastrous—her nose was straight, her jaw defined, her eyes grey, her teeth not protruding or uneven. It was just that her features seemed so completely—nondescript.

Would she look better with make-up? Surely she must? Women always did, didn't they? Not that he was used to seeing women without make-up—make-up and hundreds of euros' worth of grooming, and thousands of euros' worth of clothes and accessories.

Well, now she could have that kind of money spent on *her*. Money was not going to be a problem for her from now on. He would lavish it on her.

His mouth tightened abruptly. In his head he heard Luca's sneering at the sight of her. Anger bit him. Who the hell was Luca to sneer at a woman who had taken her dead sister's child and dedicated her life to raising him? Being a single mother on little money was no ride in the park—certainly not a limo-ride. And so what if she weren't beautiful? What did Ben care?

And I don't care either. I'll get her looking the best she can—because she deserves it. She needs all the reassurance she can get. She'll feel a lot more confident, a lot more comfortable about what we've just gone and done, if she can wipe that vile word out of her mental vocabulary.

He heard it again, cruel and ugly.

Grotesque.

Well, that word was going in the trash can. And staying there. He would never let her say it again.

CHAPTER EIGHT

'WINE for you?' Rico held the bottle of chilled white wine over Lizzy's glass.

'Um—er—thank you,' she replied awkwardly, and he proceeded to fill it up.

They were back at the table on the terrace again, but over the sea the sun was sinking in a glory of red and gold.

'Mummy, I'm really hungry,' Ben said plaintively.

'Food is coming very soon,' said Rico, pouring himself a glass of wine as well.

'What are we having for tea, Mummy?'

Rico smiled. 'Pasta, Ben. All good children in Italy eat pasta. Do you like pasta?'

'I *love* pasta,' Ben exclaimed.

'In Italy you can eat pasta every day,' said Rico.

He lifted his wine glass.

'To our first day here,' he said, looking at Ben and his mother. Ben lifted his glass of orange juice. 'Have we had a good day, everyone?' he asked around.

'Yes,' said Ben.

'Yes,' said his mother. 'It's been lovely.'

It had too, and Lizzy was grateful. It was strange. She hadn't expected it to be easy. And yet it had been. They'd done nothing except spend most of the day on the beach, coming back up to the terrace for lunch, and then, after much protesting from Ben, having a brief siesta. When Ben had surfaced they'd gone down to the beach again, returning only in late afternoon for Ben to have a quick swim in the pool, before showering and getting ready for supper.

The only awkward moment had been when Ben, splashing around in the warm shallow sea with his uncle, had called out 'Mummy, aren't you going to swim?'

Lizzy had shaken her head, the thought of stripping off to a bathing costume making her cringe. It was bad enough being on a beach with a man whose honed, lean-muscled body, clad only in swimming trunks, made it impossible to let her eyes go anywhere near him.

'I'll swim another time,' she'd evaded, and gone doggedly back to her book.

Other than that it had been an extraordinarily easy day. Now, sitting watching the sun set while they shared in a nursery tea, she realised she was feeling far more relaxed than she'd thought possible. She took a sip of her chilled wine.

'Is the wine to your liking?' Ben's uncle asked.

'Um—yes, it's lovely. I—er—I don't really know anything about wine,' she answered.

'You will learn with practice.' He smiled at her. 'And another thing you will learn with practice,' he went on, taking his own mouthful of wine, 'is to call me by name.'

Lizzy stared. She couldn't do that. The whole thing about addressing him had been so awkward that she simply hadn't done it. She couldn't address him as 'Highness', and she couldn't address him as 'Prince Enrico', or even 'Prince Rico'. And she certainly couldn't address him as simply Rico.

'And I must do the same,' he continued. 'So—' He took a breath. 'Lizzy. There, I've said it. Now it's your turn.'

'I can't,' said Lizzy. Embarrassment flushed through her.

'Have some more wine—then try,' he advised.

She took another mouthful, and swallowed hard.

'Rico,' she mumbled. She couldn't quite look at him.

'Bene,' he said softly. 'You see—all things are possible.' For a moment he held her eyes approvingly, then, with a change of tone, he spoke again. 'Ah, supper arrives.'

'Hurrah,' said Ben.

The following days were spent very largely as the first one had been. Rico made it so quite deliberately. He was giving her the time she needed—a breathing space.

He needed one too, he knew. They all did. He'd said as much to her the next day.

'We'll take this a day at a time, like I said,' he'd told her. 'We won't think about the outside world, we won't think about anything. We'll just accept the present and relax. Get used to things—get to know each other.'

It was ironic, he realised—all his life there had been a distance between himself and the world. There had had to be. And that meant, he acknowledged, that there were very few people that he ever truly let down his guard with. Jean-Paul was one, and there were a few others. Sportsmen, mostly, to whom his birth was a complete irrelevance, and all that counted was skill and dedication.

But never women—even in the superficial intimacies of the bed.

He'd bedded a lot in his time. Taken his pick, enjoying them physically. Making sure they enjoyed him, too.

But nothing more. Safety in numbers, he'd told Luca, and it had been true.

His mouth twisted. Had he proposed marriage, any of the women he'd bedded would have, in his brother's cruel words, bitten his hand off to accept. The prospect of becoming the glittering Principessa Enrico Ceraldi would have been irresistible to them.

Yet the woman he'd actually married had been horrified at the prospect.

He knew it was because of the outward disparities between

them, which she was so hung up about. Yet her attitude towards him had, he realised slowly, had another effect on him as well.

It had made him feel safe with her.

Because it made her like no other woman he knew.

It was a strange realisation, seeping through him.

All she wants from me is protection for Ben—that's all. She wants nothing else—nothing from me.

A thought came to him—another strange, new realisation.

I don't have to be on my guard with her. I don't have to keep her at a distance. Because she doesn't want anything from me—

A sense of release came over him, as if for the first time in his life, he felt—free.

Lizzy sat in the shade of the blue and white striped awning and watched Ben and his uncle play waterpolo in the pool. Ben was shrieking with pleasure. Her heart warmed. He was just so happy—every day had been a delight for him.

And for her?

It was so strange. How could it be that, despite the huge emotional upheaval she'd gone through since that fateful evening when her world had been turned upside down and she had discovered the truth about Ben's parentage, she could now be feeling so…carefree?

So relaxed.

And yet she was.

It had seemed impossible at the outset of their panicked arrival here. The enormity of what had happened, what she had done, had been overwhelming, and yet here, in this tranquil, beautiful place—so far from the rest of the world, it seemed—she had found a peace of mind she had never thought to find.

Her eyes went to the man playing with her son, and she felt gratitude welling through her—and wonder.

He was being so kind to her. And not just because of Ben.

He had gone out of his way to be endlessly kind and patient to her, for her own sake.

It was a world away from his image as the Playboy Prince. There's more to him than that. Much more, she thought fiercely.

She had misjudged him, she knew, seeing only the image, not the man beneath. He was a man who had defied his father, his sovereign, to defend and protect her and Ben. A man who had unhesitatingly married himself to the very last woman in the world he'd ever have chosen for a wife for the sake of a small child.

A child he really seemed to love.

She felt her heart warm as she watched Rico haul himself out of the pool. His lean body glittered with diamonds in the sun as he leant down, let Ben clutch his arm with his hands, and with effortless strength lifted him clear out of the water.

'Again!' shouted Ben, and jumped back in the water.

Rico repeated the process, swinging him high into the air with a laughing grin before lowering him gently to the paving beside the pool.

Ben rushed up to Lizzy.

'I scored *five* goals,' he exclaimed.

'Did you? How fantastic.' She smiled.

'Why don't you come in the water, Mummy?'

'Because she needs a nice new swimming costume, Ben. And lots of new clothes, like you've already had. Clothes for a princess.'

Rico had come up behind him.

Ben tilted his head to one side. 'Is Mummy a princess, then?'

'Yes,' said Rico casually, padding himself dry with a towel. 'When I married her she became a princess.'

'Has she got a crown?' Ben asked interestedly. He had a strong mental association between royalty and crowns.

'She can have a tiara. For when she goes to a ball.'

Ben's eyes lit up.

'Like Cinderella?'

'Exactly like Cinderella,' said Rico.

His eyes went to Lizzy's face, and then shadowed. There was a look in her eyes he did not want there, but he knew why it was.

Lizzy looked away. If there was any role in Cinderella she was ideally cast for, it was not the heroine. It was as an ugly sister.

It was Maria—Maria who had been Cinderella—swept off her feet by Prince Charming. But the coach had crashed.

Rico saw her look away. Read her thought. His mouth pressed tight. It was time to get this sorted. Time to put that cruel word in the trash once and for all.

She was comfortable with him now, he knew—and he with her. But that harsh word still remained between them like a poison. A poison that needed to be drawn.

And there was no point delaying it any longer. It was time, more than time, to do something about it.

It proved very easy to arrange. The shopping complex by the marina was designed to cater to the needs of those who stayed at Capo D'Angeli. And those needs included the overwhelming demand to attend to their appearance—clothes, hair, beauty treatments, manicures; whatever was required was available.

He would book the lot, and let them loose on her.

The following day, at breakfast, he made his announcement.

'I will look after Ben today. You will be too busy.'

Lizzy stared. 'Busy?' she asked. Apprehension filled her.

Rico only smiled cryptically. 'Very busy,' he said.

Within the hour, she found out just how busy.

Lizzy had her eyes shut. Over her head, it sounded as if the army of people who had invaded her bedroom were having a heated argument. They weren't, she knew—they were just discussing her. But in a very Italianate manner they were doing so vehemently, with many loud exclamations. She could understand why. They had been given an impossible brief—to spin straw into gold.

Make a silk purse out of a sow's ear.

Mortification filled her.

She'd known this moment must come. Known that, however desperate the circumstances of her sudden marriage to Rico had been, they could not hide here at the villa for ever. At some point they would have to emerge. Face the world.

The prospect appalled her.

She could wear all the designer clothes in the world, but it would still be her underneath. Nothing could change that. Maria had looked a knock-out even in rags, because she'd had a face, a body, that was a knock-out.

Guilt knifed through her. Guilt and grief. Oh, God, it should be Maria here, in this beautiful Italian villa, having her honeymoon with her golden prince. Looking forward blissfully to their happy-ever-after. Their own personal fairytale.

Her hands twisted in her lap. Grief and guilt twisted together. And not just guilt for her sister.

I've got to go through with this. I've got to bear it. It doesn't matter how humiliating it is, how mortifying. I have to let them do what they can. Do the best they can.

But it wasn't for her. It was for the man who had married her to keep Ben safe, the man whose reward was to be saddled with a wife in a marriage that all the world would call by the only word that suited it—*grotesque*.

A man like Prince Rico, the Playboy Prince, accustomed to the most beautiful women in the world falling for him—now married to a woman like her.

She opened her eyes. The arguing stopped instantly. She looked around at the sea of faces, all watching her expectantly.

She took a deep breath.

'Please,' she said, 'just do the best you can.'

Then she shut her eyes again—and kept them shut.

'We need another tower,' Ben instructed.

Rico considered the masterwork on the terrace table. Then nodded.

'You're right,' he said. 'I'll fit one inside this corner. How's the painting coming along?'

'Good,' said Ben. He was industriously washing stone-grey paint across the expanse of large cardboard box that had been transformed into a fort to house an army of brightly coloured plastic knights in armour which had, to Ben's ecstasy, been ordered off the internet to be delivered by courier the following morning. Ben's impatience for their arrival had been such that on their return to the terrace from the beach and the pool Rico had been driven to suggest they make a fort for the knights to live in when they arrived. Its construction also helped to divert Ben from the fact he had not seen his mother all day.

Anxiety nagged at Rico.

Was she going to be all right? It was late afternoon already, but he knew that beauty treatments took for ever, and the fact that she had been incarcerated all day did not surprise him. But how was she coping with it all?

Well, it couldn't be much longer, surely?

He reached for the scissors and began the tricky business of cutting cardboard for the requisite tower. He needed diverting as well.

'Is Mummy *still* trying on new clothes?' Ben demanded

'It takes ladies a long time,' said Rico. 'And to do their hair and things.'

'It doesn't take Mummy long,' Ben countered. 'She's always very quick.'

'Now that she's got to be a princess it will need to take longer,' Rico answered.

Ben stared down the long terrace towards where the bedrooms opened on to it. Then, suddenly, his expression changed.

'Mummy.'

He dropped the paintbrush and pushed his chair back.

Rico looked up.

And froze.

* * *

Ben was hurtling along the terrace towards her as Lizzy stepped gingerly out through the French windows from her bedroom.

'Mummy—Mummy, you've been ages! We're making a fort, Uncle Rico and me. For the soldiers—they are knights in armour. They're coming tomorrow, in a special van, and they are a present for being good. And we're making a fort for them. Come and see—come and see.'

He seized her hand and started to pull her along. She tottered momentarily, uncertain of her balance on the sandals that, although low-heeled, seemed to consist of nothing but two minute strips of leather.

'Come on, Mummy,' Ben said, impatient at her slowness.

But the last thing on earth she wanted was to go where he was leading her.

Towards the terrace table, towards the man who sat there, quite, quite motionless.

There was no expression on his face.

Her heart started to slump heavily in her chest cavity, hollowing out a space around it. She felt sick.

Sick with dismay.

Oh, God—all that work, all that time, and it's a disaster— I can see it in his face. It's awful, awful.

It had taken so *long*—hours and hours. And so much had been done to her. All over. There had been so much chattering, and agitation, and volatility, that she had just let them get on with it. The treatments had gone on and on, one after another. Spreading stuff on her body, then wiping it off again, and on her face several more times. Then she'd had her hair washed, and more stuff had been put on it, and left in, then rinsed out, and different stuff put on. And in the meantime the tweezers had come out, and nail files and buffers and varnish and hot wax, and yet more body wraps and creams. She had had to eat lunch, served in her room, with her face and hair covered in gunk and her body swathed in some kind of thin gown. And while she'd eaten yet another one of the army of people in her room had held up one garment after another, off a trio of racks that had been wheeled in—so many garments that she'd simply lost count.

'Please,' she had murmured faintly, 'whatever you think best.'

And finally the last of the wraps had come off, and the rollers had come out of her hair, and it had been blow-dried—though heaven knew what rollers and blow-drying would do for her hopelessly frizzy hair. Then yet another beautician had gone to work on her, with a vast amount of make-up, before, at the very last, she had been lifted to her feet and one outfit after another had been whisked on to her, commented on by all in the room, then replaced with another one and the process repeated.

Until one had been left on her, her hair and make-up had been retouched one last time, and she had been gently but insistently guided towards the French windows.

She had no idea what she looked like. She could see she had nail varnish on—a soft coral-apricot colour—and her hands felt smooth and soft. Her hair felt different—lighter somehow. As if it were lifting as she walked instead of hanging in a heavy clump as it normally did. As for her clothes—she could see she was wearing a cinnamon-coloured dress, with a close-fitting bodice and cap sleeves, a narrow belt around the waist and a skirt that floated like silk around her legs.

But she hadn't seen a reflection of herself. No one had asked her whether she wanted to see in a mirror, and she had been too cowardly to want to anyway. Deferring the evil moment.

But now it had arrived, and she wanted to die.

Oh, God—what had been the point of it all?

She must look ridiculous, absurd—dressed up like this, done up to the nines. All such fine feathers could do was show just how awful she was underneath.

Hot, hopeless embarrassment flooded through her. Why had

she let them do this to her? She should have just stayed as she was—accepted what she was.

The ugly sister. Who, even when she was dressed up for the ball in gorgeous clothes, was still the ugly sister.

At her side, Ben was chattering away as she walked slowly, mortifyingly forward—towards the figure seated, motionless, under the parasol at the terrace table.

Her eyes went to him, full of dread, and as she looked at him she felt her stomach give its familiar hopeless clench.

He was wearing shorts, and a white T-shirt that strained across his torso, and he was watching her approach with absolutely no expression on his face whatsoever.

She tore her gaze away from him as she felt the hot, horrible heat of exposure rise in her. She wanted to turn and run, to bolt back to the safety of her bedroom, hide there for ever and never come out again…

She reached the table.

Say something. Anything.

She swallowed hard.

'Oh, Ben—that's a wonderful fort.' Her voice sounded high-pitched and false. And coming from a hundred miles away.

'Me and Tio Rico made it. It's got two towers, and a bridge that lifts right up, and look, Mummy, it's got a porcully that goes up and down. Tio Rico made it work. Look, I'll show you, Mummy—'

She forced herself to look as Ben tugged on the string that operated the portcullis.

'That's really good,' she said in a strangulated voice.

I've got to look at him. I must.

It was the hardest thing in the world to do, but she did it. She turned her head so that she was looking straight at him. Looking straight at that totally expressionless face.

'It's a brilliant fort,' she said to him weakly.

He answered in Italian.

'Non credo—'

She swallowed, her stomach hollowing. What didn't he believe? That so much time and effort expended on her should be so wasted?

The sickness in her stomach churned hideously.

Ben was still talking, and she tried to listen, but it was impossible. Something about where all his new knights would go—which ones would be inside the castle, and which would be attacking it. His little voice went in and out.

And opposite her, still motionless, Prince Rico of San Lucenzo just looked at her, without a shred of expression on his face.

He was in shock, he realised. Shock so profound that he was still fighting to get his brain around what his eyes were telling him.

It wasn't possible, what he was seeing. It just wasn't.

It could not be the same woman. It just couldn't.

It was impossible. Physically impossible.

She absolutely, totally, completely was *not* the woman he had last seen.

Dio—where had she *come* from? That body. That fantastic, gorgeous, *lush* body. An absolutely perfect *bella figura*. With a cinched-in waist that curved out to a pair of perfectly rounded hips, and up…he swallowed…up to a pair of breasts so ripe, so luscious, so beautifully moulded by the material swelling over them that he just wanted to…he just wanted to…

He felt his body react. He couldn't stop it. It was there—urgent, irrepressible, unstoppable. A complete, total insistence on letting him know just *exactly* what it felt about what his eyes were seeing.

With an effort he did not know he was capable of, he forced his eyes upward. But it did him no good.

The reaction was exactly the same.

The rest of her went with the figure.

It was the hair—what the *hell* had happened to her hair? The frizz had simply gone. As if it had never existed. In its place, tinted to a rich chestnut, was a smooth, glossy mane that waved back from her face, pouring down over her shoulders in a luxuriant swathe.

As for her face—

How had he not seen it? Shock punched through him again. Delicately arched eyebrows over endlessly deep, long-lashed, luminous eyes, cheekbones that arced to a perfect nose, that descended to a mouth...

He swallowed silently.

A mouth that was rich, and lush, and... *Dio*, so inviting...

Someone was talking. Tugging at his arm.

'Tio Rico. You're not listening. Is it time for tea now? Mummy's come out at last and I'm *hungry*,' he finished plaintively.

Where he found the strength of mind he didn't know. But somehow he dragged his eyes to Ben.

'Yeah—sure, right. You want to eat? OK. That's fine.' He said some more in Italian, just as incoherent.

What the hell was going on? Had the universe just stopped and restarted in a different dimension? A dimension where impossible things were totally normal?

She was saying something. Her voice was more high-pitched than usual, and she was trying to sound relaxed and casual, and failing completely.

'Has Ben been OK today? I'm sorry I...er...I took so long. I...er...'

Her voice trailed off.

He was staring at her again. He couldn't take his eyes from her. It was impossible.

For a moment Lizzy just went on standing there, while the expressionless face in front of her just looked blankly at her.

Then suddenly, totally, she couldn't cope. Just couldn't. She felt as if a stone had been punched into her solar plexus. It was almost a physical pain. She turned on her spindly heels and plunged off. She didn't know where. Just anywhere. Anywhere.

She didn't know where she was going. The terrace ended in

steps, down to the swimming pool level, and she just clattered
down them, almost tripping in her desperation, past the glittering azure pool, to plunge on to the narrow stepped path that
wound its way down to the sea between the vegetation and the
pines. Her heart was pounding, and she could feel a sick,
horrible flush in her cheeks.

She wanted to die.

Why had she let them do it? She should have known it was
hopeless, useless, pointless. Hot, horrible mortification
scorched through her.

*I shouldn't have tried—I shouldn't have tried to make myself
look better. Normal. Trying and failing is even worse than just
accepting what I am—ugly, ugly, ugly...*

She could hear footsteps hurrying behind her, heavy and
pounding, and her name being called. She hurried faster, her
heel catching in her haste, so that she had to lurch and clutch
at the railing beside the pathway before trying to go on.

But her arm was being caught, held.

'Stop. What is it? What's wrong?'

She tensed in every muscle, trying to tear her arm away. His
fingers pressed like steel into her bare flesh.

'Go away.'

The words burst from her. She couldn't stop them. Her head
whipped round.

'Go away. Leave me alone. *Leave me alone!*'

There was shock and bewilderment in his face.

'What's happened? What's wrong?'

'What do you mean, what's wrong? Everything's wrong.
Everything,' she gasped.

She just stood there, frozen and immobile, tugging hopelessly away from him, while he held her, feet planted on the
step above, towering over her.

He was so close. Far too close. She tried to tug back again, but
it was hopeless, useless. Just as everything was hopeless, useless.

For a moment he said nothing—just looked at her. A look

of complete incomprehension filled his face. Then, as he looked, the expression of shock and bewilderment began to change. She saw it happening, saw it and did not believe it.

It was something in his eyes. Something that seemed slowly to be dissolving. Dissolving not just in his eyes, but dissolving *her*. Turning her liquid, like wax left on a surface that was very slowly heating up.

The way her skin was heating. Flushing with a low, soft heat that seemed to be carried by the low, soft pulse of her blood that was creaming, like liquid sugar, like honey, through her veins.

She felt his grip on her change. Not so much halting her as…holding her. Holding her in position. Holding her just where he wanted her to be. Wanted her to be because…because…

The world had stopped moving. Everything had stopped moving. She was just there, immobile, held. And he was looking down into her face—and the expression in his eyes simply stayed the breath in her throat.

She gazed back up at him. What had happened, she didn't know. Reality wasn't there any more.

And yet it had never seemed more vivid.

'Don't look at me like that,' he said, in that low, soft voice that was curling the toes of her feet, sending liquid waves down her spine in long, honeyed undulations. 'Don't look at me like that here, now. Because if you go on looking at me like that, I'll—'

'Mum-my! *Mum-my*.'

They pulled apart, jerking away from each other. It was like surfacing from a deep, drowning sea.

'He's all right. I told him not to move.' Rico's voice sounded staccato, abstracted. He took a rapid, restoring breath.

'Mummy. Tio Rico.'

Ben's insistent call came again. Lizzy could hear alarm in it.

'I'm coming, Ben,' she called up. Her voice was shaky.

'Me too,' echoed Rico. His voice was not steady either.

He cast another look at her, then pulled his gaze away. It wasn't safe to look at her. Not here, not now.

Later…later he would look.

More than look—

Suddenly, out of nowhere, a sense of exultation crashed through him.

With light, lithe steps, he led the way up to the terrace.

Emotion was surging through Rico. Strong, overwhelming and consuming. The universe might have turned itself upside down, but right now he didn't care. How it had happened was irrelevant. Completely irrelevant. It had happened, and that was all that he was registering.

Adrenaline pumped through him. More than adrenaline. Exhilaration. Something quite incredibly amazing had happened, and he didn't want explanations—he just wanted to…to go with it.

'Here we are, Ben,' he announced as he gained the pool terrace, and he waved his hand at the little figure perched obediently on the upper level, straining his eyes downwards.

'Where is Mummy?' Ben demanded.

'Here—' said Lizzy, hurrying up the steps as fast as she could in her flimsy sandals. Her heart was racing.

It had nothing to do with her rapid ascent.

As she gained the terrace Ben stared at her, paying attention to her for the first time, instead of to his new fort.

'Is that your new dress?' he asked.

She swallowed, nodded.

He tilted his head sideways, inspecting her. Then he frowned.

'You look all pretty. Like in a magazine. But you don't look like Mummy.' He frowned, confused and bewildered.

Rico put an arm around his nephew's shoulder. He knew just how Ben was feeling.

'She's the new-look Mummy. And you're right Ben.' His voice changed. 'She does look pretty. In fact she looks…' He paused, and held her eyes. 'Breathtaking,' he finished softly. 'Quite, quite breathtaking.'

For a long, endless moment, he held her eyes.

He saw her eyes flare—uncertain briefly—and then, suddenly, it had gone again.

'It's true,' he said quietly to her. 'Quite true. I can't believe…I can't believe that all this was there, all along. Just…hidden.' He paused, and then, in a low, clear voice, said, 'And you are never—do you understand me?—*never* going to hide it again.'

For one last, lingering moment he looked at her. Sending his message loud and clear.

Then, abruptly, he turned his head.

'Right, then, Ben. Time for tea.'

CHAPTER NINE

SHE was moving in a place that was completely dissociated from what she was doing. What she was actually doing was pouring out a cup of perfectly brewed Assam tea from a silver teapot, while Ben was industriously, if inexpertly, coiling spaghetti around his fork. The DIY fort had been cleared away for the moment, and the westering sun was bathing the terrace in rich, deep golden glow.

The same glow was inside her, suffused through her, so that it seemed she was part of the warm golden light all around her. It dazed her, bemused her—and she gave herself to it because she couldn't do anything else.

As she sipped at her hot, fragrant tea her eyes slipped of their own accord to the man sitting opposite her. He lounged back, his pose so relaxed that he was like a young, lithe leopard taking its ease, taking indolent mouthfuls of espresso coffee every now and then, one arm spread out across his chair-back, one long leg casually crossed over a lean, bare thigh. He was chatting to Ben, answering the child's questions with lazy good humour, but his eyes would flicker over her as he chatted, sending tiny little shots of electricity quivering through her.

Her glow deepened.

What was happening was beyond her—completely and absolutely beyond her—and she didn't care. She didn't want to question, or analyse, or examine or understand. She just wanted to give herself to this wonderful, dazed bemusement that had taken her over, filling her with this rich, warm glow that reached through every cell of her body.

After Ben had eaten his tea, they played cards. A noisy, fast game that involved a lot of slapping down of cards and crows of triumph from both Ben and Rico. Yet even in the midst of the game Rico could still find time to glance at her, still feel the echoes of that incredible shock wave that had slammed through him as she'd approached him along the terrace, her transformation so incredible he could not, even now, fully believe it.

And yet it was there in front of him, the evidence of his own eyes. A miracle.

Her hair by itself was a miracle. The frizz had simply vanished—he hadn't known it was possible, and yet clearly it was. Her skin was clear and glowing, her make-up bringing to life features which he'd thought nondescript and unremarkable.

And now his eyes kept going back to her, time and time again.

He wanted her. He knew it, and he had no intention of denying it.

It was impossible to do so. His body had recognised it in the first moments of seeing her walk towards him, displaying that fantastic lush figure which had so incredibly been there all along—invisible under the shapeless, baggy clothes she'd worn.

How the hell had she kept it hidden?

He still couldn't get his head round it. To have such a full, lush body as that, and yet to hide it.

Well, there was no hiding it now. None at all. Never, ever again would she ever hide herself.

Especially not from him.

He felt his body react again, and had to struggle to subdue it.

He must not rush this. Dared not. She was walking a knife-edge, still in a state of shock, of disbelief about herself.

I've got to take this slowly. Very slowly.

Let her get used to it. Let her come to believe it. Take her slowly, so slowly, every step of the way.

His eyes rested on her yet again, while Ben dealt out another round, his little voice counting the cards diligently as he set them down in three piles.

He could see her awareness of him even as she oversaw Ben's dealing. Saw it in the swift, covert glance, the slight tremor of her hand as she picked up her cards.

Lizzy could see him looking at her, see it and feel it. It was tangible, like the lightest caress on her skin.

She felt her heart skip a beat, skitter inside her...

What's happening—what's happening to me?

It was a stupid, idiotic question to ask. She knew exactly what was happening to her. And she couldn't stop it. Could no more stop it than she could have stopped a whirlpool sucking her down.

She was responding to the core-deep, devastating sexuality of the man she had married to keep Ben safe with her. And how could she help it?

Ever since she had first set eyes on him, that terrible traumatic night in Cornwall, she had responded to him. She had crushed it down, embarrassed by it, knowing that she must never show the slightest sign of her response because for someone like her to do so would be...*grotesque*.

It had been easy enough to do. To him, she had simply not existed as a female. Nor did she to any man, she knew. So, although her instinctive reaction to him had been embarrassing and pointless, she had also known that it really hadn't mattered at all—it had been completely irrelevant.

All that had mattered had been Ben.

And these last few days, when he had visibly gone out of his way to try and make her feel more at ease with what had so traumatically happened to her, when he'd been kind, and nice, and nothing like the Playboy Prince of his reputation, it had still not mattered. More than not mattered.

It had allowed her to start to relax around him. Start to feel at ease around him. Start to see him not as a prince, nor as a man—but as a person.

They had talked—nothing special, nothing earth-shattering, just easy conversation. About Ben, yes, but about other things too, over meals, and on the beach, and while Ben was playing, absorbed, with his trains and all the other toys that had been delivered to the villa or which he'd discovered in the playroom.

She wasn't sure what they'd talked about—nothing much came to mind—but she knew was that it hadn't been a strain, an effort.

It had been…friendly.

Easygoing, casual, relaxed.

But now—now it felt as if tiny bubbles were fizzing through her veins. Effervescing inside her.

Every time he glanced at her.

What's happening to me?

But she knew. She knew.

'Goodnight, darling, sleep tight.'

Lizzy bent over to drop a kiss on Ben's cheek. He was asleep already, she could see. On the other side of the bed, Rico reached out and ruffled his hair gently.

He had insisted on giving Ben his bath that night.

'We don't want Mummy's new dress getting wet, do we?' he'd said.

Instead, he had been the one to get wet. Lizzy could see where the damp T-shirt clung to his torso. She averted her eyes, but not before Rico had spotted her doing so.

There was a decided glint in his eye as he spoke.

'I'll go and get myself cleaned up, then join you for dinner, OK?'

He had given instructions to the chef for a proper dinner that night. Whatever the results of Lizzy's makeover would prove, he intended to make the evening special for her.

And it would be special indeed. Another wave of disbelief went over him. They had been doing so regularly, every time he looked at her.

It was incredible, just incredible.

He frowned momentarily.

Had she actually looked at herself yet? Surely she must have? And yet that initial reaction, when she'd run from him, blurting that it had all been a disaster, argued that she surely could not have seen the transformation.

He came around the foot of the bed.

'You may need some kind of wrap,' he told her. 'The nights can still be a little chilly. Let's see what you've got.'

He opened the closet door and went in. All her new clothes hung in serried ranks, swathed in plastic protectors. He glanced at them with approval. There was a lot here, and that was good. He wanted her to have as many beautiful outfits as possible. This was just the start.

She had followed him in, just as he'd intended.

'Where would you store a wrap?' he asked.

But Lizzy didn't answer him. Could not.

The whole rear wall of the closet was a mirror, and standing in the mirror, looking back at her, was someone she had never seen before in her life.

Rico straightened and looked first at the woman in the mirror, then at the woman staring at her.

He let her look. Let the look of dazed incomprehension fill her face.

Then he spoke.

'It's you. The you that you really are. The you that was hiding all this time.'

His voice was steady, level—merely stating a fact. A fact he would no longer let her deny. Conceal.

Her eyes were wide, huge.

'It can't be me. It can't.'

Her voice was faint.

He came and stood behind her.

'Oh, it's you, all right.'

Lightly, oh so lightly, he rested his hands on her shoulders.

Her skin was like satin. He felt her tremble at his touch, but she did not move. She went on staring.

'How did they do it?' she asked faintly.

He gave a smile. 'They had good material to work with.'

She lifted her hand to her hair, then dropped it wonderingly. 'But my hair—all that frizz—'

'They fixed it. There must be chemicals they use that change the hair somehow. After that, all they had to do was…do you up.' His voice softened. 'It was always there, Lizzy. Always. And now it always will be.'

He dropped his hands away.

He didn't want to. He wanted to glide them down her arms, turn her around, lower his mouth to hers and…

But he knew he must not. Not now, not here.

Not yet.

Instead, he stepped back.

'Do you think they'd have put wraps in a drawer?' he asked. 'Let's have a look.'

Rico reached out his arm and closed his hand around the neck of the champagne bottle, drawing it up out of its bucket of ice and refilling their glasses.

They were sitting at the table on the terrace, but it had been transformed from its daytime appearance, when it was usually covered with Ben's toys and books. The parasol had disappeared, and a pristine white tablecloth had been draped crisply, laden down with silver and crystal. A beautiful floral arrangement graced the centre, and the flames of long candles in silver candlesticks flickered in the night air. Above, the stars glittered in the black velvet sky. Out to sea, the lights from fisher boats glimmered in the dark. All around, cicadas kept their soft chorus, and the scent of flowers wafted softly.

The meal had done justice to the setting. Exquisitely prepared and presented, each delicacy had been too tempting to resist. And Lizzy had not resisted—nor did she resist a second glass of the light, foaming liquid that glinted in the candlelight in its tall, elegant flute.

'To you,' said Rico, and raised his glass. 'To the new you. The real you.'

The staff had gone, leaving them to coffee, tiny crisp *biscotti*, and the rest of the champagne. It was a rare vintage, and Rico savoured it.

It was not all that he was savouring.

He took a mouthful, appreciating the dry biscuit of the champagne, and leant back. His eyes rested on the woman opposite.

She had found a wrap, a soft swathe in a subtle mix of hues that blended and complemented the cinnamon of her dress. She had draped it around her shoulders, one end scooped across her throat. It did not quite conceal the rich swell of her breasts in the beautifully cut bodice.

No, he must not let his eyes drift there. He wanted to—he badly wanted to—but he knew he must not. She could not cope with that. Not yet. He must take it slowly.

Savour it.

He took another mouthful of champagne, savouring that too.

'To you,' he said again. 'To the new, beautiful Elisabetta.'

His voice was liquid over the syllables. Then, abruptly, his brows drew together.

'How did anyone think to call you Lizzy?' He said the short form of her name disparagingly.

Lizzy's eyes flickered uncertainly. 'I've always been Lizzy,' she said.

'And yet you were also always Elizabeth—Elisabetta.' There was a sudden edge in Rico's voice, which softened as he repeated the Italian form of her name. Then his brows drew together again, questioningly, frowningly. 'Was it your sister who did it to you?'

The edge was back in his voice.

'Did what?' Again her eyes flickered uncertainly.

'Was it your sister who turned you into Lizzy?'

'I don't understand,' she answered, puzzled and uncertain.

'I've always been called Lizzy. Frizzy-Lizzy, because of my hair. Or Busy-Lizzy, usually.'

'Did she keep you busy, waiting on her hand and foot?' His voice was dry.

'Maria?' Lizzy's brow furrowed, confused 'Maria was the best sister anyone could ever have.' She felt her throat tighten dangerously. 'She was truly a golden girl. Everyone loved her. She was so beautiful. She was tall, and slender, and she had long, long legs, and her hair was like honey, and hung straight to her waist, and she had beautiful blue eyes, and even when she was at school the boys were all over her, and when she became a model she was even more beautiful, and no wonder a prince fell for her—' She halted abruptly.

Rico picked his words carefully.

'Maria was pretty—very pretty. But she was…' He paused. Bimbo, Luca had called her. Cruel and callous. And yet Ben's natural mother had, indeed, possessed the kind of eye-candy looks that gave rise to that harsh dismissal.

'Hers is not the only kind of beauty,' he said.

But if Maria's sister had grown up being told that only candyfloss blondeness was acceptable, that the kind of ultra-slim figure that suited models was the only ticket in town, then no wonder she'd never tried to make anything of the looks she had. No wonder she'd settled for being Busy-Lizzy, living in the shadow of her sister.

'So who called you Busy-Lizzy?' The edge was back again.

'That was Maria,' she said with a half-laugh, making herself do so. 'But she didn't mean it in a bad way. She used to say it to me in exasperation. Because I never—'

She halted, reaching for her glass of champagne and taking a deliberate sip to cover her silence.

'Never what?' probed Rico.

What had happened to her? What had made her see herself as ugly? He had thought it might be her sister, and yet she denied it. So what, then?

He wanted to know. Wanted to find out what had been done to her, and by whom.

'Because you never what?' he prompted again.

He wanted answers. Wanted to understand. So that the poison in her would come out once and for all. Never to return.

'I never stopped,' she answered.

'Stopped what?'

'Being busy, I suppose. Being useful.'

'Who to?' he asked in a low voice.

He saw her fingers tighten around the stem of her flute.

'Maria. My parents.'

'Why did they need you to be useful?'

Her eyes wouldn't meet his.

'Because—' she stopped.

'Because?' he prompted. Quietly, insistently.

Her fingers pressed on the glass. He could see her fingers whiten where they gripped.

'Because it was all I was good for. I wasn't beautiful, like Maria, and she had all the brains, not me. She was all they needed—my parents.'

Her eyes had slid past him completely now. Staring ahead of her. Something was going wrong in her face; he could see it. She jerked the champagne glass to her lips and took a gulp. Then set it down, just as jerkily.

Then deliberately, almost angrily, her eyes snapped back to his.

'When Maria was born I ceased to have a function. Apart from that of handmaid. That was all I was good for. Looking after Maria. Helping Maria. Making way for Maria. Maria, Maria, Maria! Everything revolved around Maria. Me, I was just the spare wheel—surplus to requirements. Not wanted on voyage. Existing on sufferance—justified only if I looked after Maria, and even then barely. I wanted to hate her. But I couldn't. I couldn't hate her. No one could hate her. Because there was nothing to hate. There really wasn't. She really was a golden girl. Everyone loved her. No wonder my parents adored her.

They adored her so much they forgave her everything. Even becoming a model. There was only one thing they didn't forgive her for. Only one thing.' She stilled, then spoke again.

'Dying. That's what they could not forgive her for.'

She bowed her head, as if bowing beneath a weight.

'They couldn't live without her. So they didn't. They went into the garage, locked the doors, got into the car, and turned the engine on.'

For a moment there was silence. Complete silence. Rico felt cold ice through him.

'Your parents killed themselves?' His voice was hollow. This had not been in the dossier on Maria Mitchell.

'Once they knew she would never recover. That she would be a vegetable—in a coma until….'

She halted. Her face was stark, even in the candlelight.

'She was everything to them—their whole world. They had dedicated their lives to her. And she had gone. Left them. Left them to go modeling.' She swallowed again. 'Left them to go off with some man who had, so they thought, simply "got her into trouble"—and then she left them utterly. Left them all alone.'

Slowly, still with that cold draining through him, Rico spoke.

'But they had her baby—and you.'

She looked at him. Her eyes had no expression in them.

'The baby was a bastard—fatherless, an embarrassment, a disgrace. As for me, I was…an irrelevance. I didn't count,' she said. 'I was—unnecessary—to them.'

His eyes darkened. He felt the anger rising in him like a cold tide.

Unnecessary. The word had a grim, familiar sound.

He was unnecessary too. Had been all his life. He was the spare—surplus to requirements. To be put on a shelf and left there, just in case of emergencies. But with no other purpose then simply to pass the time, fritter his life away until and in case he should ever be needed, cease to be unnecessary.

He felt the anger lash through him again. But this time it was at himself. For having accepted his parents' verdict on him. Oh, he had resented the role he'd been born to, but he'd still accepted that that was all he was. The spare to Luca's heir.

Well, that wasn't true any longer.

Emotion swept through him. He looked at the woman sitting opposite him, who had been so horrifically *unnecessary* to her parents—but who was so necessary to the one human being to whom *he*, too, had proved necessary.

He reached across the table and took her hand. He spoke with a low intensity.

'But you're necessary now—necessary and…essential. You are Ben's happiness, and I…I am his safety. And together—' his hand tightened around hers, warm, and safe and protecting '—we'll take care of him, and love him.'

Gently he drew her to her feet. Emotion filled him as he led her down the terrace to where the French windows to her room stood slightly ajar. Inside, they stood by the bed, looking down at Ben's sleeping form.

Rico's arm went around her shoulder as they stood, gazing down at the one human being on the earth to whom they were absolutely and totally necessary.

United in that.

And more, Rico knew.

'Hang on to your hats,' Rico yelled

'I'm not wearing one,' Ben yelled back, against the revving of the engine.

'Just as well,' riposted Rico, and let the throttle out.

The boat roared off, sleek and powerful, carving a foaming wake through the still blue water.

Lizzy's arm tightened around Ben automatically, but Ben was oblivious of anything except the thrill of being in a speed-boat. Wind whipped at her hair, half blinding her, and she had to grip with all her might to the boat rail. The hull slapped and slammed against the water, bumping like a rollercoaster ride.

'Wheee!' yelled Ben, ecstatically.

Rico turned from the wheel and grinned.

His hair was blown off his face and he looked younger, carefree.

'Faster?' he asked.

'Yes, yes,' Ben cried.

'Here we go, then.'

He accelerated, and the boat picked up yet more speed. Exhilaration filled him. This might not be anything like the speed of a powerboat in a race, but it was still fast and furious.

When finally he slewed around in a great curve, and started heading back to land, he slackened the throttle and turned to his passengers.

'Was that fun?' he asked with a grin, his eyes dancing.

'Yes!' yelled Ben.

'You're a complete maniac,' said Lizzy.

His grin widened. 'No, just Italian.' He eased back on the throttle even more as they headed for land at a sedate pace. He patted the wheel. 'She's not bad, but she's no powerboat. They can get to speeds of over a hundred knots. Now, that's really moving. Still, we'll have some fun in this one, won't we?'

Annoyance flared in him. The boat he'd hired from the marina was ideal for cruising around, exploring the coastline. But that wasn't something they could do yet. He would be recognised, it was inevitable, and then the press would start buzzing with rumours and speculation about who he was with, and why. He didn't want that. He wanted his marriage officially announced from the palace. Not out of consideration for his father, who deserved none after his callous treatment of Ben and his mother, but for Lizzy's sake.

She'd had enough stress already. All her life, in fact. Thanks to her parents—and everything that had happened since to her.

But so far there had been nothing but silence from the palace. Well, he'd given his father time enough to climb down, to accept what he'd done—perhaps he should send him a reminder.

He'd get on to it today. Jean-Paul would oblige, he knew.

Smoothly, he brought the boat into shore, cut and trimmed the engine, and dropped anchor in the shallow water. Ben jumped out without prompting, landing with a splash to wade ashore. Lithely, Rico climbed over the side himself, then held out his arms to Lizzy. She got rather unsteadily to her feet.

'I'm sure I can manage,' she said.

He scooped her up, and she gave a gasp. He grinned down at her. She was soft in his arms. Soft and voluptuous. And in the couture beach shorts and short-sleeved matching azure top she looked fantastic. Her hair was windblown, but that only gave her a tousled, wanton look.

'I'm too heavy for you,' she gasped.

He laughed scornfully, wading ashore with her. To think he had thought that her baggy, shapeless clothes had meant she was overweight. There wasn't a kilo of flesh on her that wasn't in the right place.

'I can bench twice your weight,' he said confidently. He lowered her gently to the sand, steadying her with his hands. She looked amazing. Her bare arms were smooth and already beginning to tan, now that they were finally being exposed to the sun.

She was beginning to get used to the transformation, he could see. The look of bewildered disbelief was rarer now; she was accepting what had happened. She was out of the box her parents had locked her into—a coffin for her womanhood.

Well, that was a box she would never go back into. And soon her womanhood would blaze into the glory it deserved.

His expression changed. Patience, he was discovering, was a hard virtue.

'Tio Rico, I need a new sandcastle. Come and help—' Ben's piping treble pierced the air.

Rico was glad of the diversion.

He phoned Jean-Paul after lunch. 'How would you feel about an exclusive photo-shoot?' he asked him. 'Ready for the glossies…'

He would send the photos to the palace first. Remind his father that time was running out for him, that if he kept on stonewalling Rico would simply make the announcement of his marriage himself—and let the press go to town on why the palace had let that happen.

'Don't wait too long, Rico. Security at Capo d'Angeli might be tight, but even so—' His friend's voice held a warning. 'This is a story to kill for.'

'I hear you—so can you do the shoot tomorrow?'

'I'll be there. Would I miss the second scoop of a lifetime on you?' Jean-Paul laughed, and signed off.

Slowly, Rico slid his phone away. His eyes travelled down the terrace to the French windows, behind which Lizzy was attempting to make Ben yield to an afternoon siesta. His thoughts went to them.

Jean-Paul was coming tomorrow. To take photos of the happy couple—the happy family. A fairytale marriage that would set a glow over them all. A perfect ending to the tale—the Playboy Prince marrying the adoptive mother of his brother's child.

Who had turned out to be Cinderella indeed—not the ugly sister she had always cast herself as. A Cinderella whose transformation had taken him by storm...inflamed his senses.

Whom he longed to embrace...possess...

A troubled look entered his eyes.

Did he have the right to do it? He wanted her, badly. He wanted her because she was a beautiful, alluring woman and he was bowled over by her—because his body was telling him, every time he saw her, that she was a woman to desire. And he wanted her, too, he knew, for *her* sake—because she had made him feel free and because he had seen her turn into a swan. Yes, she had emerged from the box she'd been locked into, and he wanted to lead her out of it—lead her to where every woman should go.

But did he have the right to take her there?

She's my wife. What other woman in the world should I desire?

His expression shadowed. Became sombre.

Yes, she was his wife—but their marriage was not about them, it was about Ben. Everything about their marriage, including those fairytale photos tomorrow, would be about Ben. His safety—his future. Not theirs.

Why not about our future? Why not about us?

The words formed in his head, coming from the same place deep within him that told him that the woman he wanted so much now was his wife—a wife to desire…to possess…

He sat very still as he realised what he was thinking.

Feeling.

Wanting.

He had married her, promising her a marriage of convenience purely to protect Ben, to protect her. When that had been achieved, when it would not cause any scandal, then he would end the marriage. Set her free. Set himself free.

I don't want that—

The realisation seared through him. Burning its way through his brain.

And in its wake came another emotion. He did not know what it was. He knew only that he was yielding to it, that it was far, far too strong for him to do anything else but yield to it.

And tonight—tonight he would do just that.

Tonight he would make his marriage real.

Those photos tomorrow would be no fairytale.

CHAPTER TEN

QUIETLY, Lizzy slipped from her room out on to the terrace, carefully lifting the long rustling skirts of her gown.

Ben was asleep. Reluctantly, but finally succumbing. It was later than his usual bedtime, but then he'd been judging a fashion parade. He and Rico had sat on the bed while she'd tried on one after another of her outfits, to choose which ones to wear the following day.

Nerves clipped at her as she thought about it. A photo-shoot, Rico had said. His friend Jean-Paul, to whom he had entrusted the story of their marriage, would undertake it.

She was glad Rico had suggested trying the outfits first, even though it seemed odd to have finished with her in evening dress.

'I want a full-length portrait photo of you,' Rico had said.

Then, when he'd finally chosen which gown he thought would be best for such a photo, he'd told her to leave it on.

'It will get you used to the feel and fit,' he'd told her, before heading off to get changed himself, for dinner.

She'd complied, though the close-fitting strapless dusky-rose silk gown with its flowing skirts, gorgeous though it was, seemed to make her somewhat over-dressed for a seaside villa.

'Ah, there you are—'

Rico's voice made her head turn.

And then her breath caught, and stilled in her lungs.

He was strolling towards her in the soft light spilling out on to the terrace, and he was wearing evening dress himself.

He looked—

She swallowed.

Oh, dear God, he looks incredible.

The tailored hand-made tuxedo moulded his long, lithe form, and made her legs feel weak. His freshly washed hair feathered over his forehead, and as he approached she caught the faintest tang of aftershave from his newly-shaved jawline.

She gazed at him helplessly, incapable of tearing her eyes away from him.

He came up to her. His eyes were on her, but all she could see was him.

A half-smile played about his lips.

'Buona sera, Principessa,' he said softly, and lifted her hand with his, to raise it to his lips.

His mouth grazed at her knuckles, and she felt a thousand butterflies release inside her.

He tucked her hand over his arm, and she found herself clinging to it. Numbly, she let herself be glided along the terrace.

'We're dining indoors tonight. Some light rain is forecast.'

She glanced absently at the sky, which was clouding over from the west. Then he was leading her into the large, formal dining room where they'd never eaten before.

She could see, as she looked round, why he had decided for them to wear evening dress. Her eyes widened. She'd never been in here, and she was astonished at its opulence. The huge glass table was edged with a gold metallic border, and an ornate chandelier festooned with crystals shone above. There seemed to be mirrors everywhere, and more glass and gold all around.

'It's a little overdone,' said Rico wryly.

He led her to her place and saw her seated. Then he took his own place opposite her. Almost immediately came the soft pop of a champagne cork, and then one of the staff was filling her flute before performing a similar office for Rico.

He lifted the glass.

'To us,' he said softly, his long lashes sweeping down over his dark eyes, and yet again Lizzy felt the fluttering wings inside her taking flight.

The meal passed as if in a dream. The silent, swift staff placed dishes in front of her, then whisked them away unnoticed. One by one the array of glasses at her place were filled, and then removed. She must have eaten and drunk, she knew, and it must have been delicious. And yet food and drink were the last things on her mind.

Her eyes were held, entirely and only, by the man sitting opposite her.

She felt weak. Incapable of doing anything except drink him in. She must have talked, she must have said things, but her mind was a daze. Inside her veins, the wine creamed in her blood, infusing her with a strange wonder.

I just want to look at him.

Gaze and gaze.

She had never allowed herself to do so before. Had always dragged her eyes away from him. Never indulged herself. But tonight—tonight was different. She didn't know why, didn't question. Merely let herself do what she had wanted to do since the very first time she had ever set eyes on him, and felt the shock of her reaction go through her.

Then, it had been forbidden to her. Then, she had been someone who would never have been allowed to do what she was doing now.

But she wasn't that person any more. She had been transformed, enchanted, into someone quite, quite different.

Someone who could gaze at him to her heart's desire.

Because he was doing the same to her.

The butterflies swooped and soared. His eyes were holding hers, and she was breathless, completely breathless.

He was getting to his feet, standing up. Holding out his hand to her.

'Come.'

It was all he said.

All he had to say.

She stood up. She could feel the silk rustling around her. She gathered the skirts into her fingers, making her way around the table to him. The strapless bodice clung to her, her hair brushed over her bare shoulders, her naked back.

He led her out into the hallway to the interior of the house. Opened another door and ushered her inside.

It was a bedroom.

And it was not hers.

He caught her shoulders, and turned her to him.

For one long, endless moment Rico gazed down at her, into those wide eyes, gazing up at him as they had gazed all evening.

How he had waited this long he did not know.

She hadn't realised, he knew, that her looking at him like that had been a torment to him. That it had taken all his self-control not to push back his chair, stride around the table to her, lift her up and crush her to him.

But he had not done so. Not just because the staff had still been about their business, not just because the chef had produced a *tour de force* that evening and to abandon it halfway through would have been unthinkably inconsiderate. Not just because he had known that with the night to come both of them would require sustenance.

But because he had known that she needed time.

Time to give herself to what was happening to them.

Did she know how much he desired her? He suspected not. The ways of men were an unknown country to her.

A realisation came to him, plunging through him.

Will I be her first?

Emotion scythed through him, flaring in his eyes. .

'Elisabetta.' He spoke softly, so softly, letting his voice pour through the liquid syllables.

His hands curved around her bare shoulders. Her skin was warm to his touch. He rested his thumbs along the delicate bones that arched to her throat and let them smooth her minutely. He felt her tremble beneath his touch.

She was still gazing up at him, her eyes huge, and in them was a longing that was unconscious in its intensity. It jolted through him, tipping him over the edge.

He could resist her no longer.

Slowly, infinitely slowly, he lowered his mouth to hers.

She gave a soft, helpless sigh, her eyes fluttering shut.

He kissed her slowly, very slowly. It was a soft kiss, a caress of her lips with his, and he could feel them shape themselves to him uncertainly, exploringly.

His mouth glided over hers like silk on water.

He took his time, an infinity of time.

This must be perfect for her—perfect.

He mustn't rush this, must take it at her pace, take her with him slowly, exquisitely, on the journey.

His mouth left hers, left her lips parted as his moved on, across the line of her jaw, to the hollow beneath her ear, gliding like silk, like gossamer, to where with the lightest of touches he caressed the outline of her earlobe.

One hand had slid around the nape of her neck, fingers teasing at the fine tendrils of her hair, while his other hand spanned the arch of her throat.

He felt the low, soft gasp vibrating through his fingers, and then his mouth was on hers again, teasing and caressing, until, with a sigh, she opened to him.

His body surged at the sheer sensuality of it as his tongue glided within. He felt her still, as if with shock, and then, as he intensified his kiss, he felt that moment come again as she yielded to his desire.

His hand swept down from the nape of her neck, along the naked length of her back. His fingers sought the fastening of her dress and, with a skill honed with practice over many years, he released the hook, and slowly, very slowly, slid down the zip.

He felt the bodice loosening against his torso and his hand at her throat moved downwards.

He wanted… He wanted…

Dio, but she was exquisite. Full, and soft—and yet as he cupped the silken mound he felt it ripen at his touch. Against his palm, her nipple flowered.

He felt his body surge again, insistent and demanding. Slowly, sensuously, he palmed her fullness.

She seemed to gasp in her throat, and arched her back, pressing herself against him.

It was all he needed. Desire drove through him, and he swept her up into his arms.

The world tilted on its axis, and her eyes flew open.

Rico's eyes were blazing down at her, vivid even in the low light. Her heart was soaring like a bird in flight, which was strange, because she felt boneless, weak, helpless in his arms as he carried her the few strides to his bed.

He lowered her gently, tenderly, as if she were a delicate, precious flower.

'Elisabetta—'

For one long, endless moment he gazed down at her as she lay in a ruffle of silk, one breast exposed, as she looked up at him, wonder and enchantment in her eyes.

Then, with a rapid urgency that was its own message, he'd disposed of his own clothes and was lowering his long, lithe frame upon her. She felt his body crush her down into the softness of the bedding. Felt the strength, the honed, masculine beauty of his planed torso, the narrow circle of his hips, the tautness of his thighs, and the long, full shaft pressing against her.

She gasped, awareness shooting through her.

He saw her recognition.

'I have wanted you,' he breathed, 'from the first moment I saw you. Walking towards me—revealed to me—only to me—in all your beauty.'

Slowly, very slowly, he lowered his head and kissed her. Slowly, very slowly.

'Be mine,' he said to her. 'Be mine, my own Elisabetta .'

His eyes were dilated; she was drowning in their dark depths.

There was only one answer to give him. Only one answer possible.

'Rico…' She breathed his name.

Her arms came around him, closed him to her, her fingers grazing with a fierce, sweet ardour along the contours of his back.

Heat flooded through her. Her hips arched to his. A gesture old as time. The instinctive pleading of her sex. She could not speak, could not talk. She could only know that now, *now* she wanted what was the sweetest glory.

His body answered her. Sliding the silken folds of her dress from her, his hand returned, gliding along the smooth column of her leg, and then, with a touch that drew from her a breathless gasp of pleasure, he parted her.

She was lost—lost in a vortex that was taking her into another world, a world that she had never known existed, to a pleasure, a physical sensation so incredible, that her entire being was reduced to one single exquisite point. She gave herself to it, helpless to do anything but let the ravishing sensation of his skilful touch take her to the place that called to her, nearer and yet nearer, so that when the moment came it was a consummation of discovery, of such wondrous ecstasy that she cried out with it. It swept through her, overwhelming her, flooding through her to her very fingertips, wave after wave. His hand was smoothing her hair, his voice murmuring, and then, even as at last the flood began to ebb, even as she felt the pulsing of her core, he was there, seeking entrance, strong and insistent, and yet with absolute control, easing inside her.

She took him in. The pulsing of her body drew him into her,

and she felt his fullness pressing against her aroused, sensitised tissues. She gasped again, eyes flying open to see him looking down at her, his expression one of absolute focus, one of intensity.

The intensity of desire. Absolute desire.

For her.

Now. *Now.*

He moved within her, and as he did the ebbing fire in her started to lick again. Her lips parted in wonder, and he saw that wonder, and with a brief, flickering smile he moved again. And then, once more, the intensity took him over.

'Yes,' she breathed. 'Yes.' And lifted her hips to him, instinctively tilting to let him move more deeply within her, parting her straining flesh around him, moulding herself around him. He moved again, and yet again, and with each stroke she felt the bliss not just of possession, but of renewed desire.

She heard him speak again, a staccato fragment, and then an urgency took him over. Stroke after stroke, his body surging within her, he took her with him, closer and closer still, to that place where she had been.

And then she was there. Like a white heat sensation flashed through her, sweeping through her limbs. She cried out, and heard his voice too, and she was clutching him, her hands working into the smooth, heated planes of his back, her breath crying through her, her throat arching as the fire took her, took him with her.

It went on and on, until, as the final echo began to ebb, she was left with the sweet, honeyed exhaustion of fulfilment in every fibre of her being. She felt the tautness go from him, felt the full heaviness of his body on hers, and emotion flooded through her. Her arms wrapped around him, her cheek pressing against his. She wanted to hold him close, so close.

Wonder filled her, and a sweetness that was beyond comprehension. She held his warm, strong body in her arms, feeling the hectic beat of his heart gradually slow. His head was sunk against her shoulder. She felt his cheek, his soft, silky hair, the warmth of his breath. His breathing slowed, his muscles relaxing, letting go.

Languor stole through her—a peace so deep that it was like a balm, a blessing. At her hips, still conjoined, she felt his heaviness, felt the low throb within her as her body remembered the imprint of his possession, her own ecstasy. Her languor deepened as her own heart rate slowed, and sleep began to steal over her in her warm, sated drowsiness.

Her hands slackened around his back and she felt his skin begin to cool beneath her fingers. He had slipped over into sleep, she realised, and with the last of her conscious mind she pulled the dishevelled coverlet over him. Then, with a low, soft sigh, she let sleep take her.

'Principessa—je suis enchanté.'

Her hand was being taken, and kissed with courtly gallantry. Lizzy smiled uncertainly. Jean-Paul straightened and bestowed a highly appreciative look at her. He said something in French to Rico, which Lizzy did not understand.

Rico grinned.

'I am indeed,' he replied. 'Incredibly fortunate. And now, if you've finished making up to my bride, let's get on with it. Better start with Ben—before he gets bored with the proceedings.'

But Ben was on his best behaviour, and clearly determined to look angelic, which he did effortlessly, in his smart new clothes.

As for his mother.

Rico's breath caught for the hundredth time.

She sat there, on a sofa in the formal salon of the villa—a room as ornate as the dining room, but ideal for the purpose now—and looked simply—

Radiant.

It was the only word for her, and Rico could not tear his eyes from her.

As Jean-Paul took shot after shot, wonder suffused Rico.

And when it was his turn to be included—first on his own with her, then with Ben, and then with all three of them—although his pose was formal, the look in his eyes was quite different.

At the end of the session, Jean-Paul set his camera aside.

'Bon chance, mon vieux,' he said. 'And I wish you every happiness.'

He clasped Rico's hand, then let it go.

There remained only the business of downloading the digital file from the camera, and offering Jean-Paul the hospitality a friend deserved before he took his leave. And then, while Lizzy took Ben off to change them both into less formal clothes, Rico was left to e-mail Luca.

There was no text. Just a carefully selected attachment.

That would be sufficient.

For a moment after he had hit *send* he just stared at the blank screen.

Then he logged out, and went to find his wife.

She was living in the middle of a dream. A dream so wonderful she knew it could only be a dream. An enchantment. A time out of time.

The whole world seemed suffused with a glow of bliss. Every moment, every instant of every day—and, oh, every night—was filled with a happiness she had never believed possible.

How can I be so happy?

But she did not need to ask. She knew.

Rico—

She had only to breathe his name, only to look at him, hear his voice, take his hand, feel his touch upon her, to know why happiness—deep, profound, immeasurable and infinite—was in every pulse of her blood, every beat of her heart.

She did not want to think, to ask, to question. She wanted only to *be*—to be this wonderful, enchanted person, caught in her blissful, beautiful dream.

It was so strange, she mused. Outwardly, the days passed in

just the same way—easy, undemanding days, a perpetual holiday. Taking Ben down to the beach, swimming in the pool, lounging in the sun, doing everything and nothing, talking about everything and nothing.

And yet everything had changed—changed so utterly she could not believe it, could only float in her haze of wonder and bliss.

By day, the signs were subtle and unconscious—a passing caress, a physical closeness, the casual body language that was the daytime manifestation of intimacy. The hug for Ben that included a hug for her, the little touches of hands as they played with him, the warm, acknowledging glances as they talked and ate and did all the things they had already been doing since they had come to the villa.

But by night—ah, by night her heart lifted in still-incredulous wonder. By night the enchantment that suffused her with a subtle golden haze by day blazed into glory. Glory that burned like stars in its brilliance—glory that melted her body, caress by sweetest caress, touch by sensual touch, stroke by exquisite stroke, until her whole being caught flame and burned like a torch in the ecstasy of her consummation.

His consummation. Because she knew, with every cell of her being, that the strong, virile body she held in her arms, held deep within her own body, was burning too, in the same consummation. She felt his body burn with the same flame, setting him on fire as her arms wrapped him close, and closer still, their bodies fusing as one, until at last the incandescence burned away, leaving them twined about each other in sweet exhaustion.

'How…how can it be so wonderful?' she breathed at him one night, her eyes wide and bemused.

He did not answer, only smoothed her hair, lacing it with his fingers, and cradled her body against his as his hand smoothed along her back, drifting with slow, exhausted sensuousness until it slowed, and slackened, cupping the ripeness of her hip.

He murmured in Italian—words she did not understand but which flowed like honey through her. Like a balm, a blessing.

Then night folded over them and they slept, entwined, embracing. And she dreamt of heaven, because that was where she was already.

Lizzy was creaming his back. Rico lay face down on a lounger. Ben, having surfaced from his siesta, his energy levels renewed, was vigorously batting his way along the length of the pool astride a huge inflatable dolphin.

'Race me,' he called to Rico. 'You can ride the crocodile.' He pointed to a huge, inflatable crocodile with grinning jaws that was floating disconsolately in the shallows.

'Soon,' said Rico, not lifting his head. 'Very soon.'

But not that soon. It was far too good just lying here, with the sun beating down on him, the lightest of breezes playing over his skin, the drowsy sound of the cicadas, the silence of the world around him and Ben splashing happily in the pool, while warm hands glided caressingly, sensuously across his bared back, massaging sun cream deep into the muscled contours, sculpting the bones of his spine, his ribs and shoulders, with smooth, strong strokes.

Well-being, contentment—peace—filled him. He could lie here for ever.

He could be here for ever.

Life was good—so very good.

Everything—everything he wanted was here. Now. An endless now.

Time had stopped. Only day and night existed. Nothing more. There was no world beyond this.

He'd heard nothing yet from his father and Luca—and he didn't care. They belonged in a world he was not interested in right now.

Right now, all he wanted he had. He wanted nothing more.

Footsteps sounded on the shallow flight that led to the upper terrace. A shadow fell over his body. The hands at his back stopped.

He lifted his head and looked up.

Captain Falieri stood there.

Slowly, Rico levered himself up, and stood. Behind him, he could hear Lizzy doing the same. Automatically he felt for her hand and closed his fingers around hers.

'Captain Fally-eery!' Ben's piping voice called with enthusiasm. He splashed his way busily to the steps and clambered out, running up to them. 'Have you come to tea?' he asked convivially.

The Captain shook his head. 'I'm afraid not. I've come—' his eyes flicked to Rico's '—to see your uncle.'

As Falieri looked back at him, Rico could see his gaze moving past him automatically. Even so good a diplomat as he was, he could not, Rico could see, hide the flash of shock in his eyes. He knew why. The woman whose hand he was holding was all but unrecognisable. He felt her slip her hand from his and saw that she was reaching for a sarong to wind about her. Then she was holding out her hand to Ben.

'Let's go and get changed,' she said. 'Captain Falieri,' she acknowledged.

He bowed his head in return, but did not speak. He looked disbelievingly after her as she set off, hand in hand with a protesting Ben.

But Rico was not concerned that his father's chief of police was stunned by the transformation in the appearance of the woman he'd last seen looking so very different in England. He stretched out a hand and picked up his shirt, shrugging it over his shoulders.

'Well?' he asked.

Falieri's eyes snapped back to him.

'His Highness, your father, wishes to see you.'

Rico's mouth pressed together. Then, with a nod of acquiescence, he headed off after Lizzy and Ben.

'Ten minutes,' he called back to Falieri.

It was hard, punishingly hard, to take leave of Lizzy and Ben. But it had to be done. For these past days he had shut out the outside world, ignoring its existence, but that did not stop it existing. Now, he just wanted it sorted.

He took Lizzy's hands. She'd showered and changed, like him, but whereas he had put on a formal suit, knowing his father's preferences, she was wearing a simple sundress. Ben had been peeled out of his trunks and put into shorts and a T-shirt.

'What's going to happen?' He could hear the fear in her voice.

'My father has a very clear choice—he can accept our marriage with outward good grace, and keep everyone happy. Or he can have an open breach with me. I don't care which. Whichever he's chosen, it makes no difference—we're married, you're my wife, Ben is our joint legal charge, and my father *cannot* get his hands on him.' He took a breath. 'I don't want to leave you, but it's the best thing in the circumstances. I don't want you and Ben setting foot in San Lucenzo till all this is settled. I've asked Falieri to stay with you, and he's consented. I trust him. He's not my father's stoolie and he will do *nothing* illegal. He was not involved with the deception my father and brother practised on us at the palace.' His expression darkened. 'It was clever of Luca to send him to England with me—he knows I trust him, and he also knows that Falieri would have refused to be party to their despicable scheme had he been back at the palace.'

'When will you be back?' She was trying to keep her voice steady, he could tell.

'Tonight. There's a helicopter waiting for me at the marina, and the flight won't take long. Nor will whatever my father has to say to me. I'll be heading right back here.'

He gave a sudden smile, dispelling the grimness of his expression.

'Put the champagne on ice, get Ben to bed early, and…' his long lashes swept down over his eyes '…slip into something comfortable.'

For one last moment he held her gaze. Then, letting go her hands, he ruffled Ben's hair and walked out.

Lizzy watched him go. Her chest felt tight.

Ben tugged at her skirt. 'Where's Tio Rico going?' he asked.

'He'll be back later,' said Lizzy absently. She took a breath, trying to focus. 'Let's go and see if Captain Falieri would like a cup of coffee. I'm sure he would.'

'Can he stay to tea, then?' Ben asked, pleased.

'I think he can now. Yes.'

She took Ben out along the terrace. On the far side of the villa she could hear a car moving off, taking Rico down to the heliport.

Captain Falieri walked out of the house. For a moment he seemed a familiar, reassuring figure. Then he turned to look at them as they approached.

There was something in his face that made the blood freeze in her veins.

She stopped in front of him.

'What is it?' Her voice was high, and faint. The tightness in her chest was squeezing hard, so hard.

For a moment he just looked at her. His face was sombre. And in his eyes, most frightening of all, was pity.

'I have,' he said gravely, 'unwelcome news.'

CHAPTER ELEVEN

THE helicopter churned through the air, descending to the palace. Rico must have made this landing a thousand times or more—it was one of the most convenient ways of arriving and departing. He gazed down at the white towers astride the rocky promontory on which the original castle had been built. It was one of the most familiar sights in the world to him.

And yet now it seemed very alien.

He didn't want to do this. He didn't want this confrontation. But it had to be done. And the sooner it was over and done with the better.

Which way had his father chosen? Either Falieri did not know, or he was under strict instructions to give no clue. Well, the waiting would be over very soon, and then Rico would know either the best or the worst.

But it wouldn't be the worst. His father would not risk the scandal of an open breach with his son—he would accept what Rico had done. He wouldn't like it, but he would accept it. For the sake of convention, propriety. For the sake of appearances.

He felt a hardening in his guts. Appearances were all they would be. There could be no real reconciliation with his father. Not after what he had tried to do.

No one, *no one* took a child from its mother. Parted a mother from her child.

No one.

The landing pad soared up to meet them, and there was the familiar jar of impact. The noise of the rotors lessened. Rico released his seat belt, nodded his thanks to the pilot, and slid back the door. Lithely he jumped down and ducked out from under the slowing rotors, then straightened.

As he did, he saw a quartet of figures emerging from the palace. Palace guards in their duty uniforms. He paused, frowning, waiting for them to approach.

'What is it?' he demanded sharply.

The senior officer among them stared straight ahead, not looking at him. His face was expressionless.

'I regret to inform Your Highness,' he said, 'that you are under arrest.'

He was taken to his own apartments. His phone was removed from him, and he realised that all other communication devices, from PC to laptop, had been removed or disabled, including both the house phone and the phones with outside lines.

Disbelief sent shock waves through him.

What the *hell* was going on? Fury, disbelief, shock—all warred within him.

He paced, rigid with rage, across his sitting room.

The double doors opened and he snapped round. The doors had been opened by two of the guards standing outside. Through them was walking his father.

'What the *hell* is this?' Rico demanded.

His father walked in, The guards closed the doors again.

'I have placed you,' said Prince Eduardo, 'under arrest.'

'On what charge?'

Rico's voice was hollow, disbelieving.

There was a silence for a moment. His father's eyes rested on him. They were cold. Rico had never seen them look so cold.

'You have committed a crime against the principality of San Lucenzo.'

His voice was as cold as his eyes.

Rico stared.

'*What?*'

'It is a crime dating back to medieval times. It has little modern enforcement, with one salient exception.' His father paused again. 'Royal marriages,' he said.

'I don't understand,' Rico answered slowly. He was holding still, very still.

His father's cold eyes rested on him.

'Any member of the royal family requires the consent of the Prince before they may marry. You failed to obtain it. Therefore your marriage is void.'

Rico let the words sink in. Then he spoke.

'You can recognise it after the fact.'

'I shall not do so. The marriage is void. You have married without my consent.'

Rico looked at him.

'Why are you doing this? Does it mean nothing to you that the boy is Paolo's son?' His voice was strange, remote.

'Paolo is dead—because of this boy. Had that greedy, over-ambitious girl not sought to entrap him he would never have lost his life.'

Rico shook his head in denial.

'We know nothing of the nature of their relationship The girl might just as easily have been in love with him, and he with her.'

Something flashed in his father's eyes, and then it was gone. Before he could speak Rico continued.

'And whether or not it was love—or entrapment—Paolo did the honourable thing. He married her for the sake of his unborn child.'

His father's face was like marble. Cold and hard.

'He had no business doing so. His first duty was to his name. He was impetuous and self-indulgent.' His voice grew more heavy. 'I blame myself for that. He was indulged as a child—spoilt—and that was the consequence.'

A chill went down Rico's spine, like ice crystallising in his nerve fibres. His father was speaking again. Rico forced himself to listen.

'Nevertheless, when the existence of the boy was discovered—although I would have preferred to have ignored the matter, whatever repellent drivel the gutter press produced—I was prepared, however reluctantly, to acknowledge Paolo's brief marriage, and thereby accept his son as legitimate. Given the circumstances, it seemed the most…advisable…course of action. With the mother dead there would be no…unwelcome entanglements. The boy would be raised in an appropriate manner, without the indulgence that ruined his father, and accepted as a member of the royal family. Unfortunately the obduracy and ambition of the aunt proved a serious impediment.'

Rico's eyes hardened.

'She is more than his aunt, she is his mother—his legal guardian. I made it crystal-clear that she would not be parted from her son—and your attempt to do so was despicable.'

His father's eyes flashed coldly again.

'You will not address me in such a fashion,' he said freezingly. 'However, you will be glad to learn that the boy is no longer a requirement. I have rescinded my decision to recognise Paolo's marriage.' The cold eyes rested impassively on Rico. 'The boy is therefore illegitimate within the state of San Lucenzo. His future is of no concern to me.'

It was said with an indifference that chilled him to the core.

'He's your grandson,' said Rico. 'Does that mean *nothing* to you?'

His father's face did not change. 'Royal bastards are not acknowledged. He has no entitlements and can have no claim on Paolo's estate. Nevertheless, arrangements will be made for suitable maintenance, and an appropriate capital sum will be settled on him for his majority. The issue is now closed, and I will discuss it no further. Luca will handle the matter with the lawyers, and you will not be involved. As for yourself,' the cold voice continued, 'you will undertake to have no further contact or communication with the woman or the boy. When you have given this undertaking, the charge will be lifted.' He gave a sharp intake of breath. 'That is all I have to say to you.'

Rico looked at him. Looked at this man who was his father.

He was standing only a few metres away from him—but the distance between them was much more than that.

Then, without another word, Prince Eduardo walked from the room.

The doors shut behind him, and Rico was alone once more.

How long he stood there he did not know. He could feel his lungs breathing in, and out, he could feel the steady beat of his heart—but he could not feel anything else.

There were voices outside the doors. A sharp voice, and then a deferential one. A door swung open—only one this time.

It was Luca.

Rico looked at him. For a long moment the brothers' eyes met and held.

'Why did you do it?' There was almost resignation in his brother's voice as he put the question, Rico thought. 'Are you completely insane—or just extraordinarily stupid? Not just to do what you have, but then to think you could pressurise our father into accepting it. Good God, do you not know him well enough by now to know he would *never* back down before you?'

'I thought he would consider the scandal of an open breach with me more repugnant than forcing himself to do the decent thing by Paolo's son.'

'The decent thing?' A dam seemed to break inside Luca. 'God Almighty, Rico. You've lost us Paolo's son. His *son*. Do you know, do you have *any idea*, how hard I had to work to get our father to recognise Paolo's marriage? When I told him that there was a story brewing in the press, and what it was, his first and immediate reaction was to ignore it. He was so furious with Paolo that he couldn't think straight. But he finally agreed— after endless persuasion on my part—that the best thing to do would be to recognise the boy as legitimate. That meant he

could come here. That meant he *had* to come here. On his own,' he spelt out. 'That went without saying. Do you seriously imagine for a moment that our father would have anything to do with the family of the boy's mother?'

Luca's mouth set grimly. 'But how the hell could I have known that the girl would kick up such a fuss, and that you—*you* of all people—would let her get away with it? *Dio*, Rico—*you* were the one who was supposed to have her eating out of your hand, not the other damn way round. I never had you down for an idiot—let alone an insane one—but I do now. And now, thanks to your insane stupidity, you've gone and lost us Paolo's son. Thanks to you he's been declared a bastard. A bastard—Paolo's son. *That's* what you've achieved. And it's not something I'm going to forgive you for lightly.'

Bitter fury stung in his accusation. Then his slate eyes flashed again.

'It's time to grow up, Rico. To take some responsibility. Not to play infantile games and be led around by your damn over-active sex-drive! Because that's what's happened, obviously. That much is clear from the photos you sent. You had her done up and moved in on her. Well, I hope you've had your fill of her—because it's over now. You won't be allowed to go within a hundred miles of her. From now on she doesn't exist any more. And maybe finally you'll *learn* some responsibility, Rico. You'd better, because this really is your last chance. He's made that very clear, our father—very clear indeed. You came *this* close to stepping over the edge. This close. From now on, no more stepping out of line by you—not one more *breath* of scandal. From now on you learn to conduct yourself with some responsibility.'

He fell silent, his eyes heavy on his brother.

'Responsibility?' said Rico slowly. His eyes rested on Luca. Nothing showed in them. 'I've always had a problem with responsibility. Because I never had any. My sole responsibility was to stay alive, that was all. In case you dropped dead. Turned out gay. Refused to marry. Proved infertile. And in the meantime, until and unless any of that happened, I passed the time. Any way I could. Because that was all I *could* do. All I was allowed to do. Pass the time. However pointlessly. Until—' his voice changed '—until I found out there was something I could do, after all. Something, in fact, that only I could do—no one else could. I could save Paolo's son.'

His eyes never left Luca's, not for an instant, boring into him, burning into him. 'I could save Paolo's son from the hellish childhood that was being cooked up for him. The one you told me about when I delivered Ben and his mother into your tender hands like a fool—the fool you'd played me for. You wanted to throw his mother away like garbage and condemn Ben to a childhood that was going to be even worse than the one we had, Luca. Do you remember our childhood? Do you? Or has that just conveniently been blanked out of your memory? Because it hasn't from mine, and there was no way—no way on this earth—that I was going to let that happen to Paolo's son. There was no way that I was going to let him be taken from the woman he regards as his mother, *loves* as his mother, or let her lose her child. I could stop it happening—and I did. And I don't regret it for one second. Not one instant.' His voice was a low snarl now. 'Even though I've discovered just what kind of callous *scum* you all are.'

He took a harsh intake of breath. 'And now, if you don't want me to knock you out cold again, I suggest you get the hell out of my quarters.'

He saw his brother's lip twist.

'Thinking to use your *Boy's Own* secret passage and head for the hills again, Rico? It won't do you any good this time. It won't get you out of the hole you're in now. You've run out of options. Your marriage has been declared void, and you're under arrest.'

Rico's mouth whitened.

'I don't give a—'

'Allow me,' bit out Luca, cutting through the expletive, 'to explain to you exactly what San Lucenzan law in respect of royal marriages allows the Prince Regnant to do.'

In precise, exact and comprehensive terms, he did so.

Rico listened. And as he listened, his face slowly froze.

Lizzy was sitting very still. Very still indeed. She had sent Ben to the playroom, telling him to watch a DVD until she came for him.

'I am so very sorry,' Captain Falieri was saying, 'to be the bearer of such…unsettling…news, Miss Mitchell.'

Lizzy said nothing. What could she say? Yet she had to say something.

She swallowed. There seemed to be a stone in her throat.

'So…so what happens now? To Ben and me?'

Her voice was thin, and she was trying to stop it shaking.

Captain Falieri was being kind—so very kind. Somehow that just made it worse.

'I am to escort you both back to Cornwall. Perhaps you would instruct the staff to pack what you intend to take? Needless to say, all…' he hesitated minutely '…all personal effects purchased for your stay here will be considered yours.'

She said nothing. She would allow Ben to choose his favourites from amongst the toys that he had acquired here. As for herself…

She felt her heart crushed, as if heavy weights were squeezing it.

She would need nothing. Nothing but what she had arrived with.

She got to her feet. The motion was jerky.

'If you will excuse me—?'

'Of course. However…' The minute hesitation came again. 'Before you go, I am instructed to require you to sign a particular document.'

He drew a thick, long envelope from his inside breast

pocket and took out the folded document within. He placed it in front of her.

'Although you may wish to read it first—there is a translation attached to the original, as you can see—its content is very straightforward. His Highness, Prince Eduardo, requires you to agree to certain…restrictions. You are to make no claim either on your behalf, or that of your nephew, on the estate of his late natural father, or upon His Highness's estate. You are to have no contact with the press in any way. All approaches by any member of the press to you, you are to direct to His Highness's press secretary to deal with. You are to undertake never to agree to or participate in the publication of any book, or the broadcast of any programme, in any medium, pertaining to your nephew. When these undertakings have been agreed by yourself, a regular sum will be paid to you, for the maintenance of yourself and your nephew. When your nephew achieves his majority, a capital sum will be settled on him by His Highness, in due recognition of the financial obligation that would have devolved upon your nephew's natural father.'

He fell silent and extracted a fountain pen from his inside jacket, placing it beside the document, formally opening it to the final page, where her signature was to be appended.

'I will sign the papers,' said Lizzy. 'But I will not accept any money. Please make that very clear to His Highness.'

She put her signature to the document and waited while Captain Falieri added his own, as witness.

Then she turned away. 'I must talk to my son,' she said.

Gravely, Captain Falieri inclined his head, and watched her walk out.

Rain was falling. Heavy, relentless sheets of rain that swept in off the North Atlantic, rattling against the windowpanes, spitting down the chimney.

The cottage felt cold, so cold.

Damp and unused.

Captain Falieri's expression darkened as he brought her cases indoors.

'You cannot stay here,' he said bluntly. 'I will take you to a hotel.'

Lizzy shook her head.

'No. I would rather be here. I'll be all right.'

She turned to him and held out her hand.

'Thank you,' she said. 'For doing what you could to make this as…simple…as possible.'

He took her hand, but he did not shake it. Instead, he bowed over it.

'I wish…' he said, and he straightened and looked into her eyes. 'I wish that matters had been…otherwise.'

Her throat tightened. She could not cope with kindness.

Nor with pity.

'Thank you,' she said again. 'You had better go now. I'm sure the pilot will wish to start his return flight.'

A private plane had flown her to a military airfield further south, and then Captain Falieri had driven her and Ben to her cottage.

'If you are sure?'

She nodded. 'It would be best for Ben.' She swallowed. 'A complete break will be the easiest for him. As it was when—'

She could not continue. Memories pressed upon her, heavy and unbearable. Could it really have only been a few weeks ago that she had stood here in the hallway admitting entrance to two strangers?

She felt the vice close around her heart again.

She turned and went into the kitchen. Ben was sitting at the table, slumped over it, dejection in every line.

'Captain Falieri has to go now, Ben. Come and say goodbye.'

Ben lifted his face to her.

'Can't we go back with him, Mummy? Can't we? I don't like it here. It's cold.' There were tears in his voice. The vice inside her crushed even more tightly.

'No, my darling, we've come home now. Our holiday is over.'

Tears quivered in Ben's eyes.

'I don't want it to be over,' he said.

There was nothing she could say. Nothing at all. She wanted to sit at the table and howl with him, pour out all her grief and heartbreak. But she could not. She had to be strong for Ben.

She forced a smile to her lips.

'All holidays end, Ben. Now, come and say goodbye to Captain Falieri. He's been kind to us. Very kind.' She felt her voice crack dangerously.

She took Ben's hand and led him dejectedly out into the hallway.

'Goodbye, Ben,' said Captain Falieri gravely. He held out a hand to him.

Ben did not take it.

'Am I really not a prince any more, Captain Fally-eery?' His eyes were wide and pleading.

The Captain shook his head. 'I'm afraid not, Ben.'

'And Mummy isn't a princess?'

'No.'

'It was only for the holiday, Ben. Us being a prince and princess,' said Lizzy. It was the only way she had been able to explain it to Ben.

'What about Tio Rico? Isn't he a prince any more?'

Lizzy's hand rested on his shoulder. It tightened involuntarily.

'He will always be a prince, my darling. Nothing can change that.'

For one long, terrible moment she met Captain Falieri's eyes. Then looked away.

She waited as he took his leave, walking out into the rain. She heard the car door open, then slam shut, and the engine rev. The car drove off down the lane to the coast road, heading back to the airfield, to the waiting plane that would take him away.

She shut the door as a spatter of rain came in on the wind.

She shivered.

'Let's light a fire, Ben. That will warm things up.'

But she would never be warm again, she knew. A terrible, deathly chill embraced her.

How am I going to bear this? How?

The question rang out in her anguish, but she had no answer. There could be no answer.

She went into the kitchen. Captain Falieri had very kindly stopped at a supermarket on the way from the airfield and bought some provisions for her. They would do until she could get to the shops. Mechanically she started to unpack them, and then put some milk to heat on the electric cooker. Warm milk would be good for Ben. They had eaten on the plane; it had helped to make the journey pass. It wasn't really very late, though the rain made it seem darker. Only a few hours since they had left the villa. Only a few hours...

She stilled, unable to move. It was like a physical pain convulsing through her.

With all her strength she forced herself to continue, to make up the fire in the range, set it to draw, check the heat of the milk.

Ben sat at the table, head sunk upon his arms, a picture of misery.

I've got to keep going. It's all I can do. Just keep going. Keep going.

It became her mantra. The only thing that got her through the evening, got her through the following day. And the one after that. And it would get her through the one after that. All the days that stretched ahead of her.

For the rest of her life.

It was unbearable—yet she had to bear it.

There's nothing else. Nothing else I can do. Just keep going. It will pass. Eventually it will pass.

It had to.

Eventually it will get better. Eventually I will accept it. Accept what happened.

That for a brief golden time I was there, with him.

And that time was over. Never to return.

She looked around her, at the worn, shabby interior of the cottage. So short a time ago all she had wanted in the world was to be back here, without her life turned upside down, with Ben just an ordinary child, living a normal life with her.

She would have given anything for that.

Be careful what you pray for…

The old adage came back to haunt her.

The nights were the worst. The nights were agony. Hour after hour she stared into the dark. Remembering.

It's all I have. Memories.

Memories that were vivid, agonising. But memories that she knew, with even greater anguish, would start to fade. Like old photos, the colour seeping from them year by year. They would become blurred and lost. Gone for ever.

Just as he was gone for ever from her life.

Her thoughts reached for him, reached through the silence and the dark, reached across the sea and the land.

But where he was she did not know.

And what would it matter if you did? What would it matter if you could see him where he is? His world has taken him back—to the life he had, the life he has again. You were an…intermission…for him. He did what he did to keep Ben safe—and now Ben is safe again. Ben does not need him. He can have his own life back, as Ben has his.

As you have yours.

Without him.

Only memories. Memories to last a lifetime. Nothing more than memories.

A damp sun struggled through the clouds. After days of rain, the overcast skies were clearing. Raindrops dazzled drippingly on the branches of the trees, and a milder wind creamed up the coombe, bringing the scent of the sea.

'Come on, Ben, let's go down to the beach.'

With forced jollity she rallied him, filling her voice with an enthusiasm she did not feel. Nor did she meet with any in return.

'I don't want to,' said Ben. 'I want to go back to Tio Rico's beach.'

'Other people are having their holiday there now,' she said. 'It's like here in Cornwall. People come for a holiday, and then they go home. That's quite sad for them, isn't it? We live here all the time—so that's good.'

Ben looked at her mutinously.

'We could live in the house by Tio Rico's beach all the time,' he said.

'That house was only for a holiday for us. This is the house we live in. And we're very lucky to be here, Ben. Lots of people have to live in cities, where there isn't any beach at all.'

'I don't like the beach here. It hasn't got a swimming pool. And it hasn't got Tio Rico.' Ben's lower lip wobbled.

'The beach here has got waves,' said Lizzy, with determined cheerfulness.

'But it hasn't got Tio Rico,' Ben protested. He swallowed, and lifted his eyes to her. 'Mummy, doesn't Tio Rico want us any more?

She tried to find the words. Words that a four-year-old child could make sense of. But they were cruel words, harsh words for all that. Yet what else could she do except say them? To give Ben false hope would be the cruellest thing of all.

'Your uncle can't be with us any more, Ben,' she began carefully. 'He has duties to attend to. He has to be a prince now, not an uncle. It was just a holiday we spent with him. Just a holiday. That's all.'

Her words fell with excruciating mockery into her own ears.

A holiday. That was all it had been. A holiday of enchantment, magic, wonder, and such bliss that it made the realisation that such a time could never come again so agonising that she could hardly bear it.

But above all, above everything else, she must not say the words that ached to be said. For what was the use of saying them? What was the use, even in the dark—all alone in the bed she had once been content to lie in, solitary, celibate, untouched by the magic that he had strewn over her—what was the use, sleepless and despairing, of letting those words whisper in her mind, each one an agony of loss?

The only way she could face the rest of her life now was never, ever, to say those words. Never even to think them. Or they would destroy her.

Resolutely, she went on getting the beach things together.

Pain and memory clawing within her.

She took Ben, protesting, down to the beach. She had forgotten how chill the wind could be even at this time of year, in early summer. She made a camp in the lee of a line of rocks, sedimentary shales turned on their side by vast geological forces over vast reaches of time. So much time.

She looked out to sea.

Where was he now? she wondered. Was he in some fashionable high-society resort—Monte Carlo, the Caribbean, somewhere exotic? Mingling with fashionable high-society people? Fashionable high-society women, every one a beauty, the kind that he took his pick of—the Playboy Prince, leading the life he was born to lead?

Stop it. It doesn't matter.

It doesn't matter where he is, or who he's with, or what he's doing.

It doesn't matter.

It will never matter again, for the rest of your life.

She shook out the rug and weighted down the corners with a book, shoes and a bag.

'Who's for a paddle?' she said, forcing her voice to be cheerful.

'It's too cold,' said Ben, and sat on the rug and wrapped a towel around him.

She whisked it off.

'Then we'll make a railway track. Which engines did you bring down with you?'

'I don't want trains—I want my fort. The fort Tio Rico made with me.'

Lizzy's heart sank. Gently she said, 'We couldn't bring it back, Ben. It was too big—don't you remember? But we brought the knights, so that's good, isn't it?' she finished encouragingly.

'But it's the *fort* I want. Tio Rico and me made it. We made it together, and it had a bridge and a porcully and towers.'

She felt her heart catch with pain. Like a knife slicing into her memory stabbed her and she was there again, in the warmth and the sunshine—the ugly sister who had so miraculously been turned into Cinderella. Sleeping Beauty ready to be kissed awake by the most handsome Prince in the world.

No. Anguish crushed her. She mustn't let herself think, remember. It was gone, all gone. Like a dream. An enchantment.

A fairytale that was over now.

She took a breath.

She must not think of fairytales. They were just that. Unreal. This was real—here, now. With Ben. She chivvied him along, refusing to let him mope. What was the point of him moping? What was the point of her moping? They had to get on with things. They had to.

They had to keep going.

'Well, we haven't got the fort any more, but we have got trains. So let's start building this track,' she said, with forced resolution.

She started digging into the sand, carving out the railway tracks that Ben liked to make so that he could drive his engines along. The sand was cold beneath the surface, and wet. The sand at the villa had been warm, dry.

And Rico had helped Ben make the tracks.

'Come on, Ben, give me a hand,' she said.

Morosely he started to help, his expression unhappy. Lizzy

ignored it. She had to. She had to jolly him along, get him cheerful again, enthusiastic again. What alternative was there? She knelt down on the sand, facing out to sea, letting the wind whip her hair into unflattering frizzled wisps.

Her looks were going already, she knew. Without all the expensive attentions of stylists and beauticians she was beginning to revert. She didn't care.

What did Ben care what she looked like?

And there was no one else to care.

Never again.

'Where shall we make the train station?' she asked, kneeling back a moment, feeling the wind-blown sand stinging on her cheeks.

'Don't care,' said Ben. He sat back as well, beside her. 'It's a stupid, stupid track, and I don't care where the stupid, stupid station is. Stupid, stupid, *stupid*.' He bashed the sand with his spade, spattering it in all directions.

'Well, I'd put it just before the branch line goes off, Ben. That's the place for a station.'

The voice that spoke was deep and accented, and it came from behind them.

CHAPTER TWELVE

THE world seemed to stop. Stop completely. Except that it didn't stop. It whirled around her. Whirled with a dizzying speed that made her feel faint.

It wasn't possible. It was an illusion—an auditory illusion. They happened sometimes—you could hear people speaking who weren't there.

Who were somewhere quite different. Who were at some aristocratic house party somewhere, or on a multimillion-pound yacht, or flying in a private jet to a tropical island with a beautiful film star for company.

Who weren't on a Cornish beach, with the wind blowing off the North Atlantic. Making the wind feel as if it was being wafted there from paradise...

Her vision dimmed. She felt clouds rushing in from all around. The blood was thick in her head, bowing her down with its weight.

'Tio Rico!'

Ben's voice was alight. She could hear it, piercing through the clouds and the thickening blood.

'Tio Rico. Tio Rico!'

She bowed her head. It was impossible. Impossible.

'Hello, Ben? Have you been good without me?'

'No,' shouted Ben. Excitement overwhelmed him. 'You weren't here. Why weren't you here, Tio Rico?'

'I got delayed. I'm sorry. But I'm here now.' She felt him lower himself down on to the rug. And still she could not move. Not a muscle.

'Are you going to stay?' Ben demanded. But there was fear in his voice.

'As long as you want me to stay.' He paused. 'If your mother agrees, that is. Do you?'

His hand was on her shoulder. Warm and strong. Sending heat through her, a living warmth that she could not bear.

'Lizzy?'

She looked up. He was only a foot or two away from her, hunkered down on the rug. She saw him immediately, completely. She saw everything about him in one absolute moment. As if he had always been there.

'You shouldn't be here,' she said. Her voice was thick, as thick as the blood suffocating her veins. 'Captain Falieri explained to me. He said you would not be allowed to see Ben again.'

The expression in his eyes altered.

'Well, that depends,' he said. He was looking at her very deeply, very strangely, right into her eyes.

'No, it doesn't,' she said. 'It doesn't depend at all. He said it very clearly. He explained it very clearly. You're not allowed to see Ben any more.'

From the corner of her eye she could see Ben's face pucker.

'Why can't Tio Rico see me any more?' he said.

She saw Rico reach out and ruffle Ben's hair.

'Your mother's got it wrong. I'm here, aren't I?'

It was her turn for her face to pucker.

'But you *shouldn't* be,' she said fiercely. 'You *can't* be.'

His expression changed again. Something entered his eyes. Something she didn't want to see.

'Where else should I be,' he asked quietly, but with deadliness in his voice, 'but with my wife and my boy?'

'No,' she said. She rocked forward slightly. Denying it. Denying it completely. 'No,' she said again.

He looked at her. Looked at her with eyes that chilled her to the bone.

'Did you really think,' he asked, in that same quiet, deadly tone, 'that I would stay away?'

She snapped upright.

'You've got to go!' she shouted at him. 'You've got to go—right away. Right now. Falieri told me. He *told* me. So go—*go*.'

There was a steely glint in his eye. He reached for her hands and hauled her down again. Her eyes were wild, desperate.

'He told me,' she said, and there was despair in her voice. 'He told me everything. He told me about that law—the one that says you can't marry without the Ruling Prince's permission. He told me that it meant our marriage was null and void.'

'Our marriage is real, Lizzy. We made our vows in front of a priest. No one can overturn that.' Steel was in his voice now.

'Yes, they can. They can. Your father can overturn it—and that's what he's done.'

'All my father can do is refuse to recognise our marriage within San Lucenzo. He cannot overturn it. He has no power over our marriage, Lizzy. None.' He spoke steadily, remorselessly.

Her face contorted. 'Yes, he has. He *has*. Captain Falieri told me—he told me quite clearly. He's got absolute power over you. You've broken the law, and if you don't obey him he'll use that power. And he'll do it. Captain Falieri said he would do it.' She swallowed. The stone in her throat was agony. But she spoke, saying the words that had been burnt into her like an agonising brand.

'He'll do it, Rico—he'll strip you of your royalty. He'll disinherit you. He'll disbar you from the succession. Take you off the Civil List, freeze all your assets in San Lucenzo. He'll take everything from you—everything. He'll leave you with nothing.'

She heard Captain Falieri's voice tolling in her head. Saying the words that had taken everything from *her*. All hope. Gone for ever. They had crushed her, crushed her heart, cracking it in pieces.

There was a strange look on Rico's face. It frightened her. His expression was calm. Very calm. Far too calm.

'Falieri was wrong. There was something my father could not take from me.' He paused. Then he spoke. 'You. He could not take you from me. My wife.'

Her face contorted again.

'No. *No.*'

'You are my wife, and Ben is my adopted son, and no one— no power on earth—will take you from me.'

She twisted her hands in his grip.

'No,' she cried again. Her eyes were anguished. 'You mustn't say that. I won't let you. I won't. You've got to go now. Right now.'

He gave a sudden laugh, gripping her hands more tightly yet.

'What a venal woman you are,' he said. 'You only want me for my title, don't you?' His fingers slid into hers. 'Well, I've bad news for you, Signora Ceraldi—'

'Don't say that. Just go. It's not too late.'

He hauled her against him, crushing her against the hard wall of his chest.

'It's far too late. Far, far too late.'

He kissed her.

The kiss went on and on. And she drowned in it. Drowned in his arms. Drowned in the tears pouring from her.

'Mummy—Mummy?'

A little hand was tugging at her arm. Ben's voice was confused, bewildered. Rico half let her go. He swept Ben to him.

'Now, tell me—tell me true.' He stood him up in the crook of his arm, hugging his little body close to him. His other arm was wrapped tight around Lizzy. 'Which would you rather? Me not at all—or me not as a prince but still you and me and Mummy?'

'Would you go away again?' Ben asked.

Rico shook his head. 'Never. Unless you came with me. I might go sometimes—just to work, that sort of thing—maybe for the day or a few days. But you would live with me, and so would Mummy. Would that be any good?'

'Where would we all live?'

'Anywhere you liked. Well, except in a palace.'

'I want to live here and at the holiday house with the swimming pool,' Ben stipulated. 'With you and Mummy. For ever and ever.'

'Done,' said Rico. 'High five says yes.'

Ben gave him a high five. 'Yes,' he shouted. 'Yes, yes, *yes*.' His little face was alight—alight with joy.

Lizzy's face was wet with tears.

'You can't do this. You just *can't*,' she sobbed.

Rico's arm tightened around her shaking shoulders.

'Too late,' he told her. 'Done deal.' He kissed her forehead softly. 'Done deal, Signora Ceraldi.' His eyes gazed into hers. Deep, deep eyes. 'Now, don't go and tell me it was just the royal bit you fell for?' His voice was admonishing. 'My ego won't take it, you know. It really won't.'

She swallowed, hard. 'Ben—' her voice was shaky '—why not start on that station now? Tio Rico and I need to talk. Boring grown-up stuff.'

'OK,' said Ben.

His world was restored. Happily, he scrambled back onto the sand and started scooping it up to shape into a railway station. Carefully, very carefully, Lizzy undraped herself and pulled away, to the far edge of the rug.

'You can't do this,' she said again. She made her voice steady. Very steady. Calm and rational. 'I won't let you. I won't let you give everything up for Ben. He's young. He'll soon forget you. It will be hard at first, but in a year he'll have forgotten you. You'll just be a memory, and even that will fade.'

He was looking at her strangely. Then he spoke.

'But, you see, my memories of Ben won't fade. *I* won't forget *him*. And I won't give him up. He's my brother's son— and as clearly as if Paolo were here now I can hear him telling me to be the father to Ben that he was not allowed to be. Just as you—' he made each word telling '—are the mother to Ben that your sister was not allowed to be. And though the cruelty of their deaths can never be assuaged, we know that we can be the loving family to their son that he needs. Because we both love him—and we love each other, don't we, Lizzy?'

She opened her mouth, but no words came. He supplied them for her.

'You can't kiss a man like you just did unless you love him. You can't cry all over a man like you just did unless you love him. And you certainly can't tell a prince he's not to give up his title for the woman he loves unless you love him. I've got you on all three counts, Signora Ceraldi. And I've got you on more counts than that. An infinite number—not just every night we were together, but every moment we were together. Every look, every touch, everything we said to each other, every meal we shared—every smile we shared, everything.'

He shook his head ruminatively. 'It started right from the beginning—even though I didn't know it. Seeing you with Ben, seeing you love him and care for him. And when…' He paused, then went on, 'When you used that horrible, cruel word about yourself, describing our marriage, I wanted to do anything, *everything* I could to banish it.' His eyes softened. 'And I had my reward—oh, I did indeed. Ever since you walked towards me along that terrace, looking such a knockout, taking my breath away, I've been lost. And I know that makes me sound superficial and trivial, thinking with my Y chromosome, but you bowled me over. Blew me away. Knocked me for six. Whatever you want to call it—I went for it.' His voice changed again. 'But it isn't just because of that. It can't be—because even now, when you haven't got a scrap of make-up on, and your hair is going frizzy again, and God alone knows what rubbish dump you got that T-shirt out of, I just want to hold you and never, *never* let you go again. Why do you suppose that is?'

She fingered a corner of the rug and wouldn't look at him.

'It was just novelty. Kindness. Something like that.'

Rico said a word in Italian. She didn't know what it meant, but she could tell it wasn't one she wanted Ben to copy.

'It was love. Do you know how I know? Because when I heard my father telling me my marriage was void I wanted to hit him. Pulverise him.'

'He was trying to manipulate you. No wonder you were angry.'

'He was trying to take me away from you. And I wasn't going to let him.'

'He was trying to take you away from Ben.'

'Ben, yes—and *you*. Stop trying to tell me I don't love you, Signora Ceraldi.' He shook his head again, and only the glint in his eyes told her his jibe was not cruel. 'What a low opinion you have of me. The Playboy Prince—that's all you think of me, isn't it? Admit it.'

She could find no humour in it. 'You can't give up your birthright.' Her voice was low, and vehement. 'You can't.'

'I can and I have. Like I said, it's a done deal. It was a done deal the moment my self-righteous brother informed me what the penalty for my crime was. It took a while,' he said grimly, 'to convince Luca and my father that I was serious in the answer I gave them. That there was no way on God's earth that I would repudiate you and agree to void our marriage—and to hell with their damn laws. But finally they washed their hands of me. I've signed God knows how many documents my father had drawn up, and now, finally, I've been able to come to you.'

She shook her head urgently, violently.

'No. I won't let you. I won't let you do this, Rico. *Please* go back. Go back before it's too late. You can get your title restored, be reinstated, go back on the Civil List, unfreeze your San Lucenzan assets—'

But he only laughed, lounging back on the rug, propped up on one elbow. 'Yes, definitely a venal woman, Signora Ceraldi.' He gave an extravagant sigh. 'I'm only good enough for you when I'm a royal, and I'm only good enough for you when I've got my fingers in the San Lucenzan royal coffers.'

He shook his head sorrowfully. 'My sweet little gold-digger—don't you realise that since I turned eighteen it has been my life-long ambition never to be strung up by the family financial umbilical cord? I know you think I'm just a mindless Playboy Prince, but I haven't spent my youth simply philandering and racing powerboats and the like. I've made investments, taken financial interests in various ventures, played the stock markets. I may not be worth quite what I was before I quit San Lucenzo, but we can jog along quite comfortably, I promise you. We may even—' his eyes glinted again, making weakness wash through her '—run to buying that villa in Capo d'Angeli. Would you like that? But let's keep your cottage here. We'll do it up properly. Put central heating in. I'd like to spend time here. The surf looks good.'

Her hands twisted in her lap.

'The water's far too cold for you here.'

He took her hands and untwisted them. 'Then I look forward to you warming me up afterwards. Will you do that, hmm?' The glint turned into a gleam. The weakness washed through her again.

Then he was smoothing the fingers of her hands—softly, sensuously.

'Too many days without you,' he was murmuring. 'Too many nights. What a lot we have to make up for.'

She took a deep breath. Looked him right in the eyes. Those dark, beautiful, long-lashed eyes.

'Rico, don't do this. Please don't do this. I can't bear it.'

The long sooty lashes swept down over his eyes, then back up again.

'And I can't bear not to. It's as simple as that.'

For one long, endless moment he just looked into her eyes, her face, searching for her—finding her.

A little hand was tugging at him. With a lithe, fluid movement Rico jackknifed up to a sitting position.

'What's up, Ben?' he said smilingly.

'Tio Rico,' asked Ben speculatively, 'did you remember to bring the fort we made?'

It took Ben a long time to settle for bed that night. He bounced around in a state of over-excitement, until finally he could fight sleep no more. Carefully, Rico made his way down the narrow, creaking stairs, ducking his head under the low lintel. The door to the kitchen was open, and she was sitting there, a mug of tea in her cupped hands, staring sightlessly.

How long would it take her to believe? he wondered. Believe that he knew exactly what he was doing, regretted nothing. And would never regret.

He walked in, and her eyes flew to him instantly, unswervingly. And he saw in them such a blaze that it took his breath away.

Where had it come from, this love he felt for her? He didn't know. It had just arrived, that was all. Some time when he wasn't paying attention. When he was just being with her. With Ben.

My family, he thought. That's who they are. My wife and my boy. My son. I'll be the father he couldn't have. I'll take care of him. So simple. So easy. It had been no choice at all.

'Asleep,' he announced. 'Finally.'

'He's excited,' she said. While he'd been settling Ben she'd tried to do something with her appearance, he could tell. She'd put some make-up on, styled her hair. She looked good. Not as glossy, not as stunning as she had when she'd gone for the full works, but good. Definitely good.

The strange thing was, he didn't care.

I love her stunning, I love her plain.

Because I just love—her.

He sat himself down on the table, just by her.

'There's still time to change your mind. You could still go back.'

He smiled. It was a strange smile. Filled with humour, with resignation, with understanding.

'I'm here for good, Lizzy. You've just got to accept it.'

'I can't. That's what I can't do. Rico, it was just a dream—an enchantment. I was Cinderella at the ball, dancing with the Prince. Sleeping Beauty being woken by the Prince's kiss. Fairytales. That's all.'

He looked down at her. 'Has it never occurred to you that the Prince in the fairytale might like a fairytale of his own? One where he gets to quit being a prince all the time? Do you know—' his voice changed, his expression changed '—that you are the only person in my entire life to look at me and see me? Not a prince. Me.'

A look of confusion passed over her face. He gave a rueful smile. 'You don't remember, do you? But I do. I stood in this very cottage and told you we had to run from the paparazzi. And you kept saying why? Why did we have to run? Because you hadn't the faintest idea who I was. Not a clue. You just saw some man bossing you about for no good reason. Not a prince. Not the Playboy Prince. Not the spare Prince to understudy the Crown Prince. Just some man who was trying to boss you about. And even when you knew I was a prince you never really knew how to behave with me, did you? You never called me Highness, or Sir, or anything. The whole royalty thing just…passed you by.'

She still looked troubled, her hands tightening around her mug. 'It doesn't matter what I thought. Rico, you've been royal all your life—'

'And much good it's done me,' he interrupted her. 'Listen, Lizzy—I'm a lot like you.' His eyes were serious, holding hers intently. 'Like you, all my life I've been—unnecessary. Just as you were. To your parents, only your sister was important. To mine, only the heir was important. The spare was just that—spare. Only with Paolo did they ever seem to realise they had a son—not a ruling prince-in-waiting. They lavished on Paolo the love they weren't able to lavish on Luca and me. I don't know what screwed your parents up—because they *were* screwed up, Lizzy, badly, and they'd done an ace job of screwing you up too, until I got you out of that box they'd nailed you into—but I know what screwed mine up: being royal. I did a lot of thinking when I was put under house arrest by my own father, and it always came back to that. Maybe it's different for Luca—he has, after all, something to do, something to look forward to doing. But me—well, I never had anything useful to do. I represented my father or Luca from time to time, attended a few Great Council meetings, signed a few state papers when my father was ill and Luca abroad. But I was never really needed.'

He touched the side of her cheek with a finger.

'You and Ben are the first people that ever needed me,' he said. 'Just like Ben was the first person ever to need *you*, Lizzy. He gave your life meaning and purpose. And that's what you and he do for me. Give my life meaning and purpose. That's why,' he said very softly, his eyes darkening, 'we belong together.'

She was silent. She couldn't say anything. But her eyes slipped away from him. In her chest a hard, heavy lump was forming.

'What is it?' he asked, in that same quiet voice.

The lump hardened, and speaking over it was painful, impossible. But she made herself do it.

'You're offering me a life I can't accept.'

He frowned. 'Why can't you accept it?' he asked, his voice still low.

She swallowed. The lump did not go away.

'Because I shouldn't have it,' she said. 'Because it should be Maria's life. She was the one a prince fell in love with. She was the one who should have been a princess. She was the one Ben should have belonged to. Not me. *Not me.* I took Ben from her. I told the doctors to turn off her life support after Ben had been delivered, after he had grown to term inside a mother whose brain had died weeks earlier. I told them to kill my sister so I could have her baby for myself.'

Huge, anguished eyes looked at him. Her fingers were pressed so tight around the mug they showed white all the way through.

'I told them to do it.'

Carefully he got to his feet. Carefully he hunkered down beside her, placing a hand, warm and strong, on her thigh.

'There was no one else to tell them,' he said. 'Your parents had made their decision. They had gone, taken their way out, leaving *you* with that decision. Making *you* the scapegoat for that decision. They didn't even have the courage, the *love* to stay alive for their grandson's sake. Let alone for yours. And tell me something, Lizzy—tell me from your heart. Do you think your sister would have wanted to live on, in body only, while Paolo was already dead? Their deaths were a tragedy—each and every death that night a tragedy. But *we* are *not* responsible. All we can do is go on with our own lives—and remember theirs. So let's take Ben, you and me, and bring him up in a happy family. We can't change the past—but we can make the future. Together, Lizzy. *Together.*'

He reached and wrapped his arms around her, very close. Slowly she let go of the mug. Slowly she slid her arms around him, burying her face in his shoulder.

'Be happy, Lizzy. Let yourself be happy. With me. For now, and for all our lives together. Life isn't certain—we both know that. So more than anything we must live while we can—for Ben and for each other. And perhaps…' His hand slid across her stomach, warm and seeking. 'Perhaps for one or two more. Ben needs a family—brothers and sisters. Happy and loving, all together.'

He drew her to her feet. Kissed her softly. Then not so softly.

As he drew back she saw the glint deep in his dark, lambent eyes. She felt her heart turn over. The glint turned to a gleam. The gleam to a look that melted her bones.

'Come, Signora Ceraldi, time for bed. I want to find out whether it was just my title you fell for.'

Her arms went around him. Holding him tight, so very tight. Close against her.

'Prince of my heart,' she whispered. 'Love of my life. My adored, beloved husband.'

'Sounds good,' he said. 'Sounds very good.'
He kissed her once more, and then again.
And then he led her upstairs, to the bliss that awaited them.

EPILOGUE

THE photos that Jean-Paul had taken at the villa went round the world. So did the story of *The Playboy Prince Who Gave Up His Title For Love*.

And so, too, did the next set of photos that Jean-Paul came to take.

The ones of Signor and Signora Enrico Ceraldi, with Master Benedetto Ceraldi, posing in the gardens of their two favourite residences—the newly christened Villa Elisabetta on the exclusive Capo d'Angeli estate in Italy, and the newly restored slate-roofed Cornish cottage, against whose porch leant two surfboards. One fast and mean for Signor Ceraldi, and a junior-sized one for Master Benedetto. Signora Ceraldi's surfboard was in storage, awaiting such time as Master Benedetto's new brother or sister made his expected appearance—which, as could clearly be seen from the especially voluptuous figure of Signora Ceraldi, around which Signor Ceraldi was curving a lovingly protective hand, would not be long.

As for Master Benedetto, he was sitting cross-legged on the grass and attacking a heavily defended cardboard fort with an army of brightly coloured knights in armour. His smile was almost bigger than his face.

The smile of a happy child with a happy family.

The greatest gift of all.

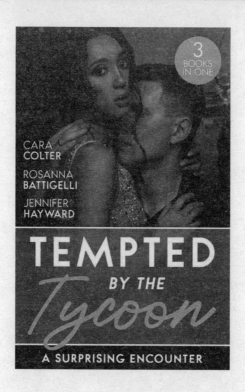

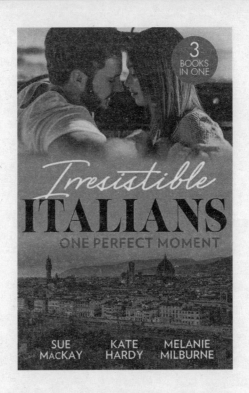

LET'S TALK

Romance

For exclusive extracts, competitions and special offers, find us online:

- **f** facebook.com/millsandboon
- **🐦** @MillsandBoon
- **📷** @MillsandBoonUK
- **♪** @MillsandBoonUK

Get in touch on 01413 063 232

For all the latest titles coming soon, visit
millsandboon.co.uk/nextmonth

MILLS & BOON

THE HEART OF ROMANCE

A ROMANCE FOR EVERY READER

MODERN
Prepare to be swept off your feet by sophisticated, sexy and seductive heroes, in some of the world's most glamourous and romantic locations, where power and passion collide.

HISTORICAL
Escape with historical heroes from time gone by. Whether your passion is for wicked Regency Rakes, muscled Vikings or rugged Highlanders, awaken the romance of the past.

MEDICAL
Set your pulse racing with dedicated, delectable doctors in the high-pressure world of medicine, where emotions run high and passion, comfort and love are the best medicine.

True Love
Celebrate true love with tender stories of heartfelt romance, from the rush of falling in love to the joy a new baby can bring, and a focus on the emotional heart of a relationship.

Desire
Indulge in secrets and scandal, intense drama and sizzling hot action with heroes who have it all: wealth, status, good looks…everything but the right woman.

HEROES
The excitement of a gripping thriller, with intense romance at its heart. Resourceful, true-to-life women and strong, fearless men face danger and desire - a killer combination!

To see which titles are coming soon, please visit
millsandboon.co.uk/nextmonth

JOIN US ON SOCIAL MEDIA!

Stay up to date with our latest releases, author news and gossip, special offers and discounts, and all the behind-the-scenes action from Mills & Boon...

 @millsandboon

 @millsandboonuk

 facebook.com/millsandboon

 @millsandboonuk

It might just be true love...

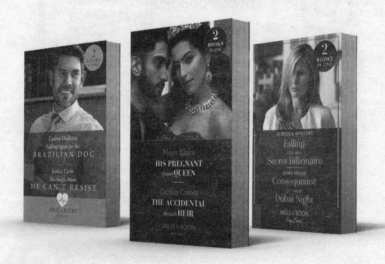

GET YOUR ROMANCE FIX!

Get the latest romance news,
exclusive author interviews, story
extracts and much more!

blog.millsandboon.co.uk

MILLS & BOON

MODERN

Power and Passion

Prepare to be swept off your feet by sophisticated, sexy and seductive heroes, in some of the world's most glamourous and romantic locations, where power and passion collide.

MILLS & BOON

Desire

Indulge in secrets and scandal, intense drama and plenty of sizzling hot action with powerful and passionate heroes who have it all: wealth, status, good looks…everything but the right woman.

MILLS & BOON

HEROES

At Your Service

Experience all the excitement of a gripping thriller, with an intense romance at its heart. Resourceful, true-to-life women and strong, fearless men face danger and desire – a killer combination!